M000306788

LITANY OF SECRETS

A Cameron Ballack mystery

Luke H. Davis

© Copyright: 2013 by Luke Davis. All rights reserved. No portion of this book may be reproduced in any form without the written permission of the copyright owner, except for brief excerpts quoted in critical reviews.

Permission to quote in critical reviews with citation:
Litany of Secrets
By Luke H. Davis

Print ISBN 978-0-9884613-2-1
E-book ISBN 978-0-9884613-3-8

DUNROBIN PUBLISHING

www.dunrobin.us

To Christy,

who knows my litany of secrets

and still loves me with all her heart.

AUTHOR'S NOTE

No writer should ignore those who have been part of the yeoman's work of composition. I owe a debt of gratitude to all who have assisted in matters great and small.

Many thanks must go to my parents who were my initial spiritual directors and whose generosity helped make this literary dream possible; to my friend and mentor Tom Foley, for broadening my faith horizons; to Theresa Robinson, who proved an invaluable resource on all police investigation details; to Tim Gibson for his expert editorial labor on the manuscript; to L.B. Graham for his generous feedback and helpful critique; to Shannon Hathaway for her verbal savvy; to Mark Sutherland at Dunrobin Publishing for his insight, assistance, and encouragement; to all my friends who encouraged me to go into writing alongside teaching; and to my wife and children who dealt graciously with me as this story became another member of the family.

Another bevy of gratitude goes to Ciarra Peters. In addition to proving herself a student of excellence and character, she is a talented artist. Her cover design is nothing short of breathtaking and captures the essence of the story you are about to read.

A massive debt of thanks goes to the reigning queen of the murder mystery genre, P.D. James. From the moment I cracked open her books, I knew I had found my literary "buried treasure." Her influence on me is incalculable, and though I will never be able to match her exquisite balance of plot, character, and setting, I am thankful she has set the bar high. It is a most worthy goal, and she is a most worthy artist of detective fiction.

As with most works of fiction, readers will wonder how much of the writing is lifted from the fabric of reality or the author's experience. While those who know me might boldly claim to ascertain some existential parallels, any connection between the characters of this novel and any person, living or dead, is entirely coincidental. Also, the institution of St. Basil's Seminary is a creation of my imagination and is not meant to parallel any real-life academic body.

Readers and residents of the town of Defiance, Missouri, should note that, although the setting of the book is laid out with reasonable precision, I have altered the landscape of Howell Road south of Defiance in order to justify the placement of St. Basil's Seminary.

Finally, the story that follows should not be interpreted as an attack on theological seminaries or the ministerial vocation or the Christian faith. I spent some of the most influential years of my life at Covenant Theological Seminary in St. Louis and am thankful for the ways in which that experience stretched and shaped my beliefs and my life story. Neither should this work be viewed as a criticism of the Eastern Orthodox Church. The Orthodox faith remains one of the most beautiful expressions of the story of Christianity, and I perpetually remain impressed by its love of creativity, pursuit of virtue, and embracing of the biblical mystery of God.

Whitsunday 2013

"I acknowledge one baptism for the remission of sins.
I look for the resurrection of the dead,
and the life of the world to come.
Amen."

From the Nicene-Constantinopolitan Creed (381),
the statement of faith for the Orthodox Church worldwide

"The glory of God is a human being who is fully alive,
and the life of such a person consists in beholding God."

St. Irenaus of Lyons (d. 202)

"Sanctify the body, engage the mind, transform the soul"

Motto of St. Basil's Seminary

TEARS FROM THE PAST

(Eighteen years ago)

Grief, he thought in verses that contradicted his ten years of age, is not a snare that can be avoided. Rather, it is a strategic ambush of the divine.

And grief was all he could feel on the bumpy ride up the grassy slope. The tent awaited them, twelve chairs clustered in two even rows. His uncles had made their way there, having borne and placed the most difficult load they had ever carried. With slow yet firm steps, his father pushed his wheelchair from behind, navigating around the soft spots on the autumn turf. Mom walked to their side, holding on to Jill's hand, and finally the short journey was complete; the blur of this day could continue.

The November wind kicked up, biting through his jacket as his father negotiated the last earthy lump and placed him at the end of the front row. Grandma and Grandpa filed in with the rest of the family. The back row remained empty, reminiscent of a forlorn pew in a rural church. To his right stood his friend Graham. Others milled nearby. Forcing himself to look forward, he noticed the pastor looking at him both kindly and sorrowfully. No words were spoken between them, but he knew instinctively that Pastor Stuart was fighting his own surge of emotions. The ride out to Bellerive Cemetery had given the cleric plenty of time to surmise the graveside comforts and ministrations that the ten-year old boy knew would neither bring his brother back nor stabilize his own cracked foundation.

Pastor Stuart's clear and placating voice carried over the breeze, "If we could, let's gather around closer, please." Slowly, the crowd began to hedge forward. There was a palpable impression they wanted to draw near, as a rabbit to a stray carrot. Yet they hung back, perhaps sensing their own mortality reflecting from the lonely little casket on the covered stand.

Sensing this hesitation, Dad turned and, with his own voice wavering, said, "Today, everyone is family." He beckoned them forward with a sweep of his right hand, and no one stayed back any longer.

As if on cue, the wind died down, and opening his Bible to John's Apocalypse, Pastor Stuart made his opening remarks before turning to the words of the twenty-first chapter of that ancient vision. And as he, the young man in the little durable chariot, listened, a colossal lament welled up within him. *Please God,* he begged, *I want Christopher to be okay. But I want to be okay, too. And more than anything, I want to believe you aren't doing this to hurt me.* Alone in his thoughts and fears, his mind drifted. But now as the pastor began to read the words of comfort, he felt the ground move under the feet of his spirit, exposing a spiritual quicksand he had never envisioned.

Then I saw a new heaven and a new earth, for the first heaven and the first earth had passed away, and the sea was no more. And I saw the holy city, new Jerusalem, coming down out of heaven from God, prepared as a bride adorned for her husband. And I heard a loud voice from the throne saying, "Behold, the dwelling place of God is with man. He will dwell with them, and they will be his people, and God himself will be with them as their God. He will wipe away every tear from their eyes, and death shall be no more, neither shall there be mourning, nor crying, nor pain anymore, for the former things have passed away."

And he began to sink. The murkiness slowly enveloped him like the morning mist coming off the Missouri River. He clawed to return to the innocent hope he knew from former days, the hope that survived even the moments when he himself had faced death. But the warmth of the divine smile faded, and the rays of that cosmic sun had been covered with the shadow of death. He was a beaten boxer receiving the finishing uppercut. He heard the words of promise in the closing verse. The words, quietly and sincerely delivered, washed over him.

And he who was seated on the throne said, "Behold, I am making all things new." Also he said, "Write this down, for these words are trustworthy and true."

True or not, the boy thought to himself, do they matter? I will live, struggle for strength and breath, and never leave this chair to walk ever again. What good does it do to wipe my tears away in the future when God has given me so many tears in the past and present?

As he swam in that ocean of brutal honesty, the last vestiges of his childlike faith vaporized, and the tattered curtain of his soul tore violently in half from top to bottom. He gazed tearfully at the glossy white box that held his beloved brother as his heart creaked open and bade him to walk the skeptic's road.

LUKE H. DAVIS

PART ONE

A FAITH DEFILED

(JANUARY 24TH-25TH)

LUKE H. DAVIS

1

The sun maintained its climb through the cloud-laced Missouri sky, a desperate salvo for mastery of the heavens on this brutally cold January day. Miles below this celestial crusade, the Reverend Tomas Zednik continued his trek across Interstate 70. Having begun his journey before daybreak, his travel efficiency gave him a momentary surge of good cheer. He had left his modest home in Liberty at half-past six, missed any semblance of traffic in the Kansas City suburbs, and experienced only a small delay on the west side of Columbia. Much to his delight, he even had time to stop at the Hermann exit. There, he walked into the Stone Hill Winery outlet store as it opened and withdrew with three bottles of his favorite Steinberg White. Now bearing southeast onto the freshly overhauled Highway 40 eastbound toward St. Louis, his buoyant spirits eroded. They were replaced with a precursor of the weariness he knew would come with greater force. Assigned to bring some semblance of order to the financial picture at St. Basil's Seminary, his shoulders slumped as he mentally projected the day before him.

It wasn't as if Zednik shrank from conflict. Nor did he find today's summit beyond the scope of his abilities. Since becoming diocesan treasurer four years ago, he found the transition from parish life to be a remarkably smooth one. The bishop's faith in Zednik's meticulous fiscal wisdom had been well founded, and the diocese was held up as a model of economic chastity. But while the larger church smiled upon his efforts, Zednik knew there was one blemish within that had to be cleansed promptly.

St. Basil's.

The seminary to which he traveled was one of the shining lights in the Orthodox faith. Zednik himself was an alumnus from a quarter century ago, and he would recommend prospective students to St. Basil's with no reservations about the school's credentials. And the reasons were legion: The best teachers in the Orthodox Church. A passion for the reverence of the ancient worship and liturgy in their beautiful chapel. The dedication to spiritual formation and pastoral theology. A community atmosphere among the small cluster of residential students. The access to a major city like St. Louis, combined with the quiet setting of a rural campus a county away. And he never heard anyone complain about the food.

But over the past two years, dark clouds had peppered the horizon of his alma mater. As Zednik steered his Ford Fusion off Exit 9 at O'Fallon and turned onto the frontage road, he let out another groan over the financial puzzle at St. Basil's. Monthly shortfalls had accumulated and snowballed. Yet vociferous alumni and donors insisted they were giving at least as much as they ever had. The administration pleaded innocence and pledged their full cooperation with the diocese. Full details had been slow in forthcoming and so it fell to him to arrive on the scene to conduct an investigation and a full audit. Zednik had never been a CPA. For those interested in his preparation, he could only claim a minor in accounting at the undergraduate level. But he combined deep wisdom with a knack for knowing when he wasn't getting the whole story. Those who crossed this normally gentle priest were known to be on the receiving end of his famous quote, "You're so full of it; your eyes are brown."

Zednik made a right turn on Highway 94 and began his southward foray skirting the Busch Conservation Area, which wasn't the most verdant territory in midwinter. He passed Francis Howell High School on his right and knew from former visits that he was within fifteen minutes of the campus. He pulled out his cell phone and made a brief call to the seminary, alerting them to his impending arrival. He coasted past bare oaks as well as pines that stubbornly held onto their needles. *Why couldn't this appointment happen in the spring*, he asked himself. He made a mental note to make his next visit during that time, in April perhaps. Then he could pull some catfish out of the lake or view some quail, hawks, and the occasional eagle.

After some time, Zednik saw the small town of Defiance appear before him. He was back in St. Louis wine country, and he swore you couldn't find a better product for miles. A collection of vineyards and shops came into view, and he slowed down for a zig-zag turn to his left and back again in the center of town. From there it was a right turn on Howell Road, and then, after less than a mile, the turn into St. Basil's.

Wearier from his thoughts than the drive, Zednik wiped his hand across his blue eyes. He rubbed his morning stubble before giving himself a gentle slap on the right cheek, a call to attention for the task ahead of him. As the Fusion began the climb up the conspicuous incline, he saw the sun's rays dance on the gigantic figure of the All Souls' Cross. The massive tri-bar edifice welcomed visitors and friends with its imposing eighteen-foot height. He turned away from the bronze cruciform as he motored past the Lake of the Protomartyr and St. Jude's Glade to his right. *Such a quiet, pastoral space,* he thought, *and yet today's talks will be anything but.* The pain in his back cried out as if in protest to his role this day, and he was glad he had remembered to bring his medication along.

As he reached the crest of the hill, the campus of St. Basil's appeared as if to lay its grandeur before him. Sadly, he thought, it was a rural splendor tainted with irresponsibility. Today would be the final battle in this long skirmish.

With a turn of the key, Father Matthias unlocked his office door on the second level of Chalcedon Hall. He had just returned from Morning Prayer, and his knees ached from the climb up the stairwell. A grimace creased his face, which caused his salt-and-pepper beard to contort. He was about to shut the door behind him when he saw his colleague, Father Andrew, approach from down the hall. He remembered, of course, that this was their scheduled Monday morning chat. Usually, they would linger over coffee and speak about the activities and challenges of St. Basil's. These encounters could get spirited, as they did not always agree on everything, but Father Matthias preferred, as he said, "working with a bucking bronco than a dead horse." But this conference would be necessarily short. The dread of today's appointment brought a cloud over Father Matthias' otherwise hopeful demeanor, and it would not be going away anytime soon. The Reverend Tomas Zednik was due to arrive any moment.

"Father Matthias," said Father Andrew, "I know that the treasurer could be here shortly, but we should meet, if for no other reason than to consider our response."

"Of course," said Father Matthias. "Come in and we'll talk." He opened the door wide and Father Andrew brushed past him into the spacious study. The rear windows always provided a sweeping view of the woods north of Chalcedon Hall, though the trees were laid bare in the bitter January atmosphere. Their inner environment, however, could hardly be described as austere. The hardwood floor gave a smart contrast to the walls, which were painted a vibrant Williamsburg blue. The polar white crown molding and chair rails that surrounded the room went well with the floor-to-ceiling bookshelves that housed a small portion of Father Matthias' personal library, including several copies of books he had written. If a bookshelf did not cover a portion of the wall, then a fresco or icon did: a painting of Constantinople here, an image of the Virgin Mary there. Father Andrew was always impressed by the sanctity of this space, yet he was equally awestruck by several items of rustic appeal. Three fishing poles huddled together in the corner by a closet door. An axe, which had belonged to Father Matthias' father, hung above the fireplace by the east wall. And there, as always, on the desk next to the printer lay the baseball glove Father Matthias had owned and used since ten years of age. Perhaps it was a strategic prop to evoke memories of a happier time. Whatever the reason for that, Father Andrew always believed the dean's office struck an interesting balance between traditional Orthodox reverence and Missouri country charm. It was like walking into a humorous intersection of a cathedral and a Cracker Barrel.

Father Matthias directed his chancellor to the armchair by his desk and mumbled something about coffee.

"Thank you, no," said Father Andrew. "I fear we may be getting interrupted anyhow." He paused and brought his hands together, interlocking the fingertips in front of his mouth before saying, "I am somewhat curious how you will begin our conference today with Zednik."

Father Matthias tilted his head back slightly and drew in a deep breath, hoping that his body language did not give away his irritation. Father Andrew had a way of coaching people toward his own preconceived goal under a veneer of concern. It was one of several ongoing tensions between the two men over the past six years. It was no secret that Father Matthias was the reigning champion of conservative Orthodox theology, having written the definitive anthology of the church fathers and their teachings. The popularity of Father Andrew—and his spiritual formation classes—was not a full-blown concern, except that Father Matthias was distressed over his openness to a more inductive study of the Bible. Father Andrew seemed more driven to update the Orthodox faith to the twenty-first century rather than understand the rich history of the church. Around St. Basil's, students secretly tagged Father Matthias as the "settler" while Father Andrew was "the pioneer." The perceived rivalry between the two was the subject of much seminary gossip and intrigue.

Pushing those notions out of his mind, Father Matthias answered, "We haven't many options. We show him the balance sheets and the list of donations. We have been very prudent and meticulous in these matters. I can't imagine how he could want much more. The bishop has made it clear that Reverend Zednik should be respected as a representative of the diocese and I am determined that our community should display that esteem to him for the duration of his stay."

Father Andrew raised his left eyebrow in muted surprise. "I certainly hope that's the case. His arrival today—indeed, any visit from the diocese—will have a polarizing effect. A great many of the students have a very firm opinion these matters should be handled independently by an accounting firm. And some of our most vocal men—Stephen, Nicholas, and Jason among them—still believe Reverend Zednik played a major role in Father Jonathan's appointment here."

"That he did, but I don't believe this needs to be brought up today. It is a side issue. And, by the way, I've never heard you object to Father Jonathan's presence here."

"I don't, Father Matthias, but like you said, it's a side issue."

The curious case of Father Jonathan Erhart was a thorny subject. His very presence at St. Basil's was one of the more hotly debated issues in the seminary community. Thirteen years ago, Father Jonathan had been caught in a heated affair with a Birmingham woman. The scandal was splashed across the religion pages of newspapers all over the Deep South. The woman's marriage of ten years imploded as a result. Father Jonathan not only was forced out of his parish, he was barred from his diocese. He found a refuge in the Kansas City area, worshipping at Holy Resurrection Church. Very quickly, the priest took an interest in Father Jonathan's well being and began a period of restorative counseling approved by the diocese. The priest's name was Tomas Zednik.

After finishing forty months of this penance, Father Jonathan had gone on to serve the diocese under Bishop Burgic for a two-year period of administrative duties, though those activities were never clearly enumerated. It was seven years ago that the controversial appointment came. St. Basil's had need of an Old Testament instructor. "Burgic's Bellhop," as Father Jonathan's detractors called him, was given the teaching role. Father Matthias was never consulted as to his feelings on the matter. Father Andrew, who came to St. Basil's a year later, believed that Father Jonathan was a sincere man, aware of his very painful shortcomings, and this often gave him a more compassionate approach to the spiritual needs of others. But Father Andrew was equally aware this appointment was a lightning rod of contentiousness. Whatever issues the students disagreed on, they were fairly united on the view that their ecclesiastical shepherds should be cleaner than the sheep.

"At the very least," said Father Matthias, "it should be a relatively brief visit. I have asked Reverend Zednik to serve Vespers this evening. He did indicate he would stay overnight rather than drive all the way back to Kansas City this evening. We'll have to have some backup to prepare the guesthouse. Cora will be visiting her mother at St. Anthony's Hospital until evening; you may remember she had a stent put in just yesterday. As such, we'll have Lainie and Dana take care of the cleaning and bedding."

"Are you sure it's a good idea to have him serve Vespers, Father? My concern is that his presence might affect the students."

"I am more concerned that we make as many offers of goodwill as possible. This is one of them. Call it a matter of strategy, if you will. Didn't our Lord tell us to be wise as serpents and harmless as doves?"

Even Father Andrew had to smile at that, "Yes, Father. I was just concerned for how the seminary community will react to his presence."

"That is out of our hands. I am just thankful we can get this meeting in before our classes this afternoon. I have asked Father Timothy to lunch with Reverend Zednik. I believe that we won't see him afterward until Vespers. With decent luck, we can get through dinner and it will be a quiet evening."

He spoke with subdued confidence, but Father Matthias had no idea how wrong he was.

LUKE H. DAVIS

Not one minute after his colleague left the office, Father Matthias quietly gathered his files and grabbed a bottle of water out of the mini-fridge he kept behind his desk. He was on his way to the door when he heard a sharp knock. The knob turned and Lainie Kale entered. The wife of third-year student Stephen Kale, she carried a svelte, athletic figure on her five feet, six inch frame. Her raven black hair, parted on the left, cascaded to her shoulders and contrasted with her white winter jacket over her dark gray sweatshirt. A fuchsia scarf covered the neck, protecting her from the brutal wind that swirled outside. She wore loose fitting cargo pants with hiking boots, and it was obvious from her entry she was in a hurry. Yet Father Matthias knew that, even if she had sprinted the hundred yards from her apartment to Chalcedon Hall, she'd be drawing even breaths. She had spent four soccer seasons at Millsaps College in Jackson, Mississippi. There she'd gained renown—both as an all-conference midfielder for the Lady Majors' team as well as a conditioned and ferociously competitive athlete. At St. Basil's, she provided invaluable assistance throughout the whole scope of seminary life. She led the seminary wives' fellowship, helped Cora Dawson with laundry, served in the rotation in preparing the bread and wine for Holy Communion, and oversaw the mailroom. Having majored in economics at Millsaps, she also assisted in the business office. Her husband remained in awe of her energy and remarked on more than one occasion that if the Orthodox Church ordained women to the ministry, Lainie would be a fine candidate for bishop. The professors at St. Basil's, to put it mildly, were not amused by Stephen's comment. But Father Matthias had always found Lainie to be a valuable "right hand" that was part of the seminary's administrative function. Thus, he did not mind this intrusion.

"Yes, Lainie? I assume there's something you need to discuss?"

She replied, "Not discuss, Father. Just being a messenger for now." Her slight Southern accent practically floated through the air like a January snow flurry. "Reverend Zednik just called on his cell phone. He's a few minutes away, so he'll be arriving shortly. He did have one request."

"I assume it's in regard to his dietary needs. I know his kidneys aren't always in top form."

"No, nothing like that," Lainie said with a slight frown. "He's asked to have the meeting with everyone involved in administration, finance, and public relations. In short, he mentioned you and Father Andrew, of course, but Mrs. Dirklage, Mrs. Porter, and myself, as well."

A confused look spread over Father Matthias's visage, and he bowed his head quickly in frustration before looking back up at Lainie. "I don't understand. Our agreement was that this would be a meeting for himself, Father Andrew, and myself. I suppose he has a reason to justify this sudden change?"

"Yes, Father. He wanted to meet with everyone who would have access to any financial gifts or the budget. Even though he knows you and Father Andrew are the only full-time personnel in the mix, he wanted anyone involved to attend."

Father Matthias let out a low groan and motioned Lainie to accompany him out of his office. As they made their way through the building, he reflected on the present conundrum. Reverend Zednik was not known for impulsive decisions, which meant he had been mulling this stratagem for some time. Now he had used the element of surprise and St. Basil's would be on the defensive. There was nary a chance the five of them would provide cohesive, perfectly structured answers to Zednik's questions. And he was certain that the treasurer would see any difference in expression as a chink in the armor of consistency. Such a threat frightened Father Matthias; he believed himself to be above board on these financial matters. If any issues were roiling, they were sins of ignorance, not of his commission.

He tore his thoughts away from these dark possibilities and spoke to Lainie. "I would ask, then, that as soon as the meeting is over, you would be so good as to change the linens in the guesthouse for Reverend Zednik's overnight stay. I am sure that he will want his bags set aside in his room upon arrival. If you need assistance, let Dana know."

"What about Mrs. Dawson, Father?"

"She is paying a post-surgical visit to her mother and so has asked for today off. Ben might know when she's returning, but I wouldn't expect her until late."

"Yes, Father. Whatever is needed."

Just as they emerged from Chalcedon Hall, a metallic silver Ford Fusion came curling around the front circle and parked in the east lot. They approached the car, and when they were within ten feet, the driver door opened. The intelligent face with the wary blue eyes appeared, set beneath the gently combed wisps of blond hair.

"Good morning, Father Matthias," said Reverend Zednik in an unnaturally forceful tone. "We have much to cover today, so if we could gather everyone as soon as possible, we can begin."

The conference room in which Reverend Zednik would conduct the meeting was remarkably spartan and utilitarian compared to the rest of the seminary. Six black stacking banquet chairs were arranged around a boat-shaped table with a Hansen cherry finish. The room, located in the northwest corner of Chalcedon Hall's main floor, was well lit and provided unimpeded views of the woods through five windows. Only two pictures graced the room. A panoramic photograph of the seminary watched over the table from the east wall, while a collage showing the progressive construction of the library hung from the south wall.

Father Matthias entered first and went immediately to the first chair on the end. He gestured that Reverend Zednik take the chair opposite him at the other end. Although Zednik would oversee the meeting, he would be the most psychologically disadvantaged. That particular chair sat a bit lower than the others, and he would be the furthest from the door. Julie Dirklage, a middle-aged widow who worked as the secretary for Fathers Matthias and Andrew, took the seat on the west side closest to the dean. Jane Porter, the part-time business manager who worked Mondays, Tuesdays, and Thursdays, sat across from her. Father Andrew slid into the chair on the east side of the room, placing him within two arms' length of Zednik. Lainie Kale arrived late after taking some time transporting Zednik's bags to the guesthouse. Once she seated herself across from Father Andrew, the group paused and then rose together with Father Matthias, who led in prayer.

"Be mindful, O Lord, of us, Thy humble servants; grant us Thy grace, that we may be diligent and faithful, avoiding evil company and influence, resisting temptation; that we may lead godly and righteous lives, blameless and peaceful, ever serving Thee; that we may be accounted worthy of entering the Kingdom of Heaven. Amen."

The other five calmly replied with a muted "Amen," and then took their seats along with Father Matthias. They had not yet settled into the chairs when Zednik spoke out.

"Over the past two years, the diocese has become more and more aware of some financial gaps here at St. Basil's. Granted, the operations of even a small seminary like this take much skill to track conscientiously. But these aren't cracks in the monetary granite. As I've said, they are gaps. And they are noticeable. The diocese requested that you perform an internal audit, which you, Father Matthias, authorized on this end."

"I did."

"And that audit failed to get anywhere."

"Now I don't see what more we could have done," Father Andrew jumped in. "We called for it to happen. We informed the entire seminary family so everyone would know something of this nature was going on. Mrs. Porter and Mrs. Kale went through pages of documents and showed us that everything was up to date on giving. We saw every deposit slip they provided. In my opinion, we couldn't have done it better in spite of the fact we didn't use a CPA."

"And you closed it off without alerting us at all. You never gave us regular reports of your progress. And like you said, you never utilized a CPA. Certainly that would have been ideal."

It was Lainie Kale who replied. "I think the bottom line is that for what the seminary was able to do, we did."

"And yet that still doesn't mean the whole system was completely above board."

Father Matthias felt the bile rise in his throat but thankfully, before he could retort, Jane Porter spoke up. She may have been a petite five feet, one inch wife of a college professor, but she backed down to no one. Her face, red with frustration, contrasted brightly with her short blond hair. "Reverend Zednik, you know as well as we do that if we are running a deficit, there may be some debate why that is, but I don't think there is any doubt that we have done our best to restrain costs and spending while we figure this out. We don't run the fountain in the Lake of the Protomartyr much at all anymore, we look for ways to cut our usage of electricity and gas and encourage our resident students to do the same. And we have stopped ordering as many consumables for use in the classroom and have pushed more digital usage of academic tools."

"I'm afraid, Mrs. Porter, that those matters are drops in the proverbial bucket," said Zednik. "Those are noble attempts. I don't debate that. But are they enough to offset the shortfall of one hundred twenty-one thousand, three hundred seventy dollars?"

With a slight growl in his normally placid voice, Father Andrew replied, "Again, Reverend Zednik, we tell you we don't know how this came about."

Father Matthias waved both his hands in an inside-out symmetrical wave, as if he were doing a breaststroke in the swimming pool. "You already seem to have an idea where you're going with this. Rather than slow dancing with your hands all over us, why don't you make your move?"

Zednik cleared his throat and winced as he felt his back tighten.

23

Once he recovered himself, he spoke in a measured tone. "The diocese has taken the liberty of procuring the lists of former donors and the amounts of what they have given. The reason for this is to lay some sort of foundation for taking over a full investigation."

"Who is taking over?" cried Father Matthias.

"The diocese, of course."

"That's outrageous! You never told us this was a possibility!"

"What would you have us do, Father Matthias? Hold your hand every step of the way? Affirm your best, yet shallow, efforts at figuring out the morass in which you now find yourselves? It's clear that after all this time something isn't above board."

The vice-like tension seemed to squeeze their gathering of any charitable dialogue, and it was by a forced miracle that Jane Porter inquired in the most polite expression she could find.

"How did you procure them?"

"What?"

"You heard me, Reverend. I'm only six feet away. How did you get those donor records?"

"I am afraid that is a private matter for the diocese."

That was too much for Lainie Kale. "I'm sorry, Reverend. But the next time you lie to us, your body language needs to be a touch more believable. Refusing to meet our eyes and shifting in your hot seat makes your deflection less than trustworthy."

"I don't think he needs to reshape his positioning," Father Matthias pronounced with barely concealed rage. "Because it's clear he's gone back to the days before Jane. It's obvious he's had someone serve as his mole! Father Jonathan swiped the records for him under our nose!"

The collective gasp that followed that statement practically threatened to suck all the oxygen out of the room. It was several seconds later that Father Andrew leaned forward, tenting his fingers together as his elbows rested on the table. His nostrils flared slowly and then he turned toward Zednik.

"Tomas, I have always known you to be a man of integrity. Even when I have disagreed with your conclusions, I have perpetually believed that you arrived at them by honorable methods. But if you had wanted to act in good faith with our seminary, this was the wrong approach. Look, I like Father Jonathan. Many here at St. Basil's were upset with his appointment. He did serve this place well as a temporary bookkeeper until we found Jane to work full-time. But for you to have him work under the radar like this is beyond unreasonable. It is unforgiveable!"

Zednik, sensing the mood in the room turning from simmering to toxic, quietly responded, "This is not that simple. And that is another matter for another time. If you want to contend the back-door, smoke-filled room quality of this action, you are welcome to do that. Complain to the diocese all you want. But I'm more interested in the hard facts we have before us."

Passing around copies of a document, he continued speaking. "Perhaps *this* is that simple. Look at the third page and especially at the highlighted amounts on the donor list. You received annual checks from the St. Herman's League, both for generous donations of thirty thousand dollars each. Then, Richard and Rosemary Sefrit, very faithful longtime donors, wrote two checks over the past two years.

One was for seventeen thousand five hundred, and the other was an even seventeen thousand. Finally, David Stange gave six thousand, eight hundred seventy the year before last. This past year he gave an even twenty thousand to St. Basil's. His restaurant business is a nice success and your school is an obvious beneficiary of his achievement. Now if you total the amounts of those six donations all together, you have one hundred twenty-one thousand, three hundred seventy dollars." He paused for effect. "The exact figure for your shortfall."

Jane Porter was quick to respond. "Coincidence. I'm not denying the math works. But the implication you're giving is just too neat."

"Mrs. Porter, is there a fantastic coincidence that you signed your name to all of those checks for deposit?"

"Who else would sign them?"

"Do you remember them? The amounts are quite significant. After all, these aren't eight year-old girls sending on the proceeds of their neighborhood bake sales."

"I see a lot of checks."

"Reverend Zednik," spat Father Matthias, "just what is this? An accusation?"

"No, a precursor to two other questions. One, why is only one signature required on such large amounts?"

No one spoke a word. Zednik continued. "All right, do you have any bank statements that will help us track these matters?"

Father Andrew cut in before anyone else could. "None of ours are on paper. Call it going green or avoiding clutter. Everything is online. It's the typical Internet entry thing. Username and password."

"Then I will require those from you as well."

Lainie was incredulous. "Wait one minute." She looked at Father Matthias for support. "Does he mean he can just demand those items by brute force?"

"Brute force, young lady," said Zednik, now sensing he had regained the upper hand, "is how this school has been operating for some time. A lack of communication with diocesan headquarters. Internal squabbling over theological emphases. And your actions show no one can tell a checkbook from a hole in the ground!"

Father Matthias was beside himself now, and he raised himself out of his chair, rigidly leaning over the end of the table. Palms flat on the surface before him, his voice shot across the space between he and the treasurer. "Zednik, if you have an indictment to make, then do it! But stop your meandering wordplay!"

Zednik raised his hands in a conciliatory gesture. "Father Matthias, do you think this gives me any joy? This is my alma mater. I preached my first sermon in the chapel here. I spent four of the best years of my life here. I love this school. But I cannot feign blindness and allow the reputation of St. Basil's to be sullied. Yes, sullied! By what is so obviously an inside job of financial sleight-of-hand."

"You're accusing one of us of stealing?" said Father Andrew as Father Matthias lowered himself into his chair.

"I think that given the present circumstances you probably can draw your conclusions about my thoughts. And that should be enough. The diocese has certain—shall we say, strong—presuppositions that we believe evidence could show to be correct. Maybe they won't. But to verify or disprove those assumptions, we will require your online banking username and password to conduct the investigation. Once we are done with that and we have some level of confidence about things, you are free to change both the username and password to something else."

There was no response from anyone at first. Father Matthias could tell the meeting had snapped everyone's emotional fibers. He needed to maneuver things toward a rapid close.

"Reverend Zednik, it seems hardly proper to do this today. Other things must take priority. And we must also talk about Vespers for later."

"Then we should begin this process tomorrow. Perhaps some passage of time and a night of rest shall do us all well. I can meet with others throughout today."

"Very well. You and I can discuss the details later."

Father Matthias rose to his feet. The conference was obviously over, though the simmering emotions were not.

At eleven-thirty, Dana Witten stepped out of her apartment on the way to the refectory in Chalcedon Hall. Her husband Dieter, as usual, would not be joining her, opting instead to work on his St. Gregory readings for patristics class. She admired her husband's work ethic and pastoral aspirations. Now in his fourth and final year at St. Basil's, he had been named student rector of the Chapel of the Theotokos. This designation was given to the senior student who combined the highest levels of academic, pastoral, and preaching excellence. In public, Dana admitted her husband had those qualities in droves. Privately, she wished labels like "compassionate," "affectionate," and "responsive" would make the list, as well. For nearly four years, she had played second fiddle to Greek translations and theology discussions. In retrospect, she felt like she had gained a priest but slowly lost her husband.

To forget her low-grade sadness, Dana busied herself in any helpful role St. Basil's could give her. Her true talents lay in gardening and landscaping. The entire staff was appreciative of how she expanded the area and usage of the Beautiful Garden at the southeast point of the campus. Her efforts had brought a steady supply of homegrown vegetables, for which the refectory personnel were unendingly grateful. She also had arranged the white hawthorn shrubs and manna ash trees around the chapel three years ago, and her careful eyes and steady hands had turned a bare plot into a heavenly garden of delight.

It was also with the linens and cleaning that Dana assisted Cora Dawson at least twice a week at St. Basil's. Knowing Cora would be gone for the day, and thus needing to check her assignment, she trudged through the bitterly cold air, drawing her putty-colored denim jacket around her. Clad in black jeans and a Missouri State University hoodie sweatshirt, she made her way through the quickening breeze faster than she expected.

She entered the building and headed straight through without slowing down. The refectory was to the rear of the main floor, where chatter permeated the facility, coming from many of the first- and second-year students who gathered for a quick bite before their afternoon classes. Some waved and even winked in acknowledgement as Dana walked by. She rolled her eyes and groaned at the cloaked flirtatiousness. *A seminary prepares men of God, but they are still men after all.* She brushed a lock of flowing light brown hair out of her eyes and approached the kitchen.

"Hi, Dana," said Mark Sadowski, the head chef at St. Basil's. "Regular entrée or is this a drive-by chow-down?"

She smiled briefly and said, "Just a small one. I need to see what Cora has for me to do, so can we make it something quick? Any greens in the fridge?"

"Three bucks and you can have the California Cobb salad I just put in there. Second shelf from the top. Right side. Plastic cover with the blue sticker."

Dana found it in no time and placed four dollars in a small wicker basket on the shelf by the east wall. Then, grabbing the salad and a bottle of Aquafina from the refrigerator, she turned and left the kitchen. "I put an extra dollar in for the water."

Sadowski looked at her with a quizzical glance. "Are we to expect your husband here for lunch? Or is it the usual drivel about having to translate St. Joachimus the Green-Eyed-Former-Butcher-Turned-Saint's query into the creation of the soul?"

Again Dana rolled her eyes and forced a chuckle. "A spot-on match, Mark. Though if Father Matthias was around, I don't think you'd be mocking the early church fathers. Even mythical ones."

"Why do you think I'm saying it now? Ah, well. You'd better get to your food. Cora did say you'd likely have to clean and change the guesthouse for that finance Nazi coming in from KC. Better get yourself as far from me as possible, missy. You come in here looking like that and I'll get the urge to take over where Dieter's ailing."

Dana frowned and raised a restraining hand. "Thank you, no, Mark. I'm blessed enough. Save your urges for dessert."

Shaking her head in mock disgust, Dana sat down at the table closest to the lobby door. She had grown immune to Sadowski's half-baked pickup lines, knowing he had no desire to follow up on them whether she was single or married. Humor, even the ridiculous type, was his way of dealing with his painful divorce of five years ago. As Dana placed a forkful of cold chicken, lettuce, and hard-boiled egg in her mouth, she grumbled to herself. Wouldn't it be nice if Dieter paid her that sort of attention?

Her thoughts were interrupted by several blurs loping past the door to her left. She recognized Father Matthias and Father Andrew steering a black cassocked man of medium build outside. Ten seconds later followed Julie Dirklage and Jane Porter, speaking in low, hushed tones. They did not turn into the refectory, but the last person did. Wheeling into the cauldron of banter with a frustrated gait, she sidled up to the table and plopped down, slamming two file folders down in disgust. Lainie Kale.

"Something wrong?" asked Dana, who instinctively knew that if Lainie was upset, it was righteous anger.

"Zednik!" replied Lainie with clear indignation. "The treasurer. He's doing a pre-meditated audit and is requiring all our bank information. He pretty much accused Father Matthias and Jane Porter of either incompetence or pilfering. Stinking meeting took about thirty of the most unbearable minutes of my life."

"That's crazy? What evidence does he have?"

"You know how the diocese works. Anything they can project into a tree to stir up a hornet's nest. And here's…" She looked around to makes sure no one could hear, and then leaned closer, "Here's the worse part. He got Erhart to find the files on our donors and their giving. He's using people on the inside to set his bear traps, for God's sake!"

"Father Jonathan?" Knowing something of the controversial priest's background, Dana had never been his most loyal supporter. But on the other hand, she had never known him to display anything but consistent pastoral kindness and wisdom. "I find it difficult to believe he's capable of this."

"Well, unfortunately, that day has arrived. And we have to be Zednik's chambermaids while he's conducting this charade of an inquiry. That's why I'm glad I caught you. I can handle the laundry and get the linens over there, but then I have to go to O'Fallon and pick up Stephen's asthma medication at Walgreens. Do you mind vacuuming Zednik's room and cleaning the bathroom? And by the way, you'll probably need to get him some bottled water. He takes medication, and he refuses to drink any tap water. I know. I feel badly that you have to do all that for a one-night stay, but I'm up against it for time."

"No, that's no problem, Lainie. You do what you need to," replied Dana. She watched her friend get up to leave when a curious thought struck her, so suddenly in fact, that it was out of her mouth before she could stop herself. "Hey, you don't think Zednik's doing this to smear St. Basil's and make it difficult for graduates to land something after May, do you?"

Lainie paused and lifted her eyebrows. Her glossy brown eyes softened with compassion as she said, "I don't know. He's a St. Basil's alum, so I don't think he'd stoop to that level. But I don't know what he'd do and Father Matthias and Father Andrew were fairly hot under the collar. It was a steam bath of antagonism in there, girl. Should make Vespers pretty interesting tonight. Zednik is leading the service. If I wasn't off campus, I'd go."

"Well, I might," said Dana. After a pause, she continued, "Might be the only time I get to see Dieter before bed anyway."

Lainie's face crumpled into a sorrowful contortion of sympathy. "Oh, girlfriend, I know." Leaning down to hug her, she said, "Your husband's just task-oriented on steroids. Give it time, babe. Today's neglect can be tomorrow's passion. You'll see."

And with that, she left. As Dana finished her lunch, she meditated on her predicament. A driven husband who loved the ministry more than her. An invading treasurer who could make the future rather unsettled. She didn't know which was worse. A dark haze of fear blew across her heart as she threw away her container and made her way out of the refectory. Instinctively, she crossed herself, as if the sign itself could drive away her trepidation.

LUKE H. DAVIS

Five hours later, a weary Father Matthias appeared from behind the *iconostasis* screen in the chapel and sauntered into the nave of the church. As he did so, the doors of the narthex opened and Reverend Zednik came walking through. A wave of fatigue rolled over Father Matthias, but he was determined that his counterpart not see his exhaustion. Zednik approached the seminary dean and spoke first.

"Good evening, Father. I assume we can change in there?" He pointed to the wall of icons and, beyond it, to the diaconicon area where the priestly vestments were stored.

With a strangely renewed combination of vigor and calm, Father Matthias replied, "Yes, Reverend Zednik. This way, please." As they made their way up the steps and approached the Beautiful Gate in the iconostasis, Father Matthias looked up at the images of Christ and John the Baptist, side by side. His voice, usually strong and booming in this intimate environment, expressed itself gently now. "Was your time with Father Timothy a productive one?"

"Quite productive," smiled Zednik, "In fact, I nearly got the entire swath of his course on the General Epistles. I'm sure if we had lingered any longer, he'd have asked me to translate the whole of James."

Despite the pugnacious tenor of that morning's meeting, Father Matthias smiled at the mental picture. "That I don't doubt. Father Timothy is our youngest professor, but he is likely our most demanding. A grade of B-minus could well be the equivalent of an A in some other courses here. I'm surprised you survived the experience."

"Oh, it wasn't a trial. We spoke of his time here, his work in the library, acquisitions, and line items. I hope you don't mind, Father Matthias. I thought since I had an audience with him, it would be efficient to speak of financial matters particular to the library."

Father Matthias sensed a bubbling up of frustration and offered a brief, silent prayer for forgiveness. "Think nothing of it, my friend. I'm glad you had the chance to meet him."

The two men had approached the diaconicon and searched through the collection of vestments before they found items that would fit Zednik. It took only a few moments for both men to complete their robing, and Father Matthias walked to the chapel on the north side of the altar to retrieve the incense for the service. He had almost reached it when Zednik broke the unnatural silence, "Matthias?"

It was the first time he had used the dean's Christian name without the usage of the title, and the quiet intimacy extended in his address gave Father Matthias a slightly peculiar sensation.

"Yes?"

In four strides, Reverend Zednik covered the ground between them so that he stood inches away—so close, in fact, that Father Matthias could clearly see the ridges in Zednik's tooth enamel.

"Matthias, I know this day has not been easy for you. I know," he hesitated, holding up a hand as Father Matthias' brow crinkled into a who-are-you-kidding look, "that is a weighty understatement. And while I feel there are things that must be done that are difficult, I want to let you know that I bear full responsibility for the tenor of today's conference."

His statement caught Father Matthias off-guard. "You are saying that you desire to shoulder the weight of today's pain?"

"This entire process has brought me great pain," replied Zednik, "because I know you are a man of integrity, and if you knew something evil was afoot, you would have stopped it. I believe there is something to be discovered, perhaps at great cost to us all. But I want you to know I am doing this because I believe St. Basil's will survive and be restored through all this."

Father Matthias pushed through his usually guarded emotions, wanting to trust this man, but needing one question answered. "But Father Jonathan? You used him. Against this school? I am sorry, Tomas, but this is so calculating, so…so…" he searched for the word he required, "so ruthless, it is out of character for you!" His voice quavered with hurt in the tranquility of the sanctuary.

"I know, Matthias, I know, and it is for that reason I wanted these minutes with you, to let you know that I have been the chief of sinners this day, that my actions today and in maneuvering this investigation have been wrongly executed despite my noble goals. I need to do my duty before the diocese and our thrice-holy Lord and Savior and carry out this inquiry. But I want to do so in the right way and with a pure spirit."

Reverend Zednik leaned forward, as if struck with a deep spiritual ache, and placed his right hand on Father Matthias' shoulder.

"Matthias, I have sinned. Before I stand in front of your family here and before I lead them before the throne of Christ, I need to be purified. Will you hear my confession?"

Stepping toward the man who had stunned him with such simple honesty, Father Matthias placed his hands on Zednik's collarbone and bowed his head.

"I will, Tomas. Tell me your sins, my brother in Christ."

Before five o'clock in the evening, the entire student body began filing into the Chapel of the Theotokos for Daily Vespers. With its starting time bound to each day's sunset, Vespers was a moveable stitch in the fabric of St. Basil's. During the winter months, given the more early waning solar rhythms, dinner was placed at half past six to accommodate the worship schedule. Despite the low growls of empty stomachs, the services remained a vital ritual for the students and, when they attended, their wives and children.

But today's rite brought with it a pregnancy of suspicion. The mere presence of Reverend Zednik had polarized the students into two groups: those who tolerated his visit like that of a passing insect and those who openly deplored his present investigation. Father Andrew was especially distressed that a Christian community could be so prone to gossip and steamy rumor, no matter how much of it might be borne out of genuine concern. In the six hours since that touchy circle of strife, someone had leaked salient details of that conference, and those elements had grown from one trickling creek to several forceful rivers of hearsay.

In that cauldron of anxiety, forty-four students gathered in the pews underneath a ceiling covered with enough painted angels and martyrs to fill the slots on a professional football team. From behind the iconostatis came Father Matthias and Reverend Zednik, followed by Father Jonathan and the student rector Dieter Witten, both of whom would be assisting. Father Matthias took his place on the left side in the front next to Father Andrew. With the robust smell of incense permeating the church, Zednik approached the congregation front and center and began with the opening greeting. "Blessed is our God always, now and ever, and unto the ages of ages."

The professors and students responded with a fervent "Amen."

The words continued their flow, the sacred dialogue and dance streaming forth amongst the congregation, the leaders, and the God whom they professed. Requests for mercy were followed by Psalms and these in turn were followed by the prayers of light. At that point, Reverend Zednik turned with his liturgical collaborators and faced the iconostatis. They gazed upon the images of the Virgin Mary and St. Basil to the left. Then, sweeping their eyes to the right, they fixed their eyes upon the solemn face of the icon of Jesus, who gestured with three fingers of his right hand up, in symbolic reminder of the Holy Trinity. Finally, lifting his hands, Zednik sent his suddenly majestic voice heavenward in petition to the Divine Mystery.

"O Lord, compassionate and merciful, long-suffering and of great mercy, hearken to our prayer, and attend to the voice of our supplication..."

The prayers continued, as ordinarily all would direct their hearts to follow the reverent road articulated for them. But out of the corner of his eye in the front row on the right, Father Timothy Birchall noticed the slightest of downward movements from across the nave. Turning his head, he noticed a small but growing commotion, taking place two pews back from Father Matthias.

Amidst the chanting and sacred wordplay, two students had sat down in the middle of the pew, refusing to participate further. Two others on either side of them were yanking them by their cassocks in a vain attempt to redirect them to a vertical base. Father Timothy might have been a relatively young priest in the Orthodox universe, but he had an uncanny ability to distinguish between intense meditation and willful insubordination. And from what he could see, the two seated students fell into the latter category. With a firm step and ignoring any sense of decorum, he scurried across the aisle in the blink of an eye and buried a pincer-like grip into the shoulders of Nicholas Panangiotis and Stephen Kale.

Neither student, even if they had tried, could resist the disciplinary pull of Father Timothy's strong hands. Nicholas retained a defiant look on his face, but Stephen glanced wonderingly about as their pew mates, Marcus Curry and Jason Hart, looked on with mocking joy. Their smiles were cut short, however, when Father Timothy glared at them and, with a backward nod of his head, motioned them outside.

When outside and with the doors closed behind them in the gathering twilight, Father Timothy half-shoved Nicholas and Stephen toward a denuded Bradford pear tree. Marcus and Jason soon joined them, forming a bemused semicircle around the priest, who raised an intimidating right hand and spoke fiercely.

"I don't care what circumstances you feel might have given you latitude for that pathetic display in there, but you men are out of line!" Father Timothy yelled. "Nicholas, Stephen, whatever you were thinking, it's inexcusable to sit down in disrespect of a visiting officiant! I don't want to hear it!" he paused as Nicholas opened his mouth to protest, "From you, or you! That action in there," he pointed back to the chapel, "was a vile, impotent and childish attempt at dissent. And don't think for a moment you can read it as anything but!"

The four students stood, stock-still and bug-eyed at Father Timothy's fury. No one doubted that he was angry enough to do them serious physical harm.

"And you, Marcus and Jason, you allowed yourselves to get draw into a pissing match. Rather than join in with the liturgy, you succumbed to a scrum of infantile pushing and scritch-fighting."

"Sir, what would you have us do?" asked Jason. "Let it go?"

"Just because you are junior chaplain, that does not give you the right to purge one problem by ignoring your greater duty to God. You and I both know that is a priest's job to intervene."

"Father Timothy, may I say something?" The request came from Nicholas. His face was red as blood, contrasting with his platinum blond hair. Whether his complexion was due to embarrassment or rage, it was difficult to tell, but most at St. Basil's would have placed better odds on rage.

Glaring at Nicholas, Father Timothy said, "Proceed. And be concise."

"If we speak of infantile pushing and a problem to be purged, then you should have gone after Reverend Zednik. Why he is overseeing Vespers is a travesty. The man wants to set up a throne of his own here and intervene for the diocese at his every whim."

"He has no respect of thinking people here," meekly offered Stephen.

"He is a priest and diocesan official and he will be given the honor due him, no matter how many objections you raise!" thundered Father Timothy.

"He's not worthy to be a priest!" hissed Nicholas.

"Spoken like someone who swims in the same pool!" boomed Marcus Curry. He had been remarkably silent since they had gathered outside, but now he gestured at Nicholas threateningly with his sturdy black hands.

"Shut up, Oreo," murmured Nicholas.

That crossed Father Timothy's line. With one fluid motion, he snatched Nicholas by the shoulder, sinking his fingers deep into his trapezoid and pulling him within three inches of his face. Nicholas' life flashed before his eyes, which were about to pop out of his head.

"It never changes, does it, Nicholas? You can't keep your big mouth shut nor can you refrain from dragging others down your impulsive paths! And you," he looked at Stephen Kale, "can't stand on your own two feet."

He released his grip on Nicholas and pushed him away. He looked at Marcus and Jason. "You two have much to learn when it comes to insight and wisdom. God does not need mercenaries to defend his honor. I would advise both of you to remember that."

Not waiting for a reply, he turned back to Nicholas and Stephen. "As for both of you, there are greater consequences for that stunt you pulled in Vespers. Until you perform some penance to be named later, consider yourself barred from Holy Communion. Your path," he gestured to Nicholas, "will be all the harder. Capping that little rebellion with a racist remark toward a fellow student made things even worse. See me tomorrow for your requirement, both of you. For now, all four of you are excused early from Vespers."

Father Timothy looked as if he was going to take leave of them and return to the chapel. Hesitating, he fixed all four of them with a level glance. "Consider this, all of you. If this is the way you solve

43

problems in your present community, that doesn't bode well for parishes that you may serve in the future. You have to ask yourselves honestly if you...how did you say it, Nicholas...are worthy to be priests. Good evening."

And with a turn of his heel, the imposing Father Timothy made his way back into the church. But Nicholas wasn't done with his classmate. Glowering at Marcus, he went after him with fists balled into stones of vehemence. Marcus, never one to back down from a fight, went straight for him. But with lightning speed and considerable strength, Stephen grabbed Nicholas from behind and Jason lifted Marcus up in a front standing tackle.

"Cool down!" Stephen snapped at Nicholas.

"Get back!" ordered Jason to Marcus, forcing him away slowly.

"Thanks a lot, you jerk!" spat Nicholas at Marcus.

"Enjoy your penance, little bishop," smiled Marcus, who backed away with a triumphant sneer on his face.

Dinner in the refectory that evening had been a subdued affair. Dieter Witten had pronounced the communal blessing, as the meal was more of an informal family gathering. Father Timothy ate his meal in relative silence, speaking only to a couple of first-year students regarding their mission trip for the next two weeks. His grilled pollock, rice, and salad were almost gone and he was tipping a glass of wine to his lips when Father Andrew tapped him on the shoulder from behind.

"Father Matthias would like to see you in his office for a few moments, if you don't mind."

Wondering if it related to the incident at Vespers, Father Timothy nodded and affirmed that he would be up in five minutes.

Dana Witten gave a sarcastic smile to her reflection in the mirror. *If the fathers want to know how to nip rumors in the bud around here,* she thought, *they could begin with lowered voices and better-insulated walls.* She had noticed Father Timothy coming down the hallway, had heard the creak of the door as he entered Father Matthias' office, and now was a hidden recipient of the tense conversation in that space. All because the linen closet was next door. She grabbed an extra pillow for Reverend Zednik's bed. Then she crouched low and listened.

"I don't understand," declared Father Timothy. "I put a stop to a brewing issue and disciplined them accordingly. You may take issue with the weightiness of my confrontation but not with my motives."

"Your motives are not at issue here, Timothy," said the visibly tired Father Matthias. "I have always been impressed with your standards and your knowledge. Your desire to produce educated priests is peerless. You are an essential pillar of this faculty. And your motives to defend the atmosphere of worship while Reverend Zednik was here are noble indeed."

"Then why am I here?"

"Because your passion for excellence does not excuse heavy-handed tactics that have a tendency to humiliate students rather than edify them. This is something that has come to the attention of the diocese, and I need you to recognize that! I am not here to bathe you in misery or critique. I am letting you know that we have men in authority over us and among us who believe a straitjacket is a better fit for this school than institutional liberty. And when you openly confront four students in plain sight of others and you place your hands on one of them, word gets around!"

Father Timothy was strangely silent as he stroked his goatee, and the words that followed were a low growl that crawled out of his six-foot-six-inch frame. "Who, then? Who reported me?"

Father Matthias knew he had said too much, but he also recognized his junior professor would eventually discern the truth anyway. "Father Jonathan had gone down the aisle with the censor during the middle of the service. He saw what happened through the front doors of the church. He reported it to Reverend Zednik, who demanded I speak to you."

"That snitch!" roared Father Timothy. "I defend both he and Father Jonathan, and this is what happens? You cannot be serious about this!"

"I have to have this audience with you, my son. Do you think I want to?"

"Father Jonathan has no right! He never asked me what it was all about! And before he comes after me for the speck in my eye, shouldn't he look at the plank lodged in his own?"

"Timothy, keep your voice down!"

"No, Father! My point is that no matter what, there seems to be a scheme afoot to remove me from employment and influence here at St. Basil's. Zednik already told me my position was on rocky footing when I met with him this afternoon, even threatening to cut the library's budget."

"He never breathed a word of that to me," said a genuinely confused Father Matthias.

Father Timothy's cords nearly burst out of his neck. "Exactly! He's telling pieces of his plan to everyone, but he triangulates things so we're all in the dark. By using Father Jonathan as his lackey, he corrodes any sense of trust I have in Zednik as a superior and Father Jonathan as a colleague!"

In that moment, Father Matthias recognized two truths. One was that, despite the financial deficit at St. Basil's, Reverend Zednik and Father Jonathan were working the circumstances like master puppeteers. The other was that Father Timothy was in full-blown wrath, and his temper and physical prowess was a potentially dangerous cocktail.

"Timothy, please," he said, searching for words he hoped his God could manufacture for him on the spot. "Calm yourself. Please go back to your apartment and do nothing for now. Talk to Jennifer about something, anything other than this. Get through tonight and be a model citizen until Reverend Zednik's departure tomorrow. Please. You, and we, cannot afford anything else."

Father Timothy raised his arms in an I-give-up expression before turning toward the door. He had reached the knob when Father Matthias put forth one last plea, "And it might help, in taking the moral high ground, if you would apologize to both men. Even if it feels less than genuine, to make peace at this time would give you a lot of collateral."

He watched Father Timothy turn the knob and open the door. Before the young professor departed the room, he turned back to his superior and targeted him with his dark brown eyes.

"Father Matthias, whatever Reverend Zednik and Father Jonathan get from me now, it won't be an apology." And he was gone.

Dana hurried down the stairwell on the east end of Chalcedon Hall. What she had just heard had simultaneously disturbed and bewildered her. She left by a side door and covered the thirty yards to Chrysostom House in a few seconds. Heart pounding, she knocked on the door and opened it when she heard the male voice welcome her in.

"Good evening, Reverend Zednik. I brought you a water bottle to take your medication."

Still smoldering, Nicholas Panangiotis knew that he was in no mood to study that night. St. Peter's First Epistle could wait, indefinitely. There were things that needed to be said, but one thing in particular that needed to be done. He would wait an hour more and then he would act on his decision. He looked in the direction of Chrysostom House and saw the light was still on. He waited patiently for it to go out, and once it did he left the library, moving across the whole breadth of the campus.

The cozy east wing at Chrysostom House was an ideal location for Tomas Zednik to pull his mind away from the day's toil and upheaval. And yet the memory of it all stayed with him, clinging to him like soot to an overused chimney. He had every desire to ignore all the planning for the next day, preferring to rise early before breakfast and lay out his checklist of items then. Yet his mind wandered back to the antagonism of the past eleven hours. Rather than put it off, he got out his files and plugged in his computer. As he waited for his files on St. Basil's to load, he went to the small refrigerator and found a bottle of Blumenhof 2010 Seyval. He preferred the wine he had purchased that morning, but he would refrain from tasting that until he returned home. He poured a glass, corked the wine, and returned to his oak work desk. A wave of extreme weariness—no, sleepiness—came over him. Perhaps numbers weren't needed, he thought. Maybe there were other matters that could keep his mind engaged. He switched into his email account and wrote a quick e-mail to Father Matthias urging action on another front. He had already discussed the possibility with the person in question earlier in the day and his suggestion had not been well received. But he could not concern himself with the volatile sentiments of others. The seminary must aim for excellence, but it also was to produce pastors, not scholarly ideologues.

He yawned loudly and thought of Father Jonathan. His dear friend, who had suffered so much criticism, found in St. Basil's a fine teaching opportunity. Yet he had discovered that grace and charity from others could be spotty at best. Reverend Zednik fought off the increasingly odious flares that erupted from his heart. He made a brief prayer of contrition. He had just confessed to Father Matthias immediately before Vespers. Why was he failing to control his urges even now?

True, Father Jonathan had been barred from all pastoral work, but to his credit he had accepted this and performed admirably in a teaching-only role. Zednik thought back to the hours of pastoral counseling and how Father Jonathan had patiently executed everything asked of him. The students and faculty here never saw all the suffering, the noble perseverance that flew under their radar. And it's not like St. Basil's didn't have complications or skeletons in the closet. The words of Jesus from St. John's Gospel echoed in Zednik's mind: *Let he who among you is without sin cast the first stone.*

He looked at the clock, which read a quarter after ten. His head felt as if he was trying to run a marathon in a snowdrift. His eyelids grew heavy, and he wondered if the alcohol was mixing badly with his medication. He dismissed that thought. None of his prescriptions he had taken that night had an alcohol restriction. His Paxil, which he took for his depression, he took in the morning. That couldn't be it. He would call it an early evening and sit in the easy chair for a few minutes of reading. It was his private custom to read before bed, even if it were only a couple pages. In the mood for Chaucer, he pulled out his well-worn copy of *The Canterbury Tales*. Even with one of his favorite tomes, he couldn't get much done. His eyelids drooped, and he could have sworn his pulse slowed a touch. Thinking of something in a flash, he wrote a brief note and placed it in his suitcase. He set the book down and prepared for bed. He knew he was a beaten man.

He woke to a barely perceptible swishing sound and, looking over at the bedside clock, saw it was half past midnight. The outside breeze had kicked up as steady gusts. He rolled over onto his right side, not knowing if he had ever felt this woozy. And as he did so, he glimpsed the invader, the one who trespassed. Even this sanctum was no true refuge. He saw clearly, even in the darkness, and in that instant, his enemy was upon him.

The drowsy priest struggled onto his elbows, but his attacker moved swiftly, forcing him back down onto the bed. As Zednik clumsily and desperately clawed away, his intruder located the extra pillow and forced it over his face. The cotton shroud pressed against his nostrils and he fought urgently for air. But his strength failed him, and he knew in his drugged state there would be no salvation from mortal harm. His raging heart waged one last skirmish, and in that moment, he laid his arms aside as Christ had on a wooden post years before. And just as his God had done so then, he now breathed his last and gave up his spirit.

PART TWO

A HOPE DISFIGURED

(FEBRUARY 3RD-6TH)

"No problem," she had said. "I'll meet you all there. No sense waiting for me. I'll see you later...Bye."

They had not only been strange words, he thought. They had also been her last.

The window into the emergency room had seemed like a chasm despite its transparency. Graham gripped him by the shoulders and whispered incoherent comforts into his ear, as if anticipating the mantle of death to drop any second. Leah with her hand over her mouth. And all three of them watching her, intubated, defibrillators earnestly seeking to revive her. And the epinephrine shots, one after another. Nothing.

He didn't know when he made the decision, but there came an instant when he knew that his presence there would do no good, that the life she had herself taken would never return. He was rolling down the hallway that led to the hospital chapel. Such places were usually nondescript, insipid rooms, but this was different. Two hundred empty seats greeted him, their composite construction at variance with the sacramental ambiance. He made his way up the center aisle and looked up at a stern crucifix, which seemingly mocked his confusion and grief.

In defiance, he pushed himself upward. He would stand before this God and ask him why. And that's when it hit him.

He was in a chapel. He was standing. That's when he realized he was dreaming again.

A groggy Cameron Ballack glided through his suburban home. Of course, it was not his, but rather his parents'. Such was your existence in a wheelchair-bound state. He slid past the den and made a left turn into the kitchen, pausing only to wave at the night shift nurse. He had given Karen a light workout, needing suctioning three times and to be turned only once. Now she could report off and get home to her husband and kids, or at least some solid sack time.

Ballack wished the gods of slumber had dealt with him more gently the previous night. For the past three years, in high definition and with heartbreaking force, the nightmare of his girlfriend's suicide landed in his sleeping mind as clear as crystal. Always on the anniversary of her final solution. And even now, he wasn't sure what upset him more. Was it that she had lied about her impending arrival? Or was it that—except for the nightmares—he had ceased to weep for her?

Pushing himself off the slippery footing of memory road, Ballack rolled into the kitchen. His father was there, rinsing off one bowl in the sink as he simultaneously loaded another into the dishwasher. Martin Ballack's stocky frame turned toward his son, who was surprised to see him still there.

"Late start this morning," said his father, as if reading his thoughts. "Oatmeal, or sausage and eggs?"

"Oatmeal, to be honest," said the younger Ballack. "I didn't sleep that well last night. I don't think I'm up for a lumberjack's breakfast. Don't you have a service this morning?"

"Not until eight. I just need to do Morning Prayer and then a tour for a psych class from MoBap." MoBap, or Missouri Baptist University, was the younger Ballack's alma mater.

"Where's Mom?"

"Out walking the Katy Trail early. She's to be back in a few to sign Karen out." He placed a bowl of oatmeal, freshly scooped from the saucepan on the stove, in front of his son. As he did so, the nurse poked her head in the kitchen. "Martin," she said, "I'll be right back. Just going to warm up my car."

Martin acknowledged her with a wave before he sat down next to his son. Taking a sip of coffee from a cobalt-colored mug, he ventured a question. "You okay today, son?"

Ballack figured this query was coming. He just didn't expect it from his father at quarter after six on a Thursday morning. He sprinkled cinnamon on his oatmeal and threw on a pinch of sugar. "I don't think that matters, Dad," he said quietly. "All that matters is that I land on my own two feet at the end of each day. After twenty-eight years, that's my bottom line."

His father smiled, probably more at his resolute tenacity than the particular way he dealt with such moments. "Well said. I didn't want to intrude or pry. Just checking." He looked at his watch. "Oh, by the way, Jill called earlier."

"Earlier? We're at six-fifteen right now. When did she call?"

"About twenty minutes ago when you were in the john. She needed to leave for work soon."

"Is it about today?"

"About tonight, I think. Something about going out for dinner. She and Ethan wanted to take you out. Might want to call her soon."

Ballack ground his teeth slightly as he slid another bite of oatmeal into his mouth. While he could never fault his younger sister for having a big heart, her need to hover over his mercurial emotions around this time of year always proved a tweak laborious. Their divergent personalities were perfect matches for their vocations. His task-oriented nature and attention to detail made him an ideal detective, the only disabled one he knew of anywhere. Jill, on the other hand, was a bubbly socialite who treated life like a gigantic game of Chutes and Ladders. No wonder she found such satisfaction in the Child Life department at Childrens' Hospital.

"I'll call her," he said, waking himself from his own reverie.

Martin made a move to pick up his wallet and cell phone and made his way towards the door. On impulse, almost by accident, Ballack heard a question come out of his own mouth.

"Dad, am I doing it all wrong?"

His father stopped and turned, his head tilted back slightly and to the right. His dark chocolate brown eyes gazed compassionately on his son's face. "What? Your job? Your emotions?" He paused, seeking to defuse things with some light humor. "Your breakfast?"

"Everything, to be honest. Life itself. The fact that I think that if I trust or become attached to anyone, some sort of disaster is imminent. One minute I'm fine with the world; the next, God, if he exists, has some Mount St. Helens going off."

His father sat down next to him and took in a deep breath before answering. "Well, I may not be the person to outline the equation. What I say won't solve that quandary cleanly and neatly. And I can't place one step in front of another for you. With me, it's different. I've always been of the mind that when the chips are down, you have to believe in something or someone. We can't be consistently cynical. It's just you're in a unique place. We've both suffered. You lost a brother when Mom and I lost a son. And on top of Christopher, you lost Michelle. Not everyone goes through a girlfriend's suicide. And you're in a wheelchair. That's a triple whammy right there."

"You're saying there's no correct way to do it?"

"I'm saying for you, me, anyone…that road would be a living hell. I'm not sure I would have handled it differently. I came out of my experiences believing. You haven't, at least not in the way some would define it. A different reaction at various times from either of us and it could be you talking to me about my lack of belief."

Ballack finished off the last of his oatmeal and slid the bowl and spoon over to his father, who placed it on the counter. "You know, Dad, you've never been upset about my lack of faith or that I've turned out like this. Has it ever bothered you that God and I aren't exactly on speaking terms?"

The Ballack patriarch shook his head several times. "You are our son first and foremost. You were our son before you started trying to figure all this out. My guess is if you keep seeking the truth in every area of your life, you'll discover it. If God genuinely exists, he's more capable than I of steering you in that direction. If God is real, and if faith is what it's cracked up to be, then he'll be able to take your questions. He doesn't need us to defend him. He doesn't need us to manipulate others, to worm them into a forced position, like some form of philosophical assault and battery. All I need to do is be honest. With others. And with you."

Both of them looked at the other, and Dad said, "Now I really need to go. Mom should be back from her walk soon."

"Kiss her goodbye."

"One step ahead of you. I already did."

He put his left hand playfully on his grown son's head. "Goodbye, Cam. Work hard, son. I'll see you tonight."

"Bye, Dad."

Ruefully, Ballack pulled out his cell phone and dialed his sister. He was slightly irked that she wanted to invade his space later that evening. He was even more displeased that he had nothing better to do.

Jill answered and, after a few seconds of small talk, got to the point.

"I was hoping you could have dinner with Ethan and me tonight at Hu Hot."

Unfair, he thought. *My favorite place. It would be like her to use a Mongolian buffet as a carrot stick.*

"Okay, count me in. Just don't expect me to be the best company…"

"I know. That's not what this is about."

Liar, he rolled his eyes. "Also, since I'll be coming from work and Tori is my ride, she'll have to be there, if you don't mind."

"That's fine, Cam. Just wanted to see you. Sorry to pop this on you. I'd just been thinking about you lately and…"

The pulses interrupting their conversation indicated a call coming in on his phone.

"Hmmm," said Jill teasingly. "Whoever this is, she must really want you."

"Shut up, Thrasher," he said, using her nickname from her youth. "I'll call you later."

Ballack switched to the other call, expecting his partner to be announcing her impending arrival.

Instead, a man's voice, scratchy yet authoritative, came through the receiver. "Cameron?"

"Scotty?" he responded. It was an odd thing to be getting a call from his lieutenant when he hadn't yet reported in for the day.

"Yeah, it's me. Listen, I need you and Tori to hustle in today. Something just broke, or at least has been put on our radar, and I need you two on it."

Ballack went through his mental Rolodex of possibilities. "Okay, what do you have for us? Mail fraud? Serial thief running amok in the county?"

"Not today. We've got a suspicious death, and I need your skeptic's nose on it. You ever hear of St. Basil's Seminary in Defiance?"

"Once or twice. Is that Catholic? Episcopal?"

"Eastern Orthodox, actually. A visiting priest was found dead in their guest room last week. The regional leadership of the church isn't satisfied with the official assessment and is pursuing further investigation. That's all I can pass on for now. I've got to set up a conference call. We'll be meeting with the bishop who's asking us to take the case. Get up here within the hour. I've briefed Tori also, so you and she need to move up here on the shake."

So here was an early beam of light in what was at first a dark day. There was no guarantee this would amount to much. It could be murder. It could be accidental death or suicide. For once, the mode of crime, even potential crime, wasn't the point for Ballack. It was that a case was theirs. Any work with purpose gave him a rush of hope.

"You've got it, chief. See you then." And wheeling out of the kitchen, he went to the den to wait for his partner's arrival.

The detectives of St. Charles County find their hub in the sheriff department facility in the city of O'Fallon. Situated north of Interstate 70, the one-story, blue and white brick building stood east of a minor league baseball stadium and a high school. The crisp exterior look was a brilliant shell for what was essentially a functional interior. Once past the reception area, there were rows of cubicles so featureless they made the set of *The Office* seem it were designed by Bernini.

Every time he met with his lieutenant to begin a new case, Ballack marveled at the miracle that was his vocation. He knew of few places—let alone police departments—that would take a chance on a physically disabled specimen. Since his youth, when his growing body gave into his unyielding disorder, he had remained in a wheelchair for transport. He knew the odds for surviving his condition. Myotubular myopathy claimed the lives of afflicted males in a steadfast tidal wave of tragedy. It was rare to have someone live past the age of ten with this genetic imprint. Ballack had lived eighteen years past that dreaded barrier. He knew that was due to several factors. The way his disorder presented itself in his body was a milder form than most in this condition. His dedication to as much weightlifting and physical therapy as possible had kept him in reasonable shape, despite the pronounced weakness in his limbs. His regular participation in a local power wheelchair soccer league helped keep his competitive edge, which supplemented his already fanatical desire to survive any odds. He knew his condition hampered his chances to participate fully in some routine police duties. He could not use a gun since the kick would be devastating, even if he could pull the trigger. He would never officially make an arrest by clamping the cuffs on a perpetrator. But Ballack had demonstrated he belonged in this job. He possessed a photographic memory that could pull details from crime scenes, files, and conversations at will. No piece of information, to him, was minor. He could see the big picture and imagine how a crime had unfolded, as if it were a movie script. Even though his voice was low and ordinarily soft—due to his disorder and having a tracheotomy tube in his throat—his JustAMP digital voice amplifier enabled him to converse and conduct interviews just like any other detective. And he tolerated absolutely no push back from anyone he interrogated.

It had been a gamble, he admitted, for the St. Charles Bureau to take a chance on him. But Scotty Bosco firmly believed the benefits outweighed the risks. Ballack was a prodigy, and though he was a crippled man desperately finding his worth in his vocation, he happily knew his department valued him.

Ballack had made the journey from his house to the sheriff's facility in twenty minutes, counting the time it took for Tori Vaughan to lock his wheelchair down in the department's Dodge Sprinter. They had used it since they had been paired together five years ago. Tori, the divorced mother of a teenage girl, was eight years Ballack's senior but she had joined the force four months after Ballack had. Whereas he loved the interrogative chase, her sharp eye noticed facial giveaways and body language at the drop of a hat. And much to Ballack's delight, Tori had been a nurse for seven years before switching gears and throwing in her lot with the police. That background meant she could attend to his respiratory needs during the day and eased his regular nursing schedule just a bit.

Neither would admit they always saw eye to eye on all matters. Tori would see intuitive details that others would overlook, and her perceptive approach rarely missed a clue. Ballack was the global thinker, his mind working several moves ahead. She would unearth the unseen jewels; he would visualize how the necklace would look. It was because of their differences that Lieutenant Scotty Bosco put them together as partners.

Bosco himself waved them back to the far corner office in the building. The lieutenant's workspace was bedecked with enough paperwork to keep him busy until the NBA Finals in June. A thirty-two inch Samsung computer monitor sat front and center on a long table behind the desk. Bosco stood lean and erect, his youthful face laced with a scanty brown beard. His gray eyes were constantly darting everywhere. Ballack would often joke that his lieutenant was the only person in the world who had attention deficit disorder in his eyes and nowhere else in his system. But Bosco was all serious now. The triumvirate gathered at the desk, and Ballack looked around quizzically.

"Where is he?"

"Who?" replied Bosco.

"The bishop. You said we'd be meeting with the bishop about the death at St. Basil's. So where is he?"

Bosco leaned forward with a smile and logged into the Skype website. "He's in Kansas City. This is a videoconference."

Ballack shot a look at Tori. She pulled her blond hair back into a ponytail and let out a frustrated sigh. Ballack knew her old-school habits like the back of his hand. Tori believed in handling stuff on the phone or in person. Cell phones were the absolute limit for her. But

Ballack surrounded himself with the latest in technology out of necessity. He flipped up his sidewinder laptop tray and logged into his Dragon NaturallySpeaking software. His muscle disorder made taking notes a dreadfully laborious chore, and the Dragon enabled him to speak into the program using his Bluetooth headset while relaying his speech into words on the screen. From there, it was no problem to print out his clear yet detailed observations. The department was overjoyed with his reports, and Bosco had personally purchased a new SoundBlaster 16 chip to make the software compatible with Ballack's laptop.

Bosco turned to both of them. "You know the drill. I'll introduce. Then the bishop will outline the situation. Ask questions when he's finished."

"Yes, dad," needled Tori, rolling her eyes at the reminder, a rule which they would break anyway.

The video connection was made, and the weathered face of a grandfatherly figure came to life on the screen. He was clearly coming up on seventy years of age. His glasses were small and didn't seem to fit his broad countenance. What struck the detectives was his beard. It was long, gray and scraggly. Shelves of books, some of which Ballack judged to be older than the bishop, stood behind him. A tri-bar cross was fastened to the wall directly behind the bishop and above his head.

"Good morning, Bishop Burgic," said Bosco. "Can you see us okay?"

The bishop nodded unsmilingly. "Yes. Yes, Lieutenant. You are coming in clearly. Thank you. Thank you for being able to meet with me on such short notice."

Bosco acknowledged with a stiff wave of his hand. "Let me make some introductions. Your Grace, seated here with me in our facility are our detectives: Tori Vaughan to the right and Cameron Ballack here in the center. They will be the ones taking the reins on this case. Tori, Cameron, this is Bishop Petr Burgic. He heads up the Diocese of the Midwest, which is part of the Orthodox Province of North America. Because St. Basil's falls in his geographical jurisdiction, he is intervening in a recent development at the seminary. I'll let him explain that now."

"Good to meet you both, detectives," said Burgic.

Tori nodded back.

"Good to meet you too, sir," said Ballack.

Bosco coughed and murmured something inaudible.

Ballack turned to him, whispering back, "What was that?"

"Address him as 'Your Grace.' That's his title," hissed Bosco.

Ballack turned back to the screen and saw the bishop waiting, almost expectantly, for the correction, as if he had not received a proper deposit of veneration.

"I'm sorry....Your Grace. Please go ahead."

The bishop cleared his throat and began. "Thank you. Ten days ago, our diocesan treasurer, Reverend Tomas Zednik, went to St. Basil's Seminary to meet with the administration there. We had noticed several financial irregularities over the past couple of years, and these matters were contributing to St. Basil's running a deficit. Both the seminary and the diocese had been in touch with regular donors. Those contributors insist they have either maintained or increased their donations, an impressive matter given the present recession. We had insisted on St. Basil's handling this with much diligence, speed, and discretion. Unfortunately, we received only general, shadowy reports from them regarding these matters. I dispatched Tomas to meet with them. When he called me Monday evening a week ago, he explained it had been a tense affair. They were not in favor of the diocese taking over the financial investigation. However, according to canon law—that is, the binding regulations for our church—they had no recourse but to accept our intervention. It was a very sad moment. We were strongly concerned, and even angry, about the monetary irregularities and the fact we weren't getting straight answers. What made it more difficult is that we have always been proud of St. Basil's as a seminary and a pastoral community. The disconnect was particularly troubling."

Tori interjected, "Just for the sake of clarity: Did the administration know or suspect you would be personally taking over this matter?"

"They knew it was a possibility. Any student of canon law would know that. However, I don't think they believed it was a *probability*."

Ballack cut in. "Not to delay your account any more, but what would be the nature of the takeover? What specific steps would you be taking? Checking deposits? Withdrawal? Anything involving sensitive information or passcodes?"

Bosco made a move to restrain the conversation. "Listen, detectives, maybe we should just let the bishop continue."

"Actually, Lieutenant Bosco, I don't mind answering that question because it might help color in my own suspicions that I'll lay out as well."

Ballack couldn't resist a slight grin of satisfaction.

The bishop continued, "The diocese, and particularly Reverend Zednik, would be receiving the seminary's online username and password for their bank account information. Tomas told the dean, Father Matthias, and the chancellor, Father Andrew, in the meeting that this would be done the next day. They knew the control would be out of the seminary's hands. After the meeting, the day went relatively smoothly. Tomas lunched with the seminary librarian. He spoke with a few students. He even led the Vespers service that evening. Except for a small disturbance during the service, everything seemed to be fine."

Burgic cleared his throat before going on, and it appeared he was getting slightly emotional. "After dinner, Tomas went to his room in the seminary's guesthouse. He called me and filled me in on the day's events. I gave him some brief counsel on how to proceed and then prayed with him over the phone. About an hour later, he sent me an email regarding a separate matter at St. Basil's, of which he desired I be aware. I can't speak to the rest of his waking hours, but I know his usual routine was to have a glass of wine and read some fiction or poetry before going to bed. And that is where it gets, shall we say, sketchy. The next morning, the housekeeper, one Cora Dawson, entered the guesthouse, wondering why Tomas had not yet arisen. He had died sometime during the night. I believe the preliminary examination said twelve-thirty, give or take an hour. The judgment was cardiac arrest. I have no problem with that. His heart clearly stopped. But the detective who was originally on the scene had dutifully scribbled some notes and when she shared the information with me, I became more and more doubtful. I believe there is more here than meets the eye."

Tori interjected, "Meaning what?"

"Part of it has to do with the atmosphere into which Tomas entered. St. Basil's is an excellent school. It's significantly more traditional than I'd like it to be, but I've never found fault with their results. There has been much debate amongst professors lately. Father Jonathan Erhart has been the center of these disputes. There were some misgivings about him coming on there as an instructor. He had engaged in some unwise activities in the past and, in our eyes, he had performed sufficient penance for those indiscretions. But there is a vociferous group of students there who don't like him. Tomas was a close friend of Father Jonathan's, so there may be some rage-by-association. Please, I know that is a strong statement. I'm only giving you my assessment. Also, many at St. Basil's believed the diocese was bullying the school. That is far from the truth, but for many, perception is reality. Tomas was the lightning rod for a lot of frustration."

"You believe, then, that someone might have wanted to get rid of him because of the financial investigation?" asked Ballack.

"The motive would have to be stronger. Someone would to have had something serious to lose," rejoined Tori.

The bishop shifted gears but showed no signs of slowing down. "Then there is the matter of Tomas' room when he was discovered. To Father Matthias' credit, he did not let anyone else enter and preserved the scene as it was. Tomas was lying on his side in bed, with a pen in his hand. To my knowledge, he never used a pen to underline things in his reading. He always used a highlighter. That was the first irregularity. Also, Tomas wore contacts. He was half-blind without them. Yet his contacts were in his lens holder in the solution. He could not have been reading. With those two pieces of information, I judged this must be more than accidental death. I'm being charitable. I'll be blunt. It is my opinion that Tomas was murdered in his room and the surroundings were manipulated to make it appear he just happened to die while reading in bed!"

It was a bold assertion, thought Ballack, and although on the surface it was plausible, he knew they were getting only one side of the story. "Any other things that might have been a tad askew?"

"One more, now that you mention it. Tomas had written a note to himself. Thankfully, he had put it in his book and hadn't laid it where anyone else could get to it. When we received his things, I found the note. It says..." and here he fumbled with a pile on his desk before he found what he was looking for, "...Ah yes, it says *Something wrong with meds. Dana W got something wrong.* Here...if you want to see for yourself." He held the note toward the computer screen. Ballack looked at it along with Tori. No doubt it said what Burgic claimed it did. The two detectives gave each other a silent, knowing look as if to say *Doesn't mean it was the victim's.*

"Your Grace," asked Tori, "Any chance we could get Reverend Zednik's notes from that day?" It was obvious to all except the bishop that Tori wanted to discover if the note was remotely genuine by comparing the handwriting.

"I can overnight them to you. I was also going to mention that I have already spoken to Father Matthias and Father Andrew about you both arriving to investigate. I have asked them to reserve their guesthouse for you both to stay. Please don't worry. You won't be in the nook where Tomas stayed. They have another bedroom with a loft. I've made arrangements already and the seminary has agreed to cover your room and board while you are there."

It was Bosco who spoke next. "And Cameron, before you ask, yes, the entire structure has full disabled access. I believe that goes for other places like the chapel, library, the gym, and the first floor of the main building. Correct, Your Grace?"

"That is right. I was informed that you, Detective Ballack, would have some specific mobility needs. Thankfully, St. Basil's can meet them. Also, the doors of the guesthouse, library, and chapel have push-button openers accessible from your wheelchair."

"I'm impressed," said Ballack.

"The seminary will be expecting you early afternoon. Father Matthias will meet with you, although I am sure most of your early face time will be taken up with Father Andrew. I am not sure how long you will need for interviews and such, but I am anxious to know your findings."

Bosco wasn't one to be pushed on time. The more important question had to do with their pool of potential suspects, if indeed this was murder.

"How many students presently attend St. Basil's, Your Grace?" he asked.

Burgic appeared thoughtful. "The total full-time enrollment is forty-four students. However, there is less than half that number on campus at this juncture. Our first and second-year classes are off campus this week and next on our annual missions trip. This year they are in Dallas, working with various ministries and charities there. So that's about…from what Father Jonathan told me, that's about twenty-six students. Eighteen remain. Plus their families, if they are married."

"So the possibility exists that if there has been foul play, the perpetrator could be baking bread right now in a soup kitchen in north Texas?"

The bishop did not like having to admit that, but Bosco had painted him into that corner. "Yes, the possibility exists. However, I would think that be less likely. The individuals who have been the noisiest about Tomas are in their third or fourth years of study, or they are on staff."

"You seem to have given this some advance thought, Your Grace," said Tori. "We might need to restart this whole thing when the rest of the student body returns."

"And, at worse," added Ballack cynically, "this could be interpreted as a pre-selected lineup of suspects."

The bishop glared at him from the screen, saying nothing. If looks could kill, thought Ballack, then Scotty would be arresting the cleric for murder.

"I can appreciate your concern, detectives, but I have implored Lieutenant Bosco to begin this as soon as possible to ensure that, if there has been foul play, you might be further along in your work than further behind."

"Thank you, Your Grace," interrupted Bosco. "We'll get started on this and we will forward an update to you after the weekend." He obviously wanted to close the conversation before it took a more acerbic turn.

After logging off the program, Bosco turned to Ballack. "Was that little production there at the end really necessary? I get you a case, and I know you're not the most pious tree in the orchard, but do you mind telling me why you felt the need to antagonize the bishop?"

"Antagonize?" shot back Ballack, "I express what any rational detective would have asked, and you call that taking a dig. He practically said he had poisoned the well! You were thinking the same thing! We can't go into a case with anything less than an open mind. So I'm less diplomatic than the average bear. So what? I guarantee we all had that comment banging around somewhere in our minds."

"And what I'm telling you is that no matter what you do or don't believe, you will act as a professional for the duration of your time at St. Basil's. I understand your beef with all this, I really do. But these folks have tradition, structure, and values, and you won't move the investigation along if you throw your antagonistic fertilizer in any soil you choose! Do you understand?"

Ballack looked at his boss. As much as he wanted to dish out a snappy comeback, Bosco was right. The job came first, and although he had only pointed out what obviously was there, it hadn't been a beneficial revelation. "Got it," he replied.

"Good. Now get down there and keep me informed."

Tori smiled at her partner as she gathered their things for the jaunt to Defiance. "Nice placement, sport."

"Wait till I get going," he replied, putting his wheelchair in reverse and backing up. Unfortunately, Bosco himself was still behind him. As Ballack scooted backward, the metal extension on the back of his headrest bisected the lieutenant's elbow joint, making him cringe from the sudden pain.

"Ouch! Why can't you watch where you're going?"

"Sorry, chief. My bad."

Ballack rolled out of the room, never imagining that in four days' time, the combination of Scotty Bosco and that metal protrusion would save his life.

The following hours were an industrious flurry. Tori drove the Sprinter south to her apartment at Westbury Place in St. Peter's. On the way, she placed a phone call to her daughter, telling her to make arrangements to stay with friends over the next few days. Ballack waited in the van while she went inside, emerging five minutes later with a large duffel bag into which she'd stuffed enough clothes for five days with the amenities she would need.

Even before they had left the police station, Ballack had called home himself with his manifold requests. Time away from home meant he'd need his respiratory equipment. When they pulled up in the driveway, Marie Ballack had everything arranged inside the front door for her son to take: aerosol medication for his breathing treatments; the vibrating chest vest he used to dislodge the mucus that could build up within his lungs; the "cough assist" machine that whooshed the mucus out of him; the suction pump to get the remainder of that mess; the ventilator he used at night to keep him inflated; the battery recharger for his wheelchair; and all the dressings and ointments he'd require. It took them considerable time to load each apparatus safely. Durable medical equipment was not the type of gear one could toss into a trunk.

"I'll call you later, Mom. Let Dad know what came up so he doesn't expect me home later tonight," said Ballack.

"Thanks, Marie. See you later," called out Tori.

Marie Ballack nodded toward her and walked to the passenger window of the van. "I'll call the nursing agency and let them know you'll be at the seminary then. I take it they would have nothing against a night shift nurse showing up there every evening."

"They shouldn't," her son replied. "If they're getting me on site, they have to take me with all the personnel accessories. Go on Mapquest and you should find directions. Here's the address. I'll call tonight. I'll be fine."

Marie turned to go back inside when she stopped and wheeled around. "Did you call Jill and let her know that you won't make it to dinner tonight?"

Ballack pulled his cell phone out. "Trust me, I'm doing it now."

On the way to their destination, Ballack took a look on his laptop and found St. Basil's website. Despite his skepticism, he still retained a high curiosity about religious details. Part of that was due to his love of learning. Even if he didn't buy into the world of faith, he liked having as much knowledge as he could. What one didn't embrace in belief could always be utilized in the context of an investigation. And if he had dirt on other people, that could serve a purpose, too. Yet much of his awareness of such matters came from years of osmosis. His father—now a chaplain at St. Luke's Hospital— had left parish and Christian school ministry behind, but was an active guest preacher in area churches. Ballack had soaked up much from both his parents—both in regular conversation and debate. In the end, he was grateful for his parents' generous latitude given him to figure out his own beliefs. Out of respect, he had explored much of Christianity even while he couldn't bring himself to embrace that faith as his own.

As Tori drove down Highway 94, past gas stations, residential areas, and occasional churches, Ballack rattled off the features about their hosts.

"Okay, here's the goods, Tor. Founded in 1934 as 'a pan-Orthodox training ground for priests and teachers of the Orthodox faith in America.' The bishop wasn't lying. Forty-four students exactly. Takes four years to run through their program. Nice interactive tour of the campus here on the site. They even podcast their special chapel services, so it's not completely in the Dark Ages."

"What does that mean, pan-Orthodox?"

"Says something here about serving the entire Orthodox community worldwide. There are different national branches of Orthodoxy, so I guess this is a way of saying they are not bound to one franchise, like the Greek Orthodox Church or Russian or Bulgarian or Armenian and so on. I guess the diocese is the regional group that is involved in long-distance governance of the school, but overall St. Basil's seems to be a rather independent entity. Looking through the academic catalogue right now. Let's see. Very heavy on New Testament, patristics, theology, and developing student leadership. Says here that one third-year student is chosen as junior chaplain for the seminary students, and a fourth-year is selected as student rector and serves as a worship leader and preacher during chapel services. Sounds like what Dad pushed for during his former days as a teacher."

"What are patristics?"

"Sort of like ancient church history and the specific teachings of guys they call the early church fathers. I think Orthodox Christians tend to prize Origen, Irenaus, Chrysostom, Gregory of Nyssa, and Basil the Great."

"Why the lecture on the history of religion?"

"Sorry. Comes from being a minister's kid. Dad had a tendency to explore the Christian practices beyond our Presbyterian tradition. He had a special fondness for Orthodoxy and their early writings. Some of that precociousness trickled down to me and I did some reading for curiosity's sake. It even got him in trouble once or twice. He made the Orthodox sign of the cross once at the end of a school chapel service and an angry cluster of puritanical folks sure gave him grief for that."

"He enjoyed pushing people's buttons, huh?"

"Don't know if he enjoyed it, but he sure had a knack for it. Why?"

"The apple doesn't fall far from that tree."

"Ignoring that," Ballack replied. "Okay, I'm on the faculty menu. Got six of them. From what I saw on the main page, two profs will be with that group in Dallas for a bit. Let's focus for now on the ones who are still on campus. Father Matthias Vova, dean of the seminary. Been there for sixteen years. One of the foremost theologians in the Church today. Author of four books, including the definitive *The Light of the Elders.* Whatever. Instructor of patristics and liturgics."

"Okay, and 'liturgics' means what exactly?" said Tori, as they entered the Busch Conservation Area that Zednik had passed through on his final day.

"Worship. Whatever goes on in the chapel or church. Readings, preaching, chanting, singing, all in one. Seems like he's got his hands in every pie there and has been there for awhile. He could be a cagey one for us to deal with."

"Or you could be totally wrong."

"I know, but I've never known a president or head of school to have landed in that position by being a milquetoast. I don't think you navigate your way through sixteen years in a top academic position without knowing how to tap dance in a minefield."

"Okay, next."

"Chancellor, Father Andrew Garrick. In his sixth year at St. Basil's, second as chancellor. He teaches spiritual formation and some preaching. Jack of all trades, maybe, and a younger guy, that's for sure. Looks about forty or below. Vova's old enough to be his father. Nothing else seems to stir the pudding about this guy."

"And then we have…"

"Father Timothy Birchall. Relatively new, compared to the rest of the staff. Joined St. Basil's three and a half years ago as librarian and assistant professor of New Testament. Alumnus of St. Basil's before going on to a PhD at Duke, and, hmm, looks like he actually *returned* to Duke for that degree since he did his undergrad work there."

Tori slowed down around a curve. "So he's a sharp cookie, huh?"

"Not only that, but he also coaches the seminary basketball team. Turns out he's well qualified to coach anybody, really. It says here that he was a reserve on Duke's 2001 championship team. Wow. Academically driven and a Coach Krzyzewski product. I'd imagine he's demanding in the classroom."

Tori said nothing. Ballack went on. "And we also have the Old Testament guy. Father Jonathan Erhart. Seventh year at the seminary.

The two years prior to that he worked for the Diocese of the Midwest in an administrative capacity."

"That's a rather blah way of putting it," said Tori, as she gunned the van up a sizable hill.

"Yeah, especially since it doesn't mention much else. Vova and Garrick have their academic and pastoral resume all over the website. Birchall, you know he eats and sleeps Jesus, Greek grammar, and hoops. There's nothing here about Erhart prior to his work with the diocese."

"What was it that Bishop Burgic said about Erhart? Something about paying for past sins?"

Ballack closed his eyes briefly, concentrating. Tori joked with him regularly that he really didn't need his Dragon software, as long as he had his photographic memory. Ballack snaked his memory back through that morning's chat, and, in seconds, he remembered.

"The words were *'He had engaged in some unwise activities in the past and, in our eyes, he had performed sufficient penance for those indiscretions.'* If the bishop wanted to steer us away from thinking it was sexual impropriety, he couldn't have failed more miserably."

"Unwise activities. That's like saying a child molester might have damaged a child," said Tori. She had a special hatred of pedophiles that bordered on nuclear.

"I wonder when it was. And with whom. And if he was ordained as a priest. I get the sense the bishop wasn't going to give us any more information than he needed to."

"But we should get plenty at St. Basil's. Remember how he said there's a cluster of students there that don't like him. That should put us on the path to somewhere."

"Until then, we're sketching with chalk rather than writing in stone. Slow down, Tor. Here we are. The bustling metropolis of Defiance. Got the zigzag coming up."

The sleepy hamlet enveloped them. It was named thusly because it competed with the town of Matson years ago when the Katy Railroad line was searching for a site for a new station. The railroad came through that area, which named itself Defiance as a slap against its rival village. Now the rail boom had long passed and only a few hundred souls were scattered throughout the vicinity. The main drag presented the typical fare of a Midwestern rural village: a post office, a bed-and-breakfast called the Elysian Field Inn, the gas station-turned-small engine repair shop, a bike rental shop, and two taverns. There was a quick left-and-right turn before they continued the final stretch to reach their destination. Several people were pedaling their bicycles up and down the Katy Trail that paralleled the highway. The Yellow Farmhouse Winery lay silent in late winter, as did the nursery just yards to the south on the right hand side. And then came the right turn on Howell Road, their final pathway to the seminary.

"Scotty said it'd be about three-quarters of a mile down on the right," said Ballack. "Just past the creek. If we hit Matson Hill, we've overshot it, but I assume there's a sign."

There was a sign, preparing them for entry, although nothing could prepare them for the steep climb up the hill, or for the blazing sun that bounced dazzlingly off the bronze cross.

"Do they know the meaning of the word *flamboyant*?" Ballack mused aloud.

Tori eased the van between the library and the chapel. "I suppose we're aiming for that building front and center?"

"When in doubt on campus, aim for Old Main," said Ballack dryly. "The wind is beginning to kick up. Probably need to put on another layer before we get going."

As soon as they pulled into the lot just east of Chalcedon Hall, the front doors opened and Father Matthias was walking purposefully toward their car.

"I am sorry that we cannot meet in my office or Father Andrew's. Those rooms are a touch more comfortable, but they are on the second floor, and the hallway is drastically narrow besides. So we are limited to a more functional location."

Father Matthias spoke the words almost apologetically, as if he normally could snap his fingers and manufacture the den of a ski lodge out of thin air. Ballack privately wondered if Father Matthias unwittingly elicited a hidden wish that he wasn't dealing with a disabled detective. Ballack, for his part, was already feeling the effects of the cold weather, coughing and sensing the sting in his upper airway. He was already wearing a turtleneck with his jeans, but Tori had just helped him put on a Kansas City Royals hooded sweatshirt that, in many sections of St. Louis, might instigate a verbal "fight" with rabid Cardinals fans.

Tori put her notebook and pen down on the table in the conference room. Father Matthias excused himself to locate Father Andrew for the initial discussion. Ballack swerved up to the table with a frown on his face.

"Now what?" asked Tori.

"It's the Father Jonathan thing," replied Ballack. "When I read his bio online, something registered. I can't place it exactly, but the name was familiar. I'm sure I've never met the guy, so this is really annoying."

"Good heavens, we finally found something you *don't* know?"

"Again, ignoring that, Tor."

It took Father Matthias more than ten minutes to locate his colleague. The room, while adequate for their meeting space, was somewhat stuffy, and Ballack's respiratory issues were kicking into gear. He reached for the portable suction machine he kept in the small cube-shaped case on the table in front of him. Flipping it on, he jammed the mini-sucker into his trach to clear his secretions. St. Louis weather had a way of making his system go haywire.

Tori fixed him with a concerned stare and rose out of her seat to help him.

Ballack waved her off. "I'm fine," he said, plunging the mini-sucker into a vial of sterile water and whooshing the tube clean.

The doorknob clicked and both the dean and chancellor walked into the room as Father Matthias spoke.

"Detectives, I am sorry for the delay. Father Andrew was finishing up a seminar and I thought it prudent to allow him to close things up. Father Andrew, this is Tori Vaughan and Cameron Ballack of the St. Charles Police Detective Bureau, here, as you know, at the request of Bishop Petr. Detectives, this is Father Andrew Garrick, our chancellor and professor of spiritual formation. After we have our preliminary discussion, I have a patristics class to teach, so Father Andrew will be your guide from then on."

"I was hoping to give you a tour of our campus so you would be able to have an understanding of the geography of your investigation," said Father Andrew. "If you like, I can handle some of your questions on our tour."

With a brief glance and nod from Ballack, Tori said, "That would be fine, Father." She preferred an interrogation behind closed doors, but knew, as Ballack believed, that sometimes people dropped their guard in more relaxed environs.

"Very well," said Father Matthias, sitting down at the head of the table directly across from Ballack. "I assume that we need to discuss the scope of this investigation and other parameters."

Ballack answered him. He knew that Tori sometimes liked listening to the initial inquiry, giving her a chance to assess body language and other intangibles, and she was more than content to have him do the talking. "This morning we Skyped with Bishop Petr, and he referenced the death of Reverend Zednik on the morning of January twenty-fifth. He accused no individual of a crime, but he did have certain concerns about the reported events of the previous day, as well as the details of the body's discovery. To be perfectly clear, Fathers, he would like to be able to rule out any scent of foul play. Our job here is to interview administration, staff, and students that we would deem essential to getting a solid picture of what happened. Those would include both of you, obviously, but we will have a wider circle than that. Perhaps if we had some idea of the events of Monday, January 24th, we would be in better shape to form an initial short list."

"Of course," said Father Matthias. "Reverend Zednik had made arrangements to come speak to us about financial irregularities here at St. Basil's. We knew from recent looks at our ledger that something strange was going on. Reverend Zednik was the treasurer for our diocese and so the task had fallen to him to call a conference. We met that Monday, in this room, as a matter of fact. Those present included myself and Father Andrew, plus our secretary, Mrs. Dirklage. Rounding out the attendees were Jane Porter, our bookkeeper, and Lainie Kale. Lainie is the wife of one of our third-year students. She leads the seminary wives' fellowship, assists in the business office, and helps in various ways here at St. Basil's."

"Why so many?" asked Ballack. "Why not you and Father Andrew?"

"We asked that question ourselves. I was not informed that the meeting would include anyone else. I was not opposed to it, but Reverend Zednik's last-minute decision to do things his way was…well, rather abrupt. It did not engender a wholesome atmosphere for a frank and respectful dialogue."

"Father Andrew, what was your take on the aura of the meeting?"

"Confrontational," said the chancellor. "We were put on the defensive and spent most of the meeting trying to figure out where Reverend Zednik was going with all this. His sole purpose was to come in and establish a beachhead from which to find out the impropriety that he thought was occurring. That, neither I nor Father Matthias had any problem with, but the way he had gotten his information was extremely infuriating."

"And that was?"

Father Andrew looked at Father Matthias, who spoke, "He had used Father Jonathan Erhart to feed him financial information about St. Basil's to make his case against us. While he did not have access to our bank statements, either paper or online, he did manage to copy our donor lists and send them to Kansas City. Reverend Zednik noticed that with the money coming in, we should have not been running a deficit."

"On the surface, would you agree with his statement?"

"What do you mean?" said Father Andrew.

"I mean do you think he had a case? Despite the fact you might think Father Jonathan is a mole, would Reverend Zednik have a case against you?"

"We have no idea!" Father Matthias responded a bit too sharply. "Our school has taken the utmost care in every matter of its existence. We put the finest academics before our students in the classroom. We desire the highest quality worship and liturgy in the beauty of our chapel. We offer admission to diligent men who take their lives, faith, and vocations seriously. We seek only the best in our attempts at financial transparency."

"Which," countered Ballack, "Reverend Zednik—and the diocese, if I might assume—didn't believe, at least in the area of money. Was he requiring any additional matters from you?"

"He was going to do an online search of our bank statements. He wasn't content with them being handed over; he wanted to handle the matter himself. We were to give him the username and password the next day. Once he used it and got the figures he needed, he was going to allow us to change our username and password without telling him what they would be. He didn't want to start on it until the next day."

"Which, for him, never came. I'm not pronouncing guilt on any individual or the school, Father Matthias, but can you see why the bishop might have a reason for sending us in?"

"I think perhaps you can tell me yourself just as well, Detective Ballack."

"A diocesan treasurer comes here. His presence is a mild annoyance to some, and quickly his actions poison the well. He's got a mole on the inside. He's getting sensitive information from you for a query that might go down a few rough roads. The next morning, he's discovered dead in his bed. No one's making an accusation, but I'm looking at what you've told me, and, on paper, it's enough to make me say that if *I* was the bishop, I might do the same thing."

Father Matthias drummed his fingers on the tabletop. "Perhaps so, once you lay it out like that." The words sounded deliberately forced from his throat.

Tori spoke for the first time. "Were either of you the first on the scene?"

"No," said Father Andrew. "That would be Cora Dawson, our housekeeper. I can introduce you to her later. I was to breakfast with Reverend Zednik that morning, and when he was delayed in coming, I started toward his room. He was staying in the east apartment of Chrysostom Alumni House; you probably saw it just past that grove of trees next to this building. Cora was just coming down the stairs and asked me what was the matter. I told her and she offered to check his room. She was headed in that direction anyway. Within minutes, she was running back into the refectory, where I had returned. She told me the news; it was obvious it was a tremendous shock for her. Her mother has had some recent heart trouble, so she is exceptionally sensitive to these matters. I ran to the room and it was exactly as she told me. I placed my fingers on his neck to confirm he was dead. That was the only thing I touched."

Ballack decided now was the time to test the bishop's suspicions. "What was the appearance of the room, as you remember it, Father Andrew?"

Father Andrew scrunched his brow, as if the facial contortion would resurrect the memory. "He was on his left side, slumped over a book. It was *The Canterbury Tales*, if I recall correctly. There was a pen inside the book. Everything else looked normal. The light was on, but, of course, it would be if he'd been reading."

"The pen was inside the book? That was the exact location?"

"Yes, inside. I judged it to be inserted at the halfway point. I called the police and a detective—I believe her name was Holloway—arrived within an hour to check the scene, make notes, and so forth. She left after thirty minutes."

Not surprising, thought Ballack, casting a wink in Tori's direction as she stifled a laugh. Though Julia Holloway had a reputation for many things, attention to detail wasn't one of them. Then again, she ought to be grateful to have a job. She had garnered a significant suspension over a year ago for an incident that was never made public. It was clear, though, that Bosco had little love for her. But since her father was a bigwig in the county, she also had a measure of job security, regardless of her incompetence. Bosco often joked privately that the detective bureau would improve exponentially if they had one key funeral.

Father Andrew went on. "The detective guessed it was cardiac arrest and we assumed it was just that. I certainly see your point about the timing, but I find it impossible to believe that members of any seminary community could have the potential for what the bishop imagines."

There was a pause, after which Ballack checked his notes on the computer screen. He had carefully repeated things as they had been spoken, and the words popped up as if on command. He clicked the save button, drew a deep breath, and replied.

"I'm not sure I share that conclusion, Father Andrew. I'm not saying you have a Hitler or Stalin behind every tree here at St. Basil's. But my experience with Christian institutions has made me very wary, and I think you should keep an open mind that even if foul play is not probable, it is possible. And though you may not see it that way, I must in order to proceed with this investigation properly."

"That's fine," interjected Father Matthias. "But I think you're wrong."

"I hope I am," said Ballack. "Shifting gears, if that's all for now, perhaps we can have that tour. Is there anything else you can tell me about the day of Reverend Zednik's visit?"

"He had lunch with Father Timothy, sat in on a class, and oversaw our Vespers service before dinner. Nothing the rest of the day was out of sorts."

Again Ballack paused, and Tori wondered where he was going with this. Sensing his need to gather his own thoughts, she announced, "Before we head outside, I'm going to need to use the restroom."

"This way, Detective," said Father Andrew. "I have to run up to my office to get my coat if we'll be outside for a bit. I'll show you the way." And in a matter of seconds, the two of them left the room.

Father Matthias rose and began walking along the length of the table toward the door, but he stopped short, turned around and sat on the tabletop four feet away from Ballack. It was obvious their conversation wasn't completely over.

"My son," said the dean, "May I ask what happened?"

"What happened?" responded Ballack.

"Forgive me for being so forward. It is not my nature to pry. I am both curious and attempting proper Christian compassion, even if you guessed the former and doubted the latter. You are in a wheelchair. Did you have an accident of some sort?"

"Only if you consider genetics and *in utero* development an accident." He gathered his emotions before going on. "I have a rare neuromuscular disorder, caused by a chromosomal tweak before I was born. It's called myotubular myopathy. That's why I've been in this chair for as long as I can recall."

"You've never walked? I'm sorry again. Those who know me will tell you I am not the best at tactful inquiry."

Ballack held up a hand in an accepting fashion. "Don't worry, Father. It's such a rare condition that I don't expect anyone to know the particulars. The truth is that I did walk for a short period. Never ran, but I walked, however gingerly, from about fifteen months until seven years of age. Then the process of getting heavier took its toll. I couldn't support my body so this wheelchair became my destination. On top of that, I had multiple—and I'm talking *multiple*—trips to the hospital for respiratory illnesses and such. Because my muscles are so weak, I can't get a productive cough. Hence all my equipment."

Father Matthias gave a look that was part sympathy, part confusion. "So is what you have a muscular dystrophy?"

"No, Father. A dystrophy would mean my muscles waste away. I have pronounced muscle weakness. The nuclei of my muscles aren't connecting at the end of the fibers, but they are isolated in the center. Because they don't fuse with each other like they should, my strength is extremely low."

"Yet you have a job and you are alive. That should at least be somewhat encouraging."

"That I do, Father, but that's because I've lived much longer than I should. Most of the boys afflicted with this—boys get it, you see, though mothers are the carriers of the gene—die early in life. I mean before they hit double digits in age. That's what happened to my younger brother."

Father Matthias' face softened. "You lost your brother?"

"Yes, I was almost eleven at the time. Christopher died unexpectedly at home. It took my parents some time to get over it. My sister went to counseling for months. I guess I just stuffed it and the result is what you find seated before you." He stopped, feeling he had shared more than he intended. He had no desire to mention Michelle.

"You stuffed it?" asked the dean. "Do you mean that you looked within yourself rather than to God?"

"Yes, Father. I guess I should come clean with you and let you know up front. God and I aren't exactly on speaking terms, and we haven't been for over half my life. In fact, it's more accurate to say I wonder if there is a God with whom I could speak even if I wanted." He waited, then continued. "Experiences, critical thinking, trying to reconcile a God of power and love with my condition. I guess things have conspired to drive me to this point. I'm sorry if this offends you, Father. I know teaching the exact opposite is your life and you would lean toward building faith rather than denying it."

"No, Detective, I do not take offense. Just reminding myself that I am not God, simply one soul who is being drawn more and more into his likeness. I would just opine that He is doing that with you, whether you know it or not, whether you believe it or not."

Ballack was quickly tiring of this. The trip down memory lane had sculpted another gargoyle of pain on his heart. And he was in no mood for a theology lesson, much less any conversation that could detract from his goal. If Zednik's death was more than initially thought, then anyone, including this scion of intelligence and piety standing before him, was a potential suspect. The pursuit of truth demanded nothing less than his detachment. It was a world he at least understood. A wave of relief washed over him when Tori came through the door.

"Father Andrew got his coat and we're ready to go," she said.

"Very well. My class was coming up in ten minutes anyway," replied Father Matthias. He stood up and offered his hand to Ballack. "Thank you for your patience with me. I will go now, but should we expect you both for Vespers?"

It was Tori who answered before Ballack had a chance. "Not this evening, Father. If possible, we'd be glad to join you for dinner."

And without a word, all of them shuffled out of the conference room.

"We will begin here and head westward," said Father Andrew. The wind had abated and the day felt less frosty. Ballack scooted alongside Tori to keep up as they approached a cluster of small, red brick houses.

"We've come out of Chalcedon Hall, the main building. All faculty have offices there, except for Father Timothy, who has his in the library. The refectory is the main room on the first floor. All meals are served there, of course."

Father Andrew was walking leisurely, seemingly enjoying his role as tour guide. "And here to the right you'll see our married student housing. Seven two-bedroom bungalows, plus the laundry facility. All residences named after either ancient and medieval councils or geographical strongholds of the Church."

"Let me guess," said Ballack. "You've at least got Nicea, Constantinople, and Antioch in there."

Father Andrew peered down at him with pleasant surprise. "Very good."

"I do some reading."

"The others are Moscow, Jerusalem, Alexandria, and Athens. They aren't flashy. No one will accuse us of running a country club here, but we believe it does an adequate job of providing for need and helping students realize the ministry is a time to 'count the cost' of following Christ."

Tori spoke up. "I'm sorry. You say you have *married* students here? Training for the priesthood? I may be speaking out of my Catholic experience, but did I just hear you say 'married'?"

"I did, Detective Vaughan. Anyone in the office of bishop or above must be single for life. Yet not only can priests be married, but the Orthodox Church also *prefers* they be married. We find it helpful to set before the faithful an example of a Christian family. What better person to display that than their local priest? And you must admit, when counseling people regarding their marriages, wouldn't it be better for a priest to be able to draw from personal experience rather than merely theoretical knowledge?"

Ballack had to admit it made perfect sense. He also knew this was a touchy subject for Tori who, despite her sporadic attendance at Mass, tried to remain as faithful a Catholic as possible. On their previous case together, they had nailed a priest in Lake St. Louis for molesting teenagers in the confession booth. It was the sort of thing that made Tori retch and that Ballack used as institutional justification for his skepticism.

They were approaching the gymnasium, on the north side of which sat a modest playground. Inside, Ballack took in what seemed to be an impressive facility. A regulation basketball court dominated much of the area, but there was also an activity room on the east side, complete with foosball, billiards, and ping-pong tables. Several couches encircled a big screen television complete with surround sound and a bookcase of DVDs. Ballack circled around the basketball floor and returned, stopping in front of Father Andrew.

"Before continuing our tour, Father, I heard that over half of your student body is off campus."

"That is true. Missions trip to Dallas. All of our first and second-year students will be there until Saturday the twelfth. That will hamper our basketball team tomorrow for their game against Concordia."

"And in your opinion, had there been any noticeable tension between any of those students and Reverend Zednik?"

"None that was overt."

Father Andrew's responses were somewhat short, so as they left the gym, Ballack kept up the interrogation. "Father, we spoke earlier about the meeting you and Father Matthias and others had with Zednik. What was the rest of his schedule that day?"

"Mightn't the bishop have told you?"

"Perhaps," said Ballack cautiously, "but I'd like to confirm any details."

"After the meeting, I took him over to Father Timothy's office in the library." Father Andrew pointed in the library's direction. Ballack thought it was a sizeable edifice for such a small institution. "They were to have lunch around a get-together regarding funding the library and our technological needs. As I wasn't there for that, you'd have to discuss the salient parts of that talk with Father Timothy yourself."

"I intend to. And after that?"

"I did not see Reverend Zednik until Vespers that evening. He led the service, along with Father Matthias and our student rector, Dieter Witten."

"Anything out of sorts during Vespers?" said Ballack, remembering the bishop's insinuation from earlier in the day.

Father Andrew looked as if he was trying to wriggle out from full disclosure, but he came clean. "Father Timothy claimed to notice two students sitting down during the service, apparently to protest

Reverend Zednik's presence. He pulled them outside, along with two others who were engaged in harassing them as they did so. The confrontation occurred with no further disruption to Vespers."

"And how did you hear of this?"

"Father Jonathan noticed what was going on. He walked down the aisle with a censer; that's the contraption that holds the incense we burn during a worship service. He saw the quarrel going on outside. As you'll see here," he gestured toward the chapel as they approached, "the doors are glass."

Ballack looked up at the magnificently tall glass doors. Above them, dominating the front of the chapel, was the seal of the seminary, which bore the motto *Sanctify the body, engage the mind, transform the soul.*

"And the students involved? Their names."

"Father Timothy can confirm this, but they were all third-year students. Nicholas Panangiotis, Stephen Kale, Marcus Curry, and Jason Hart."

"Then we'll cover that with Father Timothy."

They skirted around the chapel, taking a path around the south side. The loop led to a sign marked "Garden of St. Athansius." The flower bushes and plots were bare for now, but from the look of things it was an area normally well cared for.

As if sensing Ballack's thoughts, Father Andrew steered them south to the main road. "It is a fine patch of earth. Dana Witten—her husband is a fourth-year student—does a great job keeping it up, and springtime is when the beauty really explodes forth."

Father Andrew pointed out the locales that lay further south, toward the bottom of the hill. A small grove of trees, called St. Jude's

Glade, stood watch over the vast Lake of the Protomartyr. The lake, more like a pond on steroids, was bordered by a walking track. Just east of the lake was the Beautiful Garden where, as Father Andrew told them, Dana Witten spent a good chunk of her time growing vegetables for the seminary.

"And the log cabin in the far corner, next to the woods?" asked Tori.

"The supply shed. Ben Dawson, our grounds and maintenance man, keeps mowing and landscaping equipment there. His wife, Cora, as you know, was the one who discovered Reverend Zednik's body."

They walked north back up the main road, slowing down only as Father Andrew showed them the two dormitories, St. Gregory House and St. Irenaus House, for single students. Father Andrew served as the dorm master for Irenaus, where he lived in a main floor apartment with his wife, Anastasia, and two children. Father Timothy had a similar domicile in Gregory with his wife Jennifer. Father Jonathan lived in Gregory, as well, while Father Matthias made his home in Irenaus.

Ballack was tiring of the brisk air as they came to Chrysostom House, and he was glad when they finally entered. The guesthouse was spacious and would serve their needs well. A kitchenette with refrigerator stood in the corner near the door where Ballack wheeled in off the entry ramp. A small table highlighted the eat-in area. The bathroom stood near a queen bed, and much to Ballack's relief, there was in fact a roll-in shower. Above the bed, a loft provided space for a twin bed. An oak staircase connected the two levels. *Perfect,* thought Ballack.

"You will have a better view here than you would from the east room," Father Andrew said, nodding toward the large window that gave a sweeping picture of yet another group of trees, clustered around some low-lying benches.

"That's the Grotto of St. Jonah and All Martyrs," continued the chancellor, "which I believe brings the tour to an end. Do you have any questions about the campus itself?"

"None for now," said Tori. "If it's all the same, we need to get settled in and set up Cameron's equipment so that we're okay later tonight."

Ballack wanted one more thing. "Before we scatter to the four winds, I'd like to request that we might use this as an interview room when needed. I know it might inconvenience some, but we might move through the investigation at a better pace."

"Of course," said Father Andrew. "And if there is anything you require, please don't hesitate to contact us. We have taken the liberty of leaving a list of telephone extensions on the bedside table. If you need to make a call, press line one or two, then the star key followed by the number."

They exchanged goodbyes with Father Andrew and then set about the process of bringing things in from the Sprinter. That took the better part of a quarter hour. When they were finished, they opened a couple bottles of Propel water and began to go over their preliminary notes. Ballack pulled up his records on his laptop and began looking them over while Tori plopped down on a sleeper sofa near the window. He read his notes, always recalling the setting in which those talks had taken place. He only needed to review things once and they were carved in his mind like stone.

Tori crossed her legs, her jaws snapping loudly on her Nicorette gum. "So," she said, "Let's talk strategy. We're obviously starting with the five people in the meeting. According to my book, that's Fathers Matthias and Andrew—although we've gotten a jump on them—plus Mrs. Dirklage, Mrs. Porter, and Lainie Kale. We also need to hit up Father Timothy since he had lunch with Zednik. I'd like to know how that went."

"We also have to talk to Cora Dawson. She discovered Zednik's body, so there's an obvious starting point. Let's make a point to sit Father Jonathan down, too. I want to see where that goes." He stopped, then looked at his partner. "Anyone else?"

"This may come to nothing, but we also have Dana Witten. She was possibly the last person to see Zednik alive if she was involved in giving him his medication. We have to at least consider that note from the bishop if it is remotely genuine. So that brings the total to eight."

"If it's murder," cautioned Ballack, "then his murderer was the last person to see him alive. Let's not jump to conclusions about anybody."

"Or anything," responded Tori. "We've got a sense it could be murder, but bottom line is, we don't know for sure."

"Point taken. But regardless, we need a batting order. Let's get with Cora Dawson first. After that, let's go with Father Timothy. We may need to work around some class times, so we should be flexible about when. I want to leave Father Jonathan until later. On second thought, let's cover Dirklage, Porter, and Lainie Kale tomorrow morning. They won't be in class. I'd also like to see if we could squeeze Dana Witten in at some point, as well."

He paused, then continued. The next question had to be asked. "By the way, Tor. What was your assessment of Father Matthias and Father Andrew? Did you sense any guilt oozing out of their pores?"

"Nothing that jumped out at me. If anything, they looked confused. Not the how-are-we-going-to-cover-this-up confused. The how-did-this-happen confusion. I don't think they're hiding anything. If they are, they've covered it better than anyone."

"You sure?"

"Very sure. Almost no hand movements, no tells, no scratching of the face, no flinching, and eye contact was steady. Father Matthias did get a little upset, but that was in response to you saying the bishop made a lot of sense on investigating this further. Father Andrew looked at Father Matthias once, but seemed like he was yielding the floor to him rather than being stuck. Facial expressions? The only one of any value was when Father Andrew wrinkled his forehead. But you had just asked him what the room looked like when he saw Reverend Zednik. He could have been trying to get the details exactly right."

Ballack repeated Tori's word for his Dragon's report, then said, "Okay, how about jotting down the lineup for now?"

Tori's pen was smoking getting the information on paper. When finished, she looked out the window. A steady stream of humanity was headed toward the chapel.

"You sure you don't want to go?" Tori smiled.

"Not on your life," chuckled Ballack. "The ambiance of worship might be a comfort to them, but the greater likelihood is they are celebrating other mysteries to cover for their own."

The refectory filled briskly with students and faculty. Even the occasional female could be seen with her spouse. Ballack hung back in the narthex, unsure of which table they should take. Tori tended to be the more assertive in these situations, and so she took the lead. "C'mon, cubbie, let's find a table and hobknob with the holy Joes."

They maneuvered their way to a table on the north side. Father Andrew waved them over and greeted them. "Good evening, detectives. I'd like you to meet Father Timothy, our librarian and professor of New Testament. Father Timothy, allow me to introduce Detectives Tori Vaughan and Cameron Ballack. They are here from the county police detective bureau at Bishop Burgic's request."

Ballack did a double take. Knowing someone played elite college basketball and was six feet, six inches was one thing. Being in a wheelchair next to Father Timothy took his breath away. The librarian towered over him, with a face that reminded Ballack of Captain Jack Sparrow from *Pirates of the Caribbean*. His curly black hair dipped just past the nape of his neck, and taking one step toward both detectives, he extended a hand that looked as if it could palm a beach ball.

"Father Timothy Birchall," he said unsmilingly. "It's good to meet you both, although the circumstances could have been better." He released Ballack's digits, which felt like they had been smashed by the tires of a tractor-trailer.

Father Matthias said grace, after which everyone sat down to enjoy the first course, a creamy cold beet soup. Ballack normally did not venture much past the world of chicken noodle or chili, but he rather relished the soup, probably because he hadn't eaten since his early morning oatmeal. The soup gave way to the main course, which caused both detectives to think it was Russian night. The chef had produced a delectable supply of beef stroganoff, and Ballack fell upon it ravenously. Father Timothy offered them the option of white or red table wine, both from the nearby Augusta Winery. Tori declined the offer, and Ballack, worried that alcohol might repress his already compromised lung function during the winter, refused as well.

As they moved from the stroganoff to a dessert course of peaches and cream with coffee, Father Timothy, who had said nothing about the detectives' presence, spoke directly. "As I have heard you've come to inquire about Tomas Zednik's death, I was wondering how long we can expect your company."

Holy mother, thought Ballack, *Did everybody here fail when it came to learning tact in school?* "Can't be sure. We'll have several interviews. Typical detective work. Can't say for certain. Usually we try to stay as invisible as possible, but that might not be an option in this small of a community."

"I was just wondering," replied Father Timothy. "Personally, I don't think there is much to be made of this. True, Zednik was here to perform an unpopular task, at least it was unpopular to St. Basil's. But I can't see how this is anything but a natural death."

It was Tori who responded. "Father Timothy, how much contact did you have with Reverend Zednik?" *Good move,* thought Ballack. *Might as well get the big guy scratched off the list.* He knew Tori would be scanning his face for any guilty giveaway.

"As far as I could figure, more than most, less than Father Andrew or Father Matthias. There had been much made of his most recent and, as it turned out, last visit. A number of students were turning the seminary into a hot tub of frothy scuttlebutt. While I didn't like the idea of the diocese intruding in what I saw as a purely institutional matter, I certainly didn't care for their chasing of every rabbit trail of gossip. A culture steeped in the tea of rumor does little to enhance its attention to pastoral training. I most emphatically didn't want students to ignore their primary tasks."

"Was that a factor that day?"

"Not in my classes."

"Well, there are other classes than yours, right?"

"And according to the laws of physics, I can't be in two places at once, so I don't know," said Father Timothy with a hint of sarcasm in his voice.

Ballack was quickly tiring of the professor's edge and decided to jump in. "Did you see Zednik at all during his visit?" *I can handle your sarcasm*, he thought, *but you'd better not lie to me.*

Hesitating slightly, Father Timothy sucked in a breath of air before answering. "We had lunch that day. There were some matters he wanted to run by me regarding the pedagogy of teaching New Testament Greek and the funding of the library. As he was somewhat skilled in the issues of finance and church purse strings, I was more engaged in the funding question. Admittedly, I was less cooperative when he turned to pedagogy. I'll certainly listen to my colleagues here who have been through the teaching wars, or to the bishop, but a lifetime priest-administrator does little to conjure my sympathies. We spoke about the class syllabi for the upper-division courses until he was confused enough to seek out others and invade their space."

"How long did your lunch meeting take?"

"Forty minutes, give or take a couple."

"And the tone of the conversation?"

"It wasn't strained if that's where you're going. I had a class to prepare for, so my attention might not have fully been with him. I wasn't bitter, angry, or a bad host."

"Did he bring up anything about your position or the library that you found personally negative or professionally distasteful?"

"Those are odd modifiers, Detective. I've told you the sum of our discussion. As far as the entertainment scale goes, we were closer to the stale end of the spectrum."

"We've also been made aware," spoke Tori with strategic deliberation, "that you had to break up a disturbance during Vespers that evening. How many individuals were involved?"

"There were four in all. Two were instigators; two were harassing them while they instigated."

"And the names of each party?" asked Ballack.

"Nicholas Panangiotis and Stephen Kale were disciplined more heavily since they sat down in protest of Reverend Zednik's presence. Jason Hart and Marcus Curry got caught up in the shenanigans by pestering them. I excused all four men from Vespers and I've barred Panangiotis and Kale from Holy Communion until they do some penance."

"You don't consider that a stiff penalty?"

Father Timothy looked at Ballack with fierce confusion. "You sound just like Reverend Zednik. I defend his presence here with students but get excoriated for it."

It seemed like he was on the verge of sharing something he did not want to say. Gathering himself, he rose. "Well, I hope this might be somewhat passable for an initial inquiry. Please excuse me for the time being, for I have to pull together some things for tomorrow's classes. If you need me, you can find me in the library or in Gregory."

With that, he was gone. Tori glared at him from behind and, not taking her eyes off the giant, said to Ballack, "Well? Suspect or just plain jerk?"

"Definitely the latter until we uncover more stuff. I'd like to talk to those students tomorrow. Again, we need to hit Cora Dawson, Father Jonathan, the ladies in the financial meeting, and the Wittens, whoever they are. We've only begun. Let's get back over to the guesthouse, come to think of it. Karen will be arriving any second. I'll let you two catfight for the loft."

Karen Calabria had no difficulty finding St. Basil's and arrived mere minutes after Ballack returned to the guesthouse. In spite of his catfight joke from earlier, there was no debate over sleeping quarters. Karen was glad to give up the loft to Tori, granting herself closer access to Ballack in case he'd need any assistance during the night hours. The only bone of contention came from Ballack himself. In need of a shower, he was accustomed to parental assistance. So far from home, both Karen and Tori decided they'd tag team on getting him into the shower and the process of dressing him afterward.

"Tor, there's no way you're looking at my naked rear end," shouted Ballack in protest. "We can go without a shower tonight."

"And what about the next night, and the next?" asked Karen. "Come on. Tori's a professional. I don't think she's going to throw herself at you over such a functional matter."

"Besides, sugar bear," said Tori, "you're not my type."

"I must've missed the news report when the Playboy Mansion became handicap-accessible," responded Ballack dryly. "Fine, tonight only. But I'm calling the vendor tomorrow and seeing if they can get a portable Hoyer lift out here on the double. I'm creeped out enough as it is. All we've got here is the rolling shower chair."

In reality, Ballack knew his partner was a complete professional in this situation. The whole procedure took only twenty minutes. And to be fair, Ballack grudgingly admitted, he needed both of them for the labor of transitioning him from his wheelchair to the shower chair and back again. By eight-thirty, he was dressed in a long-sleeved T-shirt and boxers. A green blanket covered him from his waist to his toes. Tori made hot cocoa for the three of them from the supplies provided by the seminary. Ballack scanned his notes on his laptop before they processed what they had so far, but he was interrupted by a knock on the door. Tori called their guest in, and a young lady of medium-short build stepped over the threshold. She was carrying a basket of additional supplies, but that wasn't what caught Ballack's eye. Her nervous, kindly smile carried warmth he had not experienced this day from anyone else at the school. Her light brown tresses fell near her shoulder. Her fair skin stood out pleasantly, and she was dressed in an attractive black roll-up sweater, blue jeans, and brown snow boots. What really stood out to Ballack were her eyes. They were striking, lustrous pools of gray. Yet they seemed to hold a residue of sadness, as if she was a loyal soul not completely at peace.

"Hi," she said, "I'm not sure what all remained in the cupboard, so I brought over some more things in case you were running low. I'm sorry, I haven't even introduced myself. I'm Dana Witten."

"Tori Vaughan," said Tori, shaking Dana's hand, "one of the police detectives you've probably heard about."

"Hi, good to meet you," said Dana, turning to Ballack. "And….?"

Ballack was in a stupor. He had not taken his eyes off her. He snapped out of it.

"I'm sorry. Cameron Ballack. I'm her partner."

"No problem. Do you want me to put these away or let you all work that out?" said Dana.

Tori looked at Ballack, who seemed to be lost in another world, but for another reason. For the second time in eight seconds, he snapped out of it.

"Oh, the counter should be fine, Mrs. Witten. We're just getting settled and can take care of the rest later. Actually, if you don't mind, would it be okay if we spoke to you for a few minutes?"

Tori looked at her partner in surprise. He never liked forcing in an interview when bedtime approached, and to work some extra minutes now meant that Karen would have to step outside. But if it bothered the nurse, she didn't show it. She announced something about wanting to see the chapel and thought a walk might be in order.

"The chapel is unlocked in the front," said Dana, "but if you want a full-blown tour, you might want to see one of the fathers in Gregory or Irenaus."

Karen nodded blankly, as if she had just heard a lecture on thermodynamics and then quietly stepped out.

Ballack gestured to the dining table. "Have a seat, Mrs. Witten."

"Thank you, and please, call me Dana."

Tori leaned against the counter, deciding to stand for the interview. Her sharp eye noticed Ballack's scrawl on a Post-it note on the edge of the table. Two words: BISHOP'S NOTE.

Tori nodded, remembering the Skype interview with Petr Burgic earlier in the day. The note he put up to the screen. *Something wrong with meds. Dana W got something wrong.* "Dana W" was definitely here. No wonder Ballack wanted to do this now.

"I'm sorry. I should have asked," said Ballack. "Would this be an okay time for some brief questions?"

"Absolutely," said Dana, "as long as it doesn't take too long. I forgot to check the inventory sheet when I got these supplies, so I'll need to get back to Chalcedon Hall before too long and officially sign them out."

"Then I'll be brief. We're investigating the matter of Reverend Zednik's death from last week. It is my understanding, from what we've been told, that he died sometime after midnight from that Monday night to Tuesday morning. Did you have any contact with Reverend Zednik that evening?"

"I did. Lainie Kale and I had prepared his room that afternoon. We were given his luggage and so we put everything in the guesthouse for him. That evening Lainie had to drive back up to O'Fallon to get some medication for her husband. He's asthmatic and his meds were running out. She asked if I could take some water over to Reverend Zednik's room for his pills."

"What specifically was he taking?"

"Oh, I don't know. I had heard he had kidney problems, so I'm guessing some of the pills were for that. There were five pills in all that I gave him. One blue, several white. A couple of them were rather sizable. I gave him the bottled water and the pills and he took them. He thanked me, and I left. That was the only time our paths crossed."

Ballack grew curious. "The pills. Did you hand them to him? Were they from a pill box or from separate containers?"

Dana thought hard. "They were actually in the pillbox. Marked for Monday evening. Lainie had left a couple of white disposable Dixie cups on the desk, so I put the pills in one of those and gave them to him. He asked me to bring the pills over for whatever reason. The bottled water he had demanded because he never drinks the tap water."

Tori cut in. "And had he put the pills in the pillbox? Did the ones for Monday evening look comparable to other days?"

Dana looked slightly bewildered. "I don't know. I saw his meds for Monday night were there. I didn't look at any of the other days. Why should I?"

"Just asking."

Ballack decided to switch gears. "Your husband is a student here, Mrs. Wi...I mean, Dana?"

A cloud dropped behind her eyes. "Yes, Detective. Fourth year. He graduates in May."

"And did he have any contact with Reverend Zednik that you know of?"

"I'm sure he would have, though I don't know the extent, and you'd have to get the full story from him. He's the student rector here. He was selected by his peers and the faculty to be the primary student worship leader during chapel services. If he saw or spoke to Reverend Zednik at all that day, it would likely be before or after the Vespers service."

"Did you attend that service?"

"No. I thought about it, but I decided against it. Students are required to attend. Wives and children are welcome, but the faculty doesn't pressure us."

"Does that go for all services?"

"Just for Orthros and Vespers. Orthros is our Morning Prayer service, what you might know as Matins. Now, of course, Sunday services are required for all family members. Many of us attend either St. Nicholas' in the city or Assumption on I-270. If we don't attend there, then there is a Divine Liturgy here in the chapel on Sunday mornings. Dieter has been preaching at those services lately, so I have been going here."

"Would your husband have some free time tomorrow, in case we need to speak with him?" asked Tori.

"He has class until eleven-thirty, then he usually holes up in the library. If I see him before dinner, I'd be very surprised."

Again the cloud behind her eyes, darker and sadder this time. Ballack noticed a slight frown and guessed there was a story there.

"Thank you, Dana. That will be all for now." He watched her get up and decided to add a note of gratitude, anything to deflect the weightiness of their conversation. "And thanks, by the way, for the basket of goodies."

"Oh, that was nothing," she smiled. "There's an apple tart in there that's still warm. An old recipe of my grandmother's. Thought you might want something less cold than the weather we're getting."

She slipped out after saying good night. Ballack turned to his partner and spread his hands as if to say, "Well?"

Tori wrinkled her brow and spoke deliberately. "It means—as we said—we have one of the last, if not the last, person to see Zednik before he died. Gave him the pills herself. Either she didn't know what he was taking or she's hiding it well."

"She was asked by Lainie Kale to do it. I'd like to explore that connection, if there is one. Here's the thing, though. We don't know if the door to Zednik's room was locked. Lainie Kale and Dana Witten had been preparing the room ahead of time. They or anyone, if it was unlocked all day, could have gotten in and done something, if this was a suspicious death."

"Do you think it was a drug issue?"

"We've got to keep that open as a possibility. But if it was, a tox screen won't show anything for some time. Besides, it's pointless. The diocese refused an autopsy."

"I just think," said Tori, "that if this is beyond accidental or natural death, someone has covered their tracks well. The crime scene investigators couldn't find a suspicious fingerprint to save their lives. Even Holloway herself couldn't mess that up."

Ballack shuddered at that. "Okay. We've at least got Dana saying she gave Zednik his pills. Allegedly, she was ignorant of what he was taking and just did her job. I'd like to know what Zednik was taking. Is there a chance we can get a list of his meds?"

"I'll call Scotty and have him find out from the bishop."

"Also, tell him to have the bishop overnight Zednik's personal notes from that meeting and that whole day, as well as the note about Dana. We should be able to establish if that was authentic or a forgery."

"One step ahead of you. Anything else?"

"Yeah, if Karen's out there, let her know her cocoa got cold. And after you're done, I'll likely need both you ladies to get my sexy bones into that nice soft bed and hook me up to my puffer."

"Will do," said Tori, who paused before asking, "Do you think we're going to get anywhere on Zednik? Hard evidence is awfully difficult to come by."

"We're not here to wonder, just here to discern. If anyone has a confession to make, it's way out of our line of sight now."

Stephen Kale sat in the library, furiously finishing up a translation of II Peter for class the next day. No one could sense the war that raged within him. Soon after he had arrived at St. Basil's, he knew what a mistake he had made. He knew instinctively what he had to do to make everything go away. He hated the insanity of academic rigor. He hated the austerity of his two-bedroom house. He despised the distance he sensed between he and Lainie, and he cursed himself for putting it there.

Tonight however, his anger was centered on St. Peter and how that fisherman couldn't write more simple Greek. His heart clouded over as he remembered tomorrow's class would be a team-teaching event. Father Timothy would be joined by Father Jonathan. *What an unbearable hour,* he thought. *That's like choosing between a firing squad and the gas chamber.*

It was almost time for the library to close anyway. Nine-thirty was approaching, and he didn't care if his work was done. Father Timothy would have to deal with what a disappointment he was. Stephen gathered his books and stomped outside into the chilly air.

Friday morning dawned with greater cloud cover, a severe drop in temperature, and a dusting of snow on the ground. Ballack was up early, getting in a good shave before brushing his teeth. His bathroom routine was lengthier than the average person, but once done, he could normally control things until late evening. Tori was sitting in the kitchen area working on a blueberry muffin and a cup of coffee. She had set out a hard-boiled egg for Ballack, along with a bowl of Golden Grahams and a large glass of apple juice. In less than ten minutes, they were done with breakfast and had Karen signed out for the day. Ballack was bundled against the cold with a white mock turtleneck beneath a navy waffle weave Henley, and gray sweatpants. Tori wore her ex-husband's hunting jacket over a gray sweatshirt and opened the door when Cora Dawson knocked.

The woman who entered the guesthouse was in her early fifties, with an honest face, bright blue eyes, and skin tanned to a generous leathery appearance. Her toothy smile seemed genuine rather than forced, and her blond hair was pulled back in a tight ponytail.

"I'm sorry to keep you both waiting," she began. "I appreciate your patience with me. I was on the phone with the hospital last night as my mother is still there. She's going on two weeks now."

"That's quite all right," responded Ballack in his most compassionate tone. "The fathers told us some of that news. Has there been some complication with her care?"

"She had to have a stent put in. Heart trouble. One day after it was put in, her vitamin K went off the charts. So they hit her with Coumadin and it's been a challenge getting her fully balanced. I've made three trips to St. Anthony's to see her, and I might go back in tomorrow if the roads are clear."

Ballack nodded and then explained, as he would with everyone, that he would be repeating her answers for his Dragon program. He began with the usual initial queries. Name, date of birth, her role at St. Basil's and length of service, her husband. Her replies were to the point, but delivered with grace and no irritation. Only when asked about her religious background was there any expansive detail. "No, we're not Orthodox. Father Matthias did not make that a condition for employment. Actually, we live up in O'Fallon, just off the highway. We attend Messiah Lutheran in Weldon Spring. Been members there for some time now."

Ballack smiled. "I understand that you were the first to discover Reverend Zednik's body. Can you walk us through that morning? I know it might be a difficult remembrance, but anything you can remember may be helpful."

The woman pursed her lips together, allowing a pained grimace. "Yes, it was a sad morning. The treasurer had arrived the day before and was to stay until the middle of the day on the twenty-fifth. I remember going up to the linen closet next to Father Matthias' office to get some things, and, upon coming down, I ran into Father Andrew. Apparently, the treasurer was due to join him for breakfast and had failed to show. Father Andrew was quite put out by his tardiness and was set to head over to the guesthouse. I told him he could finish his breakfast because I was on the way over there and could send him right over to the refectory. He relented. When I got there, I knocked several times. The door was locked, so I had to use the house key."

She was visibly disturbed, and she had to gather herself before she went on. "I entered the room and he was slumped over on his side. He had a book he must have been reading. I called out to him from the doorway. No response. I walked toward him, thinking he might be asleep, but he was unmoving. Also, the light was on, as if he had gone even before he had fallen asleep. He was gone. I didn't want to touch him. I just placed my hand in front of his mouth and felt no breath. At that point, I felt I should check for his pulse. I put my fingers on his carotid and felt nothing."

"And then what?"

"It was a blur," she said, dabbing at her eyes, "but I knew that I needed to tell Father Matthias or Father Andrew. I caught Father Andrew and told him what was wrong. He came and also checked the treasurer's carotid. No pulse. He called Father Matthias in his office, and he arrived in two minutes. Father Andrew called the police, and within an hour an officer arrived on the scene."

Ballack had patiently allowed her to meander through her story, but now he intervened. "Mrs. Dawson, you said that Reverend Zednik was on his side. Was that his right or left side?"

She thought for a second. "He was on his left side."

"And did he have anything in the bed with him?"

"I believe just the book. I didn't see the title. I approached the bed and then ran out promptly to get someone."

Tori spoke for the first time. "You did come back with Father Andrew. Did you have a chance to look around the room and notice what it looked like? I know that might have been the last thing on your mind, but any detail you remember might be helpful."

The lady shook her head. "I can't remember much. Like I said, the light was on. His luggage was off to the side, on the rack, and it looked undisturbed. Quite organized by the look of it. He had already laid out his clothes for the next day. Now that I recall, there was one curious thing. He had a tissue near his hand, as if he had just been holding it. The tissue had blood on it, perhaps from a nosebleed. Likely possibility, as he had a dried red smear on his cleft."

The detail intrigued Ballack, who wanted to pursue a different angle. He resumed his questions. "Was there any other evidence of blood? In the bed? Elsewhere in the room?"

"No, none at all."

Which proved nothing either way. But Ballack didn't think for a moment there would be evidence that glaring. "You saw things that were—as you describe them—curious. Were there things missing from the room? Things you might have expected to see there that weren't?"

The matronly Cora Dawson had been guarded up until this point, but there was something in Ballack's question that caused a ray of illumination to shine within. "Actually, I never noticed this at the moment, but now I remember. The missing pillow!"

"Missing pillow?" asked Tori.

"Yes. When we prepare the guesthouse, we place two pillows on the bed. Since I was away that day, Lainie Kale and Dana Witten prepared the room. My standing prescription for all our guests is for there to be two pillows, both with vinyl covers and pillowcases and a sham. I do remember now that there was only one pillow in the bed. The other was gone."

"And was that second pillow put in the room the previous day?" asked Ballack.

"The girls know that's one of my major proclivities. They would have put it in."

"We'll confirm that, Mrs. Dawson, when we speak to them. But you never saw the second pillow there?"

She looked askance before returning her gaze to the detective. "No, I didn't."

Tori scratched her brow, signaling that she felt this interview had run its course. Mrs. Dawson was clearly distracted at best, perhaps exhausted from the toll on her mother's health. Ballack agreed. They had hit a wall. He said goodbye to her and Tori saw Mrs. Dawson to the door.

Ballack watched his partner go to the sink to wash their breakfast dishes. "What's your take on Cora Dawson?"

"I think she's telling the truth," said Tori. "In fact, I have more confidence in her than the priests. She was visibly upset about the whole ordeal. She only gave the bare facts until we prodded, but that seemed to be more her natural temperament than anything else. It's not like she couldn't go into detail. She did a good job noticing the missing pillow. I know anyone here is a suspect in your book, but I would think she's extremely low on that list." She finished washing the dishes and placed them in the sink rack.

"Next?" she said, as she returned to the table.

"We should take things up with Lainie Kale now. If she had a role in preparing the room, we need to check that. The pillow question may lead somewhere, and it may not. Plus, since she was in on that financial meeting with Zednik, she's one of the several we need to bug."

"We'd better start making progress soon. So far, our big break has been a missing pillow. We don't have a lot of clarity."

"Patience, Tor. Absence of evidence doesn't always equal evidence of absence. Although from the looks of things, we'll have an uphill battle getting it here."

When Tori called to arrange the next interview, she was taken aback when Lainie Kale asked for a change of venue. "I'm just finishing up a load of laundry next to our apartment. Is there a chance we could meet here so I can keep an eye on things?"

Tori didn't like others having control of the location, though this never bothered Ballack. His attitude was "anyone, anywhere, anytime," and while having people in the guesthouse was convenient for them, he relished the idea of questioning others in the place of their choosing. He gave a thumbs up signal to Tori, who relented and told Lainie they'd be over in ten minutes.

The laundry facility was a functional setting, with five washers, five industrial dryers, and an ironing board. Tori brought a portable, fold-up metal ramp that enabled Ballack to get easily through the single door. The windows were shut, trapping the scent of detergent and fabric softener inside. Lainie smiled and began to walk over in their direction. Ballack went straight for the large formica folding table in the northwest corner of the house. He had no problem meeting on someone else's turf, but once there, he called the match his way.

As before, the detectives began with perfunctory questions, which Lainie answered crisply, with a delicate Southern drawl. Tori thought it effective to ask about how she and her husband came to St. Basil's.

"Do you want the full story or the short version?" she asked.

"More is better," said Tori. "We can let you know when to slow down. What I'm asking is what got you thinking in this direction? Are there many Orthodox folks below the Mason-Dixon line, if your accent dictates your home base?"

"Well, the story goes back to our first year at college in Mississippi. April 2005. I had been dating Stephen for four months then. We were students at Millsaps; it's a Methodist college in Jackson. We were both kinda asking some questions about faith and life and stuff. Hadn't been to church together. In fact, I hadn't gone at all since I was thirteen. Stephen was an English major with an interest in journalism. He wrote for the college newspaper. I majored in economics, but I also did a column for the paper. Pope John Paul II had just died and the next election, the what-do-you-call-it…"

"Papal conclave," said Ballack.

"That's it. Anyhow, the conclave was beginning and so the focus of Stephen's article was on church leadership and how do we know our priests, pastors, and bishops are genuine men of God. He went to a variety of churches in the Jackson area, different denominations and all that, asking how they select their local, national and worldwide leadership. Much of it never got beyond local. I suggested he try an Orthodox church downtown. Neither of us knew anything about it. The place sounded about as close to Roman Catholic as possible without being in that orbit. So Stephen went there, interviewed the priest, and ended up staying for three hours…tour of the church, history of the religion, everything. We decided to go there for a service and ended up converting. It became our home church until we graduated."

"The church's name?" said Tori.

"Holy Trinity and St. John the Theologian. I know, it's a mouthful. But they were so good for us. Stephen eventually began thinking about supplementing his college training with a theological degree, so we began talking seminary soon after our sophomore year."

"What got you converting?" asked Tori. "I mean, you sort of glossed over that. Was there some aspect of the church you really liked?"

"The ritual, the mystery," said Lainie. "The fact that coming before God required some effort on your part. That he doesn't meet us where we are but that he has expectations upon us to enter into his presence. It was sort of answering a dare every week. Faith just seemed like a bigger deal all of a sudden."

It seemed to Tori to be a rather convoluted way of finding one's faith, but no two roads were the same, she told herself.

Ballack waded in. "And what made you choose St. Basil's for seminary?"

The question had been delivered with a hint of incredulity. Lainie turned her eyes to Ballack and asked, "What do you mean?"

"I'm sorry. Let me rephrase. There are several Orthodox seminaries in the country. Holy Cross outside of Boston if you're going Greek Orthodox. And there's St. Vladimir's in New York, St. Tikhon's in Pennsylvania. Not to mention St. Herman's in Alaska. All your choices are at least eight hours driving time away from Jackson."

Tori's eyes widened.

"I did some research on the drive down and some last night," said Ballack. "Trust me, I'm no expert on Orthodoxy."

"Well," said Lainie. "Location did play a role. Stephen's folks are from Memphis, so that puts us only five hours away from them. The other places would have put us far from family."

"Your family, too?"

Lainie frowned slightly. "I'm not especially close to either of my parents. Things didn't work out, for any of us. My mom lives in Owensboro, Kentucky. She works in admissions at Brescia University there. My father doesn't have any contact with her anymore, but I've discovered he's not doing well. Chances are he won't live much longer." She looked down at the table and began tracing her thumb in a figure-eight fashion. She was clearly fighting back tears.

Tori maneuvered the interview elsewhere. "You came here in the fall semester of 2008. Stephen began studies then. You've helped out in a number of areas. How did all that come about?"

"Well, Jane Porter—she's the bookkeeper—said she could use some help in the office. She doesn't work Wednesday or Friday, and with my econ major, she thought I'd be a good fit for helping with donations, elementary accounting, and so on. She handles the payroll, not me. That started in October of 2008. Three months later, Cora Dawson asked me if I could help out with some housekeeping and linens on the days I'm not helping Jane. So on Mondays, Tuesdays, and Thursdays, I am with her and Dana Witten—you've met Dana, I believe. Also, I am on the rotation for Holy Communion preparation. Baking bread, having the wine ready. For a small place like St. Basil's, there's really a tremendous amount of behind-the-scenes activity."

Tori leaned forward, almost halfway across the table, and posed the next question. "On the morning of January twenty-fourth, you were among several others in a meeting with Reverend Zednik, who was representing the diocese in a financial intervention of sorts. What was your role in that meeting?"

"Well, I don't know if I had any pre-defined role. Reverend Zednik had called ahead only minutes before and told me he wanted five people there in the meeting with him: myself, Fathers Matthias and Andrew, Jane Porter, and Julie Dirklage—she's the secretary."

"He called you personally."

"No, he called the main seminary line. Normally, Mrs. Dirklage would take the call but she had to step away, so I offered to watch the desk while she was indisposed. That's when Reverend Zednik called."

"And his reasoning for you five being there was…?"

"I can't speak for Mrs. Dirklage, but for the rest of us, it would be because we'd signed, handled, or had some access to funds and donations. Reverend Zednik wanted to take over things and forage through our books, bank records, and documentation of giving. We were running a significant deficit, and he believed there was something awry."

Ballack interposed himself. "Do you think he had a case?"

"I think he was wedging in rather unfairly."

"As much as I can appreciate your strong opinion, Mrs. Kale, that doesn't answer my question."

"I don't believe so. Chasing down records takes time, and we still had a lot to do. Why couldn't he wait things out until we released our findings?"

"Did he ask for access to your online banking?"

A pause. "Yes, he did."

"Username? Password?"

"I guess the cat's been out of the bag for some time now. Gossip travels fast."

"No, we have spoken to the bishop. Is there an issue with the diocese knowing that information for an inquiry and then allowing the seminary to re-set both username and password later?"

"Honestly, detective, that wasn't my beef with Reverend Zednik. The problem is that he was using someone here to feed him financial information in a way that made us look like the bad guys. He had a mole on the inside: Father Jonathan Erhart."

"Feeding the diocese financial information?"

"Yes."

"What type of information?"

"Exact records on all our donors."

"What was the reaction to this?" asked Tori. "When you found out about it?"

"To be completely honest, we were all outraged. I called his bluff on it and the others were ready to blow a gasket. Even Father Andrew raked him over the coals for what he did. I mean, it's one thing for the diocese to come in with an iron fist. If that's all it was, we wouldn't like it, but I think we'd move on. But what Father Jonathan did was a betrayal!"

Ballack wanted a different angle. "Who do you think was more to blame? Do you think Zednik recruited Father Jonathan, or did Father Jonathan approach the treasurer?"

Lainie put forth a sour glare. "I don't think it matters. If one hadn't, the other one would have. The truth is that we would have received major cuts and tuition hikes. That's the direction they were headed. Stephen is here on several scholarships and so if we couldn't renew them, we'd have to drop out and find something else. Other students were in the same boat."

"You've seen that hard data for yourself?"

"No, but that's the way the wind blows in higher education. We could see it coming. Everyone who met with him that day sensed it."

"Now about that evening. Mrs. Dawson was to return from her hospital visit. She asked you and Dana to oversee the preparation of the treasurer's room?"

"Father Matthias did, actually."

"Okay, and when you both set up the room, how did it look on completion? Can you give a description of the bed, the bathroom?"

Lainie looked at Ballack, then Tori, then back again to Ballack. "I guess I could. Although Dana and I worked on it separately, the final look was the same as for any other overnight guest. The bed had a gray comforter, ivory sheets, and pillows with gray cases."

"How many pillows?" asked Tori.

A confused look came over Lainie's face. "Two," she said.

"And the bathroom?"

Another puzzled gaze. "Two towels, one washcloth, a bath mat, and a bar of soap." She paused, then said, "Would you like to know which color?"

Wiseass, thought Ballack.

"Look," continued Lainie, "Can I ask why the questions about the room?"

"A man dies in a room," said Ballack. "We're going to have questions about the room." He paused. "I think for the present that will be enough. We have some other folks to interview. If we need to ask you some questions for clarification, I assume you'll be around."

Lainie nodded her acquiescence and got up to leave. Ballack nodded at Tori, who quickly said, "One more thing. Were you on campus the entire evening of the twenty-fourth?"

Lainie thought for several seconds. "I was here the whole time except for about an hour. I had to run up to Walgreens. Stephen has asthma, so I had gotten his inhaler filled. Well, I had gotten it previously, but it was a dud. Nothing in it. So I had to take it back to get the right one."

"And that was when?"

"I left around seven o'clock. I was back at fifteen past eight."

Ballack raised his eyebrows to Tori as if to say *Is that good for you?*

Tori turned to Lainie and said, "Thank you, Mrs. Kale. Before people start coming in here to do their laundry, we'd better end this. If we can leave the ramp here, I'll pick it up later."

After they left the laundry, the detectives were silent for some time. Ballack coasted down toward the Lake of the Protomartyr, Tori keeping pace with him. The sun hid behind the high clouds.

It was Tori who broke the silence. "So what's your opinion so far?"

"So far, we're spitting into a hurricane. We're not getting any clear sense on who could have done anything, if there was foul play. But we didn't expect to. But we did get confirmation on that can of worms that Mrs. Dawson brought up. She saw only one pillow. Lainie Kale says there were two the night before. I'll check with Dana Witten and see if she can confirm the two pillows when she went in that night. You'd better find out where Jane Porter is this fine day and we'll talk to her, although I doubt we can get any more distinct perspectives on the meeting with Zednik."

"I'll make the call to Porter. Meet me in the guesthouse in fifteen minutes. You'll be okay if you need suctioning?"

"I'll be fine."

As they walked back up past the chapel, Tori mused, "We still have no proof it was murder. And the real culprit, if there is one, could be miles away. And we still have more people to see."

"Patience, Tor. The truth will come out if it's there. Even if it's behind a mask of holiness, we can find it. The wall might not fall on the first assault, but if anyone here is hiding something, it's only a matter of time."

Father Jonathan was speechless.

A soft-spoken man, he nonetheless rarely received news that arrested his tongue.

But that day had arrived. He stood in the postal nook in Chalcedon Hall and looked at the neatly typed letter in his hands. He had received letters like this before but through the mail and usually from people angry over his ecclesiastical survival and promotion. To some, a sordid past meant a prohibited future. But what he saw in his trembling fingers unnerved him. The words were familiar, venomous. Seared with pain, they accused him of betrayal and wounds beyond comparison. But the most unsettling feature had nothing to do with the words. It was something else.

The envelope in which the letter came bore only his name. No return address and no stamp. That left only one possible—and very disturbing—conclusion about this epistle's genesis.

As Jane Porter did not work on Fridays, she suggested to Tori that she and Ballack come north of town and interview her at her residence. Although Tori wasn't happy about giving up their home base, she relented. Perhaps, she thought, a change of scenery would be helpful for both she and Ballack. They found their way north of Defiance, turning into Ridge Creek Estates and taking Northlind Drive until they found Matts Way. Jane Porter and her husband lived in a sizable house with an extra large back patio. The rear entrance was the best for Ballack's wheelchair. Once he negotiated the doorway with his ramp, he found himself in the expansive den, with two leather recliner sofas, a big screen television, and an ornate crystal chandelier. On the south wall hung a lifelike painting of a river view in spring. It seemed to both detectives to be a local scene.

Ballack pointed at the artwork. "Did you paint that, Mrs. Porter?"

Jane Porter followed his expression as she brought in a tray of sodas with an array of lunchmeats and cheeses. "Oh, that. Now that, my daughter painted. She's an avid cyclist and runner, and she loves the nearby stretch of the Katy Trail. That view is from the bridge on the trail that extends over the Femme Osage Creek. It's less than a mile south of here on foot."

She placed the tray down in front of them. Tori selected a Pepsi and a slice of rolled-up honey ham. Ballack chose several thin cuts of roast beef and two slices of Munster cheese. He grabbed a Fresca but had difficulty opening the can. Once Tori took care of that, he began the questions.

"Mrs. Porter, we are here at the request of the diocese regarding the sudden death of Reverend Tomas Zednik last week. We know you were part of a meeting involving him during his visit. But before getting to that, perhaps you could let us know something of your employment at St. Basil's."

"Certainly. This is my fifth year at St. Basil's as the bookkeeper. I had recently finished twenty-five years in the public schools, the last nine as a vice-principal at Francis Howell. I was done with teaching and administration. I wanted something in a school environment, but I was willing for it to be completely different from past experience. My husband is neck-deep in my former life. He's the dean of the School of Communications at Lindenwood. I didn't want to work in a university, but with St. Basil's nearby, I thought I might see what they had available. They were shifting Father Jonathan into a teaching-only role, so he was giving up any idea of overseeing the money flow. Since I had headed up budget committees and have a finance minor to go with everything else, I thought it would be worth an application. Father Matthias called me two days later, then spoke to me face-to-face, and I had the position."

"What was your impression of Reverend Zednik?"

"Well, he had been there before, three or four times during my employment, and the inherent tension in each visit increased. This last one was quite unbearable, if I might say so myself. No one doubted some money issues existed, but that didn't mean I was asleep at my post."

"Was that more or less the accusation?"

"From Reverend Zednik? Not in so many words. He did have a series of records from several donors that, when all put together, would equal the exact amount we were in arrears. Since my signature was on the checks endorsing them, he naturally felt I was at the epicenter of the problem."

"These checks, do you recall them specifically?"

"We receive many donations but these were on the moderately substantial side. As I endorse them, I am the centerpiece, I guess. But we have several people take these deposits to the bank. Father Andrew, Lainie Kale…come to think of it, Father Jonathan was kind enough to save me a trip once or twice recently, but I doubt that was out of good intentions."

"Why do you say that, Mrs. Porter?" asked Tori, who had noticed a tremor of rage in her voice.

"All I'll say about that is that if you're looking for anyone overqualified for the sort of shenanigans we were accused of, you don't need to look farther than Father Jonathan. During the meeting, Father Matthias guessed rightly that Zednik was using Father Jonathan as his mole. I guess we should have figured on that sooner or later."

"And Zednik affirmed that, correct?"

"Yes. I didn't bring this up in the meeting because there was no point setting off another bomb, but if I were a betting woman, I'd say Father Jonathan is the one sinking our funds. It's clear *someone* is stealing from St. Basil's. Father Jonathan has never been fully embraced at the seminary, but that is due to other factors that can't be pinned on St. Basil's. If he could have controlled his libido years ago, if he hadn't cozied up to the diocese and Reverend Zednik in particular, and if his appointment wasn't a classic example of strong-arming us, then perhaps we'd have a touch less rancor about him. He was the part-time bookkeeper before I came on. He knows the system;

he'd have access. Personally, I don't know why he isn't under major scrutiny."

Ballack replied, "For what? Embezzlement? Or something worse? Is there something about Zednik's fate that you're implying?"

"If you're asking if he has a connection to Zednik's death, I would doubt it. Those men were close enough to be lovers. Plus, Zednik died of a heart attack. That was the word I received. I'm talking about the money trail."

"At present, that is another matter for us. If the seminary's deficit figures into Reverend Zednik's death, then of course we'll be pursuing those facts. There may be a connection there, Mrs. Porter. But if that's the case, anyone who had access to financial information at St. Basil's could be part of that connection."

Jane Porter was clearly defensive now. Her lower lip trembled. Tori couldn't figure out if it was due to the memory of Zednik's veiled accusation or something deeper. Either way, she was becoming less likable. She packed a lot of intimidation into her slight frame. It was then that all three jumped slightly when the phone rang. She excused herself to answer it and went into the kitchen.

While she was gone, Tori sat down next to Ballack. "Well?" she asked.

"I'm still recovering from her spiteful annoyance. I was afraid she'd go postal for a second there. Regardless, it seems the more we dig, there's enough in the soil that smells funny."

They heard the sounds of hushed tones and hurried scribbling coming from the kitchen. Tori turned to her partner and whispered, "Still, if someone whacked Zednik, I can't see it being her. Why would she drive back to the seminary around midnight to snuff him out? She'd have to have keys to the guesthouse or bank on the possibility it would be unlocked."

"Which means that, unless she has a set of keys to the guesthouse, this was likely an inside job, if we're talking murder like the bishop says." He stopped, then mused, "I doubt we'll find the second pillow here."

"Come on, Cameron," she rolled her eyes. "Don't get stuck on that second pillow theory! Besides, if someone used it, I highly doubt he'd bring it back to bed to sleep with. It's been eleven days! It probably got tossed in a dumpster. But I agree with you on one thing. She was a first-class ice queen. And her eyes were anywhere but on us when she was pulling out her theory on Father Jonathan."

Jane Porter returned to the den. Her eyes were darting back and forth, but more out of concern for something else. She had obviously received some unwelcome news.

"I'm sorry, detectives. That call was from one of my husband's colleagues at Lindenwood. They were having a staff meeting over lunch, and toward the end my husband began having very sharp chest pains. He even spat up his drink because of the pain, and..." She trailed off.

"Is he okay?" asked Tori.

"Well, I need to go make sure. They're rushing him to the ER right now."

"St. Joseph's?" asked Ballack.

"Yes. Just down the street from the school. Anyway, I want to go be with him and make sure everything's okay, if it will be. I hate to have to run out on what is your job, but..."

"No, say no more," replied Tori. "You need to go. What you have going on there is more important that what's going on here. If we need to speak with you further, we know where to find you."

Ballack handed his business card to her. "If you think of anything else, please call us. But given the present circumstances, I wouldn't expect that to be priority number one."

"Thank you both. I suppose I can let you out the back?" She was clearly preoccupied with the report about her husband.

"That would be fine. And thank you for lunch."

Once they got settled in the Sprinter and backed out of the long driveway, Tori turned to Ballack. "Okay. It's ten after one. Next stop?"

Ballack was thoughtful for a brief interlude before deciding. "It seems like many roads are leading to Father Jonathan. It makes sense. He's been the center of many storms. Might as well see what all the rain and thunder are about. Let's find him as soon as we get back to campus. I wish that interview with Jane Porter could have revealed more."

"Yeah," replied Tori, "but isn't that our takeaway from most interrogations? Anyway, let's get back. Shouldn't be too hard to find Father Jonathan. Just find a cassocked guy we haven't recognized before."

"Or," said Ballack, half-joking, "look for someone with a red letter A on his chest."

"Very nice, you pretentious cripple." Tori smiled at him from the steering wheel. "Just so you know, you're not the only one who's read *The Scarlet Letter*." She gunned the van down Highway 94 toward their next surprise.

They pulled into the parking lot next to Chalcedon Hall at the exact moment that Dana Witten came out of their guest room. Tori had finished unlocking Ballack's wheelchair from the latch straps when Dana approached. The wind was picking up, which blew her hair around her face. Several wisps got lodged in her mouth and she waited to speak until she could gently extract them.

"Good to see you both back," she said, looking at Ballack only. "I vacuumed your room. Mrs. Dawson took care of the other matters."

"Thank you, Dana," said Ballack. "Everything last night was great."

"Are we to expect your nurse to come tonight?"

"Yes, around seven. Although it will be a different one. Karen has a couple nights off, so Rhoda will be here."

"Okay, I guess we'll be able to recognize her if she shows up and needs to find her way around?"

"Oh, trust me," grinned Ballack. "You'll have no problem. Young black woman, big toothy smile. Big neon yellow jacket. And her scrubs are covered with Spongebob Squarepants characters. You'd only miss her if God struck you blind."

Dana laughed in response, a sweet, lilting laugh. She brushed her hair behind her left ear before remembering something. "Oh, by the way, Father Matthias wanted me to ask you if we were to expect you for dinner tonight."

It was Tori who replied, "Well, if they still don't mind us, we'll be there."

Ballack continued, "Besides, I'd like to be there to see if tonight's entrée can top last night's stroganoff."

Dana smiled more widely this time, brushing her hair around her right ear. "Well, last night was Russian night. The refectory is doing this cuisine series, where each night we eat food from a different country in which Orthodoxy is represented."

"And tonight?" asked Tori.

"I heard through the grapevine that it's Finland."

"Finland has an Orthodox communion?" asked Ballack.

"Evidently. I think it's split pea-and-ham soup, followed by Finnish meatballs with mashed potatoes. Some sort of dessert to follow."

Ballack's mouth began watering when he remembered they needed to find their next interview. "Not to get off the subject of dinner, but where might we find Father Jonathan?"

Dana crossed her arms, more to bundle herself against another stiff wind gust. "I think I saw him go toward the library about thirty minutes ago. I don't know if he's studying there…wait. I think he's joining with Father Timothy for a class today. Stephen Kale told my husband that last night, so you might find him in the library classroom."

"Will do," said Tori. "Thanks a bunch. We'll see you at dinner tonight, then."

Dana managed one more smile in Ballack's direction. "No problem. We'll save you a seat." And then she walked off.

Ballack turned with his partner in the direction of the library. Tori stayed in step with his chair, and as they neared their destination, she asked, "So, do you think anyone here is truly a suspect?"

"Don't you think we have to assume that?"

"Even that little flirt?"

"Who, Dana? Oh, stop it! She's married, for heaven's sake! Seems like she's trapped in a future as a priest's wife. I feel bad for her, but that's her road to walk."

"Seems like a lonely one at that. I don't get the impression there's a lot of love there between her and her Socrates wanna-be."

It occurred to Ballack he'd been guessing much the same thing. He thought about what married life in an academic fishbowl might be like. He had compassion on anyone who struggled in love. His foray with Michelle had ended badly. He knew enough about Tori's life to realize a spouse could be one thing before a wedding and completely different afterward. Was that the origin of the pain behind Dana Witten's eyes? He felt badly for her, even somewhat drawn to her. He shook himself. *Oh please,* he said. *Not that. Get a grip!* Besides, the idea of any lasting relationship with his disability attached to it would be remote at best. *Do your job,* he railed inwardly. He was here to investigate, interrogate, report, and leave. It was with a renewed determination that he drove through the front doors of the library.

The Hagia Sophia Library was the most recent construction achievement for St. Basil's Seminary. Facing the Chapel of the Theotokos, the library held a disproportionately large collection of books for a community so small. The stomping grounds of Father Timothy burst with academic rigor and pride, and he never failed to remind students of the library's role in the fulfillment of that middle section of the seminary's vision, to "engage the mind." The facility also boasted a computer center fully stocked with top-of-the-line Hebrew and Greek software, along with a massive database on the early church fathers. In addition, St. Basil's was connected to other universities and seminaries across Missouri through the MOBIUS network, in which a student could request a resource and have it couriered to him in a matter of days.

The detectives wandered into the spacious atrium and peered down the bookshelves, looking for some clue of Father Jonathan's whereabouts. Only two students were in the main study area, hunched over their books and papers at a small group study table on the west end of the main room. Ballack zipped around the floor, desperately hoping Father Jonathan might materialize out of thin air.

Just as that thought crossed his mind, a voice boomed through the wall, "No, Mr. Panangiotis, that's not a participle. Notice the sigma; future tense. So how's that going to change the translation?"

Tori looked at Ballack. "Father Timothy. This way, I think. There's a ramp leading down to a door at the end of the hallway."

Ballack swung over in her direction and saw what they had missed upon their entry. A blue-carpeted hall took them on a long incline ending at an open door on the right-hand side. There was a five-foot by five-foot partition just inside the door, with, as Ballack saw from that angle, a rolling cart behind it, loaded with books and DVDs. They peeked in through the open entry and saw nine students seated in a half-moon arrangement. Father Jonathan was seated near the front, opposite the door. Father Timothy was turning away from the dry erase board at the front of the room, a Greek New Testament in his hands, which were smeared with blue ink. Apparently he had been making corrections without the benefit of an eraser.

"I'm sorry, Father Timothy," said Ballack. "We were hoping to speak to Father Jonathan, if it was possible."

A murmur and chuckle rippled through several of the students, but Father Timothy ended that with a frosty glare. He looked at Father Jonathan, then to Ballack, and replied, "Actually, Father Jonathan is helping me team-teach this class today as his first-year students are gone. We have about fifteen minutes remaining in class if you don't mind waiting."

A young man with chiseled looks and blond, almost white, hair chirped up unexpectedly. "Or for that matter, detectives, perhaps you'd want to stay. Help us solve the mystery of the aorist passive participle."

"Nicholas!" snapped Father Timothy, who suddenly changed expression and spoke to both detectives. "On the other hand, you are more than welcome to stay. If you need to speak to Father Jonathan, this would be as good a venue as any. We just need to get through a few more verses of St. Peter's second epistle, if you don't mind hearing some vicious pronouncements against false teachers."

"Don't mind it at all," said Ballack. "I've had more than a few false teachers in my day. I think I can stand hearing about their fate."

"You sure it's no problem?" asked Tori, looking first at Father Timothy and then the others.

"None at all," said Father Timothy, who seemed strangely determined not to allow any semblance of a protest from the students.

Moving briskly past Nicholas Panangiotis' chair, Ballack paused, leaned toward him, and said, "By the way, given that Father Timothy corrected you earlier, you might want to pay attention to him rather than try to impress me."

That elicited a chuckle from those gathered. Father Jonathan tried in vain to suppress a snicker. Nicholas looked as if Ballack had shucked his pants down during Holy Communion. Father Timothy gave a dry smile and held out his New Testament to Ballack as if to say, "Like to teach the class?" Ballack dismissed that unstated question with a wave of his hand.

The class turned their attention back to the passage under discussion and it was all grammar, syntax, and translation for the next ten minutes. Ballack was simultaneously unnerved and impressed. Father Timothy was an intimidating presence in the classroom. He was a demanding instructor who expected one hundred percent from everyone, regardless of ability. It was not enough to give the correct answer; he insisted one be able to demonstrate why that answer was the best option. Two years before, he had reduced a fourth-year student to tears during a senior oral examination. Yet, Ballack thought, the man's intellect was inspiring. Even in these few moments, Father Timothy was able to take complex matters from the Greek text and make them intelligible and clear. When a student did well, as Marcus

Curry did when he made several connections to a recent chapel sermon on the passage under discussion, Father Timothy at least acknowledged with token praise.

It was during the last five minutes of class that everything broke loose. Father Timothy was taking a break as Father Jonathan expounded on the end of their translation for the day, verses having to do with Sodom and Gomorrah's destruction. Here, the Old Testament professor took the class back to the nineteenth chapter of Genesis, connecting the apocalyptic ruin of the two cities to the future judgment of false teachers. A somewhat relaxed atmosphere snapped violently when he asked, "Now, what might be some criteria by which we identify false teachers?"

A tall, well-built young man sitting next to Nicholas snickered and whispered, a touch too loudly, "That's easy. You leave Sodom and get a job with the diocese."

Nicholas couldn't contain himself and sputtered a laugh on instinct. Marcus Curry and Jason Hart reeled in horror. The others put their heads down. But none reacted faster than Father Jonathan, who raised out of his chair and bellowed with more vigor than a man his age should: "What was that, Stephen? Your mouth and your heart have nothing better to do than spew poison at a serious question?!"

"I was just answering the…"

"That was no answer! That was a complete lack of grace from someone preparing for the priesthood! Perhaps when you finally commit a sin of your own, you'll know the grace of Christ in overcoming it, you hypocrite!"

The room fell absolutely silent. No one moved. Father Jonathan stood over Stephen Kale and looked as if he was about to call down fire and brimstone himself. For his part, Stephen matched his glare with a wicked gaze of his own.

Sensing the class was lost for good, a scowling Father Timothy approached his colleague from behind and placed a firm hand on his shoulder. But rather than giving a compliant response, Father Jonathan wheeled around and jerked Father Timothy's hand away, looking at him with fire in his eyes.

"You heartless scoundrel! You invite me to come here and be part of this class, and this is the reception I get! You have it out with Tomas, dispute his motives, and then you have to defile his memory by dragging me into your bog of miscreants? Someone in your shaky, greenhorn position should know better!"

Ballack immediately looked at Father Timothy's face. He was shocked at what he saw. The imposing Timothy Birchall had surely faced off against the most bruising opponents while on the Duke basketball court. Physically, Father Timothy could have taken the much smaller Father Jonathan and bent him in half with his bare hands. But the words of Father Jonathan seemed to have the effect of a twelfth-round uppercut to a punch-drunk boxer. Ballack could have sworn that Father Timothy had significantly recoiled from the sting of Father Jonathan's words. He looked over at Tori with a "Did-you-see-that?" look. She nodded her agreement.

With a slight waver in his voice, Father Timothy said, "Gentlemen, that will be all today. Refer to the syllabus for your next assignment due Monday." His eyes never left Father Jonathan's flared nostrils.

The students shuffled to the door while concurrently gathering their papers and books. Father Timothy turned to Nicholas Panangiotis and Stephen Kale when they walked by.

"You two. My office. Now."

And like defeated wildebeests, they hung their heads and followed him out the door. Ballack looked around. He, Tori, and Father Jonathan were the only ones left in the room.

Seemingly unaware of their presence, Father Jonathan went back to his chair, snatched his Bible and notebook along with his briefcase, and turned to make his way out. Upon taking a few steps, he saw and remembered that Detectives Vaughan and Ballack were waiting to speak to him, as requested. Of all times, this was one when he was most definitely *not* in the mood.

Tori gave the opening salvo. "Father Jonathan, I know that coming off the last few minutes, you might not find this to be the best timing. However, for the sake of our inquiry into the death of Tomas Zednik, it would be most helpful if you could spare a few moments of time, sooner rather than later."

"Well, it's not ideal, but I suppose you will need to speak with me before long," rejoined Father Jonathan. He looked around the room as if to make sure it was a safe zone, and then directed them both to a spot in front of the chair near the dry erase board. "Perhaps we can do it here. I'll just close the door to keep this private."

When he sat in his chair, Father Jonathan settled in with a weary groan. He looked as if he'd gone days without sleep. His blue eyes looked less like stained glass and more like faded denim. His hair, parted on the side, looked more carved than styled, but this seemed to be the only ordered part of his being. His skin looked fairly ashen, with a veneer of stubble gracing his jaw. His demeanor contrasted greatly with his scathing utterance in Father Timothy's face moments earlier.

Ballack studied him closely. Whatever might be the case with Reverend Zednik's passing, it was becoming crystal clear that Father

Jonathan was at the nexus of several storms here. It was easily apparent that, despite whatever blessing the diocese had given this man, he was deeply unpopular with many at St. Basil's. This study in duality could make for an interesting interview, Ballack thought.

Tori began the questions, asking the priest about his basic information. Father Jonathan tipped his head to the side and cradled it in his right palm, as if taking a catnap. He answered all the questions as if reading from a script.

Ballack decided to move down a different road. "Father, you came to St. Basil's under some unusual circumstances. Could you please elaborate on why the diocese sent you here?"

Father Jonathan acted at first like he didn't hear him, and he asked Ballack to repeat the question. Ballack patiently did so.

"Before I answer, can I have your word this conversation will be kept confidential?"

It was Tori who gave the answer. "We can make every effort, Father, unless what you tell us has bearing on our investigation of Reverend Zednik's death. We can use discretion, but that's our call, not yours."

"Very well. The diocese appointed me to come here and fill the vacant Old Testament position seven years ago. The hiring process was somewhat slow, and Father Jonah Nasekos had just turned down the opportunity to come here from Holy Cross near Boston. It looked as though the seminary would enter the year without the position being filled. But in June of 2004, Bishop Burgic believed that my gifts in administration, while appreciated, were winding up, and he believed I would be a good fit for a teaching post here. Through a series of talks with Father Matthias, he finally got me here."

"Was there a reason for your vocation to end up here? Was a church position not in the offing?"

"Actually, I am only allowed to teach and perform specified administrative functions, according to diocesan mandate."

"I assume," said Ballack, "there is a story behind that diocesan mandate."

Father Jonathan looked directly into Ballack's eyes. Dead silence.

"Would that have to do with the reason you want confidentiality?"

"Detective," said Father Jonathan with a swirl of bitterness in his voice, "you are hardly the picture of tact."

"Father Jonathan, my job is to protect the public and discover the truth, not to bolster your self-esteem or preserve your private history. Avoiding the question will only deepen that resolve."

The priest was clearly upset but knew he was boxed in. "Well, it appears I have no choice about going further down memory lane. I was under the pastoral care of the diocese for past indiscretions, and it was after this period of care that I received my summons to work under Bishop Burgic."

"Indiscretions?" asked Tori.

"Yes."

"If you were limited to teaching and administrative roles," said Ballack, "I imagine those indiscretions went beyond smuggling communion bread."

Silence.

Ballack was slowly losing his cool. "Father Jonathan, we can find out directly from you or we can sketch this out with the watercolors of hearsay. Your choice."

"Fine. I came under the pastoral care of the diocese soon after I moved to Kansas City from Birmingham, Alabama. I had been counseling a woman who was enduring a hard spot in her marriage. We met more and more often, but we spoke about her marriage less and less. We began an affair that lasted five months. It would have lasted longer, but we were caught in bed."

Tori swallowed hard.

Father Jonathan continued. "Her husband had been on a business trip, but he'd been fired at the midway point of the excursion. He returned early, and we were discovered in the act. It was a devastating moment. The marriage dissolved and my diocese there brought me up on charges. I accepted their censure and left the area, my parish, everything. I had a sister who lived in Excelsior Springs, right outside of Kansas City. I took a job in the bookstore at William Jewell College while I lived with her. That only lasted a year before she died in a car accident. Drunk driver. At any rate, from the time I moved to Missouri to her death, I had not dared set foot in a church. My conscience was such that if I approached the threshold of a church or cathedral, I would get nauseated. It was at this time that Tomas was purchasing something at the bookstore and we got acquainted. I overcame my ecclesiastical shame and began attending his church. He befriended me, and I told him of my history. He personally took me under his wing, not to strategically maneuver me into a church position but to befriend me. Once it came out who I was and that I was attending Holy Resurrection, Bishop Burgic got involved. The diocese here is more pastoral and less reactive than the Diocese of the Southeast. They asked me if I had any desire to return to a ministerial role. Honestly, I had not thought about it. But as I considered their words, I meditated much on the seventh chapter of Luke's Gospel. Perhaps you know the story of Jesus being anointed by the prostitute and forgiving her sins. I believe God was calling me to pay back my debt through continued service to his church. The bishop and Tomas formulated a time of penance and counsel for me, and once I completed that, I would be free to engage in a ministry position under their supervision, and it could only be administration or teaching. Counseling and parish ministry is not an option."

"The affair," asked Ballack, "was when exactly?"

"Thirteen years ago."

"You moved to Kansas City soon after?"

"Yes, once I was censured, I left."

"And your time of penance and counsel with Reverend Zednik?"

"Let's see, that would have been roughly 1999 until 2002, upon which I began serving in the diocesan office for another two years."

"Which brings us to your appointment, which brings us to now."

"Yes."

Ballack sensed where Father Jonathan would go with the next question, but it needed to be asked. "Father, was Reverend Zednik welcome here at St. Basil's?"

"Not warmly, if you ask me. The first-year students haven't yet had time to adopt much cynicism, but they are the exception rather than the rule. St. Basil's tends to have an independent spirit and doesn't like much interference from headquarters. This came to a head with the financial deficit and many students rushed to judgment, believing Tomas wanted to cut off their scholarships and spike tuition costs. It wasn't true, as those donations were earmarked towards specific matters."

"And how would you know that, Father Jonathan?" asked Tori with a touch of sarcasm in her voice. She didn't bother to hide her disgust over his adulterous actions.

"What do you mean?"

"How did you know those donations were earmarked? Did Reverend Zednik tell you and you took his word for it? Or did he find out from you?"

Father Jonathan's eyes narrowed quickly, then relaxed as the anger passed. "So you know about my role in giving him information. Neither Father Matthias nor Father Andrew said that you knew."

"Well, maybe they just didn't tell you they told us. But we know."

Ballack cut in. "Father, do you have an opinion on the death of Reverend Zednik?"

Father Jonathan clearly looked troubled. "I don't know. I have wondered that many times over. He was a dear friend, and this has given me so much shock and pain. At times I believe with all my heart that there is no way someone, here or elsewhere, could be capable of such violence. And yet I have my moments where it is clear that is a possibility."

"What do you mean, 'it is clear that is a possibility'?"

Father Jonathan held up a finger to put the conversation on pause, and while he did so, he reached into his briefcase and pulled out a plain white business envelope. He handed it to Tori, who read it before handing it over to Ballack. He looked at the ivory paper with the boldface type. Words of pain and anguish roared at him from the page:

Once again, you walk by stealth rather than by faith. Hypocrite! You have come here under a shadow you can't escape, and there are reasons for the prison in which you dwell. The sins of the past flow through the present into a future you cannot see. You fast, pray, and chant in the name of God, and yet it is God himself who will strike you down for your evil. It is an evil you created and have given tangible evidence of the filth of your heart. You have been weighed in the balances and found wanting.

Ballack looked at the page and scanned the letter again. The last line was especially chilling. He retained a cursory knowledge of major biblical events, and so he recalled the prophecy of Daniel, from the night when the Babylonian Empire fell to the Persians. Those were the exact words Daniel addressed to King Belshazzar, hours before the pagan monarch was slain.

Father Jonathan rubbed his hands as if trying to discard flakes of sin from his body. "Please," he said. "Keep it. I have no desire for it to be anywhere near me. It is that letter that has me in a vile mood this afternoon. I received it this morning in my mailbox. You see the envelope. No return address. Just a label with my named on it, typed."

"Which means," said Tori, "it is likely someone local who drove by and inserted it in your box, or..."

"Or else it is a member of this seminary community," finished Father Jonathan. "Which is an extremely disturbing conclusion. To imagine such a person is walking the grounds here at St. Basil's chills me to the bone. And yet I have not made things better with the events of the past thirty minutes. I am truly sorry to both of you for the way I acted in class today. I was out of line to speak that way in front of you to a fellow priest or to priests-in-training. To make matters worse, I don't know if they would even concern themselves with my confession."

"That might be out of your hands, Father," said Ballack, "but this letter does put some skin on what went down in class." He stopped, then added, "However, given my understanding of the church, nothing that happens among people of God would shock me. Sadden, perhaps. But never shock. Even the communities with the most holy appearances can be dens of great evil."

"I believe I am beginning to tilt in the direction of that sentiment. For the past week, I have sensed a great cloud of wickedness, a palpable evil, abroad in this place. To be sure, I can't pinpoint it. But, trust me, it is there. And we may not be able to wash it away, no matter how many tears we may use to wash our altars."

Tori had endured about enough of the conspiracy-theory platitudes and turned to Ballack to see if he had any more questions. But her partner, all of a sudden, had received some sort of revelation. She had seen that connect-the-dots look on his face before. And she knew instinctively that he wanted to get going on it as soon as possible. They thanked Father Jonathan for his time and promised to investigate the matter of the harsh letter. With a handshake and a jaunt up the interior ramp, they were soon outside in the middle of a gentle snowfall.

Father Timothy rapped loudly on the door of Father Matthias' office and was surprised to hear Father Andrew call him in from the other side. Both Father Matthias and Father Andrew were standing in the center of the room.

"I'm sorry," Father Timothy said. "I am in need of help."

"This wouldn't be about the situation in your class just now, would it?" asked Father Andrew.

How could they know already? Father Timothy wondered. All it would take would be a word in the wrong ear, and he could be out of a job. But his fears were instantly allayed when Father Matthias approached him and laid a kindly hand on his shoulder. The dean smiled broadly.

"Timothy, don't be sorry at all. If this is about Father Jonathan, perhaps this is a situation you can help us solve."

Ten minutes later, Father Timothy left, and the broad smile was now his to wear. He was secure. Father Jonathan was the one who should be worried. He was convinced. It would be easy. He had full backing. And no one would know a thing.

"Cam, slow down! Slow down! Can you…" Tori huffed as she caught up to Ballack. "Can you explain to me why you're in such a hurry just now?"

"I just remembered," said Ballack. "Remembered why Father Jonathan's name sounded so familiar."

"Had you met him before? Heard him speak? Saw his name on *America's Most Wanted*?"

"Nope, from a book. I suddenly remembered where I'd heard that phrase before. The one at the very end. You know, 'no matter how many tears we may use to wash our altars'? Well, that triggered my memory."

He pushed the handicap-access button that let them into their room. He pulled up to the kitchen table and took the cover off his wheelchair laptop. In forty seconds, he had landed on Amazon's website and feverishly typed in a keyword.

"Darren Glenn is a counseling professor over at Covenant Seminary in Creve Coeur. He and my dad are good friends. Anyhow, he's written a book on restoring people from guilt, sin, shame, the whole gamut. Dad has it on his shelf at home. Come on, come on, work!" he snapped at his laptop, which had picked an odd time for a slow Internet connection.

"While you're doing that," said Tori, "I need to run to the bathroom." She disappeared for five minutes, at one point hearing Ballack speaking out loud from behind the door, then came back to the table. "So what's the big deal you have on your mind?"

Ballack looked at her with a glow of triumph. "The notable thing is his co-author for that particular work." He gestured toward the screen. "Take a look for yourself."

And there, below Darren Glenn's name on the cover of the book, *Tears at the Altar*, were the words "FR. JONATHAN ERHART."

"Jackpot!" exclaimed Tori. "Think this guy might be able to tell us anything about him, or St. Basil's, and soon?"

"All of the above, sweetheart," replied Ballack. "I called him while you were indisposed. We're having lunch with him tomorrow in the Loop."

An early dinner immediately after Vespers gave both detectives time to touch base with Father Matthias regarding the verbal donnybrook in the classroom earlier that afternoon. Ballack was able to recall everything Father Jonathan had told him, and Father Matthias listened carefully, adding nothing, nodding occasionally. Ballack gave all the details but was concise. Nothing needed to be repeated. The one matter he omitted was the anonymous letter in Father Jonathan's mailbox. That was one item he was keeping close to the vest.

Father Matthias gave his empty soup bowl to the table server and received his main course of Finnish meatballs. "Thank you. That dovetails with Father Timothy's report of the proceedings." He sounded like a jury reporter born without a personality. It seemed to Ballack that a noticeable change had come over the dean.

The three of them were the only ones sitting at the head table on the north end of the refectory. Though it wasn't the most private of venues, Ballack decided to chance another question. "Father Matthias, in your opinion, has Father Jonathan been well-received here at the seminary?"

"In what way?"

"Across the board. As a professor, mentor, priest."

"We were asked to receive him. There was an open position. He was given that post. He teaches. He preaches in worship on occasion. He has performed adequately."

"Adequate might describe a person boxing up Kit Kats on a lazy night at a convenience store," said Ballack. "I would think in a seminary environment, you'd want more than that. I'll be direct. Does

Father Jonathan's long-standing relationship with the diocese hinder a better working relationship here at St. Basil's?"

"I don't think that has entered into our dialogue with Father Jonathan. There have been conversations about the exact role the diocese should play in many matters, including the present financial issues. There are areas of disagreement, but that is to be expected given individuals of strong opinion. Father Jonathan has been, unfortunately, caught in the crossfire of such matters, given his employment here and his previous employment with the diocese. But we do not let his unique situation influence our opinion of him."

I'll bet, thought Ballack. For her part, Tori was noticing a significant lack of eye contact. It was clear they weren't getting any more information out of Father Matthias, and they both felt a measure of professional relief when the dean excused himself. "I'm sorry for running out before dessert. I need to mark some essays this evening before heading out to the basketball game."

"I didn't know the Billikens were in town," said Tori. She was an avid fan of Saint Louis University and made certain she saw a handful of home games each year.

"No, here," said Father Matthias. "It's our annual game against Concordia Seminary. I hope the Lutherans aren't coming in here with their A-game."

"That's right," said Ballack. "Father Andrew mentioned that yesterday on our tour. I hope your low numbers won't hamper your efforts."

"We'll see," mumbled Father Matthias, and with that, he walked off.

"Now what?" asked Tori. "We've got a few hours to kill. Do you want to go to the game and see if we can connect with anyone else? Maybe use the TV room as an interrogation chamber."

"It's a possibility. Plus, I wouldn't mind seeing a game myself." He noticed Tori's cell phone lighting up. "Better take that."

Tori got up to take the call, and as she did, Dana Witten and Lainie Kale came strolling over to the table.

"Good evening, ladies," said Ballack. "It was hard to beat last night's affair, but I was delighted that this meal gave Russia a run for its money."

Dana gave her nervous smile, as if on cue. Ballack couldn't get over how mesmerizing and yet tragic that look was. He didn't have time to dwell on it because Lainie broke in: "Sir, is there a chance you'll be needing anything for your room later tonight? We're headed to the basketball game and might not be able to pull any extra supplies together until later."

Ballack thought. "No, not particularly. If we think of something, we'll call on the house line. Might even see you there, if we can get over."

"Good. Stephen is the point guard, pretty good one, too. Although I'm not sure how up-to-par we'll be tonight with only six players and half the team gone."

"I saw Stephen in class earlier today," said Ballack, hoping to provoke a discernible reaction from Lainie. "Sat in for about fifteen minutes on the Petrine Epistles in the library classroom."

Ballack could have sworn lightning flashed behind her eyes. "Hmm, that," said Lainie. "Stephen came home in a mood. What a philandering twit, that Father Jonathan. I don't know what got into him today, but Stephen was pretty shaken up. Came home ready to spit nails and tear up the place. Even a comforting chat with Father Timothy didn't do much good."

"Lainie," said Dana. "You're only seeing Stephen's side of things. I've told you that."

"Dana's right," said Ballack. "Whether Father Jonathan overreacted or not is a debate for others. But he never would have had to if Stephen had not taken liberty to talk smack about him in front of everyone else."

"He has no right to be here!" hissed Lainie, leaning close to Ballack and dropping her voice to a whisper, looking around quickly to ensure no one else could hear. "Each class Stephen has had with him has been an almighty trial. Never above a C average. My husband is a diligent worker and will be an excellent parish priest one day, but his memories of this place are been sullied by a moral hooligan who hides behind a mask of 'woe-is-me'."

"And the remedy for that is a snide comment in the midst of his fellow students and the instructor while Father Jonathan is standing five feet away?"

Lainie Kale blanched, looking as if the well of patience had just run dry. But she recovered herself and said hopefully, "That being what it is, nothing's going to happen to Stephen. Father Timothy worked it out and will require an extra assignment from him. No extensive discipline. Father Jonathan shouldn't be wagging a finger in anyone's face, be it my husband's or Father Timothy's." Her voice dropped to a nearly unintelligible sigh. "He has enough trouble of his own."

Lainie's words, spoken with supreme confidence, seized Ballack's awareness. He decided to say nothing about it. "It seems like your husband has nothing to worry about."

Lainie brushed a tear out of her eye and bit a trembling lower lip. "He's a good man, Stephen is. Funny. Bright. Loyal. This afternoon devastated him."

After a pause, she relaxed somewhat, turned to her friend, and said, "Come on, Dana. Let's go."

The gentle Mrs. Witten wasn't so ready to pull away from the table, but she relented. Before heading to the south door, she turned to Ballack and said, "Seriously, detective. If you need anything, let us know. And it might be better to call me directly. I doubt Lainie will be in a helpful mood the rest of the night."

"I can let you know at the basketball game. At least, I plan to be there," Ballack said as Tori returned to the table.

"That was Scotty. He'll be here in ten minutes. He's got the packet of stuff we requested and probably wants a progress report."

Ballack looked up at Dana and shrugged. "Okay, second half, at best, but maybe we'll see you there."

Dana blinked, smiled, and turned toward the exit. Tori tapped Ballack on the back of the head. "Come on, loverboy. I doubt the lieutenant wants to be kept waiting."

"As you can see, the scribbling on the note matches those on the rest of Reverend Zednik's handwriting," said Scotty Bosco as he sipped on a Diet Coke. Both detectives looked over the files they had requested from the bishop. There was no doubt. The note was almost certainly from Zednik, alleging that Dana Witten needed to be confronted about the identity and strength of Zednik's medicinal dosage. And that confrontation had never come.

Tori was surprised to hear Ballack say, "This certainly widens our circle of potential suspects, if there was any wrongdoing."

"That said," replied Bosco, "What do you have so far?"

Both detectives gave a summary of their investigation so far. Ballack had placed his notes in an e-mail attachment and sent it to Bosco's account. The lieutenant looked it up on his iPhone, scanning it, saying nothing but "Impressive."

Tori then handed Bosco the letter sent to Father Jonathan. "This is worth taking a look at, sir."

Ballack said, "It seems we've got something that looked like *The Vicar of Dibley* and has now turned into a soap opera."

Bosco skimmed through it and looked at his detectives. "What's your next step?"

"We've got a lunch meeting with one of Father Jonathan's co-authors tomorrow," answered Tori. "Off campus. It'll put us out most of the day, but that's a strategic break the seminary might welcome. We need to interview Stephen Kale and see what gets him in such a lather. Another refresher with Dana Witten would be helpful."

"I think we might need to bang on Father Matthias' door," said Ballack. "There's something about Father Jonathan's presence here that doesn't add up, and I'm convinced the dean is hiding something."

"What do you mean, doesn't add up?" asked Bosco.

"Something he said in class today when he practically screamed at Father Timothy. He implied that Father Timothy was on unsteady ground here. Maybe the diocese wants him out. Maybe without Reverend Zednik to protect him, Father Jonathan might feel he's on the same shifting sand."

"Well, it seems that unless someone makes a huge error in judgment, this might be a wild goose chase. Find out what you can and keep me in the loop. And who made this pie?" Bosco pointed at his empty bowl.

Ballack gave a sardonic grin. "Dana Witten. Of the last-words-of-Zednik fame. Phenomenal, isn't it?" Ballack himself had just demolished two huge slices. Given his earlier consumption of the Karelian pastry dessert over dinner, his sugar level was bound to skyrocket around ten o'clock.

As Bosco got up to leave, the door of the guest room opened, and a black woman came strutting in. She wore an ear-to-ear grin and looked as if she bought her clothes at Nickelodeon Studios. She tossed a bag on the table, stretched, and shook her hair, sending massive snowflakes in every direction.

"Good evening, peeps!" she bellowed.

"Nice to see you too, Rhoda," said Ballack. "Since you're all in the mood for excitement, how about going to watch some hoops action?"

Bosco having left, both Tori and Rhoda entered the gym ahead of Ballack, who gazed up at the scoreboard. The second half was just beginning, and the Preachers of Concordia Seminary were running away with the game. Stephen Kale was desperately trying to fire up his teammates in the huddle as Father Timothy outlined his refreshers on defense for the next twenty minutes. They were as hopeful as possible given the fact they were facing a 58 to 25 deficit.

Tori hadn't come to watch the game. She headed the length of the floor to speak with Dana Witten. Ballack let her take care of this one; his presence wasn't required. He drew his mind back to the game. Stephen Kale was a great athlete and an outspoken leader. He dove for every loose ball, hustled the ball down the court, had a deadly jump shot anywhere inside twenty feet, and slid in for a couple of nifty left-handed layups. The Concordia zone made life difficult for the rest of the St. Basil's team, and Father Timothy's troops were severely winded with only one substitute on the bench.

"Now look at him, that hot thing right there!" exclaimed Rhoda, catching a glimpse of Marcus Curry sprinting down the court for a rare uncontested lay-in. "Oooh, that boy is *so fine*! Think he'd go out with me?"

"Think he'd deny his ordination vows for someone as saucy as you?" ribbed Ballack. He was used to Rhoda's prowling humor and suggestive comments and would usually dish them right back, as long as Rhoda wasn't giving him a bath at the time. "He's probably a lonely fella here. Don't think I've ever seen, much less imagined, a black guy in such a hermetic environment."

"Gotta be a lonely brother in the middle of all this vanilla pudding!"

"You're reminding me of Pat Conroy and *The Lords of Discipline*...he's gonna stand out like a raisin on a coconut cake."

"Then I gotta help him find another heavenly body to worship. Maybe he'll start with me?"

Ballack laughed. If there was one area where Rhoda excelled, it was her sense of humor. It certainly lightened his mood during his more difficult nights.

Tori returned with a minute left in the game and Concordia holding the ball to run out a 97 to 58 rout. "Dana didn't bat an eye. I asked her if she returned to the room or if she remembered anything, however slight, about the pills Zednik took. She remembered two large round ones out of proportion to the others, but she said Zednik took them all without surprise. Nothing more than what she's told us before. Looks like a dead end."

"Until a tox screen comes back, which would be never. We're going to need another foray into dark territory. Tori, come with me. Rhoda, stand at the ready."

"Where are we going?" Tori asked.

"To pay a post-game visit to Stephen Kale."

"I really have to get back and get some stuff out of the way for Sunday," said Stephen. "I'm teaching a class at Assumption, so I would value any extra moments I can get."

"This should only take a few minutes, Mr. Kale," said Ballack evenly. Tori closed the door behind them and they were alone in the activity room. Stephen's breathing had returned to his pre-game normal level, although his face was flushed, and no wonder, given he played the entire game.

Ballack studied him. "You did well out there tonight. Perhaps St. Basil's didn't win, but it wasn't due to lack of effort. How has the season played out so far?"

It was an odd starting point for what would be a tense line of questions, but Stephen answered anyway. "Three wins, five losses. Thanks. There was no point hoping for a win. They let up on us in the second half. Even if we had the whole team here, we would have been lucky to keep it within twenty."

"Father Timothy seems to be a very driven man on the sidelines."

"He's consistent. Just like in the classroom. I've earned the grades I get with him. He's hard on me, hard on all of us. But if you master the course, you feel like you could charge the gates of hell."

"Yes, we've seen him in the classroom. That's actually why we're here."

"What?" Stephen's eyes grew slightly distrustful.

"That little performance in class earlier today," said Tori, sitting down in a recliner.

Ballack continued, "No one in the class this afternoon could mistake that you have a certain level of antagonism toward Father Jonathan. I would guess that anger has some interesting origin."

Stephen looked wary, nervous. "Even on a small campus, there will be some people with whom you don't see eye to eye. Father Jonathan is one of those."

"I'd say that went a lot deeper than being on different wavelengths. One would get the impression you were poking at his past."

Stephen raised an eyebrow. "So you know about that. I didn't realize. Well, since the cat's out of the bag: Yes, you could say I was airing some dirty laundry. The man shouldn't be teaching here. That's a fact."

"Isn't that something for the seminary and the diocese to work out?"

"Work out? He was forced onto the seminary community. That's the unvarnished truth! He's found himself and feels reborn. That's great. But let him be that way in a harmless capacity. Let him be a pencil-pusher for the bishop. But he whored himself out of the ministry! He couldn't keep his poker in his pants. And now he's training people to enter the priesthood?" He waved his hand in a dismissive fashion. "Please. He's the big sore on this seminary's face."

"Isn't that a little harsh? Doesn't the Christian faith rest on a watershed moment of sacrifice and forgiveness?"

"Okay. In truth, I wasn't harsh enough. How about 'He's a pimple on the face of the beast of Babylon?' Good enough for you?"

The interview was getting away from them and becoming unsettlingly personal. Ballack tried a new line of query. "What is the general opinion of the rest of the seminary?"

Stephen relaxed somewhat, but not much. "Mixed, I guess. Not everyone has received C's like I have, so their reports might be a little more cheery. I will say that everything was somewhat stable until Reverend Zednik's visit last month. The report went out that Zednik used Father Jonathan to feed him financial information about the school. That flew pretty fast through the student body, and Nicholas Panangiotis, he was the one sitting next to me in class today, and I decided to protest Zednik's officiating of Vespers that evening. I don't know if you've heard about that in the course of your investigation, but it wouldn't surprise me."

"We've spoken to Father Andrew and Father Timothy, who have told us some details, but we'd like to hear your side."

Stephen spent five minutes going through the blow-by-blow account. It was clear that although he felt Father Timothy was a bit harsh in his discipline, he respected him greatly. The one major detail Stephen included that the detectives hadn't been told was that when Father Jonathan had looked through the glass doors, he glared at Nicholas and Stephen and pointed at both of them, or so said Stephen, threateningly.

"You felt he was marking you?" said Tori.

"It was apparent he was riding us for some reason. Look, Father Timothy laid a heavy censure on us, but I can handle that in the heat of battle. Father Jonathan just has a spirit about him that infects this place with suspicion and discomfort. And I'm being charitable on that one!"

"I think it's quite clear what you think about Father Jonathan," said Ballack.

"Hey, I'm not saying the guy should be out of the church. He just has no business mentoring those who will serve it. He's locked himself into this shameful existence. Well, no wonder! There are reasons for the prison in which he dwells."

"Excuse me?" asked Ballack, remembering Father Jonathan's hate mail word for word. "What did you mean by that last statement?"

"What? The prison in which he dwells?" responded Stephen. "That's a quote. One that Father Timothy uses in class. Usually when talking about sin and how we choose hell in every sin we commit."

"And you find that quote appropriate to Father Jonathan?" asked Tori.

"It's a favorite of the whole class," said Stephen. "One of the potent quotables, we call it."

"So everyone would know it?"

A strange looked creased Stephen's face. "Anyone who had Father Timothy in class, including Father Timothy himself, I guess. Why? What is this about?"

Ballack recovered and redirected, "Nothing, really. The night of Reverend Zednik's death, what did you do that evening, night, and the next morning?"

Stephen frowned sarcastically. "I sulked in my apartment until dinner, ate in the refectory, and then studied in the library with Nicholas until eight-thirty. After that, I went back to our apartment and the Wittens came over. Dieter was helping me with a patristics paper, and Dana and Lainie were going over some housekeeping things while making a dessert for the four of us."

"Her apple tart?" asked Ballack, suddenly hungry again.

"No, parfaits."

"And after that?"

"Wrote half the paper on my computer until ten-thirty, did a few rounds of push-ups and sit-ups, grabbed a shower, and then piled into bed. Asleep by eleven-thirty."

"Your wife, too?"

Stephen looked quizzical. "Her, too. Do you want all the details about the entire day?"

"Thank you, no," said Ballack, deflecting Stephen's rudeness. "We've been blessed enough for one day." He fished into his card slipcase and pulled out a business card. "If you think of anything else that might bear on that evening, let me know."

"Am I free to go?"

"You're free to do anything you want," said Tori.

Stephen pulled himself to his feet and opened the door, looking out at the scoreboard, still bearing the stark result of that evening's loss. "Anything except retroactively scoring forty more points. Well, if you need me, you can find me in Chalcedon, the library, or Antioch House. Until then." And with that, he was gone.

33

Dana Witten sat, cross-legged, on the floor of her tiny bathroom. As laughter cascaded from the living room, she pulled up on her knees and leaned toward the toilet, hoping to expunge her sadness into the bowl. Yet no discharge was forthcoming.

She overheard Dieter tell a joke. Jason and Morgan Hart, along with Lainie Kale, laughed uproariously. For her, the gathering gloom cut like shards of glass, a bloodletting that would never atone for her shame.

The Sprinter rocketed eastward on Interstate 64 into the heart of St. Louis County. Ballack sat silently, drinking in the landmarks along the way. He had seen the Mormon Temple defiantly overshadowing his alma mater of Missouri Baptist University. Before long the Galleria appeared on their left near the Brentwood Boulevard exit. It took them only thirty minutes to reach Skinker Boulevard and turn north on their journey toward the Delmar Loop.

Sated after a good night's sleep and a wake-up time of nine o'clock, both detectives felt refreshed for the first time in days. A couple winding bends brought them to their first red light. As they sat in the shadow of the Amoco station at the intersection of Skinker and Clayton, beneath the largest gas sign in North America, Tori finally broke the stillness. "Okay, so this guy is who exactly?"

"Darren Glenn," said Ballack. "Been an associate professor of counseling at Covenant Seminary for the past eight years. He's done some work with my dad on clinical pastoral education credits and he's a phenomenally compassionate individual. Relates well to students. Big teddy bear type of guy. He's called Grape Ape."

"Grape Ape?"

"Yeah, like the old cartoon character."

"Okay. So he wrote a book with Father Jonathan. I wonder how that came about."

"I dunno, but when I talked with him last night, he was enthusiastic about meeting today. Seems the two of them respect each other. Plus, we get a free meal out of it. He's paying."

Tori passed a slow-moving Honda Civic, and as she did so, they both saw Memorial Presbyterian Church on the left, across from the Forest Park golf course. She looked at her partner, who gazed at the neo-Gothic structure. "You okay?"

"I will be," Ballack said. Going past the site of his brother's funeral was always difficult for him. He looked down at his hands, which were shaking slightly.

But the remainder of their drive went without any emotional detours. Tori turned left on Delmar Boulevard and they were soon within the Loop, with its eclectic swath of shops and restaurants. Normally, Ballack enjoyed coming into University City to partake of this diverse environment. However, as he and Tori liked to say, they were barely into dessert season. Ted Drewe had just opened up his world-famous frozen custard stand on Chippewa Street in the city after the traditional January hiatus, and Ballack tended to limit his culinary visits until he could combine them with his favorite concrete.

Darren Glenn was already manning a table in the northeast corner of the main floor of Fitz's. The restaurant was a city landmark, in the heart of the historic Delmar Loop on the St. Louis Walk of Fame. The table where they sat afforded a direct look through glass windows at the factory assembly line where bottles of cold Fitz's root beer and specialty sodas were filled daily.

"Dr. Glenn, how are you?" asked Ballack as they approached. They shook hands and Ballack introduced Tori.

"Pleasure to meet you, young lady," said Glenn. "Hope you brought your appetite. I've already ordered a black and bleu burger. Order what you will."

The detectives took no time to decide. Tori selected a turkey bacon melt while Ballack couldn't tear himself away from a buffalo chicken wrap. They all ordered root beer, although Ballack stuck with the diet variety. The pre-meal time was filled with catching up, reminiscing, and the usual platitudes about work and life.

"I'm working on another book," said Glenn. "This one's on ministry burnout and what churches can do to help pastors avoid it."

"Long overdue, Darren," said Ballack. "If you had written that ten years ago, you could have stopped a lot of despair." St. Louis had experienced a rash of clergy suicides over the past decade.

"Are you writing that one with Father Jonathan, too?" asked Tori.

Dr. Glenn acknowledged her question with widened eyes as he ran his tongue over his top lip. "No, we haven't partnered since *Tears at the Altar*. His memories still plagued him then, so some of the details have an autobiographical hue." He slowed for a second, then continued. "Which, of course, is why you are here. Is it about the book itself?"

"No," said Ballack. "It has more to do with Father Jonathan. We've talked with him and many others at St. Basil's. We're investigating other matters at the request of the bishop. How well do you know Father Jonathan? Are you friends?"

"Well, I wouldn't go that far. Stop short of friends. Jonathan Erhart isn't the sort of person you're chums with. He's got a high level of reserve. You get the sense he doesn't really need you, but he's professional, courteous, all that. More task-oriented than a warm style. I've been to St. Basil's to use their library, and I must say that Father Andrew is the only one with whom I could watch *The Naked Gun*."

"Does Father Jonathan seem to like it there?"

"I think for him, it has to work out, even marginally, or else he has nothing left. The good news from his perspective is that he is viewed favorably by the diocese." He paused as the waitress plopped their food in front of them. "That's not necessarily a good thing, you know."

"Why do you say that?"

"St. Basil's is either fully against him, or barely tolerates him. It's a fiercely independent place, wanting to proclaim traditional Orthodoxy but carve its own path. The diocese meddles in their affairs to the point where St. Basil's snaps back. The latest rumor is that Father Timothy could be on his way out per diocesan force."

That was news to both detectives. "You know Father Timothy?" asked Tori.

"The 'Savannah Strangler'? I do. If he was Presbyterian, we'd love to have him at Covenant, if he didn't have that one hang-up."

"What's that?"

"A complete lack of a personality. Nah, just kidding. He's abrasive at times, but there's no doubt he gets results. He doesn't get along with Jonathan, mainly because he believes he feeds information to the diocese about heavy-handed tactics. I don't know. Jonathan is a decent fellow, but he makes matters worse when he points out the garbage in other people's lives. I just think it's a bad vocational marriage. It isn't the fault of one side or another. It's just bad chemistry. Jonathan is one stable element; St. Basil's is another. But you put them together, and it's downright explosive. His friendship with Tomas Zednik was suspect. Some felt he was feeding the diocese information about St. Basil's that put the seminary in a bad light."

"Some felt? That can be dangerous, feelings."

"Well, regardless, Zednik's death, whether natural or not, didn't help. It's interesting that you set up this time to meet because Jonathan called me this morning. First time we've spoken in about a year. He asked if we could meet sometime soon. He said he felt threatened and that the danger was growing. He wouldn't tell me any more things. Just rang in and then got off the phone. Actually, he told me one more thing."

"What was that?"

"He said he needed to confess something and I'd be the one most likely to listen and not condemn him. I told him I knew everything he'd told me. I'm sure you know about his affair with an Alabama woman and his subsequent removal from his diocese there. But he said there was a darker corner of his soul he needed to speak of, and he wanted to do so in private. No one else could know."

"And he didn't give you any indication what that was?"

"None. Just that he had never shared it with anyone. That even the diocese here didn't know about it. Even his former diocese had no clue. He had just received a sign that he was in danger, and he wanted to talk about it. We're due to meet Tuesday for lunch at McAlister's on Manchester Road. He said he'd tell me then."

"Did he mention what sign he had received? Was it a moment of illumination? A letter? An email? A word of counsel?"

"You know as much as I do. I guess I'll be finding out soon enough. I don't know if he swears me to confidentiality what to say. I guess I could implore him to spill the beans to you two, as well."

"Yes, you could," said Tori, who signaled for the waitress to bring over some to-go boxes for them. "I'm surprised he allowed you to share what you did."

"He told me I could tell you, once I mentioned we'd be having lunch today. He also said he has to prepare for a sermon at Divine Liturgy tomorrow, so he wouldn't have time to speak with you today. Perhaps later, he said."

There was nothing else learned during their talk, and so in ten minutes, they made their goodbyes. Back in the van, Tori said, "Well, we still have a dark cloud over it all, but at least Father Jonathan has tipped his hand there's more to this. I wonder what this 'darker corner' is and if it connects with the letter he received."

"Can't be sure, but it's definitely a possibility. He gets an unmarked letter that has to be from an insider, possibly Stephen Kale. But anyone who heard that 'prison' quote could have used it. This triggers something within and he remembers a more grievous matter that he must confess. I'd like to know what that is. And it's clear to me that whoever sent that letter could be part of that 'darker corner.' If it's someone on campus, it's someone with a serious vendetta from the past."

"Wonder what the odds are on getting him to share that tonight?"

"Not good, especially with all that traffic in front of us."

A pile-up had brought westbound interstate auto flow to a standstill. Ballack looked impatiently around and coughed. "Let's bust a move, Tor. I'm not feeling well right now. Probably need another breathing treatment before dinner."

35

Seven hours later, Stephen Kale entered the gymnasium, picked up a basketball, and shot free throws for ten minutes. He had gone looking for Lainie, and at last he found her in the activity room, watching a movie with an alliance of students, wives, and Father Timothy. He had no desire to loaf on a sofa for two hours when he could be doing something active. He walked past the equipment bin on his way back to the basket when he saw it in there. He was wondering where it had been.

At eleven o'clock, finally finished for the evening, Father Jonathan walked out of Chalcedon Hall. He had spent time in Father Matthias' study going over some matters for the next day's Divine Liturgy. There seemed to be a thaw in their normally frosty relationship, and for this, Father Jonathan was grateful. Perhaps his premonition of danger had been inaccurate. He was looking forward to taking a long shower and pouring some fifteen-year old Scotch before getting to sleep. During his meeting with Father Matthias, he felt a throbbing sound against his hip. He disliked carrying a cell phone, but even he had to change with the times. Much of his communication was with the diocese and this proved to be a handy tool whenever they needed to reach him.

Surprisingly, it wasn't anyone from Kansas City. Nor was it either of those pesky detectives. Cameron Ballack had asked if, after the busy stretch was over, they could speak tomorrow. Today would not be good, what with Father Jonathan preaching tomorrow and Ballack fighting off a chill and cough.

In fact, his cell phone did not herald a call at all. It was a text message. Father Jonathan looked blankly at the words once he flipped open his cell:

Hi, I'm indisposed and can't get there. I'm afraid I might have left some lights on in the library. Could you check? I'd be grateful. Thanks, TB.

Father Timothy the Absent-Minded, thought Father Jonathan. Well, what was a few minutes' delay? He shuffled past the chapel and went directly toward the library. He noticed the area around Hagia Sophia was plunged into darkness. One of the lampposts was extinguished. He managed the steps and walked into the library. Oddly, it was already unlocked. The light behind the circulation desk was dimmed but definitely on. A light above a study carrel was also shining. And there was the prime offender: the classroom at the end of the hall. There were two sets of lights there, one inside the door and the other on the west side of the room.

Father Jonathan sauntered down the hall and saw that, given the radiance coming from inside, both sets of lights were on—the main lights and the language lab lights in the rear. He pulled the door further open as he entered and turned to flip off the light switch next to the door. All that remained was to get to the other switch plate, kill the language lab lights, and his work here would be at an end.

And it was at an end, but he never reached the switch plate. He heard rather than saw the swish of an object behind him, and felt the thud of a tremendous weight against his skull, knocking him into near-unconsciousness. And then there were strong hands binding something around his neck, a sharp pain in his back, and then a bitter voice he knew well whispering that the sins of the past had eliminated his future. With his last breath, he choked a final plea. "Father, forgive." And then, darkness.

PART THREE

A LOVE DESTROYED
(FEBRUARY 6TH-7TH)

Father Matthias was running low on patience. Divine Liturgy on Sundays required all personnel components working in harmony. The absence of Father Jonathan, scheduled to preach that morning, was especially vexing. Father Matthias had left a voice mail on his colleague's cell phone but had not yet received a reply. He called Father Timothy and Father Andrew, then continued robing behind the iconostasis as the first students began filing into the Chapel of the Theotokos. He looked at his watch. Six minutes and counting. Father Jonathan was never this late.

It was within three minutes of the opening of worship that Father Timothy walked in and approached the dean.

"Father Matthias, I have been to his apartment and to Chalcedon Hall, and he is in neither location."

"And he is not anywhere else on campus?"

"Guesthouse or student apartments would be unlikely. He could hardly have wandered out for long. It's below freezing and we have an inch of snow on the ground."

Father Matthias thought hard. "Given that, have you tried the library?"

"No, Father. Nor the gym."

"Very well. Take a sensible student who can help and find Father Jonathan. Go to the gym first, then to the library. I'll excuse you and whomever you select from worship this morning, and I will personally serve you both Communion afterward."

Father Timothy turned to go when he had a thought. "Would you like me to call the detectives and ask if they might be of assistance?"

The idea seemed agreeable to Father Matthias. It wasn't as if they would miss a service that neither was planning to attend. "Very well. Call them first. Let them know. They should understand."

Father Matthias watched him go. As Father Timothy passed by the fourth pew, he signaled to David Orlinsky, a shy third-year student who could probably spot a porcupine quill in a cornfield. David joined him and they walked out the front doors of the chapel. Father Timothy spoke and gestured earnestly to him as they moved toward Chalcedon Hall. The search was already in high gear.

The chapel was now one-third full. Nearly all the students who weren't at other churches that day were accounted for. Father Matthias bowed his head and said a silent prayer. He would have to shoulder the worship load by himself. His mind latched onto a homily he kept on tap for such an occasion. The words of St. Paul came to mind. *Preach the Word. Be ready in season and out of season.* Despite that biblical command, he couldn't help but feel a trickle of anger at Father Jonathan for forcing him to go into this service cold turkey. But that emotion couldn't be on display before the faithful now assembled in the chapel. He crossed himself and stepped through the Beautiful Gate with the censer, breathing in the fragrant incense. His head cleared, and opening his mouth, he heard Dieter Witten welcome the assembly with words as deep and ancient as the faith he professed. No one suspected a thing. He could only hope that Father Jonathan would arrive with the next lines of St. Chrysostom's liturgy. Yet no one came. He groaned inwardly as he made the sign of the cross and then spoke to the small congregation for the first time.

"Help us, save us, have mercy upon us, and protect us, O God, by Your grace."

It was only that grace, mused Father Matthias, that would help him get through what was already looking like a long day.

He had no idea.

37

Ballack had been up since a quarter before eight getting his breathing treatment, hacking on his cough assist, and suctioning any remaining mucus. Rhoda had left after finishing her charting responsibilities. As such, he and Tori were finishing up their breakfast when Father Timothy called them on the house phone. In five minutes, they were both outside Chalcedon Hall with the professor and David Orlinsky. The student was one of average build, with black hair combed and parted neatly on the side. Though he radiated no special confidence, he looked dutiful and it seemed he would do whatever was asked of him.

Father Timothy wore what appeared to be a black friar's hat on his head. He briefed the detectives again on the disappearance.

"Well," said Tori, "if he's off campus, he's walked off. His car is still here." She gestured at the blue Nissan Rogue near Gregory House. "If he's walked off, good luck finding him with all the student footprints. But we need to try."

"Are we to at least look on-campus first?" asked Father Timothy, who seemed to betray an attack of nerves.

"You said the only places you haven't searched are the library and the gym?" said Ballack.

"That's correct. Actually, I didn't go in Irenaus, but since that's not his domicile, I thought it was unlikely. But perhaps we should add it to the list."

"Let's do that after we check the gym and the library. I suggest we split and cover each place at once. I'll go with David to the library.

Father Timothy, you and Tori please cover the gym. If neither party finds Father Jonathan, we go to Irenaus and resume the search."

Father Timothy turned white before fishing into his cassock and retrieving a set of keys. "You'll need these to get into the library," he said, handing the set to David. "The blue-rimmed one is the library key."

"I'll call you if we find him," said Tori as they turned to go.

"Likewise," said Ballack, who rotated his wheelchair and followed David down the center drive toward the library.

They approached the ramp on the library's east side, able to hear the strains of chanting from the chapel. Ballack could sense David's resoluteness despite the fact the student was breathing heavily. "Relax," Ballack said. "We're not going to a shootout in Deadwood. Just finding Father Jonathan."

"Sorry," said David. "It's just that this is odd. It's been a strange two weeks."

They had gone up the ramp and were now at the door. David inserted the key into the lock and turned. As he did so, a baffled look came over his face.

"That's weird."

"What?"

"It's already unlocked."

An uneasy feeling washed over Ballack. "Let's go in. We're not going to find him out here."

Once inside, Ballack zoomed through the atrium, calling out the priest's name. No response. Study carrels stood empty. David looked behind and under the circulation desk. Nothing.

"I'll snoop around the bookshelves," said Ballack. "You check the restrooms, the classroom, and peek into Father Timothy's office."

"Right."

Ballack didn't expect to find Father Jonathan in the library at first. But the unlocked door had changed his assessment. He looked in each space between the bookshelves and covered his task in forty seconds. He heard both restroom doors open and close down the hallway. He was circling back to go down the interior ramp to join David in the classroom when he heard the young man's scream.

David methodically checked both restrooms, even opening the two stall doors in each. It was unlikely that Father Jonathan would be there, overcome by nerves, cowering and perched on top of a commercial toilet. But stranger things had happened. Rumor had it a bat flew out of the men's room in the chapel in 1978, darted right into the nave, and made straight for Father Thaddeus, the dean at the time. Father Thaddeus, who tolerated no chicanery during Morning Prayer, smacked the mammal in full flight with his massive right forearm, made the sign of the cross over the carcass, and then went right on to the next Psalm.

Father Timothy's office was dark but even a cursory glance through the window revealed it was devoid of humanity. David turned around and moved toward the classroom at the base of the ramp. Perhaps there was nothing to see, yet his meticulous nature drove him to investigate nonetheless. He flipped on the light switch inside the doorway and was unprepared for the graphic spectacle that lay before him. Belly down, head turned leftward, arms spread out as if crucified, and with an empty look in his eyes, lay the still form of Father Jonathan Erhart. A reddish discoloration surrounded his neck area, and his glasses lay to the side. David, shaking with fear heretofore unknown, crept unsteadily toward the body. A long, deep bruise, almost rectangular in shape, graced the left side of Father Jonathan's face. But what unlocked David's anguish was the picture on the dry erase board at the front of the classroom.

"Oh, God! Oh, please, no God! No!"

It was only a matter of seconds before Ballack glided into the classroom, but to David it felt like an eternity. The detective saw the body, then turned to the image on the board. He blanched for a microsecond, but then quietly sidled up next to David, who was trembling while sitting Indian-style next to Father Jonathan. As much pity as he felt for David, who must be buried under layers of initial shock, Ballack knew that preservation of the scene was paramount.

"David," he quietly said, leaning down and gently tapping him on the shoulder, "David, there's nothing you can do now. Let's get you out of here and sit you down somewhere else."

The young man was in a different orbit, barely able to comprehend his surroundings. It took another tap on the shoulder for him to come to. He scrambled to his feet, quivering like a baby rabbit in a thunderstorm.

"David," Ballack repeated, "Let's get you out of here. Sit yourself behind the circulation desk. Okay?"

David's breathing had grown deep and flustered, but he steadied himself against Ballack's wheelchair. "Yes, detective. I'll do that."

They left the room, Ballack leaving the light on. Upon leaving, he noticed the rolling cart of books and videos was on the other end of the room. As he followed David up the ramp, he called Tori on her cell. She answered on the first ring.

"Found him yet?"

"We did, Tor, but it's not good. You and Father Timothy need to get over here. Library classroom. I'm getting David to sit down first."

"Good Lord, is it what I think you're saying?"

"Yeah, and it's not pretty. Call Scotty and get the ME and forensics down here on the double."

Ballack hung up and went to the circulation desk to make sure David was holding up as well as could be expected. He was sitting there, head between his knees, gulping in oxygen. Someone had to calm him down.

"David?" Ballack asked.

He looked at the detective. "Yes?"

"Father Timothy and my partner will be here in a few seconds. Just remain quiet. You did fine." He stopped, wondering what might be of service for this lad when a thought struck him. "Would a glass of water or a soft drink help?"

"Ah…I'm not sure. I…Is everything okay? I don't understand. What happened?"

"We'll handle that. It's our job. You did fine. Nothing could have prepared you for that. What you're experiencing, anyone would."

At that moment, Father Timothy and Tori came through the library door.

Ballack spoke before either could: "I have David seated here behind the circulation desk to get his bearings. I have some initial questions for you, Father Timothy. First, is there a chance we could get David a glass of water or a soft drink?"

"I have some water in my office."

"Good. We can retrieve that first. If you could allow Tori to get in and tell her where it is, she can get it."

Father Timothy took the keys from David, who had held onto them through the whole ordeal, and gave them to Tori after telling her to look in his office fridge. She was down the ramp and back in less than a minute. She unscrewed the top of the bottle and placed the drink in David's hand. He thanked her in a barely audible voice.

"Second," said Ballack. "Can we lock the door? I'd like David to stay for a few moments, but I don't want anyone coming in. Use a tissue, please, as you do so."

Father Timothy grabbed a clean handkerchief from within his cassock, took three strides to the door, locked the deadbolt, and turned around.

"Let's turn the light on over the desk here," said Ballack. He didn't want David sitting in darkness minutes after finding the body. Father Timothy reached around, flipped a switch near a stamp pad, and the overhead light came on.

Ballack looked at David. "David, I am taking Father Timothy and Tori down the hall to the classroom. I am only showing them what is there. We will be back in about five minutes. Will you be okay, or would you be more comfortable elsewhere in the library?"

David answered immediately. "I'll stay here. Just don't be any longer than you said."

"If we are, then Father Timothy will come up here to check on you."

"I will," Father Timothy said to David. "I promise." The tone seemed discordantly gentle coming from the professor.

Before they went to the classroom, Ballack asked, "Father Timothy, I would assume you have a Bible close by?"

"In my office."

"On the way to the classroom, could you grab it?"

"Yes, of course."

The scriptural pit stop was brief. When Father Timothy joined them in the hallway again, Ballack spoke in a low tone.

"David is obviously in shock. He was the one who found Father Jonathan here. He was murdered in the classroom. I don't know if this will be an easy sight for you, Father Timothy, but you need to be somewhat prepared for what you see."

At the word *murdered*, Ballack could have sworn that Father Timothy staggered forward. It was obviously unwelcome news for him. Ballack gestured for them both to follow him into the classroom.

It was the first time he heard Father Timothy gasp out loud. The former basketball player buckled at the knees and fell before the dead priest. He made the sign of the cross and began whispering a prayer. Ballack did nothing to stop him. Even though they had responsibilities, he knew enough of their hosts that they required certain traditions. There would be a time to investigate. This was a time to step aside.

As he listened, he heard Father Timothy's voice return to normal, and in that room resounded words of sadness mixed with eternal hope. Ballack listened along, impressed with the fervency of this faith that he neither believed nor comprehended.

"Master, Lord our God, Who in Thy wisdom hast created man, and didst honor him with Thy Divine image, and place in him the spirit of life, and lead him into this world, bestowing on him the hope of resurrection and life everlasting; and after he had violated Thy commandments, Thou O Gracious lover of mankind, didst descend to the earth that Thou mightest renew again the creation of Thy hands. Therefore we pray Thee, O All-Holy Master, give rest to the soul of Thy servant, Jonathan, in a place of brightness, a place of green pasture, a place of repose, and, in that he has sinned in word, or deed or thought, forgive him. For Thou art a good God and lovest mankind and unto Thee do we ascribe Glory, together with Thy Father, Who is from everlasting and Thine All-Holy and good, and ever-giving Spirit, now, and ever, and unto ages of ages. Amen."

Tori joined in saying "Amen," and the room seemed quieter than ever. Ballack wheeled over and parked in front of Father Timothy.

"Father, it is important you listen to me. We will be sealing off this area to preserve it as a crime scene. I will allow Father Matthias and Father Andrew to come view the body but, as I will ask you, they must not touch him."

"I understand, detective." He rose to his feet. "Thank you for allowing me to pray for him."

"That is your tradition, and, as it did not interfere with the scene, I thought it best to let you proceed. However, we need to hurry so that David is not left alone for long. Do you see what is up here on the board?"

Tori had seen it from the moment she entered the room, but Father Timothy, overcome first by the sight of Father Jonathan's body, was taken completely aback by the sight. There on the board, held by magnets, was an Orthodox tri-bar cross made out of sections of black nylon stockings. The sight was viciously troubling enough, but Ballack was also looking at the writing beneath the cross. Block printing. A Scripture reference.

DANIEL 5:27

Ballack turned to Father Timothy and pointed to his Bible. "Could you look that up for us and read it, please?"

It did not take Father Timothy long to find the passage. As he read it, Ballack turned to Tori and raised his eyebrows. It chilled his blood to hear the words, and he knew the stakes had raised significantly.

"Here it is. Daniel chapter five, verse twenty-seven. 'Tekel: It has been weighed in the balance, and found wanting'."

The three of them had left the room and called David to join Father Timothy in his office. From there, Father Timothy could view any movement through his window and see when people began coming out of the chapel. He was to flag down Father Matthias and Father Andrew the moment he saw them.

Ballack and Tori had returned to the classroom, put on gloves, and begun the preliminary examination of the evidence. But the Scripture reference was the unnerving issue. Tori had brought her emergency bag, which contained a camera, and she stood around snapping photos of the dry erase board and the eerie cruciform message.

"Well," said Ballack, "someone is dropping a load of evil on this place. The letter. Father Jonathan is ready to make a confession to Darren. And now this, complete with the last line of that letter from Friday. And another dead body."

"No doubt it's murder. Do you think it's the second murder?"

Ballack didn't want to get ahead of the game and assume things, but he had been thinking, since the moment he saw Father Jonathan's body on the floor, that there was a connection between this and the death of Tomas Zednik. *Is it out of the realm of probability*, he mused, *that Zednik's death was a murder, too?*

"I'm saying there's a connection, Tor. I'm not one hundred percent sure Zednik's was murder, but I'm more apt to believe that now than before."

Tori snapped more photos in silence, then moved to the body.

"What do you see?"

Tori examined Father Jonathan's prone and still form. "Well, I see a nasty circle going nearly the whole circumference of his neck. Some bruising. Looks like strangulation. Here's the thing. Over on the left side of his head we've got this nasty bruise of about five inches by two inches. Really hardcore stuff, like someone whacked him with a two-by-four."

"Looks like too much bruising for a two-by-four, unless he got smacked over and over again. Might have been something heavier. I wonder how all this went down."

More silence. Tori hopped around, taking more pictures.

"Get at least ten to twelve of his neck area," said Ballack.

Tori nodded. Ballack knew it was dangerous to assume much on an apparent strangulation. He liked getting a double-digit set of pictures on victims to get a well-rounded assessment. In fact, he had written a paper on ligature investigative techniques for his Advanced Forensics and Materials class during his college days. His professor had been so impressed with his case that he passed the paper on to one of his former students. That former student was Scotty Bosco, at that time a brand new lieutenant, and this led to Ballack's eventual hire.

"Looks like some fibers dug in here in this flesh wound in the neck. There's a slight bleed, like the murderer went crazy. I'm leaving it here for the forensics guys."

"That's fine, Tor, but can you get a good look at the color of the fiber?"

Tori peered closer. "It's black, but why....oh, right," she said, turning around. Ballack was pointing at the dark nylon cross on the board.

"Odd thing. The murderer might have left his weapon at the scene," said Tori. "If he did, then he likely wore gloves and we won't get a decent set of prints."

"At best, it seems like he might have initially been bludgeoned. Stunned, he'd be easier prey for strangulation."

"I wonder what got him over here. Was he in the room and then someone came in and attacked him? Was someone lying in wait? Why here? What was the point of here?"

"Have to consider that for the motive question, Tor. Father Jonathan had some enemies here, but this is beyond the level of medium-grade frustration. There was rage, some frenzy perhaps, and definitely calculation in the attack. Heck, the murderer left his method behind. An Orthodox cross. Something in this is designed to make us think it's an attack on St. Basil's, too. Someone hated Father Jonathan, yes, but it seems to run even deeper than that."

Tori's cell phone beeped and she immediately answered, "Yes?...Yes, sir. Okay. Good. Thank you. I'll tell Cameron."

She pocketed her phone. "That was Scotty. He's on his way and so are the forensics people. They should arrive in ten minutes. Just passed the high school on 94."

"They're making good time. We'll have to alert Father Matthias and the rest of their arrival."

As if sensing he was being talked about, Father Timothy ducked his head into the classroom. "They are coming out of the chapel now. David should be okay in my office. If it's fine with you, I'll go get the other two priests."

Ballack nodded and dismissed him, then turned back to Tori. "We'll have to get everyone here assembled. Have a briefing and go from there."

"It'll have to wait until lunchtime. Some students will be coming back from other churches. Remember, Stephen Kale was teaching some class at Assumption or whatever."

They silently took more pictures, made more observations, took more notes. Finally, Tori said, "Well, what's your guess? An inside job?"

"On paper, that looks like the strongest possibility, but we need to keep our options open. The letter to Father Jonathan and the fact it happened here in this venue means that someone had access to the library. If this occurred after hours, then we're looking at people who had keys. Certainly, Father Timothy, or any of the priests could be suspects, but that goes for anyone who had a key."

"Or could get access to one."

"Then anyone is a potential suspect. But I'm not letting the people here know we think that."

There was a shuffling of feet from the hallway, and soon Father Matthias and Father Andrew appeared. They had obviously been told some minimal details on the way there, yet seeing the body of their fellow professor was a sight they were not prepared for. Father Matthias especially took it hard, falling headlong and wailing so loudly that it took several minutes to calm him down.

Ballack looked down at Father Matthias' convulsing form, the sobs racking him over and over and over. He wondered how much of this was sincere. He wondered how much of this could have been avoided. He also knew that there was only so much one could do to prevent death. *The torrent of murder begins with tributaries we cannot see until we are in the current itself.* That was from a story he had read years ago, though he could not place the storyline or author.

Yet what truly bothered him about death was that it brought the past all too close to the present. These moments of reality brought back the crushing memory of seeing his baby brother in the emergency room, long after he heard his parents' wails of abject pain when the doctor called for the time of death. The blond hair, the glassy half-open eyes, and the angelic peace upon Christopher's face. No longer would he enjoy that through future days. That was the day the wall had come down around him. And then came the moment, years later, when he got the call about Michelle. The emergency room again, this time at St. John's. The final report, that she had taken enough sleeping pills to knock out a rhinoceros, was both unbearable and yet what he expected. And then came the discovery of her suicide note telling him that she could never take care of him the way he needed. The happiness he gave her only filtered through her heart and became despair. She wasn't worthy of his love. His kindness and courage were powerless to stem the tidal wave of her depression. The history of abuse she suffered at the hands of her older brother was too much to overcome. Death would be her release from the pain. Now all he had was this vocation. It could not bring back Christopher or Michelle. Not by a longshot. But any chance he had to combat the injustice of death was a reason to live. The problem was he didn't know if he was fighting criminals who took life or fighting a God who supposedly defended life. Or if that God even existed.

"Cameron," he heard Tori say. She was nodding at Father Matthias.

The dean had gathered his wits and brought himself up to his knees. His breath came in short gasps, then slowed, then became normal again. He took off his glasses, wiped them, and then looked up into the detectives' faces.

"This is a devastating loss for our community. We have lost both a co-worker and a brother in Christ. Even if we disagreed on some personal matters, Father Jonathan was placed here by God's reasons and direction."

It seemed, Ballack thought, to be equal parts sorrow and sales pitch.

"Father Matthias," Ballack said, "Did you see Father Jonathan at all yesterday evening? I understand he was to preach today at Divine Liturgy."

"Yes," replied Father Matthias. "We spoke for about forty minutes in my office and he left a few minutes before eleven o'clock. It was a productive conversation and there seemed to be a spirit of peace between us. I can't understand how this could be!"

"Do any of you have an idea why he might have been in the library last night?"

Neither Father Matthias or Father Andrew could think of a reason. Father Timothy shook his head and said, "He had keys to the library, as all the professors do. But if he was coming here to finalize his homily preparation, he could have done that just as well in his apartment in Gregory."

Father Andrew spoke next. "Might I ask how he died?"

"At present," said Ballack, "those matters are confidential. I will say that this tragedy is something that must be shared with the whole seminary. I understand that several of your students and their spouses are presently off campus engaged in their parish responsibilities. When is the earliest we might expect them back?"

"Several are coming back from St. Nicholas downtown. They would be further away. With a 9:30 Divine Liturgy, that would put them back here within another twenty minutes. Those coming from Assumption are closer by, but they have a later service. I would expect them within thirty minutes."

Tori spoke up. "If possible, could we have everyone assembled together so we might tell them?"

"Yes," said Father Matthias. "It would be proper to disclose the situation. Would you be so kind as to allow me to make the specific announcement? After that, you may address them."

"No problem. Where would you like this to take place?"

"The chapel is not the place for sharing news of this type. And with mealtime coming up, neither is the refectory. We have the grandstand in the gymnasium. That should suffice as a place to gather."

Ballack was satisfied with this. "That seems to be the best venue to inform the community, and we can meet with everyone there sometime early afternoon. Other personnel assisting us will arrive soon and you can have the midday meal. I know this is not the most fitting atmosphere to be eating, but I think we should keep the day's activities as close to normal as possible."

"That would be wise. Is there anything else you might need?"

"We will need the library closed off. Our forensics team is coming and will need to carry out their responsibilities. We'll also need to convert the main atrium into a staging and changing area for the medical examiner and our forensics team. And I do recall watching the basketball game in the gymnasium Friday night. The bleachers will help, but I assume some will still need to stand. I would guess we'd allow the ladies to sit first and then fill in to capacity. Then, whoever is remaining can stand."

"Yes, although I believe this should not be a report laid upon innocent ears and hearts."

"I don't understand."

"Some families at the school have small children. Father Andrew's kids are teenagers and I have no problem with them receiving this news. But there are at least five children under the age of ten. We should provide some care for them so they are out of earshot."

Tori interrupted with a suggestion. "Perhaps one of the female students could watch the children in the activity room there. Five kids are entirely manageable for a few minutes. If you select someone who could watch over them, pop in a movie, or something…well then, problem solved."

Father Timothy had listened intently throughout this exchange. "That's a very good idea."

"Who would be your most reliable female to do this?"

"Come to think of it," said Father Andrew, "My wife Anastasia could handle that. We can inform her of what has transpired afterward. She could bring Thomas and Ella with her and they can help with the childcare."

Tori looked at Ballack, then Father Matthias. "Good for you?"

"That is very sensible," said Father Matthias.

"All right," chimed in Ballack. Continuing, he said, "The whole seminary community will be there. Maybe you could give that summons in the refectory before midday meal. Wouldn't most of them be there at that time?"

"On Sundays," said Father Timothy, "Everybody should be. If we are missing anyone, we can take notice and track them down. I assume you would like David to stay with us, to preclude any chance he might tell others."

"Good idea. Have him be a guest at the faculty table, if possible. And now, we should probably leave. Detective Vaughan will seal off the classroom and the pertinent areas around the library. We will also need to keep the front door locked and confirm this back entry is locked as well. That will tip our hand somewhat, but we have to make sure no unauthorized individuals muck up the scene."

"If there is nothing else," said Father Matthias, "then we should likely get busy about this difficult task. I assume there is no problem announcing one-thirty as the gathering time?"

"We'll see you then."

The company of six, David Orlinsky included, made their way out of the library into a blustery early afternoon. Ballack coughed violently, noting the temperature must have dropped ten degrees since he first entered the library. Low clouds gave the impression that snow was on the way. But he was relieved when he saw three vehicles, one of them being Scotty Bosco's Toyota Tundra, already parked outside Chalcedon Hall. The rest of the team had arrived.

The atrium of Hagia Sophia Library proved to be a serviceable place for the forensics team to change into their clean examination suits. Taking turns, medical examiner Evan Holbrook and crime scene investigator Janie Buck made the garment switch, and then drew out the necessary materials. The two of them, with Scotty Bosco and the two detectives, gathered in the classroom and set about their business.

Tori was showing Bosco the ligature marks on Father Jonathan's neck, along with the head contusion. Ballack whisked his chair around the periphery of the room, looking for a glint of any additional clue. The seminary had provided sandwiches and sodas for the entire group, with Father Timothy's assurance that they could use his office in shifts, if needed, to eat lunch. For now, nobody walked away. Buck examined around the body to check for strands of hair, blood, anything that might serve as a clue, but she would delay her hands-on investigation for after Holbrook's initial inquiry. The district attorney had been called and consulted. He was at a family reunion in Chesterfield and would be hard-pressed to leave at that moment. However, Scotty was assured, if they made the case for any warrants, he would procure them if given exact details.

Janie Buck approached Ballack. "Now who exactly is this and what's his role here?"

Ballack, surprised Scotty hadn't told them, replied, "He's Father Jonathan Erhart. Professor of Old Testament here. He was due to preach at the morning service in the chapel and was horribly late. Father Matthias asked Father Timothy to look for him. Tori and I were asked to join the search. David Orlinsky, a student, was searching the library with me and discovered the body."

Those details seemed to suffice. Ballack turned toward the dry erase board, not that he found the display upon it riveting, but because Holbrook was about to get a rectal temperature on the body. Ballack never liked these moments, even in his short career so far. Even dead people had a right to privacy, insofar as he could grant it. He waited until he heard Holbrook straightening up into a standing position and turned around. Holbrook had laid a towel across Father Jonathan's exposed buttocks. His perplexed stare went right past the thermometer to Father Jonathan's lower back. This was notable; Holbrook didn't spook or get confused easily. He had been a hard-nosed fullback at Illinois State University and was tough as nails. He must have seen something that intrigued rather than frightened him. He knew that Ballack welcomed a variety of viewpoints to paint the best picture of the incident. Some detectives believed in strict spheres of influence: the detectives investigated, the medical examiner determined time and cause of death; the forensics expert gathered evidence. For Ballack—and Tori, to a lesser degree—for someone to be this taciturn would create severe disadvantages. Holbrook and Buck were grateful for their lack of ego.

"What of it?" asked Ballack, wondering why Holbrook wore a quizzical look.

Holbrook's eyes went from the thermometer, to the body, then back again. "Well, the temperature reading tells me he's been dead for at least twelve hours, maybe just before midnight last night. That combined with the rigor mortis. The interesting thing I just saw was right here." He pointed to the bare section of Father Jonathan's lower back; the robe was rolled up just a bit to mid-spine. "There's a discoloration there that might be a contusion of some sort. Not like he was hit, but it's more like a pressure bruise."

"Do you think it's concurrent with the moment of strangulation?"

"Could be. Here. Somebody help me get his robe the rest of the way up. Gloves, please. And do it carefully."

In thirty seconds, the entire back lay bare before them. It was another long bruise, twice as long as the head injury. It went from the right center of the back and angled up to a spot in the left trapezius muscle. Though the bruising wasn't as deep as the head, it was longer. Everyone gathered around to take a look.

"What the...," began Bosco. Tori began snapping more pictures, as did Janie. It was a new wrinkle.

Holbrook looked at Ballack and Bosco and whistled.

"Did you get fibers from the ligature wound?" asked Ballack. He pointed toward the exact places as best as possible.

"We did. I guess your next question is going to be if they match that panty hose up there on the board. We'll confirm that after boxing the evidence. There doesn't seem to be much of a struggle. No blood or skin under the fingernails. Looks like someone was trying to be Albert DeSalvo and added some sort of whacking device to the mix. Can't tell if that finished him off until we get him on the table. Could be that the hit finished him first, or it was used to knock him out. Set him up to be strangled, that is. If we find the carotid, jugular, larynx, or trachea have been compressed, we'd have to say the cause of death was ligature rather than blow to the head. That seems to be most likely."

"And this bruise on the back?" Tori asked.

"Could be whatever was used on the head. Could have been the murderer's leg pressing down as he was strangling him. Or a shot with a stick, two-by-four, or whatever, after the choke-out. Or a combination of those. Hard to tell."

Ballack looked out the doorway toward Father Timothy's office, suddenly hungry. Then, just as suddenly, a vision came together. He wheeled toward the door.

"What about this," he said, his voice growing excited. "The door opens outward, into the hallway, standard for all classrooms. You walk in, for whatever reason we don't know right now, and..." he paused, gesturing toward the wall on the left next to the door frame, "we have this partition. Someone hid behind this partition to wait for him. The reason I say this," he held up a hand to ward off Tori's objection, "is because Friday when we came here, there was a rolling cart of books and other materials behind this partition. Now it's moved to the other side of the classroom. For the element of surprise, this would be an ideal hiding place to surprise the victim."

"Or," replied Tori, "he could having been hiding on the other side of the door frame."

"Only problem with that, Tori," responded Ballack, "is that's a more exposed position for the murderer. Whether the lights were on or off. The victim was more likely to be in as secure a spot as possible. Father Jonathan walks in and then gets clobbered from behind by the murderer. Hard hit. He goes to the ground. The murderer either hits him again across the back or jumps on with the stockings and strangles him, then arranges things on the board, writes the verse, and leaves here by the back door."

"Or the verse was up there," said Tori. "Perhaps Father Jonathan was drawn here for some reason."

"Unfortunately, that's the sticking point. We know that he was here. We don't know why."

"What's back here?" asked Bosco, already walking to the door on the south end of the library.

He opened it, revealing three wooden steps that went to the right, ending in front of a massive trash bin.

"My gosh, we've got to search this thing. The murderer could have dumped his accessories anywhere, but we've at least got to seal this off and comb it." He returned and placed a steady eye on his detectives.

"You two, come with me and let's get up to that meeting. I'll check in with the DA again. Evan, Janie, keep up your work here and rifle through that bin." He turned to Tori. "Is that guest room still functioning as headquarters?"

"More or less."

"Then after the assembly, let's meet in there. I want to know who you think are the prime suspects, but we do this by the book."

"Got it, boss. Collect clothes that everyone wore last night, get finger prints, and start an interview lineup."

"If Evan and Janie turn something up, we can take that in stride. We're coming up on the time. Show me where this gymnasium is and we'll go from there. After that, we meet in the guesthouse. Hopefully, I'll have heard on the warrant possibility, but it being Sunday, I may not. I need to be out of here by four because I need to check in with Stevens and Tunnicliffe."

"The kidnapping in Wentzville," said Ballack. "How's that proceeding?"

"Sluggish," said Bosco. "It's like running in a vat of day-old oatmeal."

They made their goodbyes to Holbrook and Buck and traversed the distance to the gym. Some others were already starting to file in. Bosco looked at the surroundings—the massively imposing form of Chalcedon Hall, the chapel, and the library—as if dazzled by the magnitude of this consecrated layout. "It seems like an idyllic place," he said. "From my vantage point, hardly the first place you think of for murder."

"Don't be so sure, sir," retorted Ballack. "We'll be treading carefully and treating everyone with equal wariness. It may be a Christian institution, but in my book, these places are often more institution than Christian."

After introducing the fathers to Lieutenant Bosco, Ballack went over the plan with Father Matthias once more. The dean would address the students and make them aware of the tragedy. Then, Ballack himself would come in and ask more pointed questions of the group. By one twenty-five, the bleachers were filled with seminary wives and several third-year students. The fourth-year students stood on either side of the bleachers. Ballack, Vaughan, and Bosco faced them. Joining them in that semicircle of authority were, in order, Fathers Matthias, Andrew, and Timothy. Father Timothy was still taking his colleague's death hard, much more so than Ballack expected. But truly, someone in this room was the one with blood on his hands. The spirit of mistrust. The letter to Father Jonathan. The argument during Father Timothy's class. And now a dead body in the rear of the library. Father Matthias would announce the shocking news. But one of them, Ballack realized, already knew.

Father Matthias walked into the center of the gathering, raised his hands, and a hush came over the assembly. Ballack's stony brown eyes swept over those present. He looked at David Orlinksy, still in shock from his morning discovery. He saw Stephen and Lainie Kale holding hands in the top row. There was a scowling Nicholas Panangiotis, sitting at center court. And nestled in among all that humanity was Dana Witten. She was wearing her Missouri State hoodie, a pair of Levis, and hiking boots. Her hair was down, her face haggard, but upon catching Ballack's glance, she managed a wan smile.

Father Matthias made the sign of the cross in the Eastern style, making the horizontal movement from right to left, and in a steady voice he led them in prayer: "Lord, into the hands of Thy great mercy we commend our bodies and souls, thoughts and acts, desires and intentions, all needs of body and soul, arrivals and departures, our faith and hope. To Thee we commend the end of our lives, the day and hour of our expiration, the repose of our souls and the resurrection of our bodies. Do thou, O Most Merciful God, O gentle Lord, whose clemency is ever unconquered by the sins of the world, take us, deeply sinful ones, under the wings of Thy protection, and deliver us from all evil. In the Thrice-holy name of our Savior Jesus Christ, Amen."

The group elicited a vigorously murmured "Amen." Ballack stole a glance at Tori. He knew she'd be looking for any signs of guilt or a "tell" of any sort. Scotty Bosco was rubbing his hands for warmth in the cold atmosphere, clearly preoccupied. Father Matthias glanced over the crowd and spoke.

"We are here as a spiritual family in time of great need for peace and comfort. Last night, we suffered a deep, tragic loss. Father Jonathan was murdered in the library. Detectives Ballack and Vaughan, already on campus for other reasons, are now in charge of investigating this crime. I speak for the entire faculty when I say we expect nothing less than your entire cooperation with them. At Detective Ballack's insistence, the library is closed to everyone except police personnel, until future notice. Meals will still be served in the refectory. The other aspects of our life together—classes, worship, recreation—will continue only after Father Jonathan is given a proper funeral here. In all likelihood, that will be as early as tomorrow evening. I will ask that you mind where and when you travel off campus. If the police wish to interview any of you, their needs outweigh yours."

He allowed that statement to hang in the air before concluding, "And now I will ask Detective Ballack to address a few matters."

Ballack sped into the center of the assembly. He cleared his throat to speak. It had already been a long morning and the afternoon and evening showed no sign of slowing down. His chest burned. Once done with this, he swore, it was time to return to the guesthouse and have a breathing treatment. He had to get this over quickly. But the reaction from the crowd had been noticeable. He and Tori had swept their eyes over the assembly to gauge any responses. Dana Witten had looked frankly shocked, stealing a sidelong glace at the man who must be her husband, Dieter. The Kales looked forward with widened eyes, and Tori could have sworn Stephen fought off a smile. Marcus Curry made the sign of the cross as Jason Hart lurched forward a step. Only Nicholas Panangiotis, out of all those present, kept the same pose.

Ballack said, "The St. Charles Police Detective Bureau will be taking this case. With me, as you already know, is my partner, Detective Tori Vaughan. To my left is Lieutenant Scotty Bosco. Also here on campus are medical examiner Evan Holbrook and crime scene investigator Janie Buck. They are presently involved at the murder scene. Detective Vaughan or myself will be speaking to you at some point today or tomorrow. And I would reiterate what Father Matthias said: Hagia Sophia Library is closed, as are the grounds surrounding the library at a twelve-foot radius."

He paused, wanting the words to sink in for effect. He feigned a turnaround toward the others when he whirled around and said, "However, we would find it helpful to establish certain realities. Did anyone leave their apartments or rooms after eleven o'clock last night?"

After a few seconds of silence, Dieter Witten spoke first. "I had to go over to Chalcedon Hall to check our mail. We had not been to the mailroom at all yesterday. The time was around eleven. I saw Father Jonathan heading toward Gregory and I waved to him. He returned my wave."

A long pause ensued. Ballack was about to go on to further needs when Nicholas Panangiotis spoke up, "I stayed in my room the entire night, but I'd like to know why it seems the people here are under suspicion. This place is an open campus. Anyone could have gotten in and killed Father Jonathan."

Including you, thought Ballack. But sharing his cynicism wouldn't be beneficial now. "We are simply asking for matters of fact," he said. "No assumptions are being made at present."

No one else spoke. Ballack nodded to Bosco, who said, "The detectives will require that you turn in all clothes you were wearing last night. Also, we will need fingerprints from everyone here at St. Basil's. I will assist in the collection of clothing and Detective Vaughan will be fingerprinting everyone in Christophono's Alumni…"

A slight guffaw came from the seminarians and the professors. Even Ballack let out a chuckle. "It's Chrysostom, sir."

"What?"

"Yeah, Chrysostom. You know what, just call it the guesthouse."

The name-mangling had nonetheless relaxed everyone a bit. Father Matthias dismissed everyone present to collect their Saturday clothing. As the students were leaving, the Wittens crossed paths with Ballack. Looking up at them from his wheelchair, he spoke in a clipped, business-like tone.

"Dieter, Dana. We'd like to interview you first. Two-thirty, if possible."

Dieter cocked his head to one side, looking as if offended by this command. Seeing the incipient antagonism welling within him, Dana took his arm and said to Ballack, "Two-thirty will be fine. We'll see you there." They walked away toward the door. Just before they disappeared, Ballack saw her look back with a visage of fear and confusion.

He didn't dwell on her look very long. His cell phone buzzed, and he answered. It was Evan Holbrook. "Dude, you've got to get back over here. We found something the murderer didn't think to look for."

Ballack returned to the library, having persuaded Tori he could suction himself if needed and that he would join them in the guest room as soon as he was able. Bosco was collecting clothing in extra large paper bags. Tori would get started on fingerprinting, although, as she said, they might not turn up anything. Ballack rode up the outer ramp at the library and saw Holbrook opening the door for him.

"What do you have?" he asked.

Holbrook fished out a cell phone. It was a non-descript flip phone, the type owned by people who find a mobile line to be a functional curse.

"It was on Father Jonathan's person," said Holbrook, who was somewhat excited, though his speech was calm. "He had it in a pouch attached to his cloak. I was entering some notations and Janie was getting started when we heard a buzzing sound. Janie dug it out from underneath him. Turns out it was a number from Kansas City. We didn't call back, of course. But that was twenty minutes ago. While I kept working on, Janie went through his contacts and everything. Here's what I want to show you. It's something that came through last night."

He clicked a couple of buttons and turned the phone where Ballack could see the screen.

Hi, I'm indisposed and can't get there. I'm afraid I might have left some lights on in the library. Could you check? I'd be grateful. Thanks, TB

Holbrook took the phone with his gloved hand and slid it into an evidence bag. "Don't worry, we've written it down for you. That's the only call or text he received in the last couple days, unless he deleted others. But that text came around eleven last night. It looks like we have the flare that brought him to the library. We have the number it came from and should be able to track down who 'TB' is."

But Ballack already had an idea. The library. The classroom confrontation two days ago. There could be no doubt these were the initials of Father Timothy Birchall. The question was, did the crime fit together that neatly? If he was the murderer, why leave this evidence behind?

"Thanks, Evan," he said. "Looks like a decent wrinkle. I'll inform Tori. Let me know if you turn up anything else." In a flash, he was heading out the library and back to his room.

Ballack reported the news about the cell phone to Tori back at the guesthouse. Holbrook would bring the sealed evidence over before long. Although the text message could be a damning piece of evidence, both detectives knew there was no way to prove conclusively Father Timothy had sent the message himself. Tori had fingerprinted some of the students, wives, and even children by the time Ballack had arrived. Bosco had neatly gathered a few collections of clothing in the paper bags and set them on the queen bed for now. Tori argued they would be safer in the loft, but Bosco waved her off. He was on the phone with his detectives on the Wentzville case. The guest room had turned into Grand Central Station in the blink of an eye.

Nicholas Panangiotis approached the table, which Father Matthias had donated for an ad hoc work space. He fidgeted as Tori took his digits and he was less than relaxed through the whole ordeal. As he was washing his hands with the provided cleanser, he asked, "I don't mean to sound like a crass libertarian, but if you make an arrest, those fingerprint cards will be shredded. Correct?"

"All but the individual or individuals that we arrest," said Tori with a hint of suspicion.

Nicholas gave her a low-grade glare with a slightly raised eyebrow. "Nice try, ma'am, but being as I didn't do anything, you'll be shredding that thing." He turned to go.

Ballack, never one to give another the last word, called out, "I'm one, by the way."

Nicholas stopped and turned. "One what?"

"A crass libertarian."

Nicholas looked slightly confused, then somewhat angry that Ballack had needled him. But with no comeback forthcoming, he walked out of the room.

The flood of people had slowed to a trickle, with only a few families left to go. As the Kales approached the door of Chrysostom, Tori whispered to Ballack, "What do you think of him?"

"Stephen?"

"No. Panangiotis."

"The blond Greek midget? A combustible jackass. Yet he was the only one to register nothing when he heard about Father Jonathan's death. What about Stephen Kale?"

"He and the Greek seem to be two peas in the same pod. I swear he nearly grinned when we gave them the news of Jonathan's murder."

"I think Stephen's just a regular jackass. Better stop gossiping. Here they come."

The Kales approached the table and went through the motions without complaint. Stephen actually was relatively precocious about the process.

"I actually did an article for my college paper on fingerprint reliability and information safety. It was at the height of a massive controversy where the Jackson police had their computer system hacked and many records went out to the highest underground bidder," he said. "You learn a lot about the system from that angle."

"From any angle," replied Tori. "If you're ever bored of the ministry, you should come work for us." She said this with an even tone, though to Ballack it was clear she was tired of Stephen giving them his resume.

Lainie finished her prints and patted her husband on the back. "By the way," she said, "Father Matthias told me that he wasn't sure if the two of you would be wanting to join us for dinner during the middle of...how did he put it? 'This sensitive inquiry'." She smiled. "So clinical of him. Anyhow, if you weren't going to be in the refectory for dinner, I was prepared to make you something. Nothing over-the-top. Some chicken casserole, green beans, and rolls. Do you have enough to drink? If not, we can provide some, as well."

"That would be helpful, Lainie. Thank you," said Tori.

The Kales turned and left, stopping to chat on the ramp outside with the Wittens, who were last people to arrive.

Ballack gazed over his laptop screen and then turned to Tori. "By the way, Tor, how are we going to christen our murderer?"

"Good question," said Tori. She and Ballack had a habit of assigning an appropriate name to the perpetrator on every case they worked. Ballack liked the exercise because it made the investigation a passionate, unique effort. He disliked the impersonal aspect of referring to their target as "the murderer" or "the perp." Few others on the force felt this was useful, and Ballack, of course, could care less what they thought.

"Daniel would be unoriginal, but obvious, given the origin of that Bible reference," he said. "Too common, though."

"What about Tekel?" asked Tori. "Extremely unique, but part of that verse. Something about meaning 'being weighed in the balances'. Sounds twisted enough."

"Tekel it is," said Ballack, looking at his laptop, suddenly troubled about something.

"By the way, that offer's an odd thing," he said.

"What?" replied Tori.

"What Lainie Kale suggested. Providing meals. What if the student body picks up that baton? What happens if they get on a rotating basis as the investigation drags out?"

"I don't follow."

"What are the odds that eventually the murderer could be giving us a nice pork tenderloin and mashed potatoes with a cherry pie?"

"So what are we going to do? Refuse it?"

"Not really. I was just dwelling on the irony."

"Well, stop dwelling, cubbie. And get your Dragon ready to fly. The Wittens have entered the building."

After the fingerprints were taken, Ballack directed the Wittens to sit across from them at the table. Tori cleared away the pads, cards, and cleansing solution. While she was doing that, Ballack discreetly studied the husband and wife before him. Dieter had piercing blue eyes, a scholarly face, and the build of a cross-country runner. He wore a blue sweater, chinos, and dress shoes. His dirty blond hair was wavy and gave a hint of wildness. But that was where the vivacity ended. His voice was measured, yet plain. Ballack sensed a detachment between the couple so thick it could be felt. Dana, for her part, was dressed the same as she was in the gymnasium earlier. Ballack read distress behind her eyes. Once again, compassion previously unknown pooled within him, yet he told himself he was not here as a counselor. His role had to be precise, swift, and just. Family dynamics weren't his thing to solve.

They had the recorder going and Ballack was set with his laptop. The initial questions covered the usual strata of names, birthplaces, and education.

Ballack decided to funnel the conversation more tightly. "How did you come to St. Basil's?"

Dieter spoke quickly and briefly. "I had a mind to go into the ministry. I had converted to Orthodoxy during my first years of college and inquired about St. Basil's after my sophomore year. It's been a straight shot ever since."

It was, thought Ballack, a pathetically short synopsis. He looked at Dana and his eyes asked for more color to the tapestry so far. She folded her hands over her crossed legs and began, "Dieter and I met during our junior year. There was a Greek festival, and he was part of organizing it. I helped out with the food, and we connected through that. We got engaged the same day he received early admission to St. Basil's." Her face clouded briefly, as if resenting that she had to share the memory of that day. "We came here three-and-a-half years ago and have a position lined up already."

"Impressive," said Ballack. "Where?"

"Chicago," said Dieter.

Ballack took a sip of iced tea. "Witten isn't a Greek or Russian name, and you said you were a convert. You said you were originally from Iowa, right?"

Dieter set about giving the bare facts. "My folks moved from Iowa to Grand Rapids, Michigan when I was two. We were Dutch Reformed. When I was twelve, my dad was offered a position at 3M in Springfield, right in the shadow of Missouri State."

Ballack turned to Dana. "You?"

"Maiden name is Owens. Lived in Chesterfield all my life, so this was like coming home."

"Where'd you go to high school?" Tori asked.

"Parkway West," she said.

Ballack smiled. "Go Longhorns."

Dana returned his smile. "Go Longhorns."

The preliminaries out of the way, Ballack spoke directly. "Dieter, you said that you were heading toward Chalcedon Hall last night and saw Father Jonathan. Did you exchange any words at all?"

"We didn't. As I said, I waved, he waved, and that was all."

There was smugness in his responses that Ballack didn't like. "Did you notice in which direction he was headed?"

"It seemed as if he was moving toward Gregory. But you remember I told you that before. He seemed to slow down after a bit and came to a stop. When I came out of Chalcedon, he was gone."

"And you didn't see him again the rest of the night."

"No, I would have told you that."

Jerk, thought Ballack. He imagined Tori was entertaining similar thoughts.

"What else took place last night?"

"I went back to our house. Dana was on the computer doing something. I had to go over stuff for Divine Liturgy this morning and had a question for Father Jonathan. I called his apartment but he didn't answer."

"And what did you think?"

"I didn't. I assumed he'd gone to bed."

Tori dished out the next question. "Did you have a good relationship with Father Jonathan?"

Dieter looked confused. "I don't know exactly what you mean. He was a professor who I had for several classes. He and I talked about several matters relating to liturgy and worship. I think he was a decent Christian man, flawed on some levels but misunderstood on others. Not much to that."

Ballack wanted to get back to the events of the previous night. "Did you notice any other movement outside from when you left Chalcedon Hall to when you went to bed?"

"No voices. No movement." He stopped, as if having a moment of recognition, but then a veil dropped behind his eyes. "Nothing at all."

Ballack wasn't going to let this drift away. "Mr. Witten, if you have anything to say about last night, we need to know."

"I thought your interest was in when I saw Father Jonathan and the subsequent hours."

"No, my original question stands from earlier today. Did you leave your domicile around eleven o'clock last night? You've apparently answered that. But the ripple-effect question that follows from it is just as important, and I think it's one you were thinking about just now: Did you notice anyone else moving outdoors around that time."

Dana Witten had been nervously rubbing her fingers together, and it was now that she said, "Dieter, tell him!"

Dieter gave her a sarcastic look, then turned to both detectives. "All right, on my way out to Chalcedon, I looked past the gymnasium because something caught my eye. There was someone in the distance leaving the gym and heading in the direction of the library."

Ballack leaned forward. "Did you get a look at this person? Any sense of looks? Height? Appearance? Did they have anything with them?"

Dieter answered, "Couldn't tell who it was. I figured they were headed past the library toward the walking track around the lake. One interesting thing, though. The person was wearing a hat and carried a long stick or something in his hands. Whoever it was, he looked to be striding with purpose."

Of course he was, thought Ballack. No one outside the police team and the murderer knew how Father Jonathan had died. Now here was the possible existence of a weapon.

"May I ask you why you didn't mention this before?" asked Ballack.

"Because you asked if we had left our rooms, not if we had seen someone else."

No wonder your wife seems to be miserable, given that you mix sarcasm with complete anti-social diffidence, Ballack wanted to say. Instead, he performed a minor miracle by keeping his mouth shut. It was with a mixture of relief and gratitude that he heard Tori jump in. "This person you saw in the distance, was he short or tall?"

"Probably medium height."

Just bloody great, Ballack brooded. If Witten's perspective was accurate, then it made Father Timothy a less likely suspect. Nonetheless, Ballack still considered the cell phone the weightiest evidence yet. Dieter's height assessment could be completely off.

"You're sure?" asked Tori.

"Pretty sure."

"And the object in this person's hands?" asked Ballack. "Could you tell what it was? A pole? PVC pipe? A bat? Was the length apparent in any way?"

Dieter sat back in his chair with reasonable irritation. It was obvious he wanted to leave. "At that distance, in the darkness, I couldn't tell."

"At that distance," asked Tori, "could you identify the person as male or female?"

The student rector was clearly tired of what he viewed as a barrage of questions. "I couldn't tell. If I had to gamble on it, I'd say male, given the seminary's gender ratio."

The detectives saw there was little more they could get out of the Wittens, or at least from Dieter. But Dana was clearly shaken by the entire ordeal. Looking Ballack full in the face, she asked, "It's someone here, isn't it? Someone at St. Basil's has murdered Father Jonathan?" A tear splashed down her cheek.

"We can neither confirm nor deny that, Mrs. Witten. Hopefully, we will establish that through the course of our inquiry, but please allow us to worry about that. That will be all for now. If either of you might recall any fresh memory of last night, please let us know at once."

Both Wittens rose to go, but Dieter was the quicker one to the door. He turned to his wife and said, "I need to study now because Father Matthias and I are meeting later to plan the funeral service for Father Jonathan. I'll be home later."

And with that, he was gone.

Dana leaned down to scoop up her purse. Ballack judged she was resigned to disillusionment of some variety. She looked as if she would follow her husband out the door. Instead, she halted, looked down at the floor and then collapsed into her chair.

"Detective Ballack," she implored, "be completely honest with me. Is everyone suspect?"

"I really can't put it that way. A more accurate statement would be we are working to eliminate the innocent from our list of suspects and narrow down the guilty."

"It's a process," said Tori. "All we can hope is that people understand. But it's something that will take time."

Dana folded her hands on the table and closed her eyes. When she opened them, she said, "Detective Vaughan, could I have the chance to speak with your partner in private?"

It was a bizarre request. But when Tori looked over at Ballack, he nodded yes.

"Fine, I'll be out on the porch trying not to break down and smoke." She left, taking a Diet Coke with her.

Ballack gazed at the young lady seated across from him. She looked as if she had not slept in days. Ballack was surprised now was the first time he noticed this. Her hands shook gently, and she swallowed hard.

"Detective Ballack, I'm scared."

Ballack said nothing, but gave as comforting and reassuring a look as he could.

Dana continued, "I feel like I've been on a stormy beach. I swear I've dreamed that several times over the last two weeks. And every so often, I'm overwhelmed by a tidal wave. I keep waking up, gasping as if the water has entered my lungs. And no sooner than I get over that wave than another crashes down on me. An undertow pulls me out to sea and it's all I can do to swim back to shore. I don't know why this has come on me, but I'm worried that one day I'll lay down and enter that same dream and never wake up!"

Ballack replied gently, "You're afraid someone, the murderer most likely, is going to come after you next?"

Dana put her head down and grabbed her hair, pulling hard as if trying to release some inner demon. Suddenly she sat bolt upright, crying, tears flying off her contorted face. "I don't know! I don't know! Oh dear God, this is unbearable! I have a husband who loves his studies, yet probably couldn't remember our anniversary if he even cared. I work my heart out for a school that is under attack from without and within! And now we have a murderer on this campus! What in the world am I supposed to do?!" And her voice died away into an explosive spasm of sobs.

Ballack let her cry. For three minutes he sat there, torn between turning away to give her privacy and laying his hands upon hers to exorcise some of her pain. In the end, he quietly wheeled over to the counter to grab some napkins. He returned and placed one of them in Dana's hands. Slowly, she straightened up and wiped her eyes as her breathing returned to normal.

"I'm sorry," she apologized.

Ballack shook his head, "There's no need. You're reacting the way anyone would. It's natural to think life itself is compromised. You have nothing to apologize for."

Dana blew her nose and tossed the napkin in the trash. She sat back in her chair and gave Ballack a measured gaze. Several moments passed before she said, "You don't think much of Dieter, do you?"

"It's not my place to make those sorts of judgments."

"But you don't like him. It's okay. I can read your face."

"I don't think my face is that transparent."

"You must lose every time you play poker. I'll bet if you have three of a kind, the whole table can tell."

Ballack decided it wasn't worth challenging her at this point. "Why do you ask?"

She shook her head. "I don't think he cares what I think. The sad thing is he was so different when we were dating, up through the initial months of our marriage. Even the first year of seminary was at least relatively smooth, if not tender. But since then, it's been all ambition, all about him. I think he has more passion for theologians who've been dead for a thousand years than he does for me."

Ballack wanted to stay on target. "What does this have to do with Father Jonathan's murder?"

"I don't know, but it was disturbing he barely got it out. I mean this whole thing about seeing someone last night, perhaps the murderer. When he told you just now, it was only because I forced it out of him."

She stopped, then continued. "But you're right. It has nothing to do with Father Jonathan's murder. I've just been frightened for some time. There's an evil spirit, a foul presence, if you could call it that. Something's wrong with St. Basil's. I don't mean with particular people, like the priests. But something has wormed its way in and is defiling us. And I'm worried this isn't the end of it."

Ballack looked at her with equal parts caution and curiosity. Dana's words were practically the same sentiments Father Jonathan expressed in the library two days before. "What makes you say that?"

She shivered, then rubbed her arms as if wiping them of a malevolent film. "Because there is a thread of suspicion out there. No one trusts anyone. Even for some time, the students have been jockeying for class position and recognition. The competition there is fierce. We are a loose group of acquaintances. But we are hardly friends. I'm sorry. I know you are here for a different purpose than to hear me carry on like some paranormal babbler."

"What might seem paranormal to you can be completely reasonable as the context of the investigation changes," said Ballack. "As before, you don't have to apologize."

She rose to leave. "Even so, I feel as guilty as if I had done something. Maybe I could have prevented this. Maybe not. But the world is out of control. I'm sorry. I didn't mean to go on like that. It's my way of saying I don't feel safe here."

Before she could leave, Ballack asked quietly, "And what would make you feel safe, Dana?"

She fixed him with a kindly stare. Her look was thoughtful, wistful. "If I could do the last five years of my life over again." She slung her purse over her shoulder. "Good bye, Detective. I'll let you get back to work."

Tori re-entered after she left. Taking a seat next to him, she asked Ballack, "So what was that all about?"

"Nothing that helped us clinch the case, but it recapped a lot of the fear that Father Jonathan expressed on Friday. This place is getting more kooky by the second."

There was a pile of records in a red accordion file on the desk by the bed. A laptop sat next to the file, marked "ERHART." Both were the results of Bosco's search warrants. Tori went over, grabbed both, and brought them over to the table. Both detectives began going through the paper files, hoping to find something that could shed some light on the past two weeks.

"What a way to spend Super Bowl Sunday," groused Ballack. "If I get to see the Packers play at all tonight, I'll be incredibly shocked." The door opened at that last statement. They both looked up to see Scotty Bosco, who wore an exhausted frown.

"Consider yourself blessed if you get to see any of the game," said the lieutenant. "I just spoke with Father Matthias. Bishop Burgic is due to arrive in a couple hours, and he's furious."

Weary over the imminent intrusion of the bishop, however justified, Ballack resigned himself to getting ahead of the game. He allowed Tori to rifle through the accordion file after she set Erhart's laptop in front of him. He connected its power cord, rubbed his eyes, coughed, and looked at the MacBook.

"Now comes the hard part. Figuring out his password," said Tori.

"Here's to having a knowledge of the Orthodox mosaic," replied Ballack. "It'll probably be some obscure martyr, one of the church councils, and his birthday numbers arranged backward. This could take some time." He opened the laptop.

"You're such a cynic. You could be pleasantly surpri…What?" She noticed Ballack's face had frozen in a montage of sheer animal joy.

"If Father Jonathan wasn't dead, I'd kiss him!" said Ballack, gesturing at the screen. "Look! Look at this!"

Tori looked over his shoulder. The departed priest had never logged off the night before. No hacking was required. Ballack had full access to everything.

"Maybe there is a God," he muttered excitedly. It took him less than thirty seconds to locate Father Jonathan's email account. *Microsoft Entourage. Beautiful.* "Here we go," he said. "I'll check his inbox for anything from the diocese and then go on to his 'sent' items. Be ready for disappointment, but I'm hoping we turn up a lead here."

He needn't have worried. He found a few emails addressed by Tomas Zednik sitting there as plain as day. He opened one dated from two weeks before.

FROM: Tomas Zednik <treasurer@opna.diocmw.org>
DATE: January 23, 2011   4:56 pm
TO: Jonathan Erhart <jerhart@saintbasilsmissouri.edu>
RE: Tomorrow's visit

Hello Jonathan,

Thank you once again for your carefully organized file you sent last week. Also, I continue to be alarmed by the reports about Father Timothy and thank you for the details you gave to fill in the blanks. I have shared these matters with Bishop Burgic, and he concurs that we need to maneuver Timothy elsewhere. His abilities as a teacher are not the issue here. The seminary must be a laboratory for pastoral formation and not primarily an academic citadel. While my arrival tomorrow is initially to deal with the missing funds, I also intend to speak with Father Timothy and let him know his services will not be required next year. I know he's been verbally offered a contract by Father Matthias, but the diocese must have final authority. Besides, we can use his dismissal to stabilize the funding and spread his classes among the other professors. Two birds with one stone, so to speak. It's ridiculous how Matthias and Andrew champion him as a model of teaching. It's not like our priests are going to be translating directly from the Greek when they prepare their sermons.

I have the backing of Bishop Burgic and the diocese on this one. They will likely ask why and there is no need to bring you into this. Your reconnaissance of his class syllabus and your observation report was most helpful and will be all we need.

Warmly,
Tomas

"There's a gopher in the hole," said Ballack, who had been reading it aloud for the Dragon's benefit. "We could be onto something."

"Anything else?" asked Tori, who had dropped what she was doing and was looking on with him. "Is there anything from the email Father Jonathan originally sent?"

"Doesn't look like it," answered Ballack, who had already scoped the sent items to Zednik from Father Jonathan and found nothing. He looked in the documents folder and got the same result. "If he wrote anything, it might have been snail-mailed with no paper trace. Let me go back to Zednik's pile."

The next one he pulled up was equally intriguing.

FROM: Tomas Zednik <treasurer@opna.diocmw.org>
DATE: January 24, 2011   10:11 pm
TO: Jonathan Erhart <jerhart@saintbasilsmissouri.edu>
RE: FW: Father Timothy

Jonathan,

Just wanted to pass along to you (under separate cover) what I just sent to Father Matthias about your New Testament colleague. Suffice it to say we're moving that young buck out to pasture.

> *FROM: Tomas Zednik <treasurer@opna.diocmw.org>*
> *DATE: January 24, 2011   10:06 pm*
> *TO: Matthias Vova <mvova@saintbasilsmissouri.edu>*
> *RE: Father Timothy*

> *Father Matthias,*
>
> *While this gives me no pleasure to write, I must make you aware that the diocese, according to Canon Law VI-C, has come to the conclusion that Father Timothy Birchall's services at St. Basil's will no longer be required at the conclusion of the 2010-2011 school year. This is something we can discuss in private on Tuesday. I mentioned this in a nuanced fashion to Father Timothy earlier today but am not sure he "gets it." You may disagree with these conclusions, but this is a time for greater diocesan authority in the life of the seminary, not less. We can arrange to give Father Timothy a positive reference for another position elsewhere, providing it does not involve teaching in an Orthodox seminary.*

> *Thank you,*
> *Tomas*

Tori whistled softly. Ballack drummed his fingers on the table and then pointed at the time stamp. The email had been sent within hours of Zednik's death.

"Now that," he said dramatically, "ups the ante a bit. This wasn't just a visit to investigate funds but to drop the axe on Father Timothy. It doesn't give us solid evidence, but if he knew the diocese was getting rid of him, well then…"

"Still is just circumstantial evidence. He'd have to have a stronger motive to go after Zednik."

"Yeah, I know. If what Dieter said holds true, then we're looking for someone shorter than Father Timothy. The text message is unsettling, but there's no conclusive evidence he sent it."

"We can have him in and ask for his cell phone and check it ourselves. That doesn't prove anything, but I'd like to see the look on his face if we find it."

"And if he did murder Father Jonathan, he wouldn't keep that message on his phone."

"No, but we have it on Father Jonathan's. That should be enough."

Ballack silently nodded his assent.

"There's another thing," said Evan Holbrook, who had just entered the guesthouse.

"Nice to see you," said Ballack. "How are things going in the library?"

"Janie's pressing on. I came over to stretch my legs and give you some preliminary analysis."

"Shoot."

"The cause of death is most likely strangulation with the stockings. We found those fibers and I can tell you even from a naked eye view, it's got to be the same ones as those found on the board. Most of the discoloration was on the side of the neck, near the carotid.

There's no bruising of the kind that you'd expect around the front of the throat, that is, if it was manual strangulation. Also, using the hands would most likely crush the trachea and, as you know, that requires more pressure than cutting off the carotid, which this looks like."

"So then," said Tori, "this didn't take a massive show of strength. Could anyone here have pulled this off?"

"Anyone with an average amount of strength that could overpower a man in his late fifties, as well as someone who can swing a pole, pipe, or bat. That's got to be what knocked him out."

"Anything about the stockings?" asked Tori.

"They looked old. They smelled musty. The hosiery could have come from anyone, anywhere. The brutality of the contusions, though, makes me think it's more likely someone of significant strength and ability."

"What else?" asked Ballack.

Holbrook placed an exhibit bag on the table. "Better hide this, but we found it in the far corner of the library dumpster. Wasn't that hard to spot."

Ballack looked at the clear bag. "Hospital scrubs."

Tori peered at the evidence. "Basic blues. Dusted for prints, I assume?"

Holbrook nodded, "Yep, although totally clean. I went into the dumpster myself looking for any gloves but found none. No foot covers, either. But if the murderer used the scrubs in question, you've got the whole campus as potential suspects. It's either a sizable human being, or else it's someone who wore an oversized set of clothes. You know, to cast suspicion as wide as possible. It's a double-extra large."

"Which leaves us with possibilities, but nothing narrowed down," said Tori. "Anyone with a key would have access to the library. Tekel could be someone of any size and average-to-super strength."

"Who? Tekel?" asked Holbrook.

"Never mind," replied Tori.

"Anything else?" asked Ballack.

"Only prints we got were David Orlinsky's. The library apparently got cleaned on Saturday afternoon, so we didn't have a bunch. But of course, Orlinsky, according to you, was first on the scene. He likely put his hands on the doorknob, which was the primary place we found the prints."

"We'll need to check if the seminary has a nurse's office, and if they have any scrubs missing," said Ballack, "Although I can imagine they might not have a nurse as big as Rhoda."

"So what's your assessment if you had a detective's hat on?" asked Tori.

Holbrook shrugged. "It has all the appearance of someone who hates this place. It's clear it's murder, but why this way? If the murderer wanted to knock off the priest, why go through all the trouble of luring him to the library? What's the significance there? And the stockings and the cross arrangement. That's why I say this seems to be driven by a spirit that's against the ethos of this place. There's rage in it but a high degree of calculation, too. This had been planned out for some time."

"You saw the biblical reference on the board?" asked Ballack.

"Sure did. I know you got pictures, but we left everything up there as it is."

"Thanks. Father Jonathan received an anonymous letter about thirty-six hours before his death. It ended with pretty much the same words found in the Daniel 5:27 reference on the board."

"Which are?"

"*You have been weighed in the balances and found wanting.* Basically, your life has come up pathetically short. It's an expression of accountability, of judgment. The ancient Aramaic word that encapsulates it is Tekel. That's what Tori said earlier. It's the name we've given the murderer."

"Okay, I see. You think someone paid the priest back for a past wrong?" asked Holbrook.

"Distant past. Recent past. Could be either. But whoever it was must be pissed off and felt they were balancing the scales of the world. Maybe playing God where they felt God had failed them?" The logic made sense but again, that didn't narrow anything down.

"Well," said Holbrook. "Regardless, there's no autopsy. Even the bishop refused one. He's en route, you know. I think they want to have the funeral tomorrow night. Tradition over evidence, if you ask me."

Tori rolled her eyes. "I don't get these people. What is the harm in having an autopsy and figuring it out?"

"Let's not worry about that right now, Tor," said Ballack. "We need to have Father Timothy come in and then we'll be able to pencil him in as a strong candidate or we can eliminate him."

"And how," asked Holbrook as he headed out the door, "are you going to manage to do that?"

Tori tossed her hair as she picked up the phone. "We can be very persuasive."

Father Timothy swept into the guesthouse with slow, even steps. The last few hours had aged him greatly, and the colossal individual who sat before them was not the same one he had been this morning. He removed his hat and placed it on the floor at his side. He crossed his long legs and folded his hands in his lap. He looked simultaneously mournful and jittery.

Thinking the offer of a drink might relax him, Ballack asked, "Would you like some water or a soft drink?"

Father Timothy looked down at his hands. He had the air of a little child who has received the news of an uncle who was pathetically notorious but still family nonetheless. Silently, he shook his head no.

Tori leaned forward. "Father Timothy, I know the past hours have been very difficult for you, but we must ask you some questions. I hope this is not inconvenient, but compiling this now rather than later will help the investigation greatly."

"I understand," said Father Timothy, still gazing down at his massive fingers.

The initial questions revolved around his academic record and his employment at St. Basil's. Father Timothy spoke well of his years as a St. Basil's student, referencing Father Matthias' influence. He was equally, if not more, gushing about his wife Jennifer. They had been married for four years now, having met in North Carolina. At that time, she had been an undergraduate at the University of North Carolina in nearby Chapel Hill; he was working toward his doctorate at Duke. Provided they didn't dwell on the Blue Devils-Tar Heels rivalry, he said, they got along very well.

"Seems like you've made a good go of it," said Ballack.

"Yes, we have," said Father Timothy, smiling slightly for the first time. "In fact, we just found out last week that we're expecting. Our first. Due in September."

Both detectives returned warm smiles. "Congratulations," said Tori.

"Yes," said the young professor. "We've been trying for over a year."

It was time to shift the interrogation into a different mode. Ballack took the lead. "Father Timothy, I have to ask you this. Last night, did you see Father Jonathan at all?"

"Not since dinner. I spoke to him and wished him well on his sermon, since he was scheduled to preach this morning."

"What did you do the remainder of the evening?"

"I went back to my apartment and graded some quizzes. After that, Jennifer and I went over to the gymnasium to watch a movie. That was about seven o'clock. Once a month, we have a movie night over in the activity room and we join the students."

"What did you see?"

"*Secretariat.* Good film. Have you seen it?"

"Just did over a week ago on DVD. And did Father Jonathan take the rest of the evening off, to prepare for his sermon?"

"I assume he did. Of course, he spoke with Father Matthias later, but you remember that being said earlier today."

Tori spoke next, "So you never saw him the rest of the night?"

For the first time, Father Timothy appeared to get slightly defensive. "No. I told you that. Not after dinner."

"And did you contact him in any way?"

"Contact him? If I wanted to contact him, I could just go into his room."

"You didn't call, email, or text him at all?"

Father Timothy was either truly bewildered or a fantastic actor. "No. I never saw him. Nor did I contact him in any way. Where is this going?"

Putting on latex gloves, Tori slid Father Jonathan's phone out of a plastic bag and, after pressing a series of buttons, showed Father Timothy the screen of the text message that had drawn Father Jonathan to the library.

Ballack half-expected a vociferous denial on Father Timothy's part. But instead, the professor gasped. He blinked his eyes and stared harder, as if a longer gaze could erase the evidence. He looked at Tori, then at Ballack.

"What is this?" he finally stammered.

"That," replied Ballack, "by an astounding coincidence, was going to be our question, Father. This text was sent to Father Jonathan's cell phone at..." he paused as Tori scrolled down to the date and time stamp, "four minutes past eleven last night. As you can see, it closes with your initials, which in and of itself means nothing. But this..." he paused again, as Tori worked back to the correct screen, "does mean something."

He waited for Father Timothy to comprehend the enormity of it all.

"Can you identify that number, Father Timothy?" asked Ballack.

The professor's face had gone exceedingly pallid. He groped for a reason these digits were staring at him in the face, but none could satisfy.

"Father Timothy?" demanded Tori firmly.

He swallowed. "It's my cell number." He drew in a massive breath. "But I don't understand. I never sent this text. I rarely send texts at all. And besides..." he grew suddenly angry, "if I needed the library lights turned off, I'd have done so myself! All I'd have to do is walk across campus!"

"That's not what the text says," answered Ballack. "The message clearly says you were indisposed, whatever that means!"

"It means someone else did this instead!" shouted Father Timothy, who was feverishly looking through his cell phone and found the message. "I never sent this because I didn't have my phone with me at the time! Listen. You can even confirm this with Jennifer. We went to bed late last night. She wanted to have something warm to drink, so I brewed some hot tea with lemon. Around eleven-thirty, we were going to bed and I went to get my phone. You know, plug it in and recharge the battery. Anyhow, I couldn't find it. I looked around the apartment for ten minutes, and found nothing. Of course, you retrace your steps in a situation like this, so I thought back over the last few hours. Jennifer suggested maybe I left it at the gym, so I headed over there."

"At what time?" asked Tori. "You never told us this before."

"I happened to look at the clock on my way out and it said eleven forty-five. So I got over there, checked the sofas and chairs. Finally, I saw it under the ping pong table."

"Why there?"

"At the time, I guessed because I had kept it in my coat pocket, and thought perhaps when I grabbed it after the movie, it fell out onto the floor. We put our coats on that table, you see. That was my guess last night, you see. Now I'm not so sure."

"So you're saying," said Ballack, "that you never texted Father Jonathan a thing?"

"I most certainly did not!"

"And you never noticed the phone was missing until eleven-thirty last night?"

"That's right."

"And you are saying that your wife can confirm everything?"

"You can ask her yourself. You can leave me here and go talk to her or call her on your phone so you can confirm it independently, but she'll say what I've said. Gregory 2 is where we live."

Ballack looked at his partner. "Tori?"

Tori nodded and walked outside.

Ballack looked back at Father Timothy. "Regardless of this outcome, don't think you're in the clear. Isn't it true you had been made aware that your contract would not be renewed for next year?"

Father Timothy placed a pair of trembling hands on the table. "How did you know that?"

"My sources are not your concern, Father Timothy. However, it seems like you're confirming this as true. The diocese was interjecting itself into this situation and had recommended your dismissal. True?"

Father Timothy' eyes bored into Ballack. "Yes. Absolutely. But it was not based on my performance. In fact, the diocese wants this to be a less academically-demanding place. I was their lightning rod. And, if I might say so, it was going to be a revenge firing."

"What do you mean?"

Father Timothy spread out his hands as if preparing to invisibly illustrate his account. "Two years ago, we had a disappointing mission trip with our first and second-year students. Father Jonathan was in charge of organizing it and did a poor job. Also, he was losing assignments, tests. It was a difficult time. Father Matthias asked me if, among my contacts, I knew of anyone who might be able to come in and teach Old Testament. In essence, he was asking me for a replacement for Father Jonathan."

"And did you offer names?"

"Two, in fact. I knew Jonah Nasekos would be a top candidate. We had tried to get him from Holy Cross in Boston when I was a student here. I had heard him speak at Duke once and was quite impressed. There was also a fellow Orthodox student friend, Linus Sankavikius, who had graduated from St. Tikhon's in Pennsylvania and was starting Ph.D. work at Chapel Hill. He was a college classmate of Jennifer's. I thought he would be a tremendous asset to the seminary. But Father Jonathan caught wind of what we were debating and blew the whistle on us. The next thing you know, Zednik and the bishop were on us before we knew what hit us."

"Like Albert Pujols on a hanging curveball, huh?" asked Ballack.

"Unfortunately, yes," said Father Timothy. "That was the end of that pursuit, but not the antagonism. The diocese has not forgiven Father Matthias or myself. I seem to be their target as the most junior member of the teaching staff."

Ballack studied Father Timothy as he relayed the story. Every passing moment, there appeared more layers of competition and resentment. He was about to ask another question when Tori entered the room.

"Your story checks out, Father Timothy. At least, your wife maintains you went over there. But no other witnesses saw you discover it?"

"No. That I can't help you with," said Father Timothy. "But neither will I lie and make up an alibi that isn't there."

Ballack had never had a suspect put it that way. He quickly asked his next question. "When you were in the gym, was there anything else you can remember? Anything about the activity room? Anywhere. Was anything suspicious-looking or out of place?"

Father Timothy looked up at the ceiling, as if he was searching for wisdom hidden in the planks. "Nothing in the activity room, but...yes, the equipment box! That's right."

He leaned forward, palms up, and continued. "When Jennifer and I got to the gym, we went to the activity room. You've seen it; you have to go past that box of sports equipment on the left before you walk into the room. Well, we had a bunch of sports stuff in there. Tennis balls, soccer balls, old tennis rackets, basketballs. Stephen Kale keeps an old aluminum softball bat in there. We use it after basketball practice each Wednesday night, along with the tennis balls. We play a round of batting practice. It sounds strange, I know, but the men enjoy it. It's a chance to goof off and remember that at the heart of sports is the spirit of enjoyment and fun. It had gone missing and so we hadn't done our batting practice last Wednesday. When Jennifer and I left after the movie, I noticed the bat had been put back. It was leaning in the box, grip side up, on the east side of the box nearest the activity room. When I came back to get my phone—I can't believe this didn't click before!—the bat was in the box, but it was on the far side of the box, the west end!"

"So what you're saying is that in between the time you left, which was…"

"Nine forty-five. The movie ended around nine-fifteen, but we stayed to discuss the film with some students."

"Okay, nine forty-five. You get back at eleven forty-five," said Ballack, "and the bat has shifted."

"That's correct," said Father Timothy.

"Did you notice anything else different about the bat?" asked Tori.

"Nothing. But I didn't look up close, if that's what you're asking. At the moment, I thought it was odd."

Ballack's mind was spinning, though, and he could guarantee his partner was piecing together the same matters. *If* what Father Timothy said was true, and *if* what Dieter Witten had seen was accurate—that of a figure carrying a long item around eleven o'clock the night before—then here was a small beachhead of clarity in their pursuit of the murderer. If the pieces matched up, then Father Timothy at least could be in the clear. Could be.

"And you're saying," said Tori, "that the bat was Stephen Kale's?"

"It belonged to him," said Father Timothy, "but he was not its sole user. Anyone would know where it was."

"That's correct," said Ballack, somewhat disappointed. "All of which means that we have more questions to ask of more people. Back to square one, the only numbered tile in the game."

LUKE H. DAVIS

Father Timothy had been gone for ten minutes. Ballack went outside for some fresh air, thankful Tori was able to refrain from smoking. The country air seemed to be doing her good. The two of them were hoping for a brief respite from interviews. Scotty Bosco had called Tori to let her know of his departure; the Wentzville case needed him on-site. She promised to update him around ten o'clock that night. Ballack was taking a swig of Propel when he saw David Orlinsky shuffling out of Irenaus House toward Chalcedon Hall. Time for an interception, he thought to himself.

"David!" he called out, speeding toward the now-timorous student, who waited.

Ballack came to a stop four feet in front of him. "I wanted to speak with you briefly. Is now a good time, and if so, where?"

"I suppose now would be fine, sir. I was just going out for a walk, but if you'd like to talk, I guess I can put it off. Father Matthias said he would be serving Communion to me in the chapel around four o'clock. As long as I'm there by that time, I have no objections."

"Why don't we go to the chapel, if that's okay with you?"

"That's fine."

The glass doors were unlocked, and as they entered, Ballack saw the first snowflakes of the afternoon begin to fall. The temperature was surely around twenty-five degrees and he was compromising his lungs just by being outside. The smell of incense coming from the nave was still strong.

"David, I'm just letting you know that the team investigating the murder scene found your prints on the door of the library classroom. I'm asking this as a necessary precaution: Had you entered the library at all last night? I know I asked everyone this afternoon where they'd been last night, but I want a direct answer from you right now."

David nodded. "No. The only time I've been in the library before this morning was for the class Friday afternoon. You were there. You remember."

The Kale-Jonathan bout. How could I forget? thought Ballack. "Yes. So you are saying this morning was the first time you'd been in the library since then?"

"Yes. When I turned on the lights, I opened the door further. That's probably why my prints are there."

"Thank you." The following questions had to be asked, not that Ballack thought it would reveal much, but he covered all his bases. "Did you happen to notice anyone walking around campus last night between ten o'clock and midnight? I know I asked everyone before, but perhaps on further reflection, you have been able to remember something."

Again the nervous nod. "Yes, sir. I looked out my window in Irenaus—I live on the second floor, Irenaus 13—and saw Stephen Kale walking toward the gym. It's a long way from my place, sir, but I have a good line of sight. I never saw him go into the gym, but it seemed that was where he was headed."

"Stephen Kale?"

"Yes, sir. Stephen Kale. I know his walk very well, but like I said, I couldn't be sure where he ended up."

"Did you notice what he was wearing? Could you tell from that distance?"

"I couldn't tell, but he looked bundled up. Of course, it was freezing cold."

"And this was at what time?"

"Ten-forty. I know because I set my alarm then for my medication. I have trouble sleeping, so I have to gulp down a sleep aid before I climb in the sack."

"Ten-forty," Ballack quietly repeated. Still an open verdict. But given Stephen Kale's bitter anger toward Father Jonathan, he certainly wasn't low on a list of suspects. He thanked David and wheeled himself out of the chapel. It was time for a one-on-one.

"Stephen Kale is impulsive, but I just can't see him being Tekel," said Tori, after calling the Kale residence and asking Stephen to come over. "He's a leader on the basketball court, but he's a smart aleck in the classroom. Impulsivity doesn't lend itself to this sort of behavior."

"What did you do, figure out his Meyers-Briggs profile?" responded Ballack. "I didn't get the message when we eliminated people as suspects based on impulsivity."

"Shut up," said Tori, taking a gulp of Propel and wishing it were Bud Light. The layers of questions with very few clear-cut directions were wearing on her and Ballack, and they were beginning to take their frustrations out on each other. To clear the air without the benefit of a direct apology, Ballack decided to busy himself in something constructive, so he set up Father Jonathan's laptop and went into his documents folder.

It took two minutes for him to find a file worth pursuing. Clicking on one marked CLASS OF 2012 RECOMMENDATIONS, a six-page document appeared before him. It was a series of nine half-page write-ups on the third-year students. At least, that was the average length of each entry. The outlier was the priest's commentary on Stephen Kale. It took up almost a full a page. Ballack scanned it, his wonder growing by the second.

"Tor, I think we got another possibility here."

She moved her chair next to him and followed his gaze to the screen. They read the narrative portion together.

LUKE H. DAVIS

PASTORAL RECOMMENDATION: *Stephen Kale*

I write this recommendation with a heavy heart. I have had Stephen in several classes, and he has done adequate work. His grades of C-plus and C-minus are the results of (1) late or missing translation assignments, (2) pastoral application papers of insufficient quality, and (3) test marks that display a perfunctory attempt at wrestling with the class material. While it is true that he has much potential, that still remains largely untapped. He is a very good writer whom I could see going into journalism or teaching. However, I do not believe the church to be his vocational arena. His sarcasm is especially biting and destructive. He gives me little sense that he enjoys this season of ministerial formation. He reacts sullenly when I have raised my concerns to him. I can understand this reaction. As per our seminary guidelines, one faculty dissent means that Stephen is under probation for any placement endorsement. It is completely natural he would be angry. Another dissent at this time next year and he can expect no recommendation for the ministry at all. Yet, I believe I must select a heavy heart over compromise.

RECOMMEND STUDENT? <u>NO</u>

DATE OF EVALUATION: April 26, 2010

Ballack gulped. Tori whistled. That one paragraph could put some meat on the bones of their investigation.

"That was less than ten months ago," said Ballack. "So we can surmise from those words that another evaluation was coming later this semester, if these are done roughly the same time each year. Doesn't seem to be much love lost, does there?"

"Am I off my rocker," asked Tori, "or does it seem to say that if Stephen Kale got dissed again this year, he could expect to go without any job placement?"

"It seems that way. Looks like Father Jonathan didn't think much of him but was somewhat charitable. 'Much potential', 'good writer', and he's at least done 'adequate work.' I'd say we've got a bad situation that brewed here, and Stephen might have marked the good father."

"You sure he did?"

"Father Jonathan said he raised his concerns to him. He alluded to the fact that Stephen would know what this dissenting opinion means. I wonder if that means you need unilateral agreement among the professors to advance through the kingdom."

"That," replied Tori, "can be one of our questions. Better look lively. Here he comes now."

Stephen Kale arrived in a dark mood. He had exhausted himself on his teaching assignment that morning at Assumption. He and Lainie argued the entire way home over the dearth of their finances. The announcement of Father Jonathan's death had brought a pall over the entire campus, and the restriction on recreation meant no time shooting baskets in the gym. When the call came from Chrysostom House to come and meet again with Detectives Vaughan and Ballack, he stormed out of Antioch House without a word to his wife.

Ballack sat directly across from Stephen, tapping a pencil on the table. Tori had calmed down and readied her notepad. Ballack decided she should start the questioning.

"Mr. Kale, we are trying to place everyone in reference to the events of last night. It would be helpful if you could tell us where you were from dinner onward."

Stephen, clearly still irked, looked beyond her to a spot on the kitchen wall. "I was finishing my teaching lesson in our home. Lainie went over to watch a movie at the gym with some other folks. I went over to Father Timothy's apartment about seven-thirty to ask him a question about my lesson prep, but no one was there. Turns out he was at the movie."

"Did your wife tell you that?"

"She didn't have to. I went to the gym about eight o'clock for a study break. Nothing special. Saw them over there. I just shot a few baskets to get the blood flowing, and then headed back home. I ate a snack at nine and read for another half-hour. Lainie came back around nine-thirty and we went to bed soon after. Not exactly an eventful evening."

"What do you mean by 'soon after'?"

"No more than twenty minutes."

"So you were in bed by ten?"

"It seemed reasonable given we'd be getting up early for the drive into town."

"And you went nowhere else the rest of the night?"

Stephen grew irrepressibly sarcastic. "I believe that's what sleep entails, detective."

Ballack had been feigning interest in the sports section of the *Post-Dispatch*, sitting with a bored—almost anticlimactic—look on his face, which had been turned away from the lightly acerbic dialogue. Now he spoke for the first time.

"Then, Mr. Kale, I'm interested to know how it is that you were spotted heading across campus at ten-forty at night, in the direction of the gym or the library. Certainly, you couldn't be in two places at once. Or could you chalk up this incident to sleepwalking?"

Tori saw it first—the look of absolute terror mingled with total confusion. Stephen Kale was grappling with two people who had done their homework. No longer did he fixate on a spot on the wall, nor did he intentionally avoid the eyes of either detective. Rather, his features bore the tremulous appearance of a six-year-old boy caught with his hand in the cookie jar.

"I don't know what you are saying, or if someone else said I was outside, but there's no way that could be me. I was asleep. Whoever was walking in that direction, it wasn't me!"

"Mr. Kale," said Ballack, "We have testimony from a member of the seminary population who had a good line of sight. This person claims to have seen you outside from a reasonable—not prohibitive—distance. This person claims to know your mannerisms and your movement fairly well…well enough to identify you as the traveler. I know that this person claims to be telling the truth. I can see you believe you are telling the truth. One thing I do know. Logically, you both cannot be telling the truth!"

"Then the liar is whoever said he saw me!"

Trying to throw him off, Tori asked, "How can you be sure it was a male?"

Stephen gave her what could only be described as an evil eye.

"Letting that pass," said Ballack, "There is also the matter of your very checkered relationship with Father Jonathan."

"I don't know if that's the word I'd use," said Stephen.

"I was being generous. Actually, let me ask you something else instead: Are you aware that toward the end of each school year, the professors evaluate each student in the seminary?"

Stephen grew wary, nervous about where this was going. "Yes."

"Have you been made aware of your specific evaluations?"

"Yeah." The voice had turned disturbingly flat, with a hint of a growl.

"Were you aware of Father Jonathan's evaluation, regarding you, dated April 26th of last year?"

Stephen did not answer. His glare was fierce enough to start a brush fire.

"I'll take that silence as a yes," continued Ballack. "I'd like you to take a look at this document and tell me—truthfully, mind you—if you have been aware of its contents for some time."

He turned the laptop toward Stephen. Three minutes later, Stephen finished reading the document. He straightened up in his chair, stretching his arms upward like the tendrils of a freshly potted pampas plant.

"I was aware of this evaluation."

Ballack was partly surprised at this confession. "I'd say that you were on rapidly thinning ice with Father Jonathan."

"I told you before that I didn't think he should be teaching here."

"We get that," interrupted Tori, "but you did yourself no favors two days ago in class. That little stunt surely didn't endear you to him."

"He isn't deserving of my endearment."

"Wasn't," said Ballack.

"What?"

"Past tense. He's dead, you know."

"Regardless. Given his past, it's ludicrous to think I should show him any respect. Especially when he gave me the grades he did."

"Your grades are not the issue!" exclaimed Tori. "But what is at stake is this: You received one lousy recommendation last year. Given that you certainly sank your chances of redemption—thanks to your Sodom comment in class—it's likely you would have had a repeat dissent this year."

"You know that you require unanimous approval by all the professors for vocational endorsement," continued Ballack. "You certainly realize that Father Jonathan likely stands in the way of that endorsement. The only way to gain that endorsement is to get rid of the one who's stonewalling you. Do you really believe this is not a motive for murder?"

"I don't," said Stephen. "And right now, you're going to listen and see for yourself why I say that."

"This had better be good," said Tori.

Stephen leaned back in his chair and popped a breath mint into his mouth. "First of all," he said, "I am not all hot and bothered by Father Jonathan's evaluation. I don't agree with his assessment about my work being merely adequate. But he's right. I'd be better suited for journalism or teaching English in a high school. That's actually what I prefer."

"I don't get it," said Ballack, "You're saying, first of all, that you agree with Father Jonathan's assessment of your vocation? And secondly, you'd rather go into a different career than the Orthodox priesthood?"

The tangible silence lingered for a moment before Stephen responded. "That's right. I converted to Orthodoxy because I found in the Church a reverence for mystery, tradition, and beauty that was missing from my life. I discovered the Orthodox faith could supplement my life; the rituals connected me to God and the will of Christ. I knew I would be Orthodox for life. But I also knew I would never be a priest. That was not the life for me."

"So why are you here?"

"At first, I resigned myself to the attempt toward the priesthood, in case it was what God wanted. But within a semester's time, I knew it wouldn't be. A degree from St. Basil's can't hurt, though. I've mastered some incredible critical thinking skills under Father Timothy's tutelage. I will always have a deepened sense of awe for the Church and holy tradition. But I will never be a priest."

"Do the fathers here know that? It could clear up a lot. Especially for you."

"No one really knows."

"Does your wife know?" asked Tori.

"I think Lainie chooses not to know. It's not something we discuss very much. She's so into what she does around campus. She's very helpful in many areas. Service is so much of her life. It's like her identity."

"You sound very proud of her."

"I am," Stephen said quietly, keeping his eyes focused on his hands in his lap.

There was a brief lull, after which Stephen quickly said, "Look, this has been a draining day. I know I wasn't in the best mood when I came in, and I apologize for that. I will tell you that whomever it was going across campus last night, it wasn't me. Something I forgot to tell you earlier. I have a lot of pain in my left knee. It spasms out into my quadriceps and hamstring. That's why I have that brace when I play hoops, when I run, whatever. It's really unbearable, but right now surgery isn't an option. Long story. So sometimes I have to take pain medication and muscle relaxants. Last night I took a Soma at ten after nine so I'd have a decent night's sleep. It worked faster than I thought, so I was out soon after Lainie came home. I slept straight through the night."

Ballack replied, "Is this your prescription, the Somas?"

"Yes. I take them as needed."

He looked weary, unwilling to pontificate on anything further.

Ballack looked at Tori and then across the table at Stephen. "All we have is your word that you have no ambition to go into the priesthood. While that might be a sincere statement, you do understand we have to keep in mind the opposite could be true."

"Meaning?"

"Perhaps you were angry with Father Jonathan, took matters into your own hands, and now are telling us this 'I-never-intended' story—which conveniently nobody really knows—so that you can throw us off the trace."

"Completely untrue, detective."

"I reach the universe of true, Mr. Kale, by searching the realm of the plausible. Don't think for a minute this clears you. If there's one thing my partner and I can't stand, it's a deceptive red herring."

Several calls around campus confirmed that Father Matthias was not in his office but in the conference room. The detectives locked up the guest room but brought Father Jonathan's laptop with them. Darkness had fallen, and what had been a gentle surge of powdery snow had shifted to a light barrage of sleet. Ballack judged the temperature to be fifteen degrees. Thankfully, it was only a few yards to the imposing brick structure of Chalcedon Hall.

When the detectives knocked on the door of the conference room, it was clear they were interrupting a voracious argument between Father Matthias and an equally vocal adversary. They waited as they heard a shuffling of feet. The door opened to reveal Father Matthias, who looked as if he'd been given a life sentence. Standing twelve feet behind him, with an inimical visage, was Bishop Petr Burgic.

"Welcome, detectives," said Father Matthias. "Please come in."

"I was not under the impression we were done, Father Matthias!" thundered the bishop. "We need to begin the process of preparing Father Jonathan's body for burial, and these stall tactics are unacceptable! I want to know why this is taking so long!"

Ballack, never one to back down from making a tense religious drama more explosive, rolled up to the bishop and said, "Nice to see you too, your Grace."

"This is not the place for sarcasm or humor, young man!" bellowed Burgic. "I have driven nonstop since I received the news of our brother's death. Excuse me…his murder! Detectives, I don't expect you to understand this, but we have traditions that must take place after the death of a priest. We must begin the process immediately and start a vigil of reading Psalms. Just because you don't understand…"

"The Pannikhida? The first memorial service that must be done immediately after death?" Ballack's temper was rising quickly. "After which the body is washed and prepared by the family for burial? Except that, for a priest, the clergy would prepare the body and anoint it with oil?" Ballack snapped, his frustration reaching rare levels. "And after that, the face of the deceased is covered with the same type of veil which you use to cover the chalice during Divine Liturgy? And after which, you place a Gospel Book upon his chest? No…what's that?"

Bishop Petr Burgic was stunned, his spiteful expression suddenly become docile. Nobody in the room spoke for ten seconds.

"Your Grace," growled Ballack, "Never assume the ignorance of a detective. Just because we are here primarily to investigate murder, it doesn't mean we're stupid. I'm more than capable of jumping online and learning quickly."

After a considerable silence, the bishop spoke quietly, haltingly. "Given that, then, when is the earliest we can expect the body will be ready?"

Tori answered, half-afraid that her partner would level him with another lateral blast of disdain. "Our CSI team has finished. If you desire an autopsy, then the memorial process will have to wait. If, however, you have both agreed not to pursue an autopsy and are satisfied with our initial findings, then we can't stop you from keeping your customs. Still, from a detective's standpoint, I would suggest waiting."

"Why?" said the bishop. "So you can go on trying to play your investigation game at glacier speed? No. It is clear it was murder and that is that. We don't need to drag this out any longer."

"I'm surprised, your Grace," said Ballack. "Wouldn't you want to get to the bottom of this?"

"Your job is to solve this crime. It is mine to make sure our church's traditions and bylaws are carried out."

The argument went on for five more minutes, but in the end the bishop had his way. He was helped by the fact that Father Matthias wanted the saga played out with minimal fuss.

"Would you prefer to prepare the body here or in the church?" asked Tori.

"If I might suggest," said Father Matthias, "perhaps we could do so in Father Jonathan's apartment. It is only fitting that he should be in repose in his dwelling place."

The bishop nodded in agreement.

"Is there a date and time that you intend to have the memorial service?" asked Tori.

"We should have one here for the seminary," said Father Matthias. "After that, we can make arrangements for him to be taken across the state and the diocese can make arrangements for his burial."

"If that is the case," said the bishop, "I would suggest that we prepare the body tonight. Then, we continue the wake through tomorrow, with Divine Liturgy in the chapel and the final Pannikhida immediately afterward. Would sunset be an agreeable time?"

Father Matthias said it would be. The confrontation was obviously cooling down, and it appeared to Ballack they could leave. Tori wrapped his jacket around him and they made for the door.

The bishop called out. "Officer Ballack?"

Ballack turned around and stared at Burgic.

"I am sorry that you may have found my words somewhat grating. I truly had no intention of demeaning you. Please. I am bereaved of two dear friends. It is much for an old man to take."

Ballack calmly placed himself directly in front of Bishop Petr Burgic. He looked up into his face, as if assessing how he would take the words that would be said now. He felt compassion for the man, but it was considerably muted.

"Your Grace, I am indeed sorry for your loss. As both a detective and a human being, I believe these sorts of things shouldn't happen. But I will take issue with your burden. While these days might be heavy ones for you, let me draw this out. You have lost Reverend Zednik and Father Jonathan. Both men lived at least into their late fifties. You are in your seventies, I'd reckon. All friends who have lived a considerable length of days. You have lived a full and long life. I lost a brother at nineteen months to a muscle disorder that silently stalks its victims. I lost a girlfriend to suicide when she decided my efforts to gladden her heart only brought darkness. And I share my brother's condition, so I'm certainly not guaranteed additional birthdays. I must live day to day. So must you. That is a homily you can preach to yourself as you anoint Father Jonathan tonight. Good day, Your Grace, and may your conscience be clear."

Two hours later, Dieter Witten walked out of the Grotto of St.
Jonah and All Martyrs, shielding his cell phone from the snow and
sleet. The nasty weather was slackening, so perhaps he could arrange a
meeting after all.

Entering his home, Dieter changed into long running pants and
a sweatshirt. Dana glanced up at him from the sofa with a knowing
look. Her husband would claim he was getting in a run before another
wave of bad storms came through. She shrugged, knowing he was
going out no matter the conditions. True, he probably wouldn't get a
chance over the coming days. Monday night was bringing the biggest
ice storm of the year.

Dieter glided past her, not even looking at his bride. "Be out
jogging at the track for a bit. May get in a double shot since I won't
get an opportunity for a while."

Before the last sentence was done, he was out the door, and a
fresh tear began an all-too-painful slide down Dana Witten's face.

51

The guesthouse was a refuge now. Ballack didn't want to meet with any more students. He didn't want to talk about the case at all. The bishop's arrogance and his own insensitivity riled him. Tori gave him space as she plated some of Lainie Kale's chicken casserole, then piled on some green beans and a hot roll. She fixed Ballack a plate, as well, knowing he'd be starving later. Ballack was looking over his notes on his Dragon program with a crinkled brow. Tori sat down on the sofa and noticed they still hadn't turned on the television in the bedroom area since they arrived on Thursday.

"Hey partner, since we've got some time to play with, how about watching the game?"

Ballack roused himself. "Game?"

"The Super Bowl? We've got a stretch of time to decompress. Nothing helps with that like the Super Bowl."

"I forgot all about it," said Ballack. "Yeah, put it on. Sorry."

It turned out to be a good moment to find the remote control. No sooner had the picture come on the nineteen-inch display than Greg Jennings of the Packers gathered in an Aaron Rodgers pass in the end zone.

"That's some good news at the end of a lousy day!" rejoiced Ballack. "Packers just went up seventeen points with the extra point to follow!"

Tori smiled. It was good to see Ballack back in a celebratory frame of mind.

An energetic rapping on the door jarred both of them. Tori went to see who it was and opened the door. Dana Witten waved nervously and entered the room.

"I'm sorry to keep bothering you like this," she said, "but I came over for two reasons. One, I'm going into O'Fallon tomorrow to go shopping. I'm on the schedule to make you a meal, and I was wondering if you had any allergies or intolerances."

"None for me," said Tori quickly.

"Me either," said Ballack.

"Any preferences?" asked Dana.

"Well, we have chicken tonight," said Ballack. "Although I don't mind poultry back-to-back."

"Would a small lasagna do?"

Ballack smiled, "Perfect."

"And the second?" asked Tori.

"Pardon me?" replied Dana.

"You said you came over here for two reasons. What was the second?"

Dana looked toward the door then around the room, as if fearful the conversation was being recorded. "The second reason. I was wondering if there was a chance we could speak together, all of us, off-campus. Tomorrow. I was going to be out to get the groceries, but I was hoping you could make up some reason to be away, as well. We could meet and speak then. There are some things I need to tell you, but here is not a good place."

"Afraid that Big Brother is listening in?" asked Ballack.

"More than you know," said Dana. "There is a lane that turns off Highway 94 north of town, and it leads toward the Katy Trail. It comes out near a creek. We could meet there."

"You sure you don't want to park in the lot in town?" asked Tori. "The one next to the tavern?"

"No!" exclaimed Dana. Again she looked back. "Listen, just trust me. As private a talk as possible."

"And you're absolutely certain it can't happen here?" asked Ballack.

"Trust me."

Dieter finished his sixth lap around the lake. He had gone slowly, barely breaking a sweat. He knelt down and scooped the frigid snow off the ground, wiping it over his face to refresh himself. He turned away from the lake and skirted the south end of the Beautiful Garden. His wife put in plenty of effort to make it a plot of subsistence. Not that he cared much. He had found in her a dutiful wife who would make a good priest's spouse, give them a couple of children to grant them the appearance of a respectable home, and provide enough food for health and personal space for his own happiness.

Food and space, however, were not on his mind tonight as he approached the maintenance shed. This was his sanctuary for tonight, where this confrontation needed to happen. For some time, he knew it was coming. And Detective Ballack's question early this afternoon had empowered the student rector to connect the dots. As much as this hurt, Dieter had to raise these matters now. And the shed was the most private place. It would serve well. It had for some time.

When he reached the door, he looked down and saw a brick turned up on its end on the top step. He reached out in the dark and grasped the doorknob. It was unlocked.

The only beacon in the main area was a flickering night light. Dieter made out his counterpart's silhouette near the office desk. Heavy-hearted, he could wait no more.

"We need to talk," began Dieter. "It's about something from last night."

"Okay, while the Steelers are mounting their comeback, can we at least assess progress?"

"Fine," said Ballack. It wasn't as if he was sending in the Packers' plays. The two detectives settled in at the kitchen table, notes out. An exhausting day was coming to an end, but first they needed to set up their agenda for tomorrow. Ballack had his Dragon ready to go. His cough had improved slightly, but he doubted his lungs would clear up over the next few days. More snow was expected Monday afternoon and freezing rain was due to enter the area at midday Tuesday. The temperature was not expected to budge past twenty-five degrees.

"Okay," said Ballack. "Let's set out our appointments for tomorrow. We're talking with Dana Witten off-campus. I'd also like to speak with Father Andrew, Father Matthias, and Bishop Burgic together. That may be difficult with the funeral preparations, but we might be able to snag two of those three. We need to see what the deal was with Father Timothy's potential dismissal."

"Aren't you risking setting off another bomb?" asked Tori.

"I think it's already exploded. I'm just walking them through the crater. I also think we need to get with Lainie Kale. She's married to the person who is our top suspect. She helps in the business office. She's wired in to every conceivable nook and cranny of the seminary. She's likely to have heard something or seen something. I'd also like to see what she'll say about Stephen's ministry doubts."

"If she says anything at all." Tori looked at her partner. "What?"

"Nothing," said Ballack. And he knew Tori knew he was lying.

"By the way, has there been any scrimp of hair or whatever from the classroom? Janie has been silent on that."

"Probably silent because there's nothing there. She keeps remarking how it's one of the cleanest murder scenes she's ever witnessed."

Ballack looked at his laptop screen. Nothing seemed to be adding up. They were getting snippets of truth from this school's warriors of obfuscation. Someone had to have the key, or one of the keys, that began unlocking everything. His frustration was that nothing seemed to be clicking. He could usually visualize how a crime might have happened, but he was wandering in darkness. Guilt washed over him. He had never had a chance to prevent the deaths of those he loved. Now he couldn't figure out a chess match of finality that had already ensnared one, possibly two, victims. He couldn't think here. He didn't even want to watch the game. He needed to get out.

"I'll be right back, Tor. I need to move outside and get some fresh air."

"It's fifteen degrees outside!"

"I know. I'll be just a few minutes. I'll be in the trees."

Ballack glided to a stop in the middle of the Grotto of St. Jonah and All Martyrs. A stately wooden cross stood eight feet high, surrounded by rustic country benches in a semicircle. A fire pit sat on the east end of the grotto, although it looked relatively unused. But there would be no fire tonight. Ballack had come here to get a mountain off his chest. The brutality of what he had witnessed this morning was an incubus of misery that had grown drastically. He felt pregnant with sorrow. It had been Father Jonathan face down on that floor, but from the moment his eyes graced that disturbing tableau, all he could see was a child, a sweet little cherub on his final flight home.

No matter how hard he swung the gate of his soul against that memory, the pain was always stronger. Since Michelle's suicide, it seemed to have gained potency. He remembered well laying in his bed, drinking in the final waves of a dream long since erased, the simple happiness of a ten year-old lad. He had opened his eyes in time to see three leaves, tinged with the vibrancy of autumnal hues, flutter to the ground outside. All that remained was for Dad to enter in and get him out of bed and ready for church. Jill would be coming along as well. Mom had elected to stay at home with Christopher. His recent bout with pneumonia had seemingly cleared, but since he had only returned from the hospital, it had been decided that a domestic convalescence would suffice for today. Ballack remembered stretching comfortably. He remembered craning his neck to the right, just as he had this morning in the library, looking down the length of the bookshelves. And just like this morning, he remembered the scream. Almost word for word, the pleading for understanding, the entreaties that life miraculously return, that this was not happening, and the anguished shrieks for a God who mysteriously had shut the door and remained silent. The unsettling way his stricken father gathered their things to drive to the hospital. Mom leaving with the paramedics. The silence in the car, so quiet he could have sworn he heard Jill's heartbeat as well. The undersized waiting room at the hospital, just outside the emergency room, where Graham sat next to him, as he would fifteen years later at St. John's for another death. And then the gutteral screams, the soul spasms of horror, and the sickening crash of a bedside cart thrown violently against the wall by his father. Mom choking on her silent wails. Jill looking at him in a disturbing hush. And the wall, that stony hedge, slamming down around him. His own brother. They shared a disability. They shared a common weakness. But that bond spawned love and hope rather than discouragement. He delighted in little Christopher, who would waddle up to him and wrap his arms around his wheelchair-imprisoned legs. And he knew that, in the innocence that can only well up within a toddler, Christopher felt the same joy toward him. That was the beacon he looked forward to every day.

And now that candle of delight had been snuffed out. He had wandered in the wilderness of the heart for eighteen years. He couldn't reconcile with either path before him—the God who loved his creatures but was powerless to stop suffering and evil, or the God who was omnipotent yet turned a blind and diffident eye. And so what else could he do but throw in his lot on this path, plowed by his detective profession and powered by his cynicism of divine and human nature? But where had that taken him? In the midst of a miniature forest sitting defiantly before this symbol of faith, this sign of sacrifice and self-denial by an obscure Jewish carpenter. A Roman execution device. Why indeed did he end up here, where men of God offered the rituals of hope but hid their own litany of secrets? Why did those whom he loved have this tragic habit of disappearing from his presence? And why did his vocation prove to be so intoxicating and fulfilling but his skepticism always brought him back to where he began? The questions roared together in a tidal wave powerful enough to assault the gates of hell. Ballack bowed his head. He had no answers. He hid his face in an emotional swirl of torment and fear. More than the outside air seemed cold and frosty. He had become that scared little boy in the hospital waiting room once again. And there in that arctic moment of the spirit, for the first time in years, Ballack cried.

When his catharsis was over, Ballack rolled out of the Grotto.
There was no reason to stay with so much work to be done. He
stormed toward the curve in the road, fully intending to breeze through
the cold toward Chrysostom House. Surprisingly, he heard the sound
of footsteps coming toward him. He stopped and turned, taking in the
sight of Stephen Kale heading northwest from Gregory House. Ballack
rubbed his eyes vigorously and was hit with another coughing spasm.
Kale was rooted to the spot, and—thought the detective—had to find it
incredulous that Ballack was outside in bitter sub-freezing
temperatures. They moved toward each other, Ballack anxious that
Stephen not view his red-rimmed eyes even in the darkness.

"Detective Ballack?"

Ballack halted. He looked at the shadowy profile in front of
him. "Yes. Stephen?"

The silhouette crept toward him. Although he was sure Stephen
couldn't see his reaction, he masked his initial angst. Slowly, he slid
his hand toward his wheelchair joystick, ready to bolt at a moment's
notice. It had nothing to do with wanting to return to his guest room
for a much-needed breathing treatment; it had everything to do with
the frightening montage in front of him. Stephen Kale was carrying a
thirty-four inch aluminum softball bat.

"I thought that was you, sir," said the suspect. "What in the
world are you doing out here?"

Ballack kept his hand on the joystick. No way Stephen would
try anything out here, in the open. Then again, logic would normally
dictate no one would text a priest, scramble over to the library, and lay

in wait for the unsuspecting victim, ready to grant him a dreadfully permanent peace in the bowels of that academic sanctuary.

"Something wrong, sir?"

Ballack kept his eyes on the bat. "Nothing, Stephen. I was just surprised to see you up and about. What are you doing?"

"Oh, sorry. I guess I should explain. I had just grabbed a tennis ball and my bat from the gym. Since there's no recreation in the gym until Father Matthias' ban is lifted, I thought I'd remove the temptation from the wider family. I'm actually coming back from Gregory House. I read some of the Psalms over Father Jonathan. The priests are readying his body for the service tomorrow night, you know."

"I remember," said Ballack. His eyes quickly checked Stephen's face, then went back to the bat.

Stephen lifted the bat, causing Ballack's heart to stop for a full five seconds. "It's not a top-of-the-line. I mean, it's a Mizuno Craze, but I bought it online. It was on the blemished bat section of the website. Wanna see?"

He held the bat out toward Ballack, who was holding his breath. The barrel was facing him. He reached out and took it in both hands, turning the handle upward. He rotated the barrel, looking at the logo, but keeping Stephen in his sights for any sudden moves.

"You went to the gym?"

"Yeah. Just to get that. And this," he said, waving the tennis ball.

"Missing basketball practice?" asked Ballack, desperately making an attempt at lightening the mood.

A broad smile creased Stephen's face. "Father Timothy has obviously let you in on our little traditions."

Warily, Ballack returned the grin. "Well, just that one. I'm actually headed back to my place to finish watching the game." He had no intention of letting him know about his teary solitude in the grotto.

"Ah, the game. Thanks to the events of this day, Father Matthias' ban extends to gathering in the activity room to watch the Super Bowl. Looks like we'll have to be satisfied with watching it online or on our own sets in our apartments."

"Have a preference?"

"Packers. You?"

"The same. I had Ryan Grant on my fantasy team, but his injury really shot my chances."

Stephen nodded. "Nicholas and I have a bet on the game. No money. Just the loser has to serve the winner at dinner for a week. Dress up as a formal waiter. Designed to humble without gutting the bank account."

"No money bets?"

"The fathers frown upon that. Plus, Nicholas would have considered fifty dollars child's play."

"Well, it's a close one. Pack was up 21-17 last I checked."

"Ugh. Can't have the Steelers win. I sure can't handle another bruise to my ego."

Masking his reaction well enough in the dark, Ballack nonetheless almost dropped the bat to the ground. It was such an obscure thing, and surely Stephen meant nothing by that one word. But something clicked in Ballack's mind. He thought quickly.

"Stephen," he said slowly, "Do you want to bet on something else?"

The student stood there, silently measuring Ballack's words. "Umm, what do you mean?"

"I mean do a different bet. You've been banned from recreation until further notice. The fathers won't let you gamble for money. Why not break both rules at once?"

"Here? How?"

Ballack forced a mischievous grin. He handed the bat back to Stephen, knowing full well this could be a calculated risk. He pointed in the direction of the married student housing. "You pick out three of those houses over there. Name them. Then, toss the tennis ball and whack it over there. If you hit any of your three choices on the fly or the first bounce, I've got fifty dollars with your name on it."

Stephen was stunned. "Are you serious?"

Ballack pulled out his money clip. He had just enough to cover the bet. "Game on, pal? Choose your spots."

"And if I fail? I owe you fifty?"

"I'll make your day," said Ballack, trying to make himself more comfortable. "If you fail, zero liability. You owe me nothing; you just fail to collect."

"One shot, no risk?"

"That's right, except for the risk of knocking out a living room window. But haven't you earned the right to live dangerously?"

Stephen pondered the detective's words and made his decision. "Let's do it. You want to do the short toss?"

"Nah, I trust you."

Stephen was beyond excited. Ballack guessed showing a different side of himself hadn't hurt. He gripped the bat, looked into the distance, and said, "Any three?"

"Pick your poison," said Ballack.

"Okay," Stephen replied, "we've got the lights on, so there's no problem confirming where this sucker lands. How about Nicea, Ephesus, and…oh, how about my place. Antioch."

"You sure you want that? Targeting your own domicile?"

"If I happen to crack the window, my wife is pissed, but I win the bet. That's a delicious irony, don't you think?"

"Tell you what. You pop your own window, and I will personally buy the replacement."

Stephen laughed, turned toward the houses, and threw the ball upward. He leaned into it with a clean, upward strike. The muffled *whumpf* of bat on ball cut through the crisp February atmosphere. The yellowish orb flew through the sky in a perfect arc, a streaking parabola that began to slice somewhat. The fear of breaking a window was unfounded. The ball glanced off the roof of the laundry facility and bounced back toward Chalcedon Hall, rolling to a stop.

Ballack looked at Stephen, who shrugged and held out his hand. "No such luck, but at least I'm not any poorer. Anyway, thanks for the diversion. It's a splash of humor in a dark day. No, don't worry. I'll grab the ball. I've kept you out in these conditions long enough."

He loped off in the direction of the laundry. Ballack watched him until he was sure he was headed into his house. Then the detective turned on a dime and sped toward Chrysostom. If he was visualizing this correctly, Stephen Kale was now in the clear.

The door of the Witten residence at Nicea House opened wide, and Dieter strolled through the living room.

"I'll be in the shower," he said, not even looking at his wife. "It was a lengthy run." The door of the bathroom shut, and in seconds, there was the familiar hissing sound of the shower.

Dana Witten never even looked up from her book. Her glances out the window over the last half-hour had told her all she needed to connect her suspicions. "Whatever you were doing out there, darling," she whispered to herself, "your goal wasn't to go running."

The door of Chrysostom slowly opened and Ballack shot into the guest room. "Tori! We've had it all wrong. It's not Stephen Kale! He's not Tekel!"

Tori was coming out of the bathroom at the news. "Where have you been? Are you trying to land yourself in the hospital by staying out in this weather? And what's this about it not being Stephen Kale?"

"Drop everything, girl. We're going to the library. You got Father Matthias' key? Good. Let's roll." He was headed out the door, oblivious to the celebration surrounding the Packers' fourth touchdown on another strike to Greg Jennings.

"Hey, wait..." called out Tori, scrambling to get her jacket on and grab Ballack's portable suction at the same time. It took her a thirty-yard sprint to catch up to him. "What do you mean it's not him?"

"Ssshhhh!" hissed Ballack. "I'm saying that if I'm putting this together correctly, it's not him. Let's get to the library. I'm not comfortable speaking in the open air. Let's get to the classroom and we'll talk."

They ducked underneath the police tape and entered the library. Ballack had another coughing fit, so hard it seemed his lungs would turn inside out. Tori turned on the portable suction and Ballack took care of the rest. They continued down to the classroom.

Compared to the boisterous tragedy earlier on, the classroom was eerily silent. All that was left of the incident was a tape outline of Father Jonathan's prone repose. The stockinged cross had been taken as evidence; Tori's pictures would suffice. Tori walked toward the center of the room and turned toward her partner. "Alright, you have an idea. I'd like to see how you painted this one."

Ballack walked through his previous depiction from that morning, emphasizing the space behind the partition stand as Tekel's likely stealth position. Tori grew impatient quickly. "You said all that before, but how can you be sure that the initial strike, if it was from there, was *not* made by Stephen Kale?"

"Do you remember the bruise?" asked Ballack. "The one on his head?"

Tori thought back. Five inches by two. From the base of the ear to the forehead. Or as a St. Louis native would say, southeast to northwest. "Yeah? So?"

"Evenly distributed contusion, right?" asked Ballack. "Hit him flush. If the murderer is coming out from behind the partition, to make that kind of bruise, what sort of swing would he be making?"

Tori didn't see at first. "What do you mean?"

"Tor, if you're up at bat during the police benefit softball game in July, show me what you'd do."

She was getting a sense of where her partner was going. She assumed a mock batting position and swung. "How's that for form?"

"Not bad for the police benefit," replied Ballack. "You normally swing that way, correct?" Tori nodded.

"Good," continued Ballack. "Now, get behind the partition and show me how you would make a swing at Father Jonathan and make that same exact bruise on the side of his head."

Tori walked through the exercise. Twice. Unsuccessfully.

She looked at Ballack. "I couldn't."

"And why, Tor?"

"Because I swing right-handed. To come from behind there at that angle and make a bruise like that would mean the attacker is likely a left-handed swinger."

"Exactly."

"Let me guess. Stephen Kale is right-handed?"

Ballack nodded, that irrepressible smirk spreading on his face.

"Mind telling me," asked Tori, "how you figured that out?"

Ballack told her of his chance encounter with Stephen just minutes before: the discussion of Stephen's bet with Nicholas Panangiotis and the hope it wouldn't bruise his ego, how the word *bruise* triggered something with Ballack, which led to his spontaneous batting challenge, and how, when Stephen sent his attempt clattering off the laundry hut, he had swung right-handed.

Tori shook her head. "I don't disagree with your observations. I just don't want to jump to conclusions. And besides, you saw how he shot in the basketball game. Left-handed."

"He *shot a basketball* left-handed. That doesn't mean he does the same thing with hitting a ball. Or throwing a ball."

"What do you mean?"

"Plenty of people will do some activities with one hand, yet be stronger with the opposite hand for others. My uncle Dan shoots a basketball and throws a baseball left-handed, but he golfs, plays tennis, and swings a bat right-handed. My other uncle Andrew swings a bat, golf club, and tennis racket left-handed, but he's right-handed for throwing a ball and shooting hoops. Dad is much like them, all mixed up, depending on the sport."

"What if Stephen's a switch-hitter? Couldn't he be good either way?"

"Possible, but unlikely," said Ballack. "If you want to put those suspicions to rest, I can always ask him directly. But in all likelihood, when he swung tonight, he went with the most comfortable stance."

"And another thing. There's no evidence the head shot was the first one. The back bruise could have been the first hit."

"Again, unlikely," responded Ballack. "That contusion was longer and not as deep, which—granted—could be from a bat or heavy stick. But remember the angle also went from mid-spine on the right to the left of the neck. Same general angle as the head shot. If done from behind, it's hard to imagine that being from anyone other than a lefty. If the back bruise is even the result of a bat."

Tori had cupped her chin in her right hand. "It's possible, but it's too neat. And besides, how are we going to tighten the noose on our suspect without making it obvious? Are we going to precede Father Jonathan's funeral with a round of batting practice and demand everyone on campus take three swings?"

Ballack waved her off. "No, I'm not proposing that. Tekel would deliberately swing differently given that situation, anyway. But it's much less likely Stephen Kale is Tekel. I'm not saying impossible, but I think those odds have greatly diminished."

"Then what's your proposal?"

Ballack rubbed his hands together. "Maybe we need to cast the net wide to pull it in tightly. What if this has been building, not for months, but for years? I'm inclined to think these two deaths— Zednik's and Father Jonathan's—are connected. The question is how. I say we focus on the one that is clearly murder and look for a history. We already have rumblings between Father Jonathan and Father Timothy. That's a definite possibility. But we need to go through some additional documentation. Beyond Father Jonathan's recommendations. Something that is common to every student here."

"And that would be?"

Ballack raised his right eyebrow.

"You're kidding, right?" asked Tori.

"Let's go, girl," replied Ballack, already zipping out the door and up the interior ramp.

58

Tori jogged alongside Ballack's wheelchair as they made their way back to the guest room. "If we're headed in this direction, we'll likely need to get a search warrant. That could take time."

"Or not," said Ballack. "Father Matthias might give us what we need when we ask. If he senses we can get it with a warrant, he might as well hand it over. If he knows the information could damage him, he probably knows any delay could raise suspicions."

Tori looked to her right and saw Father Matthias and Bishop Burgic leaving Gregory House, headed back to Chalcedon Hall. "Hey, looks like they're saving us a trip. Let's ask them now."

Father Matthias and the bishop approached the detectives, the chilly gusts billowing their black robes in ferocious waves. They had been speaking in low tones, but upon seeing the detectives Father Matthias loudly—in fact, almost too cheerily—said, "Good evening, friends. Out and about in the wind and cold?"

"We are," said Tori, "and I am not sure if this finds you at a bad time, but we have one additional request to make of you."

"Ah," replied Father Matthias, "Before you make that, I have to let you know of a change in plans. It seems that…well, Your Grace, would you care to let them know?"

The bishop drew himself to his full height. It seemed, thought Ballack, a remarkable maneuver clearly designed to intimidate. Not that it worked with him. After all, everyone towered over him since he was perpetually seated.

"Yes," said the bishop, "Due to the inclement weather that is coming, the diocese is requiring that the Divine Liturgy and Final

Pannikhida for Father Jonathan will be tomorrow at eleven o'clock in the chapel. We desire to have continual services in Kansas City before Father Jonathan's final burial, but to avoid any delay the coming ice storm will bring, we need to move up the time."

Ballack wasn't surprised. Another chess move by the diocese. Whether it was a practical reason or a sheer power play wasn't the point. They now had to move ahead and rearrange their schedule at the same time.

He stifled another cough and looked Father Matthias in the eye. "That is the diocese's wish, and given there will be no autopsy, we will not prevent that. However, for our purposes, there is something we will require of you."

Ballack sped into the guest room as Karen pulled up in the parking lot. Tori looked at her watch. "Is your nurse late?"

"On time, actually," Ballack said. "I texted Karen and told her she could come at eight-thirty. I figured we'd be settling down by then."

"Hardly settling down," said Tori, throwing a massive file of papers down on the table. "We're going through all this tonight?"

"A cursory run-through," said Ballack. "I want us to do two separate searches. I'm going to get back on Erhart's laptop and see if there's anything left to root out. You rifle through those application materials and collate contacts under each person's name. Name, phone numbers, locations. I want to know if there is a past connection between Erhart and anyone on our list."

"The whole seminary is our list, thanks to Stephen Kale being a right-handed hitter."

"I'm not necessarily eliminating Stephen. C'mon, Tor. Let's stop and put the pieces together."

Karen had entered the room.

"Hi, Karen," said Ballack. "Is it possible to iPod things for awhile?"

"Will do," said the nurse, putting her ear buds in and hiking the volume. Even at that distance, Ballack immediately recognized she was listening to Coldplay.

Ballack turned back to his partner, lowering his voice. "Let's look at the facts. Zednik comes here for a tongue wagging, dressing down three priests, the business manager, and a student. He never makes it out. The deathbed scene looks suspicious. The day after we arrive, Father Jonathan receives the letter that alludes to some kind of past indiscretion. From the tone of the letter, it doesn't appear to be a remote matter. Whoever passed that on seems deeply affected by Father Jonathan's actions. There's pain in that communiqué, a pronouncement of doom, and it seems like whoever was the originator of that piece wants to speed up God's wrath and help the Almighty balance the universe's justice. Given the anonymity of that letter, the lack of identification on the envelope, and the murder scene bearing the last line of that letter, Tekel is someone here. That, we don't doubt. I just think there's a massive vibe pulsing through all this: that one of Father Jonathan's past sins hit someone here pretty hard. I know I'm grasping at straws, and all the evidence is circumstantial, but what else do we have to go on?"

Tori was silent for ten seconds.

"Let's do this," she said.

"First things first," said Ballack. He signaled Karen over. "Bath first. I smell like a Lithuanian gutter. If you two can transfer me in, perhaps you can call Dana Witten and arrange our walk-and-talk for earlier in the morning. I want that done so we can get back for the service in time."

"We're going to the funeral?" gasped Tori.

"Me, you, and your perceptive skills. If there's someone in the house of God looking smug or guilty, you'll be able to tell. Karen, bath. In case he exists, I'm sure the Lord doesn't want to be repulsed by my carcass."

60

The Katy Trail is literally the longest, most narrow state park imaginable. Starting at Machens in eastern Missouri and running over two hundred miles westward to Clinton, the Trail is a favorite of hikers, cyclists, walkers, and joggers. The portion running north of Defiance provided adequate tree cover from any sun, although given the swollen clouds that were rushing up from Oklahoma, there would not be much in the way of glare this Monday morning. The temperature was the same as the night before, and Ballack hoped the power would stay on through the ice barrage they would receive tonight.

They had followed Dana Witten to their starting spot, a secluded area just off the highway. She got out of her car, wearing a gray North Face sweatshirt and black windpants. She took off her crocs and eased on her cross-training shoes. Ballack rolled down the Sprinter's ramp and pulled up next to her blue Chevy Aveo.

"Sorry about the early start, Dana," he said.

"That's okay. More time to make the lasagna for later," she responded. "Shall we go? How about heading back south?"

The three of them walked a ways in silence. The nearby creek remained frozen. Every once in awhile the wind would kick up. Ballack was glad to be going into the breeze at the beginning of their constitutional rather than the end. Finally, he couldn't take the silence any more.

"I assume that you brought us out here for more than recreation, Dana. If you expect us to be able to digest anything this morning, you probably need to start sharing with us now."

She wouldn't, or couldn't, look at him. She had added a red thermal earwrap to keep her head somewhat warm. He started to think she hadn't heard him when she spoke for the first time.

"I have no idea who my husband is."

Ballack measured his response. "I believe you've intimated that before."

"I mean he's a walking jumble of contradictions. I was reading in our living room last night when I saw him approaching our house from beyond Chalcedon Hall. He was speaking to someone on his cell phone. When he got home, he announced he was going out for a run around the lake track. Said he might be gone for a while. After he left, I checked his cell phone to see who it was he was speaking with."

"And who was it?" Tori spoke for the first time.

"No one. At least no one I could tell. I went into every folder: calls made, calls received. He must have just deleted it. Deleted everything, in fact. Totally covered his rear end. That's when I came over last night to see you. On the way, I tried to look over by the lake, and I saw him jogging. Then when I went back after speaking with you, he was gone. I figured he was back home, but, when I arrived, the house was empty. He didn't show up for another thirty minutes. Didn't look like he broke a sweat, yet he went straight for the shower."

Ballack tried to process where she was going with this. "Dana, I'm sure you didn't just bring us out here to report on your husband's movements. You've got a few conclusions under that statement. You've already told us you feel like you're in peril. Now you've got a husband who sneaks out on you. Care to tell me what you're really thinking?"

They were approaching a bridge. Ballack recognized it as the one over the Femme Osage Creek, the same one depicted in the painting in Jane Porter's den. Dana pulled up and stopped, grasping the railing and looking out in the distance.

"I think my husband is either cheating on me, knows who the murderer is, or is himself the murderer," Dana said in a voice weighed down with tragic perplexity. "I believe that whoever he is, he has compromised himself. He is either killing our marriage, knows who has killed someone else, or has killed Father Jonathan." She looked as if she might cry again, but instead she merely held onto the railing, searching the sky with a crestfallen glance. "The disturbing thing is that I am more resigned to that than angry. I am not sure what precisely is going on, but it can't be good. He's become even less approachable than he ever was."

Tori's cell phone rang, and she answered it, walking down the pathway to ensure some solitude. She was twenty yards away when Dana spoke to Ballack.

"I can't talk to him this way."

"Which way?" asked Ballack.

"The way I'm talking to you. Where I have the confidence you'll at least listen to me. I can't explain. There's something about it. You have a way about you, where I know that even though you're here on a murder issue, when I approach you, you put everything out of the way and you listen to me. I know that should be the bedrock of my marriage but Dieter is either unable or unwilling. Even when I make suggestions or if I ask him why he preaches on something or explains an issue a certain way, he's hardly the paragon of receptivity. More often than not, he blows me off and tells me I would never understand.

He's totally withdrawn from me. We haven't had sex in months. There are days I'd give everything to put my marriage back together again. But more often, there are days I want out. And now I'm looking at a future as a priest's wife who will play second fiddle to the church. Forever. And I resent him for that journey."

"And you tell me because you can't tell him?"

Dana looked at him full in the face. "Because I feel like I can trust you. Because you care about the truly important things. Life. Justice. Hope. Anyone can see that. He whittles away his time with obscure saints and readings so he can make a name for himself. You do your job to make the people around you better, to make the world around you better. And Dieter has always had it easy. He's been given so much and gotten by with just enough charm towards the right people. I can't imagine you've clawed your way through life by the path of least resistance."

"No, that is true," said Ballack.

"Look, I feel unsafe. Something's really wrong with Dieter, and he's involved in this issue in some way. I can't tell him or anyone else at St. Basil's my thoughts. You're the only one I trust telling."

"You're absolutely sure?"

"Yes. This goes beyond a crumbling marriage. It's a matter of life or death. I don't want my nightmare to become a reality."

It was at that point that Tori came back. "That was Scotty. He's coming for the funeral service and wants a briefing of where we are going before it all goes down." She turned to Dana. "I'm sorry we have to cut this short, but maybe we can start this up again soon?"

"No need to apologize. I need to get shopping anyway."

"Cameron, I'll run ahead and start up the Sprinter and get it ready for your arrival."

And she did. Dana walked alongside Ballack as the two proceeded to the parking area. "I'm sorry you have to see St. Basil's at its low point," she said, frowning. "Although it's not the warmest environment, it's normally not the den of hopelessness it's morphed into."

"Maybe I need to come back when it's not murder season," Ballack joked. He smiled as Dana broke out in a laugh. The explosive snicker caught him off guard, and, before long, he slipped into laughter as well. But just as suddenly, the cold intake of air forced a spurt of coughing. He attempted to slow his breathing in a vain attempt to recover. Nothing. He took off his trach cap and still could not coordinate a single breath. Mucus bubbled in his upper airway.

"Cameron? Cameron?" Dana asked, then pleaded, before noticing Ballack pointing at his trach and back toward his portable suction bag attached to the rear of his wheelchair. Swiftly, she lifted the bag and set it on his lap, grasping the long, flexible catheter and flicking the button to bring the machine to life. Ballack's blurred eyesight cleared as he felt the expulsion of his airway secretions through the tubing. He cleared his eyes in time to see Dana point inquisitively at the small sterile water bottle, looking at him as if to say, "Rinse it in this?" His quick affirmative nod was followed by her efficient rinsing and replacing of the tubing. Realizing that he couldn't use the catheter again, she took a latex glove from his emergency pack behind his wheelchair and stuffed the dirtied conveyance in it. Ballack pulled himself together, stunned both by the suddenness of his coughing attack and how naturally and quickly Dana had acted. His new medical hero circled in front of him and leaned downward, checking his face for signs of distress. They locked eyes for a few seconds that seemed like forever. She reached forward and, placing her hand on his left cheek, wiped some moisture from the corner of his eye.

"You okay?" she asked.

He nodded. "Yeah." A painful pause. "Thanks."

Her hand remained on his cheek.

"Don't scare me like that," she smiled, removing her hand and straightening up. They restarted their journey toward the cars. Not a word was said until they made their goodbyes at their vehicles. Nothing needed to be said. His ears were still tingling from hearing her call him by name.

Ninety-nine times out of one hundred, Scotty Bosco would have been early or on time to meet with his detectives. He lived by the adage, "To be early is to be on time; to be on time is to be late; to be late is to be forgotten." Today, however, was the hundredth time. A four-car smash-up at Highway 94 and Pitman Hill Road was the culprit, and Bosco cursed his way through a twenty-minute standstill. His attempt to make up time south of the Interstate was stalled when he got behind an elderly antique dealer in a rickety moving van. It wasn't until he hit another straightaway that he gunned it past the van and cruised unimpeded the rest of the way to St. Basil's.

But an open route over the last six miles still meant he showed up with only eight minutes before the Pannikhida. He had called Tori and alerted her about his tardiness. She confirmed they would wait for him in the narthex. He would rather have skipped the funeral service, but his detectives were insistent on observing their surroundings, and, if that meant spying on others at the nadir of their grief, so be it. Bosco had a few moments to spare. He wasn't due to check on his other case in Wentzville until mid-afternoon.

The three of them entered the nave at one minute before eleven. The priests, including the bishop, were in their full garb, assisted by Dieter Witten. Chanting had already begun and soon the assembled students, with some spouses and several children, were following in locked liturgical step. Ballack listened along, holding back from making the sign of the cross or from verbalizing any portion of the responses. Psalms and chants came and went with rhythmic regularity. The atmosphere was charged with a swath of joy. The majority of the congregation was following the Orthodox adage that Father Jonathan, in the presence of his Divine Advocate, was more fully alive in heaven than he had been on earth.

One matter remained before shifting the service into the final Pannikhida: Holy Communion. Tori had spoken to Father Andrew before the service and assured him they would not be coming forward to join in the sacrament. Ballack examined the looks of those interspersed souls in the pews. Marcus Curry. Jason Hart and his wife. Nicholas Panangiotis. The tense-jawed David Orlinsky, more jittery than ever. And Stephen and Lainie Kale, hand-in-hand. He couldn't swear to a guilty look on any of them. He turned his attention back to the platform in front of the iconostasis, where Bishop Burgic, blessing the open casket with the sign of the cross, walked over to do the same with the bread and wine. He lowered his voice to a murmur that only God could hear, lifted his head, and partook of the sacred bread. He then took the remainder of the consecrated bread and placed in it what must have been the Holy Cup. He approached the iconostasis and spoke in a loud voice.

"Having beheld the resurrection of Christ, let us worship the holy Lord Jesus, the only Sinless One. We venerate Your cross, O Christ, and we praise and glorify Your holy resurrection. You are our God. We know no other than You, and we call upon Your name. Come, all faithful, let us venerate the holy resurrection of Christ. For behold, through the cross joy has come to all the world. Blessing the Lord always, let us praise His resurrection. For enduring the cross for us, He destroyed death by death."

As if on cue, the congregation began to move forward to receive the wine, one after the other. The priests would wait to drink from the Holy Cup until later, so Dieter Witten first went forward to eat and drink. Within minutes, everyone who moved from their seats had been served. A strange look crossed Father Andrew's face, but nothing else seemed odd. All that remained was to move through the final Pannikhida. Ballack sorely needed to debrief with his lieutenant, but knew that the disrespect in leaving at this stage would be unforgiveable.

He wouldn't have the chance at all.

Partway through the prayer service for Father Jonathan, Dieter Witten went to the lectern to lead in the recitation of the Lord's Prayer. Heads bowed through the nave as the student rector led in the ancient entreaties that Christ himself had passed on to his disciples like precious spiritual cargo.

"Our Father, who art in heaven, hallowed be thy name. Thy kingdom come…"

It was at that point Ballack could detect a change in Dieter's voice. It was hoarse, scratchy. A hint of fear had annexed his normally flat tone. Ballack looked up. Dieter was clearly attempting to complete the prayer, but there seemed to be an obstruction in his throat. Imploringly, he cast a glance at Father Andrew, as the congregation begged the Almighty to "forgive us our debts." He grasped at his neck, clawing desperately at thin air, then reaching around for an instrument he clearly expected but had vanished.

Father Andrew started toward Dieter as the congregation began noticing the bizarre activity at the lectern. Ballack quickly motored his wheelchair down the aisle, wanting to beat everyone to the site. It was when the lectern came into view that the front rows let loose a horrifying collective gasp. Dieter's face had gone bright red, as if oxygen was cut from his entire body. His eyes bugged, then rolled back in his head. His legs trembled and gave way underneath him, his knees slamming violently to the floor and his legs bending back on themselves. As the priests surrounded him, Father Andrew tried to take off Dieter's collar. He turned and screamed, "Epi-pen! Where's his Epi-pen? He's having a seizure!"

Dieter's body went into spasms, and the entire congregation broke into loud screams and wails. Stephen Kale jumped one of the pews, diving in to attempt resuscitation. Marcus Curry and Nicholas Panangiotis, in a rare show of solidarity, kept the crowd at bay, giving the fallen rector a chance to get air.

But one look at Dieter's face told Ballack that air was one commodity he wasn't getting back. Stephen's chest compressions were ineffective. As the shocked community pressed closer, Dieter's form gave one last lurch. Then quiet.

Silence. Then an explosion of grief, the likes of which seemed so unnatural in a house of worship, erupted from the students and faculty.

"Oh, please God! Oh dear God!" screamed Lainie Kale. "What is going on? It can't be! It can't be!"

"Dieter!" called Father Andrew, shaking the dead man gently. "Dieter, please, come back!" All to no avail. Surrounding the still form on the floor of the chapel, those assembled broke down in an acute tumult of sorrow. Wives shielded their little children from the horror before them. Scotty and Tori were throwing elbows, trying to join Ballack at the front. They were cut off by the moving scrum of Bishop Burgic and Father Matthias.

"What is this? Another death?" roared the bishop. "You are not satisfied with taking one life?"

"This is not my doing, your Grace!" screamed Father Matthias above the cacophony of suffering voices in the church. "I refuse to have you accuse me and poison this place with your lies!"

"Please, Father! Stop it!" Scotty said through gritted teeth. The dean and the bishop had gone after each other in the rage of the moment and would have fought there on the spot had it not been for Scotty and Tori physically intervening. Chaos was in full gear, and nothing seemed likely to quell the terror.

Nothing, that is, until the labored voice of Cameron Ballack, strengthened by his vocal amplifier and coupled with his wheelchair horn, shushed the crowd's fury.

"Stop it! Stop it! LISTEN!"

And as if a word of God had been spoken from heaven, everyone stood stock still. He wheeled toward the platform.

"Nobody, and I mean nobody, move a muscle," he slowed down for emphasis. He looked at Dieter's body. "Stephen, thank you for your attempts, but he's gone. Please move back and step away. Fathers, Your Grace, please step back. Scotty, Tori, please come forward."

The detectives moved forward. Bosco was impressed with his young detective's cool demeanor.

Ballack looked at the assembly. "This place must be vacated immediately. We have no choice, given the events of the past two weeks and especially the past couple days, but to treat this as a suspicious death. Please leave immediately. I understand that this is a sudden matter and grief is appropriate. Grief is your duty and responsibility. But you must let us do ours now."

The bishop moved toward the altar to remove the communion elements.

"I meant everyone, Your Grace!" snapped Ballack. "The bread and wine are part of this area and must be part of our inquiry! Please step down!"

"They are sacred elements, having been blessed! They are the body and blood of the risen Lord and we cannot subject them to any other use!"

Bosco, sensing where Ballack was going with this, intervened to support his detective. "Your Grace, they are part of an investigation. As significant as your doctrines and traditions are to you, our needs outweigh them for now!"

"I forbid this!" howled Bishop Burgic. "This is stripping this place of its holiness and dignity!"

"Oh, for heaven's sake," shouted Tori. "What is this accomplishing? Get back, get out! Everybody!" She slyly slid open her jacket, exposing her gun. Not that she would have used it, but no one outside of Ballack and Bosco knew that. She was that desperate for order.

Thankfully, there was a small procession of folks already leaving the nave. The fathers remained up front, unsure of what to do in assisting the bishop's exit. He looked around, sensing the tide of opinion had turned against him. "This is an outrage! God is a God of order, who has blessed these elements by sacred tradition of his Church! Why is no one else speaking against this?" His eyes alighted on Father Matthias, Father Andrew, and Father Timothy. Their resolute glares showed they were firmly in the detectives' camp.

Ballack scooted in front of the bishop, barring him from advancing toward the bread and the wine. For the second consecutive day, he went off on the aged leader. "Stripping this place of its holiness and dignity? Your actions, while commendable in your sight, are only stripping Dieter Witten of his dignity. And let me remind you, Your Grace: If this God does exist, he'd better not be one who ties his hands by the morass of church tradition. I would remind you that your God should be one who seeks justice. And if you won't seek it yourself, then clear out of our way so that we can!"

Ballack's normally moderate, coarse voice practically boomed in the nave. An awed hush fell over the seven living souls interposed between the two corpses—one aged, one young.

"That was his polite way," said Bosco, "of telling you to leave."

The bishop glowered a toxic look through the lieutenant. "You might have the power of the state to do so, but I will report this outburst to your superiors!"

"That's enough, Your Grace," the voice of Father Timothy thundered, and he promptly took him by the arm, pulling him up the aisle, not slowing down until he had forced him outside.

The detectives, shocked by this fortuitous turn of events, could hardly believe their good fortune. Bosco drew a quick breath and turned to Fathers Matthias and Andrew.

"Obviously, we need to act quickly. Treating this as a suspicious death and possibly murder means calling in our CSI team. We will need the chapel cordoned off. I suppose you can make this announcement to the seminary?"

"I can," said Father Matthias.

"However," cautioned Father Andrew, "there are some who are not here, whether in their houses or off-campus. I know we told the Dawsons to take today off, so they will not be in until tomorrow. We'll need to check who else is not here and make the rounds."

"Oh, my gosh," said Tori, recognizing there was one key person who had not been here to view this tragedy. "Dana."

Ballack had been leaning forward to get a look at Dieter's mouth for any clue of the distress that had terminated his life. When Tori mentioned Dana's name, he shut his eyes tightly. The grief mounted, one layer on another. The lamentation rocketed through his heart. Not for Dieter, who was past caring for. For Dana. She had doggedly and patiently suffered through a loveless marriage, always hoping for the best, that perhaps her man would right himself. She showed kindness and compassion to others even if she was not often a recipient of such attention and goodwill herself. Now she would receive the devastating blow of knowing this marriage could never be redeemed. She would never know what could have been. And this fatal strike had been no fault of her husband. Her grief would be both replete and denuded. It would simultaneously feel like everything and nothing.

He opened his eyes. Tori had just tapped him on the shoulder. No one else was in the room.

"Scotty just called Holbrook. They're on their way. We need to check things out in here."

"Okay," he said weakly. "Let's start with him."

Tori pulled out her camera and began snapping pictures. Ballack lifted his laptop to begin the tragic craft of post-mortem analysis. He craned his neck and felt something pop loose and give him instant relief. He looked at Dieter's body. He thought back to the vision of Father Jonathan, face down in the library. And though he was not witness to it, he imagined the sight of Tomas Zednik, lying in perpetual repose. Three deaths, three separate places. And as his mind whirred to coagment the pictures of mortality, he recalled the vision, the declarative seal above the front doors of this very chapel. In a place of rest, Zednik's body had been violated. Father Jonathan's life was snuffed out in the library, the venue of the mind. And here, in this arena of the soul's nurture, Dieter Witten had fallen into the waves of eternity.

"Sanctify the body, engage the mind, transform the soul," whispered Ballack, repeating the seminary motto from memory. It was a vision under nefarious attack from within. He could only hope this was the final fusillade.

PART FOUR

A JUSTICE DELIVERED
(FEB. 7TH-8TH;
APR.23RD-24TH)

Evan Holbrook arrived thirty-five minutes after receiving Scotty Bosco's phone call. The lieutenant directed Holbrook into the chapel while he himself went to speak to Father Matthias in the refectory. He found Ballack furiously dictating into his Dragon and saw Tori snapping pictures with cautious regularity. It was with a disquieting clunk that Holbrook set his materials down on the floor and began drawing his observation gear on.

"Another one?" Holbrook queried.

"Unfortunately so," said Tori, not moving her face from behind the camera. "So when is Janie getting here?"

"Woke up this morning not feeling well, but she threw down a load of sore throat lozenges and chicken noodle soup. She'll be here in an hour. So what's the name and your initial gut reactions?" he asked.

Ballack replied, "Name is Dieter Witten. He's the student rector here. Fourth and final year. He was leading the Lord's Prayer during a funeral service just under an hour ago when his voice changed and he began slurring his words. He then got hit with a massive seizure and collapsed. Right in that position, too. Legs folded underneath him and everything. Looks a lot like anaphylactic shock from something, so we barred everyone from touching the communion bread and wine. Had some traditionalistic backlash at first, but they finally capitulated."

"It was amazing," said Tori, still focused on the body. "Cameron was a frigging brick wall to the bishop. You're my new hero, brother. By the way, what'd you think of Father Timothy getting Burgic out of here?"

"Made me the number one Duke fan in the world," replied Ballack. He pointed toward the platform. "Bread and wine undisturbed since the last person who took it."

"Brought my little chemistry set per the boss' instructions," said Holbrook, negotiating the platform steps in a single bound. He approached the cup, pulled out a small, clear flask, and poured the remnants of the wine into it. As the liquid settled, he grabbed the loaf of bread, raised it to his nose, and sniffed. His face crinkled, and he sniffed the bread again. He looked at the flask, took out a penlight, and shone it toward the bottom of the glass. He turned to the two detectives.

"Tori, I know this is quick, but can you call Scotty and ask him to bring one of the priests here ASAP?"

"What's the deal?" asked Tori.

"I want to know if Dieter Witten had an almond or tree nut allergy. We may have hit the bullseye already."

"Almond allergy!" Ballack exclaimed. "Are you sure?"

"When you said seizure," Holbrook replied as Tori pulled out her phone and dialed Bosco, "I wondered if we had some sort of allergic reaction. When you said you had shielded the communion stuff, my antenna really perked up. And now…" he placed the bread in front of Ballack's nostrils, "my thoughts are pretty well confirmed."

Ballack sniffed. "You've got to be kidding me."

"That's right," said Holbrook, offering Tori a whiff as she walked over. "Someone put a load of almond extract or something in here. And look," he pointed at the interior of the loaf, "these speckles look suspicious. Almost like someone crushed some almonds and added them to the mix."

"And the wine?" asked Ballack.

Holbrook grabbed the flask and looked closely. "It appears to be some sediment that isn't normal for wine. I'd have to get a better look at it to confirm, but given what's in the bread and…" he paused, taking a smell of the wine-bread mixture, "Wow. This is like inhaling a Zero bar, nougat and all."

"How could he not have known, if it's that pungent?" Ballack said. "I would think the stench would be an absolute giveaway."

"Perhaps Father Matthias can answer that question," announced Scotty Bosco. He and the dean had just entered the nave and were approaching the scene up front. The lieutenant introduced Father Matthias to Holbrook as Tori and Ballack drew close.

"You were asking a question when I entered, Detective Ballack?" said Father Matthias. "Something along the lines of how could he not know? Of whom were you speaking?"

It was Holbrook who spoke up. "Father Matthias, did Dieter Witten have an allergy of any sort?"

The dean's eyes widened slightly and he lifted his head. "He did, I'm afraid. Almond and tree nuts. Quite severe. To the degree that our cook ran the food selection process under a fine-toothed comb." He stopped, visibly shaken. "Is that what you are guessing is the case here?"

"Unfortunately, yes," said Holbrook. "And he didn't have an adrenaline shot or Epi-pen on him?"

"I can only guess," said Father Matthias, "that he felt he wouldn't need it here. He went into shock only once since he was here and that was his first year. He was in class and a friend gave him the shot immediately. But I can't understand why he would just go into shock here! We have no almonds within yards of this place!"

"I would dispute that, sir," said Holbrook. He held out the loaf of bread. "Do you recognize this?"

"It was our bread for the Divine Liturgy this morning."

"Smell it."

Father Matthias held the loaf to his nose for a few seconds. "This is odd. It's not the type of bread we normally use."

"Not normally use?" asked Ballack. "What type do you normally use?"

"It's slightly rounder and less dense. I figured this loaf got overbaked. Is this what killed him, when the bishop offered the bread to Dieter?" Father Matthias was obviously crushed at the prospect of administering a fatal Communion.

"It wasn't just the bread, sir," cut in Holbrook. "The wine smells like it's been messed with. If someone had put an almond-flavored liqueur in the wine, much like amaretto, it would smell like almond but would still be completely safe for Dieter. What you have here…" he raised the flask and illuminated it once more with his penlight, "is almost certainly ground almond dust, given the very slight smell and the sediment in the bottom of this flask."

"Are you saying," said a tremulous Father Matthias, "that someone has sabotaged our bread and wine to do this? Someone has besmirched our chapel, our worship, and has…has…*murdered* this young man?" His voice shook with rage.

Bosco moved in to calm him down. They needed Father Matthias to think as rationally as possible. "Sir, before we proceed, can you tell us one more thing? If Dieter was so severely allergic, how would he have missed this? Wouldn't he have noticed something wrong with the elements?"

"Not necessarily. He was very dependent on us for assistance. Dieter had a very bad sense of smell."

"Were only a few individuals privy to this information? Or was this common knowledge to anyone who knew him?"

"Closer to the former," the dean elicited in a sad whisper. "A few of us knew. But the bishop served Communion today. He would not have known. And it may not have immediately registered to those in the know when they took Communion."

Father Matthias said no more. He looked from Father Jonathan's coffin to Dieter's body on the floor. He shook his head and put his face in his hands. Bosco drew next to him and placed a comforting arm around his shoulders.

"Sir, we promise you. We will find whoever did this and bring his work to an end. Whatever it takes to do it, to connect what dots are there, we'll do our level best."

A blue Aveo sped past the chapel on its way to the married student homes. "Forget about that for now," said Tori. "Dana Witten just came back. Does anyone want to come along with me to break the news?"

"I'll go with you," said Father Matthias. "I am not sure how she will take this, but I must be there at her side. This will be devastating. I can't imagine how we will recover, but what she is going to endure is much worse."

He got that right, thought Ballack, watching Tori exit the nave with the dean. His gait seemed to have unsteadied, and the crushing load of the last twenty-four hours seemed to have sucked the life out of him. So great was the loss, so disconsolate was Father Matthias, thought Ballack, that he even forgot to pray over Dieter's body.

Dana Witten had placed the ground beef, ricotta cheese, and spaghetti sauce on the small counter top of her kitchen. She thought it odd that some people were milling around the front of Chalcedon Hall rather than remaining at the chapel. By her estimations, the Pannikhida for Father Jonathan should still be going on. She shook her head. Just another odd day in God's country. She was putting the beef and cheese in the refrigerator when she heard a knock on the front door. *Probably Mrs. Dawson, come to ask me to round up the laundry.*

"Hang on. Just throwing some stuff in the fridge. Be right there."

More knocking. Four stiff raps. Each harder than the other.

Dana lost her cool. "I said I'm putting stuff away!" She marched out of the kitchen toward the front window. "Can't you have just a touch of pa—?"

She froze. Father Matthias and Tori Vaughan were standing at the door with heartbroken faces. Her eyes drifted to Father Matthias' lowered hands, which shook slightly. They held a small cross on a chain.

It was Detective Vaughan who spoke. Her speech was low, quiet, and yet held a twinge of practiced, durable comfort. Even before she began, Dana knew what the words would be. The aroma of death had entered the house since the moment she saw them.

"Mrs. Witten, we're afraid we have some very sad news."

Thirty minutes later, Ballack was sitting in the guest room, poring over admissions files for the Class of 2012. He expected Tori to return at any moment and put her recording skills to use. Bosco had checked in with him before calling his Wentzville kidnapping case for an update. Ballack ignored the cellular conversation and tried to see any overlap between the letter to Father Jonathan and the pages of applications before him. No student provenance intersected with Father Jonathan's past locales, be it Kansas City or Birmingham. Ballack's head began to throb slightly. The third death added to his anxiety and the cascade of muddlement quickened the pain in his temples. The impending ice storm, bearing down on them from the southwest, would arrive in three hours and looked like a killer. Bosco excused himself and stepped outside and Ballack continued his labor for another ten minutes.

The door rattled and Tori walked in.

"So? How'd it go?" asked Ballack.

Tori walked over to the sofa, plopped down, and laid her head back. "You know how these things are. They never go well; they aren't designed to. Dana Witten is caught in the vice of several emotions and she doesn't know which one is legitimate. For a woman snagged in an empty, emotionless marriage, she sure is bawling a lot. And yet, for all her tears, she strangely looks resigned to his death."

Ballack looked at his laptop screen, trying to avoid Tori's glance. He knew all too well that inner conflict. The sadness of relational angst often intersected with the desertion of hope that it could work anyway. It was the primary reason why Michelle's suicide—though more recent—would never be the millstone of gloom that Christopher's death was. Resignation had a way of being the soul's eclipse.

"Is she still in her house?" he asked.

"No, we took her over to the chapel. She wanted to see him. Even she needed closure. She didn't stay long. I think she wants to be alone. I saw her heading into the trees, that whatever-it-is, the grotto."

Ballack turned on his chair's power and moved toward the door.

"Where're you going?" Tori pleaded.

"Just for a minute," Ballack said over his shoulder. "I won't be long."

He burst out the door and finessed his way down the ramp through the stiffening wind. There was no trouble finding Dana once he entered the grotto. She was sitting on the front bench, facing the cross, hands clasped right over left. She was still in the clothes from their walk earlier in the day. Ballack crept closer, not wanting to disturb the thick calm of her fresh bereavement. Yet he felt compelled to be there, even if he could not exactly explain why his presence felt appropriate.

"It shouldn't have ended like this," said a voice. Dana's.

Ballack hesitated, unsure if he should respond. Finally, Dana turned to her right and looked at him. "It shouldn't have."

"I'm sorry."

Dana shook her head. "I've lost my husband. It's hitting me that I'm twenty-six and a widow. He wasn't a good man, Dieter—he acted selfishly and his ambition for success never extended far beyond his own orbit. But this was my battle. If our marriage was to be over, this shouldn't have been the way."

She gently placed her face in her hands. She sniffed loudly. It was apparent to Ballack that the dam was about to burst. He tried to deflect it.

"Did Father Matthias allow you to see him?" he asked, knowing the answer.

She nodded.

"Did he explain the situation?"

Silence. Then a nod, more slowly.

"I'm sorry," Ballack said, now fighting back tears himself.

Dana could not control herself any longer, and her gray eyes spilled forth in all their vigor, fomenting against this cataclysm of loss. "Why? Why? Oh God, what are you doing? Murder? This is never going to end!!! I can't take this! I can't take this! I..."

And she pitched forward, practically landing in his lap. Her head convulsed spasmodically, sucking in the cold winter air as if the draughts could provide defense against the abyss of pain. Ballack wavered, unsure of how to react. He was a policeman, a detective, there to protect and analyze, to see the case to the bitter end. To offer the touch of peace to this beautiful young lady seemed to splash over the reservoir of acceptability. Yet he could not turn away. Even if he had no faith to offer, surely he could touch her heart with some comfort. He slowly reached down and placed his right hand on her head. As if on instinct, she pulled her hands from her face and grasped his fingers, wetting his nails with her tears. Before he knew it, his left hand had reached down to embrace her. And her tears were not the only ones that flowed.

Ballack returned to the guest room, already exhausted from the morning's events and shaken from his pastoral moments with Dana Witten. As such, he was entirely unprepared for the sight of Nicholas Panangiotis sitting at the table across from Tori. Evidently they were the only ones in the room. Bosco was nowhere to be seen. Ballack put his palms up as if to ask where the lieutenant had gone.

"Scotty had to run to the other case. Lineup identification was a big disappointment and so they are back to the beginning," said Tori. "He said call the minute we have anything big."

"Tell him not to hold his breath," replied Ballack. Turning to the Greek firebrand seated across from his partner, he asked, "What brings you here, Nicholas?"

Tori looked at the student and nodded. Nicholas cleared his throat.

"I want you to know, first of all, that although I'm not the easiest person to deal with, I do think you've done a great job with everything that's gone down here. I'm scared just like anyone else and wouldn't know how to react. I know I acted like a total ass during the fingerprinting as well, and I'd like to apologize for that."

Ballack looked hard at him, wondering where this was going. "While we appreciate your humility, it seems you've come to do more than apologize."

Nicholas looked down, then back up at the detectives. "Two weeks ago, Stephen Kale and I were in trouble for an inappropriate action during Vespers when Reverend Zednik was here. Father Timothy disciplined us by barring us from Holy Communion for the next two Sundays. I felt the punishment was strict, but, out of respect for Father Timothy, I decided not to make trouble. That night I actually decided to go over to Marcus Curry's room in Irenaus and confront him about his part in the Vespers disturbance."

"Refresh my memory. Marcus is…?" asked Tori.

"The one black student here at St. Basil's. I was still rather steamed because he wasn't punished like I was. I felt he should know that. In fact, I was so overloaded with rage, I was set to fight him. It wouldn't be the first time. We had been suspended from classes for a day for a rumble after he accused me of cheating on a mid-term exam. It wasn't true, but I overreacted. He got a black eye, and I cracked my knuckle."

"Mr. Panangiotis," said Ballack impatiently, "Exactly what does this have to do with what we are presently dealing with, might I ask?"

"I'm sorry. I'm leading into that. Along the way, I had a change of heart, and so when I got to Marcus' room, we ended up talking for two hours and sort of made peace. We'll never be friends, but we do need to find a way to co-exist. We called Father Timothy in to speak with us and he suggested that as part of my penance and a display of goodwill that we put some of our reconciliation into practice. Long and short of it is, one of those 'practice events' was preparing Communion together with faculty oversight."

"For chapel services?"

"Specifically for Divine Liturgy. The thing is, we were also asked to prepare the bread and wine for this morning's service."

"The one for Father Jonathan?"

"Right. Father Andrew and Father Timothy were with us last night as we placed the bread and the wine on the altar and laid out the adornments. We were about to pray over the elements when Stephen Kale walked in. He said he'd been looking for Father Matthias, so we directed him to Gregory House. The bishop and Father Matthias, of course, were involved in the preparation of Father Jonathan's body. Stephen had taken a long, hard look at where we were putting the bread and wine."

Ballack interjected. "The bread you placed on the altar. What did it look like? Be specific as possible."

Nicholas thought hard. "Round. Golden-brown. Puffy. You know those big yeast rolls like they have at Ryan's or Home Town Buffet? Like those, only about eight inches in diameter and three inches thick."

"You said golden brown and puffy?" asked Tori.

"Yes."

"You're sure?"

"Absolutely certain. Why?"

Ballack decided to risk it and show a card off the deck. "All we can tell you is the bread on the altar for the service today is not the one you just described. A naked eye view is enough to tell us that."

"Are you saying someone switched the bread?"

Ballack raised his eyebrows, remaining silent.

Nicholas continued, "That has been vexing me all morning. I have been feeling guilty and wondering if we had provided something in either the bread or wine that might have caused Dieter's reaction and death. I just talked with Marcus about it. He said we needed to mention to you both that we were the ones preparing the elements last night. But he's scared to leave his room. He's downright terrified! But I swear to you, I remember what loaf we placed on the altar and that we poured the wine. Father Timothy can verify that. And he locked the church behind us."

"Do either of you have a key?" asked Tori.

"No, the only ones who have keys to the church are those in need of leading worship or cleaning and repairing the nave, narthex, or bathrooms."

"Which means that would include the priests, Dieter, the Dawsons...who else?"

Ballack thought hard. "Would it also include Jason Hart as junior chaplain?"

"No," said Nicholas. "The junior chaplain is not given a key. He can only involve himself in the church environment under the oversight of a priest."

"Which means," said Ballack, "barring individuals hocking the keys and making copies, the only others would be Lainie Kale and Dana Witten."

"So why was Stephen there?" asked Tori.

"I guess that's our role to find out," said Ballack. Turning to Nicholas, "Thank you for coming by. You've helped to confirm a few things."

Nicholas nodded, put on his coat, and walked out. Ballack turned to Tori. "What say you? Looks like we have a bread switcheroo."

"Yeah, and given what Evan said about the wine, we're looking at someone breaking in and wrecking that, too. Nicholas looked completely sincere, too. He's scared."

"What about the odds that we're chasing down someone who made a copy of the church key? Can we discount that?"

"That's a question I usually ask, Cam. And your normal response would be…"

"That we play the hand we're dealt and hit the most likely circle of suspects first. Add Stephen Kale to that because he walked in on them and knew they were prepping Communion."

"You're kidding!" Tori exclaimed. "Are you bringing him back in the lineup? You practically eliminated him last night!"

"I didn't eliminate him. I downgraded him from a Category 5 hurricane to a tropical depression."

"Okay, okay!" Tori was growing exasperated. "Back to the files to check for overlap. Let's hustle. It's three o'clock. I like the idea of making progress while there's still light outside."

The next three hours proved tedious. One admission file followed another with nothing of note. Tori read through the applications and emergency forms for Stephen Kale, Jason Hart, Nicholas Panangiotis, Marcus Curry, and David Orlinksy. Cross-checking all the data with the vast array of documents and files in Father Jonathan's computer took much patience, and Ballack felt any degree of meticulousness trickling away. He was chafing at the prospect of spending more time staring at a MacBook. Tekel was nowhere in sight.

"Okay, nothing in these files suggests that any of these men knew Father Jonathan before coming here. We're about to hit the rest of the third-year class. Before we do, is there any other page here we're missing? Is there anything…" he gestured for Tori to look at the laptop, "I'm missing here?"

"You've gone bug-eyes on this thing for two days, partner," she replied. "If nothing's on there, we're swamped." She went to look at the next application when a single light-blue card fell from between two stapled papers.

"What the heck?" she said, picking it up and looking closely. Ballack got into Father Jonathan's email to search for anything he might have neglected.

"Hmm. This could be nothing, but it should have been with Stephen Kale's application and forms. It's a change-of-information card with his name. Only thing on there is a request to add a secondary emergency contact. Meg McNerney."

"Okay, why am I listening to this?" asked Ballack.

"The request wasn't filled out by Stephen. Unless he developed some very legible, effeminate loops and whirls in his cursive writing." She handed him the card.

Ballack looked at the card. "That is weird." He looked at the information. "No address, city, or state. Just a phone number. Area code 270."

"Never heard of it."

"But it will take just a second to locate it." Ballack logged onto the Internet and, in a matter of a few keystrokes, had his answer. "Covers the west-central counties of Kentucky. It originally split off the 502 back in April 1999."

"Well, what good is a Kentucky number? It carries no association with Father Jonathan or where he's been before."

"Hang on, Tor, hang on," Ballack said as he tried to jumpstart his memory. There was something remotely familiar about all this. He shut his eyes, rotating through each of the residents at St. Basil's. It took only a few seconds, and suddenly he opened his eyes. "Let's make the call."

"Okay, sport," said Tori. "I'd like a reason why you think this is so special we have to drop everything and ring someone we've never heard of."

"I'll give you two. Date and place."

"What?!"

"Let's take the place first. I have no idea if it's the exact location, but it's worth a shot. The 270 area code covers Bowling Green, Elizabethtown, and…" He paused for effect. "Owensboro."

"Meaning?"

"Do you remember our conversation with Lainie Kale in the laundry room on Friday? She said her mom worked in the admissions office at Brescia University…in Owensboro, Kentucky!"

Tori's eyes widened slightly.

"Now," said Ballack. "Date. Do you remember when Lainie said she started working with Jane Porter in the business office?"

"I remember the month was October."

"Yeah, of 2008. Take a look at this page. Do you notice when this secondary contact was added?"

Tori looked. "November 3, 2008."

Ballack looked straight ahead. Tori knew him well enough to recognize he was starting to write a screenplay on his presuppositions.

"Okay, Cameron," she said. "I realize this could be something. But we don't know if it's Owensboro, and the date of the contact info change could be a coincidence. How does this connect with Stephen, anyway?"

"Who said we're thinking about Stephen? I'm talking about Lainie."

"Why?"

"Remember how I said Lainie was in every nook and cranny of life at this campus? What if there was a reason for that?"

"Cam, where are you going with this? Besides, if you look at Stephen's application, he lists Lainie as his wife, and there's a slot for her maiden name. It's Wilkins, not McNerney."

"Who said Wilkins has to be her mom's name? She practically told us she came from a dysfunctional home. Her mom could have any name other than Wilkins."

"How about if we look up the number online or look up the name first to confirm the number?"

"Care to make this interesting?"

"You mean bet on the outcome?"

"I say it's Owensboro. This smells like Lainie Kale. You doubt me. Fifty bucks says I'm right. Tread carefully. Stephen couldn't take me last night."

"Deal," Tori said as she took the laptop and went to the White Pages website.

Two minutes later, Ballack was laughing uncontrollably as he dialed Meg McNerney's number on speakerphone. "No worries, Tori," he chuckled. "Just get me tickets to for the Cardinals' home opener, and we can call it even."

Stephen Kale was sharpening his hunting knife. It was one of his guilty pleasures. He had fully intended to go hunting tomorrow, but the initial sheets of snow and freezing rain for the past two hours had pushed that out of his mind. There was still enough to be done around the house.

He heard a knock at the front door of Antioch House. Looking from down the hall, he saw the towering form of Father Timothy. Discreetly, Stephen tossed the knife onto his bed and motioned for the priest to come in.

"By the way, make sure you get wheelchair-accessible seating for the game," Ballack guffawed as he waited for his call to be answered somewhere near the banks of the Ohio River.

"Oh, shut up," Tori said half-sullenly. In truth, she was glad. This could be the break they needed.

A husky female voice answered. "Hello?"

"Hello, is this Meg McNerney?"

"It is. May I ask who is calling?"

"This is Cameron Ballack. I am a police detective in St. Charles County, just west of St. Louis, Missouri. We are in the midst of a criminal investigation at St. Basil's Seminary and your number is one of the many before us as we are casing out some details."

"May I ask how you got this number?"

Ballack grinned. "Miss McNerney, during our compiling of evidence, we saw that you are a secondary contact for one of the members of the seminary community at St. Basil's. Are you aware of that?"

"I am most certainly not! What sort of game are you trying to pull?"

"I'm sorry. I didn't mean to alarm you. But the contact information sheet doesn't lie. Are you certain you aren't aware?"

"If you're so confident you're right, who is the person's name I supposedly know?"

Ballack had enough, so he chose to cut to the chase. "Stephen Kale."

Complete silence.

"Miss McNerney?" he asked.

"I'm here, I'm here. I'm so sorry. Did you say Stephen Kale? Susan's Stephen?"

"Susan? Who's Susan?"

"Susan Sexton. My roommate. We work at Brescia University in town."

Brescia, thought Ballack. *We're getting warmer.*

"Your roommate? Both of you at Brescia?"

"Yes. I work in Alumni Relations. She's an admissions counselor and she organizes all the tours for prospective students."

Admissions. Bingo. Closing in.

"I'm sorry," continued the woman, "what does this have to do with me or Susan?"

"I think it appears that whomever named you as Stephen's contact had it in mind to be connected to Susan instead. Let me ask this. When you said 'Susan's Stephen', what did you mean?"

"That's his mother-in-law, right? Is this what this is about? He's got his mother-in-law as his secondary contact?"

"You're listed as the contact. But I'm sure that's the case, that she's the real contact."

"Then you said this has to do with an investigation?"

"It does. We're just going through some…" Ballack then heard some static, before hearing a popping sound. Wondering if she had dropped the phone, he asked, "Miss McNerney? Are you there?"

After a few nervous seconds, she was back on. "Yes, sorry. It's just that Susan pulled up in the driveway. Home from work. Would you like to speak with her?"

"Would I ever," said Ballack, as the wind roared outside and the ice slammed down from the sky.

The woman who picked up the other end of the line sounded as lilting and feminine as her roommate was sturdy. She took no time identifying herself as Susan Sexton. "You mentioned that this was part of an investigation at a place called St. Basil's. What does this have to do with me?"

Ballack decided this would not be the time to drop the "M" word. There was no telling what Susan Sexton knew and what she didn't. "Everyone walking around on two legs is breathing just fine," he said, swallowing on the half-truth. "I understand that you are Stephen Kale's mother-in-law. Lainie Kale's mother?"

"Yes, although it's taken awhile for Lainie to admit that. We're not exactly close. Again, what is this all about?"

"Is there any reason why this number would happen to be their secondary emergency contact?"

"I have no idea why. Has this been the case for some time?"

"Since November of 2008."

The words hung in the air, as if choked in the phone line. "November 2008. The only reason I can think of is to be able to contact me regarding their account."

"Account?"

"Yes. I wasn't in on a whole lot of Lainie's college life. We didn't hit a thaw in our relationship until she and Stephen moved to St. Louis for graduate school. They were able to get in only by snagging a boatload of scholarship money. They've lived on the bare minimum ever since they were married. They applied for food stamps and, of course, that comes with income restrictions. The state will watch you like a hawk. Anyhow, around November 2008…um, I…you're not going to report me are you? Please, before I go on, could you assure me that nothing I say will get reported to the state?"

Ballack wasted no time. "Ma'am, I'm a detective conducting an investigation that—trust me—doesn't have to do with shifting of money to beat the government's watchful eye. And besides, as a disabled person, I know the difficulties involved in getting medical care and other resources with limited financial means to procure them. But given what you've said so far, I think you'd better tell me the rest of the story. I am involved in a criminal inquiry here and I don't want anyone being able to trace obstruction of justice back to you. It's less involved than me getting a warrant to check the details anyway."

"So you won't tell?" She had bought Ballack's bluff—hook, line, and sinker.

"I never promise one hundred percent, but if it has no bearing on my investigation, you have nothing to fear."

"Thank you for your honesty. Well, in November 2008, I got a call—out of the blue, mind you—from Lainie. She said she had come into a steady job, but the income would disqualify them from Medicaid if discovered. She asked if we could have some sort of agreement to help them. It was clear that a less frosty relationship between her and I was in the offing. At that point, I knew it was emotional blackmail, but I hoped it could grow into something better than that."

"What was the deal?"

"We were to open a bank account in my name. Lainie would send the funds to me every month, and I would deposit them. They would have access to the funds because they were signed onto the account as secondary account holders. Only my name appeared on the checks and debit card. Practically untraceable. That way, they'd be a little more financially independent during grad school."

"So there is enough to disqualify them from food stamps?"

Susan Sexton was silent.

Tori was silent, too. Ballack turned her direction, covered the speakerphone, and whispered to her, "And there's the stash that Zednik couldn't find." His eyes narrowed, sensing the kill. He decided to circle around for a different look.

"Why were they in graduate school, Mrs. Sexton?"

"Well, if you've met them, you would have discovered that. Stephen's obviously in journalism school and Lainie is pursuing a master's in economics. At St. Louis University. That's why they're in need of scholarships. I don't know what this has to do with a place called St. Basil's."

The deception runs deep, thought Ballack. *She's reunited with nothing but lies.*

"Mrs. Sexton, when did you and Lainie start having issues?"

"Well, in a sense, we've had a checkered relationship most of our lives. Definitely since the divorce. My husband and I split when Lainie was thirteen, and it was a major earthquake in our lives. Lainie never forgave me; it was my doing, and I guess she had every right to be angry."

"She seemed to be angrier with her father when we spoke with her. She said he didn't want to speak with her, and he'd probably not live much longer."

"What?" Susan exclaimed. "How would she know? She's only seen her father once!"

Ballack shook his head, genuinely confused. "Excuse me? I thought you said you and your husband divorced a while back."

"Yes, my husband and I. But Jake wasn't Lainie's father. She actually liked Jake and never forgave me for the divorce. Her rage is justified, though. I cheated on him. It was stupid and sad."

"Then what's this about her father being on the verge of death?"

"Again, Jake's not her father. He's still alive and well. He's a shipping accountant in Mobile and we keep in touch. There's no way he's about to die."

Ballack felt his headache returning. He looked at the clock. Seven p.m. "Then who is Lainie's father? I'm confused."

He felt the guilt surge on the other end of the line. Finally, she said, "I cheated on Jake with Lainie's biological father."

"Excuse me?" said both Ballack and Tori at the same time.

If Susan was shocked by the voice of Ballack's partner, she went on undaunted. "We were caught in bed. It was bad enough that Jake saw us, but Lainie was with him. It was dreadful. It had been going on for some time. We were bound to get caught."

What in the blue devil...thought Ballack. The puzzle had come together at last. "And you said this was Lainie's father?"

"Yes," Susan sniffed, clearly weeping on the other end. "After the affair, I came clean and told her that she was the result of a relationship I had with her father years before. At the time of that relationship, I was going through some issues with my parent's divorce, and he was a counselor I had gone to. He also happened to be a priest."

The detectives exchanged glances.

"During our sessions we became more intimate. We ended up having sex, several times a month. Lainie was the result of it. Johnny never told his church. I never told Lainie until after Jake and I split. It devastated her. It was one thing to know that Jake wasn't her real dad, but another to understand her biological dad had caused the rupture."

Indeed it must have, thought Ballack.

"Lainie and I had a deteriorating bond throughout high school. She couldn't wait to get out and go to college. I, in turn, needed to find another place to put my guilt behind me, so I've been here the past six years. In spite of it all, I let Lainie know where I was in case things took a positive turn, because I haven't seen her since she left Birmingham."

"Uh-huh," said Ballack, a triumphant smile blazing across his face. "Birmingham, huh?"

"Yes. We lived there before Lainie went off to Millsaps."

"Birmingham, Alabama."

"Um, yes."

"Mrs. Sexton, you said the name of Lainie's father was John."

"Yes, that was his name."

Ballack looked at Tori. Neither could believe that her accidental find of that card had unlatched this door.

"Mrs. Sexton, listen to me carefully and above all, don't lie to me. I know that's not J-O-H-N, as in the Apostle John."

Their key to the lock, standing two hundred miles away and leaning on the counter in a recently remodeled kitchen, hesitated, wondering how this would culminate.

"It's like the actor, Jon Voight. J-O-N. Correct?"

Again the aggrieved pause.

Ballack moved in for the kill. "Short for Jonathan."

They heard a gasp.

"Father Jonathan Erhart," declared Ballack.

Nothing. Then a firm *click.*

"I don't think it will ever be the same, sir. I can't fathom a situation in which I would end up going in that direction."

Stephen Kale paused, then looked directly at Father Timothy before continuing. "I'm sorry."

Father Timothy shook his head vigorously. "My son, you have nothing to be sorry for. Why would you even think of apologizing for going in the direction you knew God wanted you to go? So you're not to be a priest! There are other paths, Stephen. Your studies here can enrich your life no matter what field you enter!"

"So you're not disappointed?"

"Disappointed? No! I'd be disappointed if you continued to pursue the priesthood for the wrong reasons. The ministry is not meant to be a time of treading water to see if life shakes out for you under this canopy. Now, I'd suggest you remain and get your degree. You've sacrificed too much not to. Dieter's death is a heavy blow. It's natural you'd have second thoughts. But not finishing your degree would not honor your friend. I think Dieter would agree if he were alive."

"I think so, too, Father Timothy," Stephen replied. "I've underestimated you, sir. I thought for sure you'd be upset. Instead, you've given me one of the kindest re-directions I could've asked for."

Father Timothy raised his eyebrows and spread his hands out in a humorous display of mock triumph. "I baffle expectations. This is what I do."

Their talk was coming to a proper and happy end, but they could hardly have guessed what was coming. At that moment, Tori

Vaughan had sprinted through the ice and practically slid across the front deck, slamming into the door.

Stephen was up in a flash. "Officer Vaughan, come in, come in. Gosh, you gave us a fright! Are you okay?"

Tori caught her breath, hoping her next question wouldn't arouse total suspicion. "I'm sorry to interrupt whatever deep thoughts you both were having. I was just wondering, Stephen, if you could tell me where your wife is."

"Lainie? Why?"

Tori grasped for a decent half-fib, but nothing specific was coming to mind. She'd have to throw out the first thing that popped into her head. "I just need to ask her something about a line item in the budget. We're not able to get hold of Jane Porter on the phone. Officer Ballack was going in search of Father Matthias in Chalcedon Hall to ask him the same question. Whoever got the answer first, wins."

"Well, sorry she's not here," said Stephen. "I'm sure you just missed her. I think she was heading over to Gregory and Irenaus to round up what they would need for linens tomorrow."

"Thanks," said Tori, running right back into the rain without giving Stephen the chance to ask why Lainie was needed. She was trotting across campus when she saw the light coming from their guest room. The seminary golf cart sat next to the ramp. *That's strange*, she said to herself, *I'm sure we had turned those off and locked the doors. What's going on?*

She dashed onward toward Chrysostom Alumni House, wondering if she was barking mad or if someone was in the room. So quickly did she skid all the way there that, in her nerve-racked state, she forgot to keep her promise: to wait for Ballack outside Chalcedon Hall.

She unlatched the door and immediately saw Lainie Kale.

"Hi, Officer Vaughan," she said cheerily. "Did you nearly break your neck coming up that ramp like I did? Looks like the pellets haven't had enough time to melt the ice, huh?" She turned toward the dresser near Ballack's bed, clean folded sheets in hand.

Tori, the trepidation within her churning into overdrive, took off her jacket. Perhaps giving the impression she was settling in for the night wouldn't give anything away. She laid the jacket on the kitchen table, forgetting she had left her gun within the breast pocket.

Lainie remained crouched at the dresser, arranging the flat sheets at the end of one drawer and the fitted sheets at the other end. Tori quietly moved three feet behind her.

"Mrs. Kale," she said, a bit roughly, "We'd like you to stay. Once my partner gets here we need to ask you a couple of questions."

No response. She shifted the pile of flat sheets a quarter turn.

"Mrs. Kale!" The words were considerably sharp.

Lainie turned, remaining in her squatted stance. "I'm sorry, Officer. I heard you. That's no problem." She looked back toward the picture window and pointed. "Could you, uh, hand me those towels on the sofa for the bathroom?"

Tori turned and wondered if there was some mistake. There were no towels that she could see. "Are you sure? There's nothing…"

She never completed that thought. A sharp pain followed the massive thud to the back of her skull. She was unconscious before she hit the ground. Quickly, Lainie Kale extinguished the lights in the room and replaced Ballack's heavy battery recharger, plugging it into the wall from which she had removed it seconds ago. She pulled the shades. In pantherine fashion, she took Tori's insensible form by the wrists, pulling her across the floor and outside to the golf cart.

Ballack scooted through the expansive calignosity that was the refectory. He called out for Father Matthias down both hallways. He had noticed from the outside that the dean's office was unlit. It looked to be a dead end, so Ballack headed back outside. Before he did, he dialed Scotty Bosco's cell phone, leaving a message that they intended to arrest the murderer in a matter of minutes.

Thankfully, the ice had quit pelting the countryside, but the temperature still had to be in the teens. Yet that wasn't the only challenge facing Ballack. Tori was nowhere to be found. He pushed the joystick forward and headed toward the Kale residence. His eyes swept through the scene before him. Stephen and Father Timothy. No one else.

So Tori was likely done here. *Where could she have gone?* He decided to return to the guesthouse and wait for her there. Seeing the lights were out, that didn't seem too likely, but he desperately needed to limit his exposure to this weather. Not to mention his wheelchair was finding these pathways to be treacherous footing indeed. He jacked his speed control to the highest level and rocketed back to Chrysostom.

There was some difficulty getting up the ramp, but he was able to reach the access button and open the door. He had a more brutal go of it lifting his arm to turn on the lights. When he did, he immediately knew something wasn't kosher.

Her jacket on the table.

Yet she was nowhere.

Bathroom door open. Not there.

"Tori?" he called up to her loft. No response. The stillness of the room unnerved him. He wheeled into the living area when he noticed the bottom dresser drawer was slightly open. Even with his consternation alarm going off, his obsessive-compulsive streak was still intact. *Why can't people leave stuff closed?* He rolled his eyes and approached the dresser, nudging it shut with his footplate when he saw it.

On the carpet.

Near the foot of the bed.

Fresh blood.

And that scene elicited a spontaneous entreaty that even Ballack's agnosticism couldn't hinder.

"Dear God, please. Not Tori. Please!"

He spun around, making for the door. Pulling out his cell phone, he dialed Scotty Bosco. It went to voice mail. Ballack stifled a curse and waited for the beep.

"Scotty! It's Ballack! We've fingered Lainie Kale, but she just might have done something to Tori and I need to find her before it's too late! Get down here! Get your ass down here! Now!"

Ballack's first thought was that he was insane for going out into the swirling wind that was bringing a fresh supply of winter mix. But concern for his partner overwhelmed any personal danger to his health. He shot down the ramp and turned left, heading south toward Irenaus House. Perhaps Father Matthias was there and could assist.

The wind kicked up again, stinging his eyes. The fire in his lungs stoked to biblical proportions; nonetheless, he stumbled on toward Irenaus. *Please, Father Matthias. Anyone. Be there.* He was nearly to the dormitory when he realized there was no way in. No ramp. No access. And he had forgotten Father Matthias' extension off the list in his room. Not to mention, with the wind and throttling sleet, there was no way Ballack could be heard, no matter how much volume his chair horn would make.

Ballack sat there, the despair going from a waterfall to an avalanche. He was out of options. And if he happened to find Lainie Kale, what then? How was he supposed to make an arrest? He was the one detective on the force who couldn't fire a gun. With his muscle weakness, the kick would be devastating. He knew that wasn't an option.

Wait a second, he thought. *Maybe the lack of choice is my one choice.*

He knew he couldn't use a gun.

But Lainie Kale didn't. And that could buy him, and Tori, a chance.

And he wouldn't have long to wait. Tekel was coming.

In the distance, chugging up the lane between the chapel and

St. Jude's Glade, came a golf cart. Even at that distance, he could make out the raven black hair, the determined look, and the furtive demeanor. Unwilling to wait on a messiah to bolster his chances, Ballack gunned his wheelchair down the path, heading directly toward the cart. The two vehicles were within twenty feet of each other when the cart pulled up and screeched to a halt, the headlights switching off.

Instinctively, Ballack reached for the only tool that would give him any prospects. His only hope was that she wouldn't notice it in the dark. Deftly, he grabbed his cell phone, inauspiciously clicking the volume off, and pointed it directly at the wide-eyed figure of Lainie Kale.

"Get out of the cart, Lainie!" he barked, a bitter, vile acerbity to his words. "Get out with your hands up! Get out! Now!"

And Lainie Kale, in a smooth and controlled motion, slid out of the front seat, stood by the cart, and glared at Ballack.

"So," she scoffed. "How did you know?"

Seven minutes before, Scotty Bosco ran his fingers through his hair, impatiently waiting for the space cadet behind the counter to put his order together. The McDonald's at Highway K and Crusher Drive in O'Fallon was normally more efficient than this. Two McDoubles, a small order of fries, and an iced tea shouldn't take long, but this person was showing all the incompetence of a UN military operation.

His cell phone buzzed against his waist. This was the second time, and he figured this should at least be a working meal. He fished out his phone and looked at the caller ID, having just missed the call. His spirits lifted. Perhaps there was a break. He connected to his voicemail. He smiled at the first message. Then the second one began.

The blond sophomore placed the tray on the counter. "Order three sixty-two? Order three sixty-two?"

Order three sixty-two was nowhere to be found. He had just bolted out the door, making a dash for a maroon Toyota Tundra in the parking lot. His heart thumping against his chest, he shot out toward the highway as fast as he could. He just hoped he could get to St. Basil's in time. On the icy roads, that was no guarantee.

"Where's Tori?" asked Ballack.

"What do you mean?" smirked Lainie. "I haven't seen her. Isn't that your job to keep tabs on your partner?" She began to lower her hands.

"Keep them up!" Ballack barked. He'd learned enough in his short time on the force to know when a culprit was lying. "I asked you where she is." The weariness in his debilitated arms began to mount. *How long can I keep this up?*

"And I asked you, how did you know?"

Ballack stared at her, matching hate for hate. He spoke slowly and distinctly, "If you leave a foul enough stench, eventually we'll find where the landfill is."

She spat on the ground, the icy mix now at a drizzle. "I'd like to know. You're arresting me, you're pointing a gun at me. So why can't I know?"

"Meg McNerney. The secondary contact on the blue form. Called her, got your mom. Her little secret."

Lainie's eyes blazed in the darkness. "Figures she'd spill that. The dirty little tramp."

Ballack kept the phone pointed level, but his strength was beginning to drain. "So the letter to Father Jonathan. Also from you."

Lainie nodded, smiling fiercely. "You recognize my work. The fusion of various lines from fiction novels over the years, plus a biblical judgment. I thought it was supremely appropriate."

"I thought it was sickening."

"You?! What in God's name would you know about it? I went through my teenage years knowing my mom's husband wasn't my real dad. From the time I was in diapers, she said my father had died in a car wreck. I swallowed the lie! Imagine my surprise when Jake brings me home years later to find my mom in bed with that liar! To see your parents break apart like that? To hear that your whole life had been a lie? You're the one who is sickening! You have no idea! And then he turns tail and runs out here, away from me. With no thought of accepting his responsibilities!"

"I think maybe being censured had been bad enough," said Ballack. "Whether you agree with that or not is up to you. But my concern is that you played God to hunt him down."

She stared at the phone. Ballack wondered how much longer he could continue this charade. His arms burned. "Didn't you?" he screamed.

When she didn't respond, he practically thundered as loud as his vocal cords would allow. "Lainie Kale! Whether you realize it or not, this is your confession booth! So if you don't want what my gun's itching to do, you'd better start telling me your sins!"

Lainie, looking scarily triumphant now, tossed her head back in pride. "I tracked him from the moment Jake left us. If I didn't have a man in the house, then the one who caused that rupture wasn't going to survive his evil, by God! I had my ways. The Internet is such an easy road map if you know what you're looking for. I met Stephen around the same time I discovered Father Jonathan had come here. I know that Stephen told you about his conversion to Orthodoxy. That was the step I needed to bridge the gap, to get Father Jonathan back for what he did."

"What?" growled Ballack, squinting through the drizzle. "You worked that whole situation to convince your husband to go to seminary?"

Lainie raised her eyebrows. Ballack had to admit she looked pretty in an aggressive Southerner type of way. Thankfully, he never considered that his preference.

"Let me get this straight," he continued, his shoulders throbbing with pain. "You manipulated your husband into coming here, convincing him that he had some sort of potential to serve God and others, all so you could position yourself against your father?"

"Don't call him that!" shouted Lainie. "He was a monster who destroyed my life!"

"And the money?" said Ballack. "Let me guess. You were so driven to hate a school that would take on Father Jonathan as a teacher that you decided the best revenge was to rob the school bit by bit. There never was any need for Medicaid. You were on scholarship, but not to the extent you let on. We saw everything in Stephen's student file. The whole thing was a smoke screen! A complete and utter hoax! And you lied to your mother about graduate school. She had no idea you and Stephen were here!"

"So you wired the diagram perfectly, huh? Isn't that sweet? Poor Detective Ballack! A gimp that can't walk to save his life but can run right through the maze of evidence and cinch the present with a beautifully colored bow. Yes, the money. It was nothing compared to the dignity and innocence Father Jonathan took from me. Zednik only legitimized his pathetic existence by restoring that hustler to ministry! That makes him as bad as Father Jonathan."

"And all you needed was a reason to knock him off, too?"

"No, but Zednik sure gave me one. Getting the seminary's username and password was going to lead him down the path to discovery. I couldn't take that chance. He had to go. I'm sure you can guess how."

"Explains the missing pillow. You must have smothered him, he bled from the nose, and so you had to get rid of the evidence."

"Yes, which only was an appetizer to my real intent. Saturday. The anniversary of when Jonathan was caught in bed with my mother. Justice. Full circle."

"Justice? You call sending a spineless, anonymous letter justice? You call lying in wait for an older man justice? Smashing someone with a softball bat and choking the life out of him with panty hose? You call that justice?" Ballack's arms screamed for mercy.

"Justice? Yes, detective. When you consider it was done with the same black stockings that belonged to my mother, it's called justice."

The icy tone with which she had delivered those words sent a brutal chill through Ballack's bloodstream. "Even if that meant Father Timothy was implicated because of that text message? You were the one who snatched his cell phone during the movie. You sent the message to Father Jonathan and then put it back in the TV room so that Father Timothy would think he'd just left it there. You signed it 'TB' to throw suspicion in his direction!"

"You wouldn't understand!"

"Even if it meant your husband was accused of Father Jonathan's murder?"

Lainie spat again. "Talk about spineless. Stephen didn't want to be here. Hardly the epitome of manhood."

"Which is why," responded Ballack, putting the pieces together with a final educated guess, "you were having an affair with Dieter Witten."

"How did you know that?!"

"I didn't. That seemed to be the only connection between the first two deaths and his. But allow me to connect everything. You two were secretly together. The night of the murder, he sees you heading toward the library. He tells Tori and I enough of the truth to get it off his conscience, yet not enough to implicate you. He meets with you to inform you of what he saw. He gives you an ultimatum, maybe not to turn yourself in. He might still believe somewhat in your innocence. But he at least wants you to say something to us. You get pissed off and realize that to get out of this, you need to knock him off. Knowing he has an almond allergy, you spike the bread and wine with enough stuff to implode Busch Stadium. And so we have our third murder."

"He never gave me an ultimatum. He met me in the shed and told me he had seen me out the previous night, going toward the library. He never accused me of anything, but I could read him. He was suspicious. He'd put the pieces together like you did. So I couldn't take any chances."

"Which is why you switched the bread and doctored the wine. You sent Stephen on a scouting mission, when he was none the wiser, to see if there were people in the chapel preparing for Communion. And now Dana's a widow because you killed her husband."

"He told me he didn't need me anymore! Last week we met at the shed, the place where we always met in the past, and then he told me he needed to end it! That he needed to have a respectable image and going off to Chicago would change things anyway. That he needed to give Dana the impression that he was a faithful priest. What a load! She's pathetic. Probably couldn't even find her way around the marriage if she had a manual."

That comment nearly blew all Ballack's circuits. The adrenaline surged into his tired arms, and he pointed the cell phone at her. *Where's Scotty?* He suddenly wished the phone was really a gun and the Miranda rights were a figment of his imagination.

"Pathetic?" he roared. "You're pathetic. You whine and moan about an affair ruining your family life, and you go engage in one yourself! You've systematically poisoned this place! You've defiled, disfigured, and destroyed the fabric of a community. And that makes you a monster! Not Father Jonathan. Not Reverend Zednik. Nobody else! You!"

His words were delivered with such a vehemence, with such toxicity, that they surprised even him. Even Lainie seemed to think he was capable of shooting her between the eyes, so her raised arms stiffened. *I need to act quickly*, he thought. *I need to make sure Scotty or Tori can get here soon.*

He pointed the phone at her leg, threateningly. "So get face down on the ground and cover the back of your head with your hands." He pointed again. "Now."

He regretted the words as soon as they were out of his mouth. Emotion had overcome him, and he had ordered her to get into position to get cuffed although he couldn't execute that operation. But none of that mattered, for in that moment, his hand vibrated. The freezing mist had slowed drastically, and through the night air Ballack could see an equally icy, cruel smile form on Lainie's lips. He kept his eyes on her, but he sensed something had gone horribly wrong.

"I thought you were wondering about your partner," she sneered. "You know, the one bound and gagged and likely at the bottom of the lake?"

Liar, thought Ballack. *No way you could have pulled it off that fast.* But in that moment, his hand vibrated strongly again and he knew from Lainie's look that his fingers had glowed in the dark.

"Because whatever your plan might be," she continued, "that sure isn't a gun in your hand."

And in that instant, she was running toward him.

Fishtailing through the heart of Defiance, Scotty Bosco let loose a stream of profanities. His junior detective wasn't picking up the phone. He had tried numerous times to break through before but his phone repeatedly gave him the "LOOKING FOR SERVICE" banner. He threw the cell phone on the seat beside him. In that instant, his truck hit a patch of ice, sending the Tundra careening off the road and knifing through an A-frame sign outside of the plant nursery. He cranked the wheel to the left and cursed the sleet for choosing this night out of all others. Throwing caution to the wind, he jammed his foot on the accelerator, looking out for the turn onto Howell Road.

If there hadn't been an ice storm tonight and if Lainie Kale was wearing better-soled shoes, thought Ballack, he would be a dead man.

He had managed to escape her grasp when she stumbled and fell on the slick ground. Skirting her outstretched fingers, Ballack swerved to the left side, jacked up his power level, and poured on the steam. He raced westward, past the south side of the chapel, hoping to get to the main road for a right turn. Everything was pushed out of his mind for now, including Tori's fate. He had to secure Lainie Kale's capture, and he'd need the help of others.

He heard his adversary get to her feet and sprint after him. He was ten yards in front of her but her speed and conditioning would close the gap quickly. He could only hope that the footing would prove as unreliable for her as it was on his short jaunt so far.

It was just as that thought crossed his mind that his wheels hit a slick spot on the polar lane. Pitched to the left, he swerved to avoid flying directly into the trees. He stayed on the road, but he veered too far to its south side. He was going to be cut off by the fast-closing Lainie. His heart popping against his sternum, he made an impromptu turn to the left and shot down the road toward the Lake of the Protomartyr. The swerve bought him a little space, but his gambit would only purchase him a minimum of time. It had also separated him from the rest of the campus. He heard the rhythmic sound of her feet drawing closer, nearly on top of him. She had managed to run fast without falling on the ice. He wasn't going to beat her to the lake. The gap was three yards, two yards, her arms flailing, her body towering over him on the steep drop. He sensed her eyes bugging wide, anticipating the opportunity to send him to a watery grave. That was her only option. What she didn't realize was that Ballack had a few items remaining on the ingenuity smorgasbord.

He felt her reach for his headrest; he sensed her fingertips pierce the padded area like an eagle's talons, transferring her weight to his rate of speed. At that precise moment, Ballack reared back, forcibly yanking back on the joystick and jamming his Quickie into reverse. The impact was colossal; the steel rod extending from the headrest skewered Lainie in the midsection, lifting her six inches off the ground and knocking the wind out of her. Falling to the pavement, she twisted her ankle and Ballack heard a distinct crack behind when she landed. He shoved the joystick forward and increased the distance. He knew he couldn't waste a second. She'd be in full pursuit before too long. She might be hobbled, but he couldn't afford any more chances. His last shot was to get to the track around the lake and hope for the best.

That was his plan, but Ballack never got the opportunity. As he went full tilt, bearing left, he misjudged the pathlink to the track. Instead of landing flush on the track surface, he overshot it by a foot. The left front wheel dropped off the road first, causing Ballack's weak torso to jerk in that direction, capsizing the wheelchair. It lurched savagely, tottered for a second, then flipped over, slamming down on Ballack's humerus. His muffled scream was immediately prefaced by the shattering of his upper arm.

It was pointless, he knew, to hope for anything more. He fumbled with his belt buckle, though it would do no good. Just before he could click himself loose, he felt a woman's fingers tear into the collar of his jacket. He tilted his head only to be met by a brutal punch that nearly crushed his right cheekbone. He felt a constriction at his waist, then the liberation of his body from its seat. Lainie Kale grabbed him by the back of his windpants and flipped him in a complete somersault. He landed smack on his tailbone, his feet splashing into the icy reservoir.

"You demon! You heartless demon!" she spewed at him. Grabbing him by the waistband and the scruff of his neck, she edged him toward the wintry water, stomping on the thin ice by the lake's edge to make an opening, his liquid grave. His trach cap flew off, and the subzero air plunged into his lungs with a stinging rush. Dead-weighted, he heard the sound of a motor in the distance. He couldn't be sure if it was a dream or not. The truth was he was past the stage to pinpoint that with any certainty.

He knew death was seconds away, and that he was powerless to stop it. His only hope—indeed his proactive prayer—was to delay the inevitable. His limp arm flopping to the side, he used all his limited reserves to catapult his right arm upward, wrapping it around Lainie's right knee. As he did so, he noticed Lainie's left hand was within reach of his mouth. His teeth wrapped around her middle finger, clamping down as tightly as he could, inducing a shriek of pain he swore could be heard in Arkansas. With his life on the line, he found strength unknown. And as her bloodcurdling howl ended, Ballack looked up, his hopes rewarded. It had been a motor he heard, from the vehicle he had desired. The piercing headlights of a familiar pickup truck had just appeared through the gate entrance. That was the good news. The bad news was the truck had hit the sheet of ice at the base of the hill and was streaking toward them. It was coming at an incredible speed.

Noticing the rapidly shifting luminescence behind them, Lainie Kale looked back with equal parts of rage and fear. A Toyota Tundra rocketed over yet another ice sheet, screeching and twisting, slamming into Ballack's wheelchair with tremendous force and launching it out of its supine position. With devastating speed and an astounding crunch, the wheelchair flew directly into Lainie Kale's legs, bringing forth yet another ungodly cry, this one worse than before. Murderer and detective tumbled together, one over the other. And the knee of the killer crashed into the throat of her final intended victim.

Ballack, every bone in his body screaming out for mercy, lay on his side, the frosty waves lapping into his face. His eyes closed shut, his ears perceiving a familiar voice encouraging him to hold out, and his heart tendered a drastic prayer he was sure would be his last.

"Daddy, daddy!"

"I'm here, buddy."

"Daddy, I'm scared."

"I know, son. It's not wrong to be scared."

"I'm afraid I'm going to die. What if I die?"

"We won't let that happen. We're not going to let you go."

"You promise?"

"Never will let you go..."

"Daddy, take my hand."

"I'm here, son."

"Will you pray with me?"

"I'm here, son...I'm here, son."

"Daddy....daddy...daddy..."

"Cameron? Cameron! Hey...over here!"

White ceiling. Nondescript walls. Muted lighting. Perpetual beeps. A throbbing pain on his face, in his neck, in his lower back. And a cafeteria tray on a table by his bed.

Wherever I am, thought Ballack, I'm a long way from a semi-frozen lake in St. Charles wine country. His vision cohered as he cleared his throat, and as he did so he was able to turn his head slightly and see who had been speaking to him just now. It was a clearly exhausted—but even more elated—Martin Ballack.

The young detective blinked, unsure if this vision was reality. His father wore a black cardigan sweater vest over a white starched button-down shirt. The well-worn khakis gave him a classic

399

professorial look. He reached over and took a sip from a coffee cup on the nightstand before rubbing his eyes and looking directly into those of his son.

"You sure visit some interesting places in your sleep," he said. Cameron Ballack recognized the phrase, a line from one of his favorite novels in *The Binding of the Blade* series. He swallowed painfully.

"Where am I?"

"Progress West Medical Center."

"What's today?"

"Tuesday, February the eighth."

"I've been here overnight?"

"Barely. You almost didn't make it. We almost lost you."

"We?"

"Mom and I. And Scotty. We've been here all night. First in the ER, now here since they got you a room."

The younger Ballack winced, wanting to move.

"Hang on, son. Let me do it." His father pushed a bedside button and the head portion raised slightly.

"What happened? Where's Mom?"

"She went down to the cafeteria to get breakfast. Jill's not here, but she will be soon. She's driving in from a conference in Memphis. Knowing her, she likely drove all night. Scotty is downstairs, dealing with the media."

"What?"

"*Post-Dispatch.* Channels Two, Five, Eleven, and Thirty. The whole buffet of public information. You're quite the sensation."

The son was dazed by the news. "So what all went down? Ow!" He had forgotten about his broken arm. Much of the rest of his body seemed to be heavily bruised.

"Careful, buddy. If you need to move, let me handle it or get a nurse in here. Here's what I know. I was headed home from St. Luke's last night when I got a call from Mom, who had gotten the scoop from Karen, who had just talked to Scotty."

"I follow," said Cameron, rolling his eyes at the winding trail of humanity.

His father smiled. "She was hysterical. Said you'd been in an accident and you were on the way to Progress. Scotty was here and filled us in on everything. He had gotten your call and tried responding but couldn't connect. He got to St. Basil's as fast as he could. He saw you and Lainie Kale struggling next to the lake and turned that direction, but he was going full speed. He hit some patch of solid ice and slid across the base of the hill like it was slicker than snot on a doorknob. He smashed into your wheelchair, which he's incredibly embarrassed over. But the impact sent it into Lainie Kale and knocked her down. He got to you first and dragged you out of the lake. Apparently, the crash was heard all over the school and everyone rushed down. Quite a few spills and tumbles, but the ones who got there first assisted in subduing Lainie and calling the paramedics for you. You were knocked out and turning blue. One girl gave you CPR and got you kickstarted. Can't recall the full name. Dana something-or-other."

"Dana Witten?" asked Cameron, his heartbeat elevating.

"That's the one. Anyhow, it was a community effort. Scotty had already cuffed Lainie. Father Timothy and Father Andrew asked if they could take you here given the medics might be slow. Father Matthias prayed over you. It was a group effort.”

“What about Tori?”

“She survived. She’s three doors down, actually. Lainie bound and gagged her and tossed her into the lake. But she didn’t weight her down or anything. That lake isn’t too deep, and the only part that was frozen that night was the edge. So, when Tori’s feet hit the bottom, she pushed off and sprang upward. Broke the surface, went back down, sprang back up. Kept hopping that way until she got out and wriggled to the edge. She landed on the opposite end of the lake from you. Scotty found her after the medics arrived. In some respects, you’re better off than she is.”

“My neck is killing me. I guess that’s from Lainie’s knee spearing me in the throat.”

His father looked dreadfully somber. “That’s why we thought you might not make it. The medics got you up here fairly quickly, considering the roads. The docs started working on you immediately. It was like George Washington Hospital when Reagan got popped by Hinckley. All hands on deck. Your throat was purple and they were worried your trachea had been torn by the impact. If so, we knew it wouldn’t be a happy ending.” He paused. He was clearly fighting back tears.

“Which room, Dad?”

His father closed his eyes.

“Dad?”

“I heard you.”

“Was it *the* room?”

His father nodded, eyes still closed. The memory was too strong.

"How long was I in there?"

"Felt longer than it was, which is saying something. The long and the short of it is your trachea was bruised, but not torn. They nearly changed your trach tube because you were unbelievably bubbly in your airway, but just suctioned you instead. They had you on the vent when they could. Neurological exam was fine. Biggest worry on that was you might have sustained a concussion. All in all, you came out of it pretty well."

"Then why am I in pain from head to toe?"

"Severely sprained right knee. Broken right wrist. Cracked cheekbone. And your left humerus is broken and angulated. Just like what happened to your left femur when you were seven years old."

"The arm break I sustained when the wheelchair tipped over. The cheekbone was Lainie's work. I must've gotten the other injuries on the second impact. I suppose the chair isn't salvageable?"

"Scotty was trying to bring his truck from forty miles an hour to zero in the blink of an eye. All I can say is be glad you weren't in it when he slammed into it. He was awfully torn up about it and could barely speak to us. He was relieved when you pulled through. He was just on the morning news. Couldn't shut up about what you did. He's incredibly proud of you."

Cameron smiled.

"And so are we," came a feminine voice from the doorway.

"Mom," gasped Cameron, "I thought you'd prefer sausage and eggs over this view. But I'm glad to see you guys again."

His mother walked to his bedside. She leaned down and gently hugged him around his neck, kissing him on the forehead. She backed slowly into the tender embrace of her husband and clasped his hands as he enfolded her. "Thank God....thank God," she whispered.

They remained in silence for two full minutes before the younger Ballack spoke.

"It's just been a draining few days. I've always been a tornado of cynicism, and then this case was all set up to justify my views further. I just hated seeing a place that spoke for God, that trained people to speak for God, doing the sorts of things we uncovered. I mean, it went beyond murder. Backdoor shenanigans, sexual impropriety that went way back, sketchy dalliances between students, bickering and backbiting. You name it, it was there. And yet, the more we got into it, the more open about their shortcomings people became. Not all of them. But after a while, the aura of the place seemed to be less and less hypocrisy and more and more the garden-variety brokenness of everyday life."

He looked at his parents. "Care to explain that to me?"

His father pulled the recliner up for his wife and sat down on the straight-back chair. "It might not be an explanation. More an observation of fact. You know that. Hypocrisy is pervasive all across the religious spectrum. Liberal and conservative. Christian, Muslim, and Jew. It's in every layer of soil in the human heart. That doesn't transform things, but it gives an honest starting point and you at least can expect disappointment will happen eventually."

"Is that why you got out of the church world and the school world?"

"I'm a hospital chaplain because I find a beauty in being on the front lines where faith meets the ultimate questions of pain and suffering head-on. I do that, not because I have all the answers, but because I can be a fellow pilgrim alongside others with whom I feel a common bond."

"It's not because you can avoid the political, hypocritical hokeyness of the other spheres?"

His father looked down at his hands, then back at his son. "It's not a question of if you deal with it, but when and how much. The balance of my vocation is such a blessing that it helps me to overlook the down side of things with a certain amount of grace. Cameron, you're talking about a problem that's been in the world for ages. The church, the parochial school, any ministry or religious organization of any kind—you have con men and Mother Teresas, savages and saints, knaves and knights, those who use God for their twisted desires versus those who live for him and for the good of others. My guess is you found some of each at St. Basil's. And that's got you thinking again."

"Which has to drive you crazy. I would think you'd want me to hurry up and land somewhere already."

"Of course what you think and what you believe is important to us, Cameron," said his mother. "But the journey you take toward those values is important, too. I would say—and I'd guess I speak for both of us," she gestured at her husband, "we desire that your faith should be authentic. We've tried to speak and live out what we believe, but we never wanted you to put yourself in the club just to please us. You're our son, and nothing can make you otherwise."

"You almost lost another son last night," he said.

"Yes, after thinking Dad and I would never have to bear that pain again. I was waiting it out for so long thinking, 'Not now, not again, not the same room all over again'. When the doctor came out and said you would make it, I felt like God removed a sword from my heart. Not that it would bring your brother back, but keeping you is blessing enough."

"A blessing that will require rehab, recovery, and all the trimmings. And even at one hundred percent, I'm still bound to a chair for life."

"Which," his father said, "we'll take with no complaints."

"Every transition, every lift, every suction, every drive to the hospital or a doctor's appointment, every drop of medication," said his mother, "is worth it if you're the recipient. Every day that we wake up and you're alive is a victory."

Cameron shut his eyes, failing in his efforts to hold back the salty discharge coming from them.

"You're not crying, are you? You're crying?" The grinning form of Scotty Bosco filled the doorway. "The stone heart of Detective Ballack has melted at last!"

"Hey, Scotty," laughed Martin. "We've just been bringing him back. You look like you've been having fun with the media droves." He hopped out of his chair and warmly shook the lieutenant's hand, slapping him on the back.

Bosco looked at his detective, then the Ballacks. "I got them all warmed up down there. Now they want to talk to you two."

"What? Why?"

"I made the mistake of telling them you were here."

"Oh, sweet fancy Elijah…thanks!" Martin said in mock exasperation. "Well, we'd hate to make a liar out of you. Let's go, sweetheart. Our fifteen minutes."

Marie Ballack got up to join her husband and winked at her son. "We'll be back soon."

Cameron Ballack gave a sarcastic look. "Where am I gonna go? Please."

Bosco sat next to the bed as the Ballacks left the room. "You look good."

"Shut up. I look like I've been through a meat grinder. So what've you got?"

"Two rescued, though nearly dead, detectives and one bitter confession from Lainie Kale. She let loose a half-hour spew that confirmed your accusation. Turns out she got Reverend Zednik by drugging him first."

"Drugging him?"

"Zonked him out by switching some of his meds with her husband's Somas. That made him easy prey for when she got into the guest room."

Ballack grimaced. It was a horrible way to die. Of course, that was the case with Father Jonathan and Dieter Witten as well. Though none of them had clean hands, murder was no solution to their iniquity.

"So what's going to happen between her and Stephen?" he asked.

"Can't say for sure, but if a jury convicts her, would you see Stephen remaining long in that marriage?"

"I can't see them remaining hitched under any circumstances. He wasn't headed for the priesthood, so a divorce wouldn't ruin him vocationally. She was cheating on him. The embezzlement, too. Going forward under the same roof would be unthinkable."

"Well, enough of them, Cam. There's a few other reasons I wanted to catch you the minute you woke up."

"Fire ahead."

"First, I called Bishop Petr Burgic this morning with the news that we nailed Lainie Kale. He was very gracious and generous in his praise."

"Nice to see he can have that disposition once in a blue moon. Why can't he be that way in person rather than through the phone line?"

"Well, whatever the case, there seems to have been some peace forged between the diocese and the seminary over this."

"Of course. Lainie Kale was the hub of all this filth, not the seminary itself. She was the one who stole the money, who murdered three men, one of whom was her own father. I know St. Basil's wasn't exactly welcoming toward Father Jonathan, but the diocese hadn't done any favors in circumventing the hiring process."

"Point being, that was the first thing. Second item: your wheelchair."

"Scotty, you putting this at number two doesn't exactly fill me with confidence."

"It's bittersweet. You might need a new wheelchair. I tagged that thing so hard it tore my front bumper to shreds. The chair itself took a nasty whack. The good news is your laptop was covered and avoided any water, and your software is safe as well. Barely. But you want a miracle, you got one."

Ballack coughed, his throat feeling cracked and dry. "I guess I shouldn't complain. If you were one minute later and if you *didn't* hit the wheelchair, Lainie Kale would have succeeded in dumping me in that lake."

"Speaking of surviving the lake," exclaimed Bosco, "look who arrived from down the hall!"

Tori Vaughan—measurably weakened, visibly shaken, but very much alive—shuffled in from the hallway. She was wrapped in a thick blanket and wore hospital scrubs over a long sleeve tee shirt. The back of her head bore a nasty cut from where Lainie creased her skull with Ballack's wheelchair recharger. Unsteadily, she sat down next to Bosco.

"You okay?" asked Ballack.

"I'm here," replied Tori.

"Holy smokes, she speaks," said Bosco. "That was more than I got out of her."

The three engaged in small talk for a few minutes. Ballack got all the details from Tori as to how she stayed alive. In her haste to get rid of her victim, Lainie had failed to tie Tori's ankles together tightly enough. She was able to wriggle free of the duct tape after the initial bounce off the bottom of the lake. From there it was a matter of controlling her breathing while timing her jumps in one direction.

"Maybe Father Timothy could use your hops for a few extra rebounds next year," said Ballack.

"Okay, guys, let's get to the last thing I want to say. You were called to this case to investigate one suspicious death. Over the next few days, you had to take on two more murders. You slogged through a less-than-conducive environment to nail the perpetrator. You both exhibited bravery, professionalism, and perseverance. There were some moments along the way that might be referred to as lucky breaks. I don't see it that way. My perspective is that your teamwork and your instincts created your own luck, and you followed them to the bitter end."

"Is this a commendation?" asked Ballack.

"I would think you'd leave this for the press conference," said Tori.

"No, what I said is a precursor to this: Because of your actions, I'm immediately recommending you both for the Special Investigative Division of Metro St. Louis. You'd still be under the jurisdiction of St. Charles, so you won't have to move anywhere. Just need to do some additional training. But you're aware of the SID, of course?"

"Yeah," croaked Tori. "Best investigating talent from each department, responding to specific crimes in the Metro area. Teams of four work on sensitive cases. I'm thrilled, but why us?"

"Sensitive cases, specifically those of a spiritual bent, require detectives who know the religious system and have a healthy pessimism. You need to believe people are capable of immense evil. I believe that's what helped with the St. Basil's case. I think you'd bring a lot to the SID. It would be a provisional assignment, in limited cases. You'd be part of a small team, not a large canvas, due to the nature of your cases. But it's a great opportunity. And it's not one extended to many officers so early in their careers."

Ballack could hardly believe his ears. "It's an opportunity, no doubt. But I hope you don't expect us to be up and running around anytime soon. It'll be some time before we can strum the banjo."

"Whenever you're ready," said Bosco.

"I never knew getting my head cracked open could lead to such opportunity," said Tori. "Disaster seems to open up the golden road. Next case, I'm walking out on Interstate 70 into oncoming traffic."

Her response brought muffled laughter from the two men. It seemed like a good time to go their separate ways. Just as Bosco got to his feet to assist Tori out of her seat, the door opened yet again and a brown-haired girl bounced into the room, clutching a paper bag and rushing to the bed, wrapping her arms around Ballack and hugging him as tightly as he could handle.

"Jill!" he exclaimed, "Dad said you were driving all night. I'm surprised you made it through with all the ice."

"Nothing was stopping me, brother, especially when I heard what had happened. Most of all I figured you needed to start getting your strength back, so let's start lifting." She reached into the bag and tossed an object on his bed.

Ballack looked at it, giving his sister a confused look.

"A plastic spoon? Is this some sort of joke?"

She laughed. "It's just a little something to help you…" She reached in the bag and pulled out a yellow-and-green pint-sized container, "…lift this out of the carton."

Stunned, Cameron Ballack found himself staring face to face with a massive helping of Ted Drewe's frozen chocolate custard.

"If this isn't the smile of God, I don't know what is," he replied hungrily, reaching for the carton.

"I got plenty for both of us," Jill said, giggling, pulling out another smaller carton.

"Then let's open them up," he replied, "As hungry as I am, this carton will be gone in sixty seconds."

Ballack returned to St. Basil's on a calm Easter weekend, or as the Orthodox tradition termed it, Pascha. His parents drove down with him, wanting to experience the Divine Liturgy for themselves at this apex of the church year. Even a slew of severe weather that blew through the St. Louis area the night before could not dent Ballack's buoyant spirits. Tori would join them later that Saturday evening. The arrangements were for Martin and Marie to take the loft with Cameron sleeping in his bed below. Tori was willing to take the room where Zednik had slept. Ballack smirked at the irony.

"I hope no pillows go missing," he said aloud to himself while they were getting settled in.

"What's that?" asked his mother.

"Nothing. Just an inside joke." And he said no more about that.

It was just over an hour before Vespers that Ballack decided to call on Father Matthias. The seminary's strict fast on Holy Saturday meant that the refectory was not an option, but food was not Ballack's reason for entering Chalcedon Hall one more time. He needed closure. Father Matthias had been the first person to greet him when he arrived at St. Basil's. It would be imprudent not to speak with him now.

The dean was coming down the stairs to the main level of Chalcedon when Ballack spotted him.

"Officer Ballack, welcome back. How good to see you."

Ballack shook Father Matthias' hand. His wrist had healed and he felt no residual pain. "Thank you, Father. And please, call me Cameron."

"It will take some getting used to, but I'll attempt it. I have a few moments available. I try to keep a silence on Holy Saturday, but for you I think I can make an exception. Shall we go back to the conference room?"

They sat, side by side, in the room where they had begun their whole saga. Much of their conversation revolved around the completion of the second semester and a bright future. The students had performed very inspired work, given the earlier tragedies that befell the community. Dieter Witten's post as student rector was left unfilled out of respect for his memory. Ballack wondered how much of his secret life Father Matthias knew. On an extremely surprising note, St. Basil's was looking at an increase for the next year. Enrollment was expected to rise from forty-four to over fifty. Now, said Father Matthias, their most vexing issue was how to have room for the burgeoning student body.

"Have you found a successor for Father Jonathan?" Ballack inquired.

"We have. Linus Sankavikius is coming from the East Coast, on a recommendation from Father Timothy. Very promising. Thirty years of age. Completing his doctorate at the University of North Carolina. I read a manuscript of his dissertation. He has to be the only man alive who can make the comparative hermeneutics of Jonah and Nahum sound interesting."

Ballack swept his hand over his head, as if to say that was beyond his comprehension. There was another question on his mind. "Is Stephen Kale returning?"

"Yes. Was there some doubt?" Father Matthias replied.

"Stephen has been humbled by the events of this year. He told us all of his decision not to pursue the priesthood. Of course, we were stunned at first, but on the whole we were impressed by his honesty. Not everyone has that calling and, as Stephen reminded us, God does not waste any of our wanderings."

"Those seem to be good terms to live by."

Father Matthias looked at him, his head resting on his palm. "And are you back on terms?"

Ballack didn't follow. "Pardon me?"

"When we first met, you said you weren't exactly on speaking terms with God. I was wondering if this experience has changed your perception."

An uncomfortable pause followed. It was one thing, Ballack thought, for him to speak about his doubt. It was another to be asked.

"Father, I don't know. I'm not even certain. But I do know this. If you had asked me three months ago, before everything broke loose here at St. Basil's, my reaction might have been 'I don't know and I don't care'. That was then. But now, I'd merely say 'I don't know'. There's something at the root of my heart that seems to tell me that I can't accept my unbelief any more than I can believe. Both seem problematic now. I can't directly disprove God's existence, nor could I prove it if I wanted to."

"I hope that you would leave room for something more."

"Something more?"

"One of the heroes of our tradition, St. Irenaus, once said we can never know God through direct speculation, never in his greatness, but only in his love. You are a detective, Cameron. An excellent one, I might add. Of course, you analyze, you study, and you use critical thinking skills and reason. Those bring you to a certain point in every crime, every case. But what you also do, what makes the difference, is know the suspects—and the others touched by your investigation—as people. Detection must be a personal, relational game as much as a rational one, I would think."

"What's your point, Father?"

"We can speculate if God exists, but that speculation leads either to unbelief or pursuit. If we 'go for broke' and seek God, then we either are loved by him or not. If he's not there, we lose nothing. But if he exists, then we gain everything."

"That's a wager you think is worth taking?"

"I take it every day when I wake up. It sustains me through days of hope. It also upheld me through the darkness of this past year."

"Your faith seems to swim through the questions rather well, Father."

"Well, some of those questions are my own. The problem of suffering, the brokenness of a world God is restoring slowly, the problem of evil."

"Even that," said Ballack, "has a dual answer. If there is a God, why is there so much evil in the world? On the other hand, if there is no God, why is there so much good in the world?"

Father Matthias gave him an awed look. "Magnificent."

"It's not my quote. St. Augustine, actually."

"Not from our tradition, but we celebrate the truth wherever it's found."

"More good terms to live by," said Ballack with a generous smile.

"Indeed," replied Father Matthias, returning his smile. "It is good to have you back. Are we to expect you for Divine Liturgy tomorrow?"

"You can count on it, Father."

"Good evening, then."

Ballack drove back in the direction of Chrysostom House. Looking to his left, he caught a glimpse of a figure sitting in the Grotto of St. Jonah and All Martyrs. Wheeling into the now-green woodland space, he swooped in next to Dana Witten. She turned toward him. She was sitting on the same bench as that February afternoon when she bewailed the news of her widowhood.

"Hey you," she smiled at him.

"Hi yourself." He smiled back.

She looked up at the cross, then at him, pausing to brush her fingers through her hair. "I heard you might be coming this weekend. You picked a nice one."

"Better than last night," remarked Ballack. "How close did the tornadoes come?"

"A few miles north was the closest one. We definitely fared better than Maryland Heights, Bridgeton, Ferguson, or the airport. Not your typical Good Friday."

Ballack said nothing, and Dana sensed his reticence. "Not that," she said, "it would have been a typical Good Friday anyway."

"I suppose not," Ballack said quietly. "What is going to happen with you—you know, after May? After graduation?"

"It's time to leave. I've known that. I actually left right after Dieter's funeral, but I return from time to time. It felt right to come back for Easter. I stay at Jane Porter's place up the road on weekends like these. The fathers have offered to have me stay on. Something about assisting Cora, serving as a hostess, revising the promotional literature. They were very kind to offer. It would have been a small stipend, with free room and board. But I said no. I think they knew I wouldn't accept it. This place has been a refuge for me, but it holds some terrifying memories."

"So where are you headed?" Ballack hoped the quaver in his voice wasn't noticeable.

"Oh, I'll be around. I'll live at my parents' place until I can get on my feet. The last two months I've been drowning in resumes and applications. Turns out I won't have to go far. I'll be teaching sophomore English at Whitfield next year."

"Teaching. Nice!"

"And I'll be the assistant coach for girls' soccer."

"I didn't know you played."

"I wasn't the star Lainie was," she said, her face darkening as she mentioned the name. "But I played all four years at Parkway West. Started at full back my senior year. I didn't play at Missouri State, but I kept my skills warm with intramurals."

"So you'll be somewhat close by."

"You sound happy about it."

Ballack blushed slightly.

"It's okay," Dana said, touching his arm. "You think I mind? It's been a long time since someone has been excited about my presence."

"Now that's impossible," said Ballack, embarrassed at how clumsily he was putting out the charm.

She sat on the end of the bench, facing him, their knees almost touching. She looked full in his face and spoke in a placid yet tender tone. "Listen to me. It's important you hear me. What happened weeks ago was horrific. It devastated me. The murders, the suspicion, losing Dieter—even though he wasn't the ideal husband. It forced me— caused you—to confront deadly things about this place. There is so much about that time I will never understand. It was such a dark time: the nightmares, the loneliness, not being able to trust anyone. But you being here gave me the sliver of peace I could claim. I thought there was so much you did that no one here was willing to do. You risked your life to stop Lainie. When I heard about what you had to do, I cried for hours. No one here shows that kind of courage and love. I don't say that to condemn them. It's just that you don't realize how different you are from others."

"I was just doing my job," said Ballack.

"Maybe that was what your official report said," replied Dana. "But you're forgetting the hidden impact. You brought justice. You brought peace. Your courage meant I didn't have to live in fear any more. Don't expect me to forget that, Cameron."

She leaned toward him. Her hand on his face. Again. She tilted his head and kissed him on the cheek, her lips barely grazing the edge of his own.

"And don't ever expect me to forget you," she whispered. And with an even stroke of his hair, she arose to walk toward the chapel as the bell rang for Vespers.

LUKE H. DAVIS

Dinner at the guesthouse was a festive occasion. Ballack talked with Tori about their upcoming SID training while his mother prepared the shrimp paprika. His father tossed a salad while opening a small cooler packed with ice and beer. Tori happily got started on two bottles of Schlafly Pilsner. In a celebratory mood, Ballack bypassed the Schlafly and, along with his father, opted for a Radler combination of Beck's Light and Sprite. His mother poured a glass of white wine and brought the steaming entree to the table.

"Does it bother you guys," asked Tori, "that we're noshing on this while our hosts are fasting and going through self-denial in honor of Lent?"

"No," said her partner. "I'll have another roll, Mom."

"They're welcome to come over," said Marie Ballack.

"Do you Presbyterians ever stop eating?" asked Tori, already chortling, though that was likely due to the fact she was on her third drink.

"Presby-Lutheran," said Martin Ballack. "I'm declaring myself a new hybrid. Solid theology and German brew. The best of both worlds. What do you think?"

"I think that should be your last beer, honey," said his wife, sending the group into peals of laughter.

With a beautiful Easter service behind them, they drove eastward on Highway 40. Jill had promised she'd come from church to meet them. Ballack had made heartfelt goodbyes to all the fathers, to Stephen Kale, and, of course, to Dana. He had to admit her point, there was much pain in the offing. But St. Basil's had also given him a sense of renewal. Justice, even the limited scope of human justice, had been done. A murderer had wrought suffering, but stopping such cunning evil prevented so much more. And it had brought about the possibility of advancement. It was what Tori had been hoping for. It was a stunning achievement for him, being unable to walk and yet now a major player in fighting area crime. When Scotty Bosco summoned him to the bureau office over seven weeks ago, he could not have dreamed it would have played out this way.

Yet what Father Matthias shared with him continued to gently assault his mind. He had been analyzing this mystery for years, had been slamming himself against the wall of doubt—a barricade that originally came down in sadness, but a hedge he maintained for protection. But what indeed was he protecting? A heart insulated from pain. A moated life detached from another chance at love. Now he felt that castle opening up to new possibilities. Yet he couldn't blindly make that leap. He couldn't place that faith in a Creator unless he believed that Presence to be there, to be here. And yet, he knew his present locale was no answer, either.

Shielded from his parents' conversation with his iPod in his ears, he allowed his thoughts to drift and let Linkin Park be his sermon for the day. As they turned on the Mason Road exit, he felt the words wash over him, shaping him, convicting him.

> *I know what it takes to move on*
> *I know how it feels to lie*
> *All I want to do is trade this life for something new*
> *Holding on to what I haven't got*

He couldn't bring himself to believe. That he knew. But neither could he remain still. The chorus flowed through him again. *Amen, Chester,* thought Ballack, *Amen.*

The sun had peeked through the clouds and vaulted over the expansive grounds before them. The Honda Odyssey rolled to a stop and Martin Ballack turned off the engine. A series of clicks and releases later and a new power wheelchair rolled down the ramp and began the climb up the knoll. They were back at Bellerive, all of them, for a moment of hope, a moment of shared affection.

Again, they made the climb. Once more, Jill held her mother's hand, and Dad walked behind his son, who needed no one to push him now. The canopy was gone, but the memory of Pastor Stuart's voice rang clear and true. They came to their destination, and stopping together, they looked upon the headstone, one foot square, graced with a Latin cross.

JOHANN CHRISTOPHER BALLACK
Isaiah 40:31
Our little eagle...child of grace

As if the sight triggered the remembrance of one of his father's sermons, Ballack recalled the verse his mother had chosen for the headstone. *But they who wait for the LORD shall renew their strength. They shall mount up with wings like eagles. They shall run and not be weary. They shall walk and not faint.*

His mother handed a bouquet of lilies to Jill, who walked forward and placed them in the bronze vase set in the headstone's marble foundation. For several minutes, no one spoke. Then, his father walked behind Mom and wrapped his arms around her. She smiled, never taking her eyes off the headstone, and a tear slowly traversed down her cheek.

"One day," Dad whispered. "One day." There was nothing more to be said.

After another minute, the son looked up at the sky, then back at his brother's stone, and quietly said, "One day."

He turned to his family, who straightened themselves and readied to go.

"Can I stay, myself, just a few more minutes? I won't be long," he said.

His father looked at the females, then back at his son. "No problem. Will you be able to handle the bumpy ride back down?"

"Yeah," he said. "Thanks. All of you." He added, "For everything."

"Everything?" Marie Ballack asked.

"For the strength to lift a cripple like myself. For giving space to my frustration. For being the family I always needed. And...oh, for loving a son and brother who is still trying to figure out what he believes."

Martin squatted next to him, gripping his shoulder affectionately. "You'll always have us. Whatever you need. And as far as what you believe, seek truth with all your heart, and you'll find it."

"And don't worry about having to discover some hidden particle of faith that's escaped you, son," said his mother. "There is some faith that you might have to find, but just as much, perhaps faith will end up finding you."

They turned to go.

"Don't be long, brother," said Jill. "Frozen custard calls. I can't wait forever."

They both smiled.

He turned back to the headstone in a swirl of emotions. He shut his eyes to the warm spring breeze. So many incidents, so many people, so much evil and so much good had all come together in a conspiracy of the soul in the past months. He could not tell where it would lead. But he knew that he was not the person he was before. And perhaps that would turn out to be a good thing. Perhaps one day he would discover the burst of light that blinded every angel and be at peace. But as his mother said, perhaps that light would find him instead. For now he was in this place, not to say goodbye. Rather, for the first time in years, it was to say hello.

He opened his eyes, and his heart saw the form of his baby brother before him. And he saw the smile and heard the laughter. No litany of secrets. Just love. And grace. And hope.

"Hi, Christopher," he whispered. "It's me…Cameron, your brother."

LUKE HERRON DAVIS is the author of the Cameron Ballack Mystery series, of which *Litany of Secrets* is the initial volume. He is also the author of the poetry book *Through a Child's Eyes*, a tribute to his late son. Luke has taught in the ethics and religion departments at private schools in Missouri, Florida, Virginia, and Louisiana. He lives with his wife Christy and their children in Saint Charles, Missouri.

CPSIA information can be obtained at www.ICGtesting.com
Printed in the USA
BVOW02s1709140515

400141BV00010B/680/P